Nut Hollow
The Knife and Nefairious

MICHAEL SANDS

To order additional copies of this book, contact:
Xlibris Corporation
0-800-644-6988
www.xlibrispublishing.co.uk
Orders@xlibrispublishing.co.uk
300190

CONTENTS

PART THE FIRST

PART THE SECOND

PART THE THIRD

For Catherine

Acknowledgments

I would like to thank Katie and Dara for being two very special girls and for helping to inspire this story. A big hug too for Tóla, our magical wee son.

Thanks to my parents Ben and Barbara and my sisters Kellie and Ryanne for all your encouragement.

Thanks also to Pádraig (RIP), Mary, Patrick and Marie McLean for helping me find Nut Hollow.

A special word of thanks to the brilliant artist currently known as Randall Stephen Hall . . . get your pig on!

Thank you to all the readers for lending their eyes and finding all those little mistakes.

Thank you to the team at Xlibris Publishing.

Finally, to my beautiful wife Catherine. Thank you for so many things over all our years together but most of all for believing.

PART the FIRST

Come away, O human child!
To the waters and the wild
With a fairy hand in hand,
For the world's more full of weeping than you can understand

WB Yeats—The Stolen Child

Prologue

Many mornings ago . . .

He knew he shouldn't do it but he didn't care. He didn't care that it broke the rules, every single one of them. Breaking rules was something he was very good at especially after all the commotion at his father's party. The others would just not expect it and once he had it they could say whatever they liked, he would not have to listen. He would have what he needed to shut them all up for good!

From his front door he watched them, including his mother, walk towards the Learning Tree.

"Close up behind you please," she said.

"Aye, ok."

His thoughts had more to say,

Yes on you go, my fairy friends, just another Ceremony, just another day in the Hollow. Well not likely! Not if I have anything to do with it!

He stretched his fingers, toes, arms, legs and most importantly his wings.

"When I have it, I'll get him out and then they'll feel the full force of the Duveline," he snarled.

His own Ceremony had been celebrated only a few weeks ago but everything had changed within him since he had held the Knife.

Why should I wait? I'll get it now and that will be that. They'll never catch me, none of them . . .not even Greagle.

His wings fluttered quickly behind him and he was up. In the distance he could see the Ceremony reach it's climax; the handle of the Knife was coming out!

"C'mon Nef, this is it", he said.

There wasn't much time. He pushed on now, circling up around the nut tree that grew above his house. He was out of sight of the crowd who were all staring at the young fairy on the stone. Up into the early branches he went. Only a few seconds now . . .

There it was, the Knife, the blade, the handle, the wonders of it's sharp promise, beckoning him. His wings were now beating at full power. In the morning light he swooped down and sped along the top of the river. Not far now and still the crowd did not see him. He flew towards it with the sun behind him to help cover his arrival. Faster now until the wind howled in his ears.

"Don't do it," it said.

But he did not listen. He pushed on again, his vision focused solely on the handle. He moved his hand in front of him. It would be over in another second. He would have the Knife and all the power that went with it.

"Yessss," he hissed.

He reached . . .

"I have——"

Suddenly his world was spinning out of control . . .upside down and round and round . . .

*   *   *

1

Preparation

This morning . . .

The rain came straight down from the dark sky. Straight as the edge of a ruler, there was no wind to slant it. The drops bounced off Hollow River only to fall back again and be consumed. It was not night but not quite light and things were beginning to stir around Glenmak Mountain. I had my duties to attend and thought of them as I stood at my front door. I live just under the Learning Tree and my name is Graneff. Now living under a tree might seem strange but when you're only the size of a little (human) boy or girl's little finger it makes perfect sense.

The mayor's residence has always been here and it suits us down to . . . well, underneath the ground. With my wife Gráinne and children, son Pog and daughter Fer we live here quite contentedly. This day was a special day indeed. One of the neighbour's children had reached thirty three and the Carving Ceremony was due to take place at Sun's Height that afternoon.

I shook my head,

"I hope the rain stops or else there will be a lot of fancy hats for the bin."

Gráinne agreed. She wasn't really one for dressing up but the Ceremony was always a good excuse.

"Water and hats do not mix," she sighed.

Pog and Fer were not long up and getting out of their night clothes, ready for the wakening wash. We always wash in the river. There is nothing like river water first thing, even if it is a bit cold.

All along Nut Hollow the sounds of morning could be heard, starlings, robins, blackbirds and thrushes all taking turns at alarm calling. Then there were the green frogs, a lazy bunch that don't do very much at all except give the odd croak now and again. They edged along to the water and complained about the rain. Moles, mice and snails all yawning and stretching and having a small moan about getting out of bed, I'm sure humans are far too polite for that.

Fer and Pog unfolded their wings and walked slowly to the river's edge.

"You ready?" asked Pog

"S'pose so," replied Fer and in they jumped.

"Goodness gracious, chilll-ly!"

Gráinne and I bent over and took a handful of water in our hands and poured it over our heads. Ah there's nothing like the water running down your back to wake you up. We had left our jumping in days behind a while ago.

Beyond the Learning Tree down to Cross Rivers the neighbours greeted the morning. We have a lot of neighbours and thankfully we nearly all get along well. Sometimes there are rows about flying too fast or dropping nuts on peoples' heads but not today.

"Good morning Graneff, how's tricks?"

It was Shest. He and his wife Lirna live next door, at number three Nut Hollow in around the roots of the first nut trees. They were just married and every day was as new as a snowflake. Ah, young love.

"Grand, thanks, just getting things in order for the Ceremony, you'll be there of course?"

"Wouldn't miss it, see you later."

As I turned I heard them splash and the "Ooooh!" that always comes next.

So things proceeded well and light gradually filled the glen. I never tire of the view as green and brown shapes emerge from the grey blanket of early morning.

After a quick dry off using handfuls of moss we headed back to our home. The dewdrops on the grass at the front door are sweetest first thing and we all had a healthy sup. I shouldn't laugh but the young ones nearly always go for a blade of grass with a big droplet and get soaked. This morning was no exception and Pog and Fer giggled at each other after another tasty liquid mishap.

We went back inside and gathered around our riverstone table in the kitchen. If you leave a stone in moving water long enough it becomes wonderfully smooth. The stone sat steadily atop four nut tree branch legs. Our plates were the empty nutshells, carefully shaped by myself. I learned this at the Learning Tree from my father. After a breakfast of crushed nuts and mole milk we got our special clothes from the Ceremony wardrobe. A fine wooden construction it was and stood quietly in the hallway behind the front door. The doors of the wardrobe were only opened on such occasions and were a bit stiff but I used snail oil and they soon creaked outward. I lifted my robes off their hanger and called the others to do the same.

"Oh not again," said Fer, "I look like a buttercup in mine."

As the morning progressed and we got our good clothes on the rain that had threatened to spoil the whole event began to ease. This cheered Gráinne no end as she carefully lifted her hat from it's box. This hat was given to her by her mother, Verin and was her pride and joy. It had been a present from Gráinne's dad, Grast to her mum on their engagement. It caused a stir at the time as it was made of crushed duck down which was squeezed into an empty nutshell. Duck down is not easy to come by in the Hollow.

The nutshell was polished until you could see all the colours that ever there were through it and was as delicate as a fairy kiss. To finish it off Gráinne's father added threads of web that were made especially by an elderly spider, Spindler, with whom he was particularly friendly. When the sun shone they glistened and flowed. There wasn't a hat like it in the Hollow. Gráinne placed it on her head like a crown and she looked every bit a fairy queen. I pulled my coat over my shoulders and checked on Pog and Fer. They were busy annoying each other as youngsters do, pulling hair, pulling wings and all that sort of thing.

"OK," I said, "let's go."

2

A Gathering

As is the law at these events everyone must be aware of outsiders. Should a human see the Ceremony it could spell disaster for the whole community. Thankfully there were none around. I looked down the Hollow and saw a great gathering of the fairy folk. They were all heading towards the Learning Tree, the young in the care of the old and the old in the energy of the young. The sounds were of the ever present river mingled with fragments of conversations relating to the grand event.

"Turned out OK in the end," said Blalim. "Nothing worse than the rain at a Ceremony."

Blalim was one of our eldest and most respected fairies. He had seen nearly one hundred carvings in his days in the Hollow.

"Sure you were only bouncing off trees when the Great Wetting occurred. Do you remember, Graneff?"

I had to be honest with him,

"Bits and pieces, Blalim, I heard there was an awful furore amongst the ladies."

Blalim's eyes sparkled as he had a quiet giggle to himself,

"Goodness knows Rephenne wasn't too happy that day. Hat ruined, makeup all over her chin, her second shoe was pulled from the mud after a week . . . the first one was never found. I never saw as many colours in the river before, and all of us of course drenched to the skin. Ah may she rest easy, you know I miss her Graneff but she's always with me, especially on a day like this."

"I know Blalim, she was wonderful woman."

"Aye," he sighed.

Away on he went looking a little sad. His wings were heavy on his back but he kept them in great order. He always said,

"You have to look after the wings, you never know the minute you would need them!"

As Blalim walked on towards the Learning Tree, I could see the young one for whom today would change things forever, Druhin. He looked a bit confused. His parents Aldarn and Suerna were as proud as two full bags of corn and were telling him to,

"Pull up those britches. Comb that hair. Straighten your wings immediately," and asking, "Did you brush your teeth? Have you practiced your carving? Can you spell your name?"

Poor Druhin, he would learn that parents couldn't help themselves sometimes. The fairies of Druhin's family were a little excitable to say the least.

His father had to be asked several times to stop night flying without a light. Whenever he and Suerna had a disagreement he would head for the sky in a huff and she would start to clean the house. Flying without a light around the Hollow is extremely dangerous what with birds, bees, bugs and branches. Should you do it often enough you could get your wings clipped. Nothing worse than the sting of the clipped wing!

As for the washing? Well on a few occasions poor Druhin has been chased from his bed in the middle of the night.

"Must get these sheets clean, must get these pots clean 'cos when your father lands he'll get one round the ear and then he'll be needing something soft to lie down in."

I suppose Suerna was caring in her own wonderful way. It all left Druhin a bit tired now and again. He was the sort of fairy whom you thought could just do with a few hours extra in bed. Still this was his big day and he looked quite bright. No rows last night then.

The only person allowed to fly on a Ceremony day was the First Flyer, in this case Druhin. We all treat it as a day off our duties. Of course in an emergency that law could be broken but that hasn't happened for ages. This meant that some of the wings were not in their optimum condition, except for Blalim's of course.

On they came, the fairies of the Hollow in all their grandeur. Some of the neighbours had gone to a good deal of bother. There were waistcoats made from bluebell petals, trousers made from dandelion stalks, dresses made from ivy leaves and not a dirty pointed ear amongst all the fairy children. The shoes were all shining and reflecting the sparkles of the stream and to say you never saw such a display of hats would be an understatement. Pointy ones, flat caps, round heads and square berets with midgy feathers.

"You're looking well," or "You scrub up rightly," and "You don't look a day over two hundred," and even "A Ceremony and a big gulp of Cuckoo spit, I can't wait!" were just some of the lines to be heard.

The excitement was building for sure as each family took their place in the seats on the Seating Stone. Each family had been sitting in their place for hundreds of years and no one dared to break that tradition, not even courting couples. No, the Ceremony was very special and this one was just about to start!

3

A Major Hiccup

We numbered one hundred and twenty eight. It's important to be precise when counting. I don't know anyone who likes to miss out on sandwiches and Nut juice after one of these dos. Of course we don't have to stand and butter bread or boil, cool and shell eggs or peel spuds or dice carrots or cry over onions like humans. No, fairies have magic that can be used to whip up everything from yellow oranges to green bluebells.

The Honour of the Sandwiches belonged to Clumser. I had heard that he was keen to make up for his efforts after the last Carving. Oh I suppose that would be thirteen years ago now. Well everything had proceeded perfectly that day as I can remember.

The First Flyer, Herchia looked beautiful dressed up in a mixture of petals. Her family were beaming with pride and she had said her special words very eloquently. Her nerves at take off were replaced with the grace of the wind under her wings and her smile would've shamed the sun. Her First landing was excellent and she carved her name perfectly. With the excitement everyone was ready for the food. Up stepped Clumser. In a steady voice he began,

"To all from all food for the ball

In dark and light I have the right

To yummy the tummy in the Flyer's hall

None to hunger at all tonight!"

Well that's what he should have said. He was speaking beautifully until he got to the last line when just as he was about to say 'hunger' and seal the spell he let go as loud a hiccup as had been heard in the Hollow.

Uh oh! I thought. *This could be bad!*

You see fairy magic is fine, if you get it right but if you get it wrong! Well of course he had tried to say hunger but all we heard was a mighty 'Hic!' The problem was that the magic decided that the hiccup was of special significance and because the magic is stronger on a Ceremony day it was no time at all before we were all hiccupping!

Oh the state of us. Now you know that if you have to hiccup you suck in wind and of course if you do that often enough the wind will have to get out. It wasn't long before the rumbling started in tummies and didn't we sound like a winter gale. But that was not the worst of it, the escaping of the wind started and not from the way it had come in. Oh no, it got out the other end! I think you know where I mean.

Some of the loudest parps and poops came from the women fairies. They couldn't believe it. Women fairies never parp in public, many don't even parp in private but now from their lower reaches came 'phipps', 'frapps', 'poopaloops', 'blubbedings', blarfalups' and worst of all you know that sound when you put your tongue between your lips and blow?

Of course this was all a scream to the younger fairies who joined in with great gusto. The parents were helpless; all their many attempts at instilling good manners took a severe knock that day. Oh I don't think there was a quiet night in the Hollow for a week. I won't even mention the smell.

Thirteen years was a long time to ponder on that unfortunate moment. We hoped Clumser would have more luck today. I couldn't help but notice a few pre-packed lunches bulging in pockets just in case.

Now if I can just describe the Seating Stone itself. Positioned right alongside the Learning Tree it slopes at a very pleasant angle, perfect for fairy backsides! The elder fairies like Blalim get to sit right at the top where there is most moss. I would like to be that comfortable but it would mean I was really old and I don't like the idea of that too much. Despite the moss for some there just was never enough,

"Not as much as last Ceremony. Nothing is as good as it used to be. My behind won't be the better of this for a week," said Grochin, he was fond of a good moan.

"Ah give over you old goat! Nothing wrong with the moss, it's your back end. There's more fat on a knitting needle," replied Frenel, his long suffering but loving wife.

Indeed they were a bit of a double act when they got going. I was looking forward to their verbal hurling today. I hope Gráinne and I can have as much fun because they always give each other a kiss at the end of the day no matter what.

We got ready for the First Flight and Carving. Silence slowly lowered around us and the talking died down until there was only the river to be heard. The never ending whoosh of the water and the splash as it falls down and ever onward. Then the white foam that bubbles up and the glittering sparks of light that catch your eye as it smoothes the great boulders. There was magic in the air no doubt.

A minute or so passed allowing everyone to gather their thoughts. The younger ones wondering how their big day will turn out, the rest of us remembering back and thinking at how it felt like yesterday but knowing it was much longer ago. I broke the silence with our traditional words,

"Friends and fairies here we meet

A Ceremony now to complete

A young one here to begin

A higher journey from within

No longer bound the soil to walk

But take the air like dove and hawk

A privilege of the fairy race

And honour not to misplace

So who now dares to take First Flight?

A voice it takes to claim the right."

Druhin stood up and walked slowly to the edge of the stone as generations of fairies had done before. Suerna was beside herself with excitement and her face was getting redder by the minute. Aldarn had his work cut out holding her down. She didn't say a word though, she knew better, only one voice was allowed.

"Here is the voice that claims the right

It is I, Druhin, who earns First Flight

I stand beside the Learning Tree

Having today reached thirty-three

My wings are ready for the air

To ride the wind and take good care

So friends and fairies this is my task

Your blessings on me now to ask

So from the stone and to the heights

I fly into the days and nights."

Very well spoken young fairy, I thought but I had one further thing to say,

"Then Druhin, I command you, take first flight!"

No sooner had I spoken when his wings stretched out and shone clear behind him. They started slowly up and down but quicker, quicker, quicker. They were now a blur of energy building, building, building. The crowd on the Seating Stone began to cheer and clap.

"Go on Druhin, get up there son," yelled Aldarn.

Poor Suerna was screaming at the top of her lungs, "Yes my boy yahoooo! Go oonnnnnn!" The fairy voices were as one,

"Fly!"

Up he went, as if shot out from a bow. He flew straight up to the height of the Learning Tree and whizzed back down over all our heads as proud as could be.

Good man Druhin, I thought, *this is going to be some night!*

Well if he didn't do cartwheels and somersaults and wing skims for the next ten minutes. Of course being egged on all the while by the fairy folk and the loudest voice was Suerna. She was ecstatic with pride. Here was her boy zipping around in the sunlight, thirty three years old today in the middle of his First Flight.

"I never thought I'd see it!" she gasped. "I never thought I'd see it!"

"Did you think you'd see it?" she asked Aldarn, grabbing his arm.

"'Cos I certainly never thought I'd see it! Look at him go, that's my son you know," she shouted and nudged her next door neighbour. "Do you know that's my son, look at the flys of him!"

"I know Suerna, you can be proud of him today," replied Sherene.

"We've been neighbours for many's a summer; sure it's like watching my own son scooting around up there."

Sherene had never been lucky enough to meet the right fairy man. There were several nearlys and a few almosts but something just didn't fit each time. But as she often said,

"Don't feel sorry for me for each child in the Hollow is like my own."

This meant she had a lot of birthday presents each year but she never forgot a single one. Of all the elderly fairies the children liked Sherene the best because not only was she very generous but also could tell a story like no other. Certainly like no other lady fairy because her stories would make your hair curl and your toes cross and your fingers snap and grab out for the nearest hand. She often giggled at the number of young fairies who first held hands at her story nights and indeed many of them ended up as husband and wife.

When the energy and nerves of the occasion began to fade ever so slightly, Druhin calmed his wings and gracefully headed back to the spot from where he had taken off. The Ceremony wasn't finished yet.

It's a common enough thing that the First Flyer forgets the Carving what with the excitement of the air and all. Indeed Blalim's brother, Greagle, had to be escorted down from his first flight. He whizzed around for nearly a half hour. The other fairies were quite restless but restrained nonetheless, all but Grochin,

"In the name of all Fairydom, come down out of that Greagle, my backend is near frozen clean off. I won't be able to move for a month!"

It was a sign of things to come for Greagle but more of him later.

Back to the Stone and the final part of the Ceremony.

Druhin was positively beaming with pride and his cheeks were flushed from his aerobatics but he regained his composure and knew he had more to do. The crowd fell silent again after many congratulations,

"Great first flight son!" "Mighty bit of flying there!" "By the life of me I thought you were going to hit the tree head on!" and so on.

"Flyer, give your wings a while to rest
Your carving skills now to test
Take this blade and shape the wood

Your name will here be understood

History follows your letters now

Forever learning the secrets how

For all the Fairy folk to see

Carve your name into this tree!

I stood beside Druhin and took his left hand. Together we knocked on the bark of the Learning Tree three times. I then did the same with his right hand and waited. A matter of seconds later the bark began to peel apart to reveal the inner tree. It was the most perfect white. It would remind you a bit of the snow on top of Knock Layde on a winter's morning. From this inner white the Carving Knife pushed it's way through, handle first. This was really old magic and everyone was enthralled at the sight.

"Druhin, are you ready to take the Knife?"

"I am ready."

"Then carve!"

He raised his hand and took the Knife by the handle slowly drawing it out from the inner tree. The handle was made from white wood and fitted his hand perfectly. The blade was made of solid gold and shone in the sunlight. Druhin had often heard about this moment and now here he was about to carve his name forever into the Learning Tree.

With great care each letter was written into the white wood of the inner tree. He could see the thousands of names before his all moving around in the inner tree like icicles in a bowl of milk. When he had carved the final 'N' he replaced the Knife and it slowly withdrew back from where it came. The outer bark healed itself as if it was being zipped up by invisible fingers and the Learning Tree was as it always was.

"Fairy friends I declare the Ceremony over, let us celebrate!"

As I said this I noticed a nervous Clumser getting ready for his big moment.

Now, says Clumser to himself, *this is it. You've waited thirteen years because of one little blunder. Anyone can make a mistake but you had to starve the Hollow for a week! Just breathe deeply and let the words roll off your tongue. There'll be food for a month and all will be forgiven . . . hopefully.*

Poor Clumser, if he had said this to himself once he had said it a thousand times. He would surely be made to sleep in a cow pat for a year should he make a mess this time. We gathered ourselves in a loose circle. Knowing humans you maybe thought there'd be a big table and chairs to be carried out. No need. One of the benefits of getting the magic right is that the food appears ready cooked, the table already laid and everyone gets a big comfortable chair with lots of holding space along the arms for plates and drinks.

"Ladies and gentlemen, it is time for a second chance. Some of you will remember Clumser's last effort, an unfortunate click of a hiccup, eh Clumser?" I said, winking at him.

Clumser looked straight up and twiddled with his fingers behind his back. There were a few mutterings in the crowd.

"However, as long as we learn from our mistakes we should be OK. Clumser will you call for food for the folk?"

Clumser cleared his throat and took a deep breath,

This is it, he thought, *you don't want the cow pat.*

All was silent again except the river, Grochin was about to warn that he'd better get it right but he didn't.

Goodness my stomach couldn't take another attack of wind!

Clumser took a deep breath.

"To all from all food for the ball (*The first line safely away, phew!* thought Sherene)

In dark and light I have the right (*Good man, keep it going,* thought Gráinne)

To yummy the tummy in the Flyer's hall (*Don't hiccup now!* thought Shest)

None to hunger at all tonight!" (*Yahoo, yahoo, the bums are safe, the bums are safe!* thought Grochin).

A large round of applause and the food, table and chairs all duly appeared. I gave Clumser a look of approval and he had a smile on him as wide as a half moon.

What a feast we had! Nut cake, buttercup bread, grass ice cream (a delicacy), rush soup, sloe gin and whin bush beer for the adults, dewdrop lemonade for the children. There was roast snail, grilled beetle and my favourite, pickled minnow with daisy salad. We must have eaten for hours. Then the songs began and good old Suerna belted out at least three at the top of her voice. She and Aldarn were enjoying the sloe gin rather too quickly.

Soon enough the effects of the day began to show on us all and yawns replaced yarns. The sun had had enough and was bidding it's farewell behind Brea Height. The Fairy Folk moved steadily back to the Hollow, with everyone commenting on the proceedings. It was a good chance to hear a good story, especially from the older fairies. The younger ones were excitedly getting on their pyjamas as the doors slowly closed. I walked up behind Blalim and Greagle. They seemed to be reflecting on something more serious and not in the mood of the day at all. They spoke very quietly. Indeed the lines on both their brows were quite wrinkled.

"Ah now, surely you haven't fallen out on the day of a Ceremony?" I asked.

Well I got quite a look. Not a 'don't be silly look' as I was expecting but something darker.

"What did you hear?" asked Blalim sharply.

"Tell us, Graneff. It's important. Did you hear what we were talking about?" demanded Greagle.

Well if this didn't confuse me even more.

"To tell you the truth lads I didn't hear a word you were saying, I just came over to say hello."

"Good!" they replied together.

"No point in worrying the folk yet Graneff, we'll talk later. Good night and sleep well, you will need it!" said Blalim.

4

A Warning

Blalim's tone bothered me all evening. I hardly spoke as Gráinne and I got the young ones ready for bed.

"Are you OK?" she asked.

"Oh I'm fine it's just something Blalim said or more the way he said it."

We bade our goodnights to Pog and Fer and went into the kitchen. Gráinne put the dishes away and brought me over a steaming cup of mushroom tea.

"Here, this should calm you down. What do you think he meant? Is there something wrong?"

"I don't know, I'm going over to see him," I answered.

"At this hour?"

"I know but I have to find out, for my own peace of mind."

I took a hearty sup of the tea then put on my waistcoat and headed for the door.

"I'll see you later love," she said, "say hello to the lads for me."

"Aye, will do, night night."

I set out into the Hollow and it was as dark as dark could be. Treacherous for humans of course but we fairies love the dark. In fact the darker it is the more we can see. I walked slowly through the clover and grass stems. The clover is the softest in all Ireland and I rubbed my hands gently over it as I walked. As ever the river was good company.

The moon appeared, splintered by the branches of the nut trees and briefly lit up my path but the clouds soon put it back to bed.

I wonder if Odhran has heard any rumours?

No one knew what age Odhran was and most of us had given up guessing. Some say he is the oldest owl that ever there was. No one knows where he lives but he seems to know everything that's going on and we all sleep happily at night knowing he's looking out for us. As children we used to stay awake looking out the window to see if we could catch a glimpse of him but we always woke the next day in strange positions with a crick in our necks.

I walked up to Blalim's door. A grand solid door it was, made from nut wood with a large bronze knocker. Blalim's father, Crevus, helped Blalim make it at the Learning Tree. What a fairy for sculpting and carving he was. I gave the door a rap and waited. I knew they would be awake. I half hoped they would be playing draughts and surprised to see me. Rigid footprints approached and I knew it would be Blalim.

"You best come in, we've been expecting you," he said.

I followed him in to the living room (no sign of a draught board) to see Greagle looking quite serious. He had moved in with his elder brother a year or so after Rephenne had passed away. I bid him good evening and apologised for the lateness of my visit. Blalim cut straight to it.

"It's important you know who we are dealing with; Nefairious and I go back a long way."

"Nefairious!"

"Indeed," sighed Greagle as he drew deeply on his pipe.

The wisps of smoke drifted gently towards the ceiling of no. eight Nut Hollow.

"I really thought we had heard the last of him," continued Blalim.

He looked quite agitated and stared into the depths of the fire.

"I mean how could he come back after his skulduggery, not to mention being eaten by Brandon?!"

"You mean Brandon the buzzard, don't you?" I said.

"Yes he was his judge. We clipped his wings, flew him to the top of the Learning Tree and called on the buzzards to decide his fate. Brandon must've been extremely angry because the last we saw of Nefairious was his ankles sliding down Brandon's throat", said Blalim.

"But he knew the magic," said Greagle, "his father taught him."

"I know," replied Blalim, "but to survive that and to return to the Hollow? There's trouble ahead and no mistake."

"Forgive my ignorance," I interrupted, "but Nefairious is long digested, surely?"

"Yes, that was the last we thought we'd ever see of him," said Greagle, "but the rumours of him are on the wind . . . somehow he escaped. He'll be wanting his revenge on us all. It was your father after all that flew him to the top of the Learning Tree along with me. Did he never mention that event or the time leading up to it?"

"Not very much if at all. I mean I remember hearing about the trial and all but we were young then and had all manner of things to be getting along with. I suppose we felt sorry for him in a way but life goes on you know, homework, chores, girls!"

"Yes quite," said Greagle disapprovingly.

"One of my best pupils or so I thought."

As he said this I noticed him run his fingers down his right side (an old injury or wound perhaps). He went on.

"We had our ceremonies on the same date, though many years apart of course. I taught him special flying tricks around the Learning Tree itself. He really was a fabulous flyer. He had all the moves in no time and some he invented himself. Sure his First Flight was the talk of the Hollow for weeks. It would make young Druhin's look like a belly flop."

"I never liked him," said Blalim, "too cocky. Always pushing it with everyone and bragging about how fast he could fly."

"Aye but we sort of got used to him," I said.

"He was fast though," said Greagle

"Humph!" answered Blalim. "Little did we know he was planning the theft of all time."

"What do you mean?"

"Well," said Greagle, "you recall his habit of flying as fast as he could toward the Learning Tree and you would swear he was going to get his wings through the back of his head but at the very last moment he would just twist away. He was practicing the whole time under our noses. Amazing really, wasted talent."

"But what's the sense of that, I mean the only thing worth stealing would be the Carving Knife and no self respecting fairy would dare to do that."

Greagle fired me a look as if to say, 'Yeah right."

"Graneff, my boy," said Blalim, "never underestimate a fairy gone bad."

5

Nefairious

The damp logs hissed and spluttered a steady stream of grey smoke up the soot covered stone chimney. The flames danced about and tickled the large black pot that hung over them. Inside the pot, which swung gently from three gold chains, a white and mucky foam had formed on the surface of the boiling water. Around the hearth lay the remains of a few large slugs, half a caterpillar and two skewered frogs' eyes.

Hmmm, kebabs, thought the cook, *my favourite.*

The sound of the bubbling water calmed Nefairious. It reminded him of his former home down in Nut Hollow. It was this memory that drove him and his sense of revenge.

Sixty years. Sixty years on the top of this mountain with no one for company but slugs, dung beetles and all other manner of creeping, crawling, cowering things. My time is drawing near and then my friends there will be changes in the Hollow, mark my words!

He stirred the pot, spilling some of the water onto the fire. It caused a puff of smoke and both the fire and Nefairious hissed in unison.

"Twenty minutes should do it."

He moved away from the fire and left the silver ladle in the foul smelling mixture.

"Ladle, keep an eye on my dinner."

He knew it would. The ladle was one of the many things he had practiced his magic on since his expulsion. It knew when to stir but shouting at it made him happy. He would be stirring a whole pile of trouble soon enough.

The years had transformed this athletic and talented fairy to a wizened shadow of his young self. All his brightness and ambition had been diverted down a path of treachery and trickery. He had been often warned not to break the laws of the Hollow but of course would not listen. Occasionally though, he did listen to his memories. He closed his eyes.

"Aw! Come on you cowards, eat some, what are you afraid of?" he said. "No one will ever know."

Graneff and Gráinne looked at Nefairious,

"You can't mean it," said Graneff. "I don't mind stealing a few gooseberries or even pulling a few birds' feathers but we were expressly forbidden to eat toadstools. They're cursed."

"Away with ye! Old wives' tales, if you believe that you'll believe anything. C'mon Gráinne it's just me and you."

"No way! Do the stories not bother you? Warts and madness and the eternal itch? That's what happens when you eat toadstools, everyone knows that."

"Well well and here was me thinking you were both game for anything. Turns out the pair of you are nothing but . . . *fairies*! I have heard that eating toadstools makes you fly faster and see into the future. C'mon . . . try one."

"I haven't eaten any and I can see your future heading nowhere fast," said Gráinne.

"Ha! Rubbish and boloney. Away back to your flying lessons and wing washing, I'll be whizzing past you with even greater ease than I do already . . . losers."

So the young and determined Nefairious crossed the boundary of the Hollow and headed up river into Fernglen, the densest and most dangerous townland that anyone knew about. Nothing but ferns, frogs, dung beetles and stickybacks. But he didn't care. He had a point to prove and wouldn't be happy until everyone was feasting on toadstool tart.

As it happened he collected his fair share of toadstools that day and dung beetles too come to think of it. On his way home again his temper had cooled a little but unknown to himself he was chewing on slugs' eye stalks like chewing gum.

Suddenly the water bubbled over the side of the pot again to another grand hiss. This sharp noise invaded Nefairious's recollections and he was back in his stone cabin waiting for his food to cook.

"What a feast! Must build my strength. Frog's eye kebabs and slug stew. Fabulous."

Although this meal may not have appealed to everyone, the slugs were cooked to perfection and with a slight seasoning of crushed moth and dried butterfly it was a culinary masterpiece. As with most things, Nefairious excelled when he put his mind to it and his mind was keenly focused on the residents of the Hollow. His efforts to escape the confines of Brandon's stomach were a very painful memory.

If I ever have to perform a Softening again, he shivered at the thought of it. The spell to weaken ones bones to the point of liquid is the ultimate last resort but he'd had to do it.

"Water, mud, sludge and slime
Distract my bones a little time
Make them hear what softness says
To melt inside for several days
Make them see the liquid state

Is better than a stone or slate

But like the lava when it's cool

Heed again their solid rule."

That was bad enough but there was only one escape route. Yes, he crawled into the bowels of the mighty buzzard and waited. Now Brandon had a serious appetite for mice and voles and hedgehogs but a rat was his favourite and on the morning of the judgement he'd had two.

Into the brown, white and creamy goo he went and the smell was horrendous but what else could he do? As bad luck would have it the old buzzard had been blocked up in that department for some time and had been having great difficulty in releasing and for three days and nights in a semi liquid state Nefairious lay in the poo sack. But as is the way of these things his presence had caused a loosening of affairs and he was unceremoniously deposited from a great height and at great speed onto the top of Knock Layde, where he now lived.

Thank you for the dark magic, father, he thought. *Thank you for the lessons at the Learning Tree, I understand now. No one could have guessed the secrets you told me about the old ways. Secrets that will help me claim my rightful place as ruler of Nut Hollow and the owner of the Carving Knife.*

He allowed himself a loud and repugnant laugh and rocked back excitedly in his chair.

6

Neroh's Party

"I don't think I've ever had a worse night of sleep since we got married," said Gráinne.

"What on earth was on your mind?"

Despite my best efforts at slumber the conversation with the brothers had entirely filled my head and left no room for calm sleepy thoughts. Nefairious had been planning to steal the Carving Knife! That is the lowest thing a fairy, if he can be still called that, can even think of. Not only did he think of it but if it wasn't for the intervention of Greagle that sunny morning he would have succeeded.

Blalim had informed me that treachery ran in his blood. His father Neroh had been a figure of suspicion for many years. Numerous attempts to get to the source of his wealth were made by the elder fairies of the time but to no avail. And to confuse the issue he gave the impression of being the friendliest fairy that ever was. Sure if he didn't help out with collecting crops or milking moles for folk or making clover rope to name but a few things people felt something was wrong.

However, over confidence can lead to carelessness. A long time ago Neroh had invited half the Hollow to his fine home for an end of season party. Normally he would have locked all the doors but didn't bother about one little door round the back.

Sure no one would even get in there, never mind look, he thought.

The party was going well when some of the smaller fairy children decided to play hide and seek because the company of adults is intolerably boring for youngsters of all kinds. Now what better place to get a hiding place than through a little door round the back? Well, in went Dellaphin with her cousin Keferly and waited. They waited for such a time that they thought they would never be found and decided to explore.

"What a strong smell of nuts," said Keferly, "do you think there might be a few lying about?"

"Certainly smells that way." replied Dellaphin. "I think I can see one round here a bit."

Of course it was pitch black in their little hiding place (no point hiding where someone would see you and anyway the ability to see in the dark improved with age). Dellaphin reached out and plucked the first available nut and quickly munched it and crunched it.

"Hmmm!" she mumbled.

"My turn," said Keferly.

She did the same and soon the girls were filling their faces.

"What a day!" they said together.

Magic nuts were always welcome, especially with no grown ups to tell you that you'd had enough. As it turned out the nuts were stacked high like a massive pile of ripe white apples just out of view of the two youngsters. The loose ones had been thoroughly enjoyed but the youthful appetite isn't easily satisfied.

"Any more?" asked Dellaphin.

"Hold on, I'll just reach round and see. Wait . . . oh . . . yes, got one, phew!"

No sooner had she said that when they both felt the ground shake beneath them. Suddenly nuts were cascading around their ankles, up to their knees and within two flicks of a lamb's tail the girls were being carried along on a river of magic nuts. Out through the little door they spilled taking all their seekers with them. When the furore had settled down a thousand nuts lay scattered with the children like little winged islands in their midst.

"Are you OK?" asked Dellaphin.

Keferly nodded her head slowly.

"Mmm, think so. What about you?"

"Oh, I'm fine."

The other fairy children were picking themselves up from the deluge of nuts. Any minor injuries were quickly forgotten as they realised just what had engulfed them. The sound of munching was all that could be heard. Truly a First Flight, twenty birthdays and a Ceremony had all come at once. The rumblings had not gone unnoticed at the party.

"I knew it, I just knew it?" said Grochin. "It's the end of the world, we're all for the high jump!"

"No I don't think so Grochin, not yet anyway," said Blalim. "Sounds more like something has caved in or given way."

Oh no, thought Neroh. *It can't be!*

He had to think quickly or else his secret stash would be a secret no longer. He would deal with the disturbers later. For now there were a lot of curious fairies asking questions.

"Ladies and gentlemen, there is no cause for concern. The noise you heard was simply my latest invention, a mechanised nut collector. I'm still working on the finer details, such as vibration control. You see it's designed to rattle a branch very quickly and dislodge the ripe nuts into our baskets. If you will continue with your drinks I'll go around and sort them er . . . it out."

"Are you sure you don't need a hand?" asked Grast.

"Not at all, it's always happening. I'll be back in five minutes."

Neroh smiled as he left the garden and headed round the back of the house. It seemed that his story had worked, well why wouldn't it? No one had cause to doubt him.

"You know," said Grochin, "old Neroh is just great, there he is running to fix a machine that will help us all in the middle of his own party. Not a word of help or anything, just make sure you enjoy yourselves, great host altogether."

Graunad was a little perturbed.

"It's probably just me but did anyone think that Neroh reacted just a bit too quickly? He never mentioned a nut collector before and normally he does like to keep everyone well informed of his activities."

"Well if he is in trouble he probably didn't want any fuss. That rattle sounded like a lot of cleaning up was required, I'm going to help, who's coming?" asked Grast.

As is the way among the Hollow folk the thought that one of them might be in need of help was enough. It was drummed into all that you never know when your rainy day might come so it's wise to keep a spare umbrella. It was a good feeling to open it up and keep a friend dry. With this in mind the party gathering, which accounted for pretty much all the neighbourhood, put down their drinks and plates and rolled up their sleeves.

"Kindly lower your plate Grochin, and come on!" said Frenel (well it was more of a threat truth be told).

"Umm! Umm! Never know where the umm next umm bite's coming from," mumbled a discontented Grochin.

Almost ninety fairies ready for action walking determinedly round the clover adorned roots that made up the outside of Neroh's home. The picture they witnessed would stay with them for a lifetime, what they heard would haunt them. Neroh had lined up the fairy hiders and seekers; seven fairy children with tears in their eyes and awaiting some dreadful retribution.

"This will be the last day your inquisitive fingers ever touch a thing in this Hollow. I'm going to remove them all with a blunt knife. Your legs will be replaced with wooden stumps and nailed to the bottom of the river. Your heads will make footballs and I shall use your hair for fishing rope . . ."

His temper had been well and truly lost so much so he didn't even notice the crowd gather behind him. He began to shout,

> "Darkness in deed
> Blackness of heart
> Gather at speed
> Now to start
> Magic so deep
> From down below
> Punishment steep
> And full of w- (oe)"

"Stop this!" roared Graunad before Neroh could finish. "Children, run!"

They didn't need to be told twice. The seven little fairies dispersed as if blown by the wind. Immediately Greagle was up and flying directly at Neroh. As he cut through the air he quickly loosened the rope that was hanging in a loop from his belt. In an instant he was circling it round his head ready to let it go.

Neroh quickly realised that events had taken a twist from which there was no turning back. His mind switched to the approaching crowd and he let his façade of civility fall. His wings burst open and he too was airborne. Greagle had to flick left as fast as possible just to avoid him. Neroh was a big fairy and an impact would have had disastrous results for Greagle.

"So you think you can catch *me*? *Neroh*! The wind itself is too slow, think again. How dare you think you can compete with a Duveline master?"

"Duveline!" thought Graunad. "Black magic."

"Where did you think I learned to do the all the things I can do? The Learning Tree? Ha! There are quicker ways than that. I have bartered much for these skills and you will soon feel their power."

He positioned himself above the crowd flying backwards slowly, never losing sight of Greagle who himself was hovering with his rope at the ready.

"I am to be your keeper and you will obey my law. The Hollow will echo my rules and the river whisper my name. The time has come!"

A terrible whistling wind began to whip up around the children's ankles knocking them over like corn stooks.

Let the north wind take care of them, thought Neroh.

The wind at his command rushed around their heads and was pushing them back toward the river. Those fairies still on the ground were in a state of shock. There were screams and shouts of terror as the wind pushed and pulled them. They grasped frantically for any root or flower stem that might save them.

Surely this could not be Neroh, their friend and whose son went to school with their children. This must be a practical joke just for the party. Any moment now he would descend and laugh heartily at the fright he had given. But no, his eyes were fixed on their faces with such anger that no one had seen before.

Among the amazed onlookers was Vifell, Neroh's wife of many years. To complicate matters her son Nefairious stood at her side as the whole episode unfolded. He couldn't speak but felt his loyalties being ripped down the middle, along with his heart.

"Neroh," she called, "what is this madness? Why are you doing this?" her voice just loud enough above the wind.

But Neroh did not have time to answer. Wherever the last shred of decency had been hiding it had reappeared in his eyes as he looked at her. It is thought he truly loved her once but the Duveline had changed him. He held her gaze long enough for Graunad to hit him behind the head with his hurley stick. He had flown up from behind as first Grast then Vifell caught his attention. Down out of the sky he fell into a crumpled heap of nastiness and the wind calmed as suddenly as it had risen.

"We have no time to lose," said Graunad.

"We must get him to the only place that will hold him."

"Oh aye," said Greagle, "and where would that be? His brand of magic is twisted and exceptionally strong."

"Exactly what I mean," answered Graunad, "the Fairy Thorn of Carey is the strongest most twisty thing I've ever seen. Not even Neroh will be able to escape. Between our magic and those branches we'll be safe."

There was a hush about the company. The Fairy Thorn of Carey was the place where the older fairies told their children they would end up if they were bold.

"It's the strongest and darkest prison we have. There is no escape for any fairy once imprisoned," exclaimed Graunad.

"You're right of course," said Grast, "but what about the humans? They've been known to knock them down and not even our magic can withstand that."

"Aye, sometimes they do but we have them so scared of snapping a branch they'd never knock one down as big and dark as the Carey Fairy Thorn."

"Huh! Humans," snapped Graunad, "they're capable of anything. We're going to need the help of the animals to be doubly sure. Bee stings, worm traps, spiders' webs, blue bottle droppings (truly foul) anything and everything to keep that fiend at bay."

Graunad, Grast, Greagle and Blalim headed for the Carey Fairy Thorn with Neroh still out for the count. The rest of the Hollow folk tidied up the horde of nuts. With a few magic spells each larder in the Hollow filled with these most precious items and Neroh's secret room was soon empty. The general mumbling faded as the four carried Neroh down past Cross Rivers and up through the long grass. It was an arduous task as Neroh was too risky to fly with and none had walked so far for a long time.

Each small creature they met was put on alert against this bad fairy and each promised to fulfil their duty. On they went until they stood at the foot of the Thorn itself.

"Let's be quick," said Graunad, "this is no place for us. Too long here and the tree would claim us all. Put him down and go."

No sooner was Neroh laid on the ground when the first of the Thorn runners slithered along the ground through the grass. It wrapped itself slowly round his body and lifted him to the space between the leaves and the trunk. Soon other thicker branches came and surrounded him drawing him deeper into the foliage.

The four turned to watch from a safe distance. Deeper into the darkness he went. The branches closing about him like a deadly serpent. The thorns on the thicker branches glistened in the evening sun. He would feel their anger before long.

"It's done," said Graunad, "let's go home."

7

Feathers

Time moves slowly and shows it's passing in any number of ways. For the Hollow folk the leaves on the trees disappear and re-emerge. Flowers bloom and fade and bloom again. The cry of babies fills the air along with the buzzing of bees and the flapping of birds. Even Odhran's feathers fall out and grow back again. After the incredible incident with Neroh most of the fairies in Nut Hollow were in a state of shock. During the days that followed hardly a sentence was uttered that didn't refer to those events. However, each day brought a little more light than the last and the air seemed easier to breathe. Chatter returned to topics more suited to these gentle folk. Graunad, Greagle, Grast and Blalim continued to meet and check up on the rogue in the Fairy thorn but each summer thickened the branches around Neroh and his threat diminished until his name was only ever used as a means of keeping younger fairies in line at dinner times and bed times and any other times youngsters get into mischief.

The sun spread it's light all over Brea Height and as far as the eye could see was clear. The sheep along the tops of Glenmak Mountain wished the humans would hurry up and chase them. The cows strolled happily down to the river each day and drank their fill, swishing their tails at flies and wasps (and the occasional sleepy fairy) and discussing the prospect of a long summer. They weren't too hopeful as good weather is as fleeting as the chances of true love. Nonetheless the Hollow was doing well and no storm clouds could be seen.

"I'm not happy with those thistles," complained Grochin.

Oh here he goes again, thought Frenel.

"What do you mean 'not happy with those thistles'? No one likes them, forever catching your clothes and pulling you out of the air."

"Ha!" said Grochin, "the last time you flew there were two moons in the sky."

"That's not the point and you're no Greagle yourself!"

"Listen woman, we've been in the Hollow a long time and can you honestly remember seeing so many? It's almost as if they're surrounding us. Whoever is in charge of trimming them back should get a large thistle around the backside," he moaned.

"You old goat, are you completely mad? Thistles surrounding us indeed. You'll be seeing nettles in your pyjamas next."

Grochin took a long look up the hill and in spite of his feelings he reluctantly agreed with his wife, although he didn't say as much.

*   *   *

Nefairious paced impatiently around the kitchen of his house on the top of Knock Layde. He was now pretty much back to his physical strength but in need of some practice with his magic. The air around the mountain top where he was exiled was a poor comparison to Nut Hollow. Any spells that were to work up there would have to be extremely strong. Although Nefairious found this a terrible frustration his magic was attaining a strength he didn't realise (a strength that would surprise many in days to come).

I need to be able to fly, he thought. *I need to be faster than the wind, this spell has to work.*

Since the softening his wings had shrivelled up and rather worryingly for him fallen off in much the same way as the dry skin over a cut would do. They showed no sign of returning. This caused him many sleepless nights on Knock Layde gazing at the stars and in spite of the tranquility his temper was under such severe pressure he thought he might explode at any moment. The spell in his mind was the one his father had shown him at the Learning Tree. He recalled the scene.

"Now Nefairious," said Neroh, "if for some reason you should lose the ability to fly there's one spell that will help, and keep this quiet, do you understand?"

"Yes father."

"Some folk around here would never use this spell; they think that any fairy who has lost the ability to fly isn't worth the name . . . so righteous I'm sure. However, these things happen. Now listen."

Neroh took from his back trouser pocket a black wallet. It was made from beetle back leather and had a large N decorated on the front. It folded outward to reveal an inner pouch held down with a silver clip. From within the pouch he removed seven tiny feathers, each one a different kind.

"These are the Seven Feathers of Flight," he said, "they have been taken from the most agile flying birds in the Kingdom of Carey. I had to shrink them down as you can see. I also had a time collecting these I can tell you, so don't lose them."

He introduced each feather with great reverence and spoke these lines,

"Ah Swift so named you tame the wind,
That flows along your gentle skin
And Swallow's tail in time of need
Gives me courage for the deed
And mottled from the singing Thrush

Disguise the host in any bush

Red breasted Robin the noble one

Yield pride when the task is done

Morning's favourite the Starling's song

Make me sound like nothing's wrong

Fear the Buzzard's pointed claw

I will now defy gravity's law

And Owl so clever give to me

Wisdom for my trickery."

"Each of these feathers has been used in many spells and is very powerful but to use them all together will give you incredible skills. With these you will be able to do just about anything your heart desires. But be warned the power is fleeting and you will be in need of much rest when your task is accomplished."

Nefairious recalled gazing up at his father in complete awe and not really understanding what exactly was going on. However, with the passage of time he now appreciated just what powers where within his grasp; powers that would help him to release his father and take over the Hollow. Oh how sweet would the revenge be on those do-good fairies.

"Stop day dreaming boy!" his father's voice jolted him back again to the Learning Tree.

"I entrust this wallet to you in the hope you will never need it because if you do you will have passed through dreadful times."

"But why can't you keep it?"

"Nefairious, you will learn to accept gifts from me without question but if you must know, the feather spell works only once and I used my turn many years ago."

"You got your wings clipped?" asked a shocked Nefairious.

"Of course not," snapped Neroh. "There were frequent battles in these parts at a time and I was badly injured. Sure if you look at the older fairies, they nearly all carry a wound or two."

"Why were there battles father?"

"For the nuts of course! They contain powerful magic, too tempting for some creatures, like rats and crows and weasels too. Someday you will learn to use this magic but for now, no more questions. Now let's hide this somewhere safe."

Of course Neroh forgot to tell Nefairious that he was in league with the attackers. Only the leadership and bravery of Greagle and Blalim and friends thwarted his plans. His wounds were nearly all self inflicted, except for the time a young crow unaware of who he was pecked him in the back. He flew into a branch and broke his wings in the fall. His mastery of deception even then was second to none and he played up his escape from death no end. Neroh enjoyed the attention and no mistake.

He walked down from the Learning Tree through the Hollow smiling at his neighbours with Nefairious trotting and tripping along behind.

"Why don't we leave it where they'd never think to look?" asked Nefairious.

"Exactly son, you're learning."

Neroh had the run of the Hollow; there wasn't a door that didn't give him a warm welcome. As he thought he hummed, the darker the thoughts the louder the hum. What he produced was no recognisable tune, but Nefairious was sure he had heard it before.

"What's that tune you're humming, Dad?"

If you picture the scene at that moment they could've been any father and son in the world but of course they were not. They were far from normal, and getting further away with each step. Nefairious walked in his father's shadow, a shadow that would cast over him greed, pain and desire. Today however, the shadow meant adventure and the wallet.

"Oh I learned that tune many years ago and used to rock you to sleep by it. I hum it most days. People never know what you're thinking when you hum. Now smile and no more questions."

Neroh turned and faced into the Hollow, his long brown coat flicking up the leaves as he walked. His black boots were the finest beetle leather and cost a considerable sum but being Neroh they were given to him for services by the cobbler, Brógun. He always wore a red waistcoat and today was no exception. All this suited his white shirt and black britches that had creases sharp enough to cut mole bacon! He smoothed his fingers around the wallet that waited in his waistcoat pocket.

This would have to be just right, no one could ever question his motives, for his son's sake, or at least until it didn't matter. He looked around expecting Nefairious to be right there. He wasn't and instead was standing some way behind watching Graneff wave his arms about explaining what he would do if he could fly like Greagle.

"Come here, Nefairious," he shouted. "We have work to do."

Nefairious said his goodbyes and rejoined his father keeping his eyes down as he approached. His excitement immediately quelled by his father's tone.

"When was the last time you heard a good story son?"

"Sure, last Saturday, we always go to Sherene's for a good yarn."

"Well, it's Saturday again and you're heading back right now."

8

That Night in Sherene's

The weather had been so hot that the sun so often looked for was now almost feared. The grass and growth was as dry as a thirsty mole after a day pulling the plough through the daisy fields. Daisy fields are hard work for a mole but they do yield up the finest ingredients for daisy jam, butter, cakes and all sorts of wonderful things.

In her youth Sherene had walked through the daisies with her parents. Mostly she went with her mother, Alene, collecting the white petals that fell from the daisies after the ploughing. Her father, Sherf had often told her the dangers of the ill-tempered mole and that 'the whish of those whishkers could do permanent damage!'

She had fond memories of her youth but lately that was all she had. Her parents got older and slipped away peacefully within a few days of each other. She turned her thoughts away from marriage when it became clear to her that that was one road she would not be taking and instead devoted her time to her house and garden. These were maintained in the finest manner for her real true love . . . stories.

What a yarn spinner she was. She found herself the centre of attention at many gatherings, be they happy or sad. Her way with language carried her listeners off into another world for an hour or two and they often told her they were the better for the journey.

As it was a Saturday (Fairy week days—Moon Day, Yous Day, Weddings Day, Stars Day, Free Day, Saving Day and Sun Day, for handiness we'll use your human names) she was busy as usual getting her living room prepared for the weekly invasion of the local children. She had spread ten yellow and blue cushions that she knitted herself of course and filled with the downy feathers of the older midges. These provided the best stuffing for pillows and cushions and as no one else had the way to persuade midges give their feathers Sherene's cushions were the talk of the Hollow. Old Grochin had pleaded for some for his crinkly rear end but to no avail, they were for children only.

Each of the four walls of the room was covered in books. All sorts of books, big ones, little ones, round ones, square ones, triangular ones, rectangular ones and even inside out ones! She firmly believed that the imagination was the best place for inquisitive young minds to find answers. Her father had carved the shelves from the autumn fallen branches of the Learning Tree so what better thing to put on them than books.

The dark purple couch was as comfortable as the cushions and the two chairs on either end as comfortable as the couch. Sherene herself sat in the rocking chair beside the fire. Rocking to and fro helped her tell the stories and it was noticed a few times the more exciting the story got the faster she rocked (she had once nearly tipped over backwards but finished the story just in time).

Her house was on the other side of the river and as most of her audience couldn't fly yet they would jump across on the stepping-stones nipping the bums of the lazy frogs as they went. Her front door was made from Rowanberry wood and was covered in velvet green moss except for the post box and the knocker. It was made from two old mole bones and made the grandest of raps. As with most fairy dwellings it was out of human sight safely tucked away under a large flat stone. It was six o' clock on Saturday evening and the children were on their way.

"KNOCK KNOCK!"

Ah that'll be the start of it, thought Sherene. *Who will we have today?*

She put down her cup of buttercup tea and went to the door. As ever she found a troupe of eager faces staring up at her.

"Well well, can I help you?"

"Ha ha," replied Graneff, "it's story time!"

"Oh! Of course it is, I nearly forgot, you'd better all come in," she smiled and winked at them.

The children bundled in excitedly and spread themselves out on the cushions and couch and waited without a sound. This was for two reasons. Firstly the anticipation of the adventure ahead and secondly the large bowl of fairy toffee. It sat there on a wooden table just scrumptiously. It was the sort of stuff that'd make your teeth fall out just by looking at it. Best of all they didn't even have to ask 'please and thank you' to get at it and no matter how much they ate there was always enough. Perfectly wonderful indeed.

The little mouths were busy negotiating this sticky feast as Sherene sat down on the rocking chair beside the fire. She threw on a lump of hairy turf and began her story with an explosion of embers and blue smoke. Nefairious put his hand in his pocket. The feather purse sat quietly there but his head was aloud with ideas and anxieties as to where he might leave it. He was glad no one could hear him think.

Sherene began,

"Once upon a time in a dark part of the forest lived a troll. A hairy old gnarled bad tempered egg of a troll. He had black hair that looked like a crow's nest on his head and two squinty eyes. His brow always wore a frown and his lips were always turned down. His nose was like a month old carrot and he had three teeth. Two on top and one on the bottom and they were all rotten. His clothes were made from old nut sacks and his shoes were toeless and heelless. Now this is not to say the troll was poor. No, far from it. He was a miserly old devil who had lots of money but refused to spend any of it."

As Sherene took a breath Nefairious wriggled uncomfortably in his seat. He could hear his father's voice sternly in his head warning him to leave the purse without getting caught. He gazed at Sherene's face and felt guilty that this wonderful woman was being used in a nasty plan but he had no choice. He'd have to wait a little longer.

"The troll took great delight in scaring the other creatures that lived near him in the wood. He would sneak up behind a moose and bite it squarely on the bum! He would sometimes trap the birds and pull off their wings! You know I've even heard of him cutting the tails of newborn calves and using them for his sandwiches! A thoroughly nasty piece of work and no mistake. We're lucky in the Hollow not to have anyone like that."

Nefairious stared straight down not daring to catch her eye in case she would know. In the room the chewing had slowed as the story took hold. The fire breathed and coughed occasionally and the room got hotter.

"Enragad was his name and some of the other trolls would ask why he was so nasty but all they would get in response was, 'Humph! Because I **can** be!'

So for years he brought fear to the forest until no one would pass his way at all. However, he had built his dark little house beside the most beautiful lake you could imagine and the other animals wanted to go back and use it. Sadly they were too afraid to approach Enragad and had to watch him swim and splash and drink the beautiful water while they had to rely on puddles and oul' sheughs. Well, what were they to do?

As it happened along their way came a beautiful lady troll called Birgid. She was amazed to hear that Enragad had taken over the lake and was frightening the animals.

'This just can not continue, now everyone gather round,' said Birgid, 'this is what we'll do.'

Well poor Nefairious was in a right state now. He loved stories and even noticed Sherene beginning to rock a little more in her chair.

Oh father, why? he thought.

If there was a moment you could say Nefairious went bad this was it. He asked Sherene could he have a glass of water (so as he wouldn't miss the story) and excused himself and went to the bathroom. Sherene duly obliged and headed into the kitchen as tiny hands reached again for the toffee bowl. Nefairious went into the bathroom and looked around.

'Now where can I leave this purse?'

He noticed a fine cabinet hanging up above the sink. He opened the mirrored doors and saw three shelves on either side. They were full of soaps and ointments, no room there. Then as he closed the doors he noticed the cabinet move slightly. He looked round the back to see a nail and the hook on which the cabinet hung. He carefully took down the cabinet and gouged out a small hole in the wall, just big enough to hold the purse.

'I'll see you later,' he said.

He replaced everything just as it was and as cool as you like he sat himself down with a handful of toffee just as Sherene returned. She gave the fire another lump of turf and continued the story . . .

"Suddenly the creatures had some hope. Here at last was someone who would confront Enragad. They felt stronger and braver than ever but how would they get rid of the cruel little troll? Birgid looked at them all in the eye and said,

'What I ask of you will not be easy but it is vital we work together. We will have to ask the snake for help!'

'The snake!' they replied. "Are you mad, sure he's worse than Enragad!'

'Are you sure about that?' asked Birgid. 'He doesn't bother with anyone in this part of the forest and I know he has a big appetite but also likes to be the scariest creature around. If he heard that there was another more frightening than he, do you think he would be pleased?'

The animals shook their heads. They knew she was right but how would they get the snake to come to their part of the forest? After some discussion Birgid told them the plan. The fastest animal would take Birgid to the snake's lair where she would ask very politely if he would grant them an audience with his scariness. She would relate the story of the scary troll being even scarier than the snake. He would then hopefully like to meet the troll and see just who was the scariest creature in the woods.

So Chevalon the horse and Birgid headed to the lair of Snaryk, king of snakes and hoped he wouldn't eat them.

They stood at the front of his underground lair and called 'Snaryk the most Frightful' we have word of one even more frightful than you!' There was no sound, then suddenly from behind them he appeared,

'Who are you to call on Snaryk, why I should eat you both right now!'

He hissed terribly and made to gobble them both but Birgid said,

'Stop O terrible slitherer, you are no longer the scariest creature in these woods and if you eat us you will never know who is.'

Snaryk thought a moment then hissed,

'Scarier than *me*? What rubbish! Take me to this impostor immediately.'

Birgid rode swiftly back to the lakeside with Snaryk's foul breath on her shoulder. The other creatures cowered as he slid past them licking his lips.

'Where is this foul pretender to my throne?' he snarled.

Birgid was happy to point him in the direction of Enragad's house. Away he crawled cursing and spitting and spluttering.

Sherene's chair was moving at some speed now. The little fairies were enthralled and several had huddled as close to the rocking chair as they dared without getting their toes squashed. Even Nefairious was caught up in the tale, though he did wish to have Snaryk for a pet. Graneff was sitting beside a lovely little fairy called Gráinne. She didn't like the thought of all that nastiness and Sherene noticed her reach out and grab Graneff's hand. No one dared move, the fire roared up the chimney and all eyes focused on Sherene.

"Well as soon as each of these examples of nastiness laid eyes on each other the battle began. They were soon rolling, fighting, kicking, punching, cursing, throwing, wrestling and biting away at the other. On went the fierce spectacle hour after hour. 'I'm the nastiest,' said one,

'No I'm the worst of all,' said the other.

Gouging and nipping and ripping all the way to the edge of the lake they went like two demons at work. Birgid and the animals watched the spectacle in awe. Then the largest splash that ever there was filled the air and the two disappeared in a foam of bad temper. Silence regained the day. They were gone to the depths, fighting all the way to see who would be the worst. Sadly for them and happily for the forest they never returned and neither seemed to realise that being the nastiest was no prize at all. The smaller creatures returned to their chores and were glad that the forest was safe once again."

Sherene gazed directly at Nefairious as she finished her story.

"Does she know?" he wondered.

She slowed the rocking chair and every little fairy began to cheer and clap. It was now time for bed and they all bade Sherene thank you and goodnight. She waved from her front door making sure they all made it safely over the river and listened to the excited recantations giggle off into the evening. As he reached his home Nefairious turned and looked at Sherene's now closed door. He was content that the purse was safely hidden and would not be discovered.

9

Two Little Girls

Above the Hollow was another world, a world of stuff and nonsense. That world was where the humans lived. What a frantic bunch they were, forever talking about school, homework, mortgages, cars, work, money and clothes and window boxes. They dwelled in huge houses that could comfortably sleep every fairy that ever lived or was ever likely to live. They travelled about the place in things they called cars, tractors, trucks, jeeps and JCBs. Possibly the loudest collection of polluting tomfoolery you could get.

However, they were a civil sort mostly and some had an appreciation for plants, animals and trees, what we consider the important things. Of the crowd that lived above the Hollow two were particularly nice. Little girls they were and often seen rolling down Brea Height, flattening all in their paths. This occasionally led to thistles being removed by their parents and the application of creams (ice creams of course) for nettle stings. As is the case with most summer days the sun was out drying after the rain had been out soaking.

The Wellington boots were quickly retrieved from under the sofa and the pair of them were on their way down the Brea. If you were to see them from a few puck outs away you would see a splash of brown and blond hair bouncing along inside red and black polka dotted raincoats and yellow and white striped wellies.

"Well Katie," said Dara, "race you down to the river."

"You're on", and away they went tearing down through the long wet grass doing their best to avoid the numerous cowpats. For these two, the Hollow was a big adventure playground. Plenty of branches to be swinging on, the river to get wet in and the bridge to scare each other under with tales of gruff goats called Billy and a little girl in a riding hood with Grannies that looked like wolves. Today would be a different day, who would need bedtime stories to be afraid of when you had *Fairy* tales?

"I win, I win," said Dara. It was always a great victory to get the first splash and Dara claimed the honour today.

"Oh, you cheated, you're not allowed to stand on the cowpats," replied Katie, a little miffed. "You have to go round them or else you clean your boots with your fingers," she insisted.

Dara's first splash had cleaned off most of the offending material and Katie's splash, which half soaked Dara, soon cheered her up. Both were giggling away in no time. The river swept past as they caught their breaths and looked around. The raindrops clung to most of the long grassy stems on both banks of the river; large liquid prisms bending sunlight and making magic. The branches of the Learning Tree hung lazily down and moved gently in the wind trying to hold on to their many leaves. Katie and Dara ducked under the branches and headed up river to a little clearing they had designed on previous visits. The grass was well flattened and so thick that you could easily be sitting on a big green cushion. They both had removed some smooth river rocks and used them as little tables for any sweets or crisps they wanted to eat.

"Well," said Dara, "do you think we will have any adventures today?"

This was a common question posed by the girls. Their heads were full of the stories and tales they heard each night before going to bed.

They wished something fantastical could happen to them some day but doubted that it ever would.

"Oh I don't know," replied Katie, she had become attracted to what looked like a little fly in a spider's web.

"I suppose this would be the place for an adventure but everyone says that those sort of things only happen in fairy tales and Narnia books."

She fell silent for a moment.

"Dara could you come and look at this, it looks like . . . well . . . it looks like a fairy!"

"Oh ha ha ha!" snapped Dara. "Very funny I was just telling you what I was thinking, there's no need to be sarky."

"I'm not," replied Katie. "Promise. Look."

Dara pushed her hands down into the soft green grass, leaned forward and stood up.

"You'd better not be having me on or you'll be going back in the river."

"Shhhh! C'mon over to you see this."

Dara took the few steps she needed and soon was looking into the spider's web. The web itself was a silver secret clinging on between two branches in a shadowy part of the tree. The lines of webbing were so thin you could hardly see them. But they were there alright and stuck in the middle was . . . well . . . well it certainly looked like a fly to start with, but it only had two legs and two wings. It had blue shoes and green trousers and a yellow shirt and an orange waistcoat and at this particular time appeared to be fast asleep and not in the slightest bit bothered about becoming spider soup.

"My goodness," exclaimed Katie, "I've never seen a fly like that before, have you?"

"I don't think it's a fly," answered Dara

"Well if it isn't a fly or something like a fly what else can it be?"

"I don't know at all," said Dara, "but this little fellow certainly is in good health, the buttons are bursting on his waistcoat. Do you think we should wake him up?"

"Are you mad? He might turn us into goats or slugs or who knows what," gasped Katie.

"I think we should let him . . . it . . . lie on and head up to the house."

"Oh I don't think he would mind too much and we'll be very nice. Now what can we use to wake him?"

Katie wasn't convinced. She had heard stories about fairies all her life and knew there were good ones and bad ones. How would they know about this little chap even if he did look cute?

"What about a wee splash of water? I reckon that would do the trick," said Dara excitedly.

"I'll get a long piece of grass and let a drop from the river roll down and splash him on the nose. What do you reckon?"

"Well, I suppose it'll do no harm but if we end up with three legs and two heads it'll be your fault."

Dara stepped back from the web and gazed into the long grass for just the right stem.

"Ah ha! You'll do the job," she said

"Are you ready Katie?"

"Oh why not?"

Carefully, Dara held the piece of grass over the little fairy's head. Katie returned from the river with her hands cupped to hold the water they needed.

"Here goes!"

The water drops trickled from Katie's outstretched hands backways over her palms and onto the stem. One or two drops fell over either side but soon a large wet one was on it's way. Bull's eye! The little fairy was splashed fairly and squarely on the head and he woke up with a shiver and a shake. He rubbed the water from his eyes and tried to remember how he had got there and what or who had soaked him. As the water cleared he got he most frightful shock.

"Odhran preserve us!" he wailed. "Please don't eat me . . . pleeeaassee!"

He set himself up on his elbows and scrambled to stand up. However, he couldn't do it because he was stuck in the web. A double shock! Now with all the commotion the owner of the web began to edge toward him.

"Oh help me please I do not want to be eaten thank you very much," he shouted.

Neither Katie nor Dara could release him quickly enough and suddenly the spider was right beside him. Katie was about to stick her hand around him when another strange thing happened.

"My good fairy, I have had my breakfast today and besides I'm not really one for fairies. Don't you remember what happened?" asked the spider suddenly.

Well, thought Dara, *this is some day . . . a talking spider too if you don't mind.*

The spider went on,

"My young fellow I mean you no harm, so please don't look so worried. I haven't seen a fairy in my web for some time and besides I don't think I could eat a whole one!"

As he said this he winked with half of his many eyes at Katie who was also quite shocked at the turn of events.

"For some reason you were climbing on the branches above my home, looking for nuts I'd say, when the branch snapped under you. Down you came in a heap of youthful extravagance, rapped your head off that branch above you and landed safely where you now find yourself."

"Oh! Now that you mention it I do recall something about a nut or two and stretching out for a real juicy one on the end of that branch," said the dazed intruder.

"Now my good fairy, what is your name and who are your people?" asked Spindler the spider.

"My name is Clumsill," replied the somewhat confused fairy.

"Hmmm Clumsill eh? Would you be related to Clumser and his wife Silleyn?"

"Yes they're my mum and dad."

"Yes, I'm sure they are, that explains a few things," laughed Spindler

In spite of his best efforts Clumsill could not free himself from the web. Spindler gently cut the sticky threads from under him and carried him to the edge.

"Well Clumsill, this has turned out to be quite a day and there's still a lot of daylight left. I will have to trust your care to these two little human girls. My lunch will be flying along at any moment and I don't want to miss it if you know what I mean?"

"Oh all right then," replied the fairy.

Katie and Dara looked at each other then at Spindler. It didn't matter that they were about to talk to a spider. There was something about him that demanded respect.

"Your Spiderness," started Dara

"Oh now away with that nonsense, Spindler will do very well."

"Ok then, Spindler, we promise to look after this little fellow and take him back to his house even if we don't know where or what his house is."

"I can help you there," said Clumsill feeling altogether happier, "it's just over there across the river, number twenty four Nut Hollow."

Katie and Dara had never heard the name Nut Hollow before. To them they were just down at the river at the bottom of the hill. As it turned out they were about to learn lots of new things.

10

Well Watered

The three new friends bade farewell to Spindler. Katie had Clumsill in her right hand and was trying not to squeeze him too tightly. Both she and Dara raised the overhanging branches from their path until they were down at the edge of the river. The afternoon had meandered toward evening without anyone noticing and the sparkles on the water were not as bright as before. However, the river swept past and as inviting as it looked the girls knew it would be cold if they fell in.

"So whereabouts is this house of yours?" asked Dara.

"All I can see are rocks and grass and midgies which are now having me for dinner!"

"Ha! Listen to you," said Katie, "aren't you the clever clogs who said 'lets wake the fairy'?"

"Alright alright, but I'm hungry and I can't imagine fairy plates holding enough to fill my tooth."

They had walked a few steps back towards the Learning Tree when Clumsill interrupted,

"Ok we're here, sort of. I mean it's over on the other bank. You can cross the bridge or jump using those stepping stones."

The two girls decided together that bridges were for old people with too much sense and an unhealthy fear of mud.

"I'll go first," said Dara, and away she skipped without a thought.

No surprise really as she had crossed them many times. She was on the other side in no time at all.

"Well c'mon then."

"OK, just a sec," replied Katie.

Clumsill wasn't particularly happy about his situation. First, if this giant who was holding him slipped he'd be in for a soaking and secondly, even if he did make it home dry when his parents heard his tale he'd be in for a 'spin'. Fairy children don't like to be dizzy, so sometimes if they have misbehaved their parents line up wooden cups of water along the hall on both sides about a footstep apart. They then ask the children to turn around with their eyes closed as many times as they have years. Next they must walk along the line of cups without spilling any. If any is spilled they must clean it all up and go straight to bed without any supper. Clumsill had done this a few times and always ended up on his knees mopping up. So he feared he would be wet no matter what tonight.

Katie skipped over the first few stones without incident. Then about halfway over she saw a large green frog out of the corner of her eye. They were on a collision course. Katie didn't want to squash the fat little fellow and tried to jump to the stone next to the one she meant to. Well her foot landed on the stone but her momentum was such that the rest of her kept moving and she spun around in mid air and landed bum first in the middle of the river. The frog looked at the strange creature splashing about in the water, wiped some of the splash from his brow and continued steadily along his path.

"Oh for goodness sake!" said Katie, "I'm soaking and one of my wellies is away down the river."

Clumsill was also dripping. Katie's hand had dunked him fairly and squarely under the water. They were a pair to be seen alright. Katie clambered out of the river to the side and was pulled the rest of the way by Dara. Clumsill coughed and spluttered on resurfacing in among Katie's soggy fingers.

"Oh what a day this has been. I've never had anyone like you home before. Who knows what my parents will make of it," he fretted.

Katie was not worried about fairies at that moment. Her Wellie boot was floating somewhere downstream and her exposed foot was in mud up to the ankle. Still she knew she hadn't too far to go to get back to her house. She would see Clumsill home, say goodbye and that would be that.

"OK," said Dara, "where is your house?"

"Are you joking?" asked Clumsill, "Your foot is at the front door."

Dara looked down at her foot but beside she could only see roots and stones and grass. Certainly there was nothing resembling a door of any kind.

"Are you sure?" she asked, "I mean to say there's nothing here but muddy grass and a few stones . . ."

Ah humans, thought Clumsill, *blessed with big, bright, beautiful, colourful eyes and yet they can't see through them.*

"Look again," he said.

Both girls looked at each other as much to say 'OK daft little fairy' then they looked around their ankles again. Slowly the ground on which they stood seemed to change. There were little marks all about their feet, footprints like you might see on a beach on a sunny Sunday. There were stone paths neatly designed to stop just at the water's edge. Many of these paths had flowers along each side and most had gardens attached and hedges and some of them had pools and waterfalls and all sorts of wonderfulness.

"Do you see this?" asked Katie.

"I do, I do indeed . . . it's beautiful," replied Dara.

Now with their eyes truly open the splendour of the Hollow revealed itself to them. As far as they could see the land on either side of the river was carefully carved and shaped into gardens, vegetable plots, hedges, paths and allotments. All the paths led into the overhanging grassy banks. No wonder they hadn't noticed this before. They had looked around the Hollow many times but hadn't really seen anything apart from what they expected to see. Suddenly the bees were flying in a new pattern as if they were being herded or guided. The larger flying insects that they thought were just more potential biting things were actually flying fairies tending the insects! The overhanging branches of the nut trees were beautifully adorned with seats, couches, and hammocks made from moss, leaves and spider webs. The girls were in a state of wonder. Everything in their midst had some previously hidden detail now singing out in front of them. It was almost too much for their eyes to appreciate.

"Clumsill! What is going on?" came a voice suddenly.

The girls were shocked to hear such cross tones in amongst this beauty but cross they were,

"Those creatures are standing right on top of my daisies . . . in the middle of my garden!"

It was Clumsill's mum, Silleyn, and she wasn't pleased.

11

Introductions

The water dripped slowly off Katie's hair but she didn't notice. She wasn't bothered that her wellie boot was long gone and her foot was soaked inside her muddied sock. She cared little that her lovely dress now had a distinctive soggy streaky pattern all down the front. No she didn't care at all because here at the bottom of the brae she was getting the scowl that only a cross mother (or cross wife perhaps) can give to a child (or husband) who has misbehaved. Silleyn was hovering just in front of her eyes and occasionally would fly quickly round her head. Too quickly for Katie to move because she'd be back as fast as you could blink.

"Humans!" she said. "Humans, and that means a magnificent muddy mess, which is exactly what I've got. Not enough you bring one of these disastrous creatures to the door but you've brought two!"

The scowl shifted down to Clumsill who folded back his wings and bowed his head in shame.

"Two humans of the little girl variety. This will never do," said Silleyn.

So much for nice fairies, thought Dara, too shocked to speak.

"I heard that," said Silleyn

"But I didn't say . . ." blurted Dara.

"Of course, you are still tied to the spoken word. For a creature so big to have such a small mind."

Silleyn thought this was great fun. Unknown to the three comrades now at the end of her temper she had seen their escapades from the start and hadn't moved to rescue her son when she realised that the girls meant no harm. She did however think that a lesson would be best administered with her present course of action.

"You're just lucky my husband didn't catch you, you'd be all croaking like those useless green frogs over there!"

(As we know Clumser and magic don't mix very well so they were fortunate indeed that he didn't get to use any).

Katie and Dara could only look at each other. There was nothing else for it. What with all the excitement of the day plus a cross fairy mum, they did well to remain standing up. A few moments later when Silleyn was all glared out a smile slowly tickled it's way to the edges of her mouth. Her eyes closed ever so slightly and her tiny pointed ears slid back on her head a fraction. Her face changed wonderfully and warmly to that of the beautiful fairy she was. Her white teeth gleamed like milk on cornflakes and she flew carefully to Dara's left shoulder. The two girls were now totally confused.

Oh dear, thought Katie, *she's going to change us into goats with two tails and is laughing at the thought of it.*

"No, no, don't worry my dears," said Silleyn. "There will be no magic of that sort today. I just thought a little fright might focus your attentions. Now would someone like to do the introductions?"

As she said this she turned her gaze again toward Clumsill, who looked up in relief and started to clamber up Katie's wet sleeves until he reached her shoulder. Katie was too surprised to learn that some fairies can read human minds to even notice the youngster by her ear.

"Well Mum," began Clumsill, "I was climbing the tree next to Spindler's nest when I saw the juiciest nut I'd ever seen and well I reached and reached and . . . well . . . the next thing I remember is Spindler's giant jaws heading my way and four large human eyes glaring down at me. And with all the running about I didn't even get a chance to ask them their names although they know mine and now they know where we live and . . . and . . . oh what a day!" he gasped.

"Ok, son, ok slow down, you'll do yourself an injury going on like that. Now take a deep breath."

"Well the next thing they were taking me home when the small one here slipped on the rocks and got her backside all wet. Then you came out and started shouting and I thought I was going to have to walk between the glasses again!"

"Excuse me, 'the small one' did you say? Of all the cheek! I'll have you know you're in no position to be calling anyone small and anyway I happen to be three feet and two inches. You have two feet and are barely three inches, so there," said Katie a little irked at such a description.

"Well you are a bit smaller than the other one," said Silleyn.

"My name is Dara, Mrs Fairy and I'm four foot one which is very tall for my age, which is seven by the way."

"Seven, eh?" replied Silleyn, "I'm one hundred and fifty three and don't feel a day over one hundred."

"One hundred and fifty three!" said Katie and Dara together, "but that's impossible."

"No not really," said Clumsill, "that's what fairies of my mother's age call 'the prime of life'. Now if you want to see someone really old just turn around."

The two girls did just that. Flying in with speed and elegance came another fairy. But this one was not smiling or pretending to be cross. He looked very worried and quite angry and amazingly was carrying two more soggy little fairies in his arms.

"What in all manner of wonder is this? Get inside immediately, there is trouble coming from Knock Layde this very minute, get inside now!" he shouted.

It was Greagle and he didn't have time to ask any questions. He pulled a handful of powder potion from the pouch on his belt. He quickly sprinkled it over Katie and Dara. Within a few breaths the girls began to feel quite strange. Stranger still when they realised they were shrinking. The trees grew around them with the leaves and bushes. The fairies suddenly were able to look them right in the eye. The stones from which they had jumped several moments before were now enormous boulders.

"Today is the day we thought we would never see," shouted Greagle, "now run!"

He flew off in a flash of wings. Katie and Dara were now frightened but had wit enough to follow Silleyn.

"Quickly, this way," she said.

12

Trouble Brewing

Nefairious often had trouble sleeping after leaving the wallet in Sherene's bathroom. He doubted it would remain unfound.

She's too clever, she'll find it and start asking questions and she'll know it was me, he thought.

However, as time past his mind settled and his confidence grew. With his confidence came arrogance.

She's not clever enough for me. Ha, she'll look in that mirror everyday I bet and not know the secret under her silly old nose.

The seasonal changes which numbered sixty since then, had turned the once curious and shy Nefairious into the fairy his father had always wished he would become. The thought of his father kept him going and built in him a need for revenge that was doubling each day since his expulsion from the Hollow.

My attempt at the Knife was unprepared but I almost got away with it. I've grown in all sorts of ways since then, stronger and faster now and even Greagle is slower and weaker. Father soon you will be free and we will reclaim the Hollow as our own.

The excitement of the forthcoming attack made him tremble and cackle with delight. He hadn't been idle these last few years. Any manner of scratching plant, stinging insect, smelly potion or winding weed had been collected and experimented with. No one could see his little lights flicker into many early mornings on top of Knock Layde. He had now the ability to call upon a hundred rats in a moment. His command of plants meant that the thistles and brambles all listened out for his every word. The blue bottles which are the most hideous and annoying members of the fly family had built houses near his own. They buzzed and hummed all day press ganging unsuspecting little creatures into Nefairious's army.

The black smoke snaked out of his chimney and the fire underneath the stove glowed red.

"Soon father the Hollow will know the voices of those that they have silenced too long. They will learn the true cost of interfering with our family."

No sooner had he said the word family when a picture of his mother flashed into his mind. She was smiling down at him as she picked him up after a fall.

"Ah mother," his voice cracked slightly but swiftly his mind banished the thought of her.

"Mother indeed, friend of the enemy you will not be spared . . ."

If there was any decency left in him maybe his mother could've found it. Sadly her time amongst the fairies of Nut Hollow had passed in his absence but her influence was stronger than he knew. He didn't dwell on such soft images too long and stirred the black pot of foulness that was bubbling beside him.

His thoughts were interrupted by a loud thud on his front door. He replaced the ladle and went to answer it. His kitchen was a dark place. Many creatures had been given a quick end in there and bits of bone and wing littered the stony floor. He enjoyed kicking them out of the way as he walked. On reaching the door he withdrew the dusty grey curtain that served to block the light from it's sad little window. He peered out to see Préak, captain of the crows.

If ever you wanted to know what black was all you'd have to do is look at this crow. His feathers swallowed up the light like an empty wardrobe. His beak was as sharp as a sword and his feet had talons like an eagle. He stood tall above the other crows and they were nervous of him. They had good reason too for his temper and anger were renowned amongst all crow kind. His body bore the marks of many battles and he walked with a limp. The story goes that he got into a fight with Greagle and the great fairy wounded him with his knife. Greagle's skill in that fight was only matched by Préak's hatred of the fairy folk. He swore his revenge and it was natural that he became embroiled in Nefairious's plans.

Then there were his eyes or rather, his eye. He had one black eye which sat in his skull like a deep well of cruelty. His other eye was white (the strangest sight ever recorded in crow lore to that point). The white eye on this blackest of crows made him appear all the more sinister. Worse still for his enemies was that the eye had the power to see things, things that no normal eye could ever see. It could see the thoughts of other animals as if they were written down on a piece of paper. It also had the ability to hypnotise weak animals that had the misfortune to look into it. A swirling white pool of greed and desire, waiting . . . watching.

"I trust everything to be in order, Nefairious," he cawed.

He was one of the few creatures who dared to look directly at Nefairious and say his name to his face. In fact there was very little trust between these two. The only thing that bound them was there desire to wreak havoc on the Hollow.

"Not long to go now, my winged friend, patience."

"I hope so, for your sake. My birds grow weary of waiting. Surely a swift attack would be enough. A hundred well trained and eager crows against those pitiful flying bugs."

"Caution, Préak, they may be small but since when was size a decisive factor? You should know that." He glanced down at the crow's leg.

"They have knowledge of the magic that demands the utmost precision. I will not risk everything just to satisfy your bloodlust. The time *will* come and you *will* wait."

Préak was not impressed and even if he was he wasn't going to let this fairy see it, no matter how bad he was.

"We'll see and it better be soon," squawked the great crow.

The sound of his voice was jagged and dark. There was no music in it at all. Crows do not care much for songs. He flew straight up and over Nefairious who had to duck slightly so as not to be hit by his wing before landing in a black temper just a few caws away.

Your eagerness for revenge will be the death of you someday crow, he thought.

He smiled to himself then returned to his dark little house. He had made the best of it on top of the mountain since his undignified landing. He had gathered many large stones and covered them with sods of grass. For all the world his house looked like a grassy mound in the middle of nowhere on which sat a clump of haggard rushes. It suited him though. The years of waiting and planning would soon be at an end.

He closed the door with a bang and returned to the black goo he used for soup. His spoon was carved from the wishbone of a robin redbreast which he had killed because he dared to land several times on the rushy top of his house. His bowl which now spilled over with the steaming awfulness was the shell of an unfortunate snail who had also passed his way once to often. Over he went to the table in the middle of the grey room at which he plotted and planned. He had two chairs both shaped from the stones he found on the mountain top. He never sat in the one opposite him now, that one was for his father.

Father you will soon be free, free to reclaim the Hollow, free to rule over those treacherous folk who abandoned you to the Thorn, he thought and sipped his soup

"Hmm! Lovely but a little more rabbit's blood I think . . ."

Away over to the efficient bog wood cupboard with it's jars of plants, bones, weeds, powders and potions he went and found the bottle he required. The red black sticky blood poured into the bowl and he was content.

"Got to maintain my strength for tomorrow, tomorrow will be the day."

If anyone could've heard him then they would have said he started to sing. Nefairious would of course say he never sang.

The sun painted the sky with blotchy clouds intertwined with red, yellow and orange streaks. It's work had been done for the day and was making way for the moon and the other creatures of the night with a splash of easy colour. Hints of purple clung onto the edges of the shadows cast by the small copse sitting atop the hill between Knock Layde and Nut Hollow. We called it Two Hour Wood because it took that time to get up to it, play in it and get home again. We often did this in the days before tomorrow and never thought of the difficulties we would face getting back the day after that.

13
Unlucky For Some

The night had been busy on the mountain top. Nefairious had summoned a meeting with Préak and several other slinking sorts. The old weasel, Welset, was annoyed at missing out on his night's sleep but the idea of having a new Hollow in which to roam delighted him entirely. He headed a group of forty or so other weasels, all with similar notions. Behind them there was a large collection of rats, hungry and greedy as ever and led by the fearsome Rant. Then came the smaller but no less tricky creatures . . . wasps, beetles, blue bottles and of course slugs. The slugs were some way behind due to their need to eat any green thing they found. There were lots of tasty things for them that night and eventually they took their place in the congregation.

The moon shone down as if it was the only light on a stage before the play. The wind had decided to blow somewhere else but that night it would blow no good. Nefairious put on his dark green velvet coat, pulled the hood up over his head and proceeded out through the front door. The assembled crowd let their conversations fly away into the blue light of the night and waited in silence.

"My friends, I'll keep this short. You know my claim on the Hollow to be true; you know my duty to free my father Neroh, the very one who welcomed you no matter where you met. You can kill whoever you like, take whatever house you like or eat what or whoever you like but I *must get the Knife*. Welset, I'll need the sharpest teeth you have at your disposal."

Welset grumbled something and looked coldly at his men, then nodded at Nefairious.

"The future of you all will be truly golden but you must be wary of the magic. The elder fairies will wield it without mercy to defend themselves, isn't that right Préak?"

The crow shifted uneasily for a moment from one foot to the other saying nothing. His white eye stared straight at the little fairy making these grand promises and he hoped they would cross paths when all was said and done.

"Make this your grandest achievement; tell your children of the day you banished the fairies. Make their wings into ornaments for your halls."

As Nefairious spoke his voice grew louder. He moved around in front of them as if in a dream hardly stopping for breath.

"Time for you all to live the sweet life, enjoy all the secrets of the Hollow. Feast on the nuts you have so long desired and feel their power course in your veins. Drink from the river and feel it's strength fill your senses. Get rid of the do good fairy folk once *and for all*."

He screamed these last words as if his life depended on it. The congregated mass swayed and oozed applause as best they could. Greed was their common bond. The moon wiped it's brow behind a cloud and returned to light the mountain top. Nefairious called the leaders to him and they returned to the house.

They followed him into the dark space that Nefairious used to contemplate and plot and plan and sleep and eat and rage. The table in the centre was a mess of dirty dishes and bits of goodness knows what.

Fur filled the cracks and black stains slithered along the grain. Without any warning he leaned over the table and swept everything off. They all watched as the various shapes collided with the floor and smashed and clattered in their own separate ways.

"Sit down and listen," urged their host. "I suggest we make the most of the attack tomorrow. Leave any alive and they will come back to haunt us, be sure of it. However, killing is not uppermost on my mind. My errand lies above the Hollow, at the Thorn itself."

Several of the gathered breathed deeply and uneasily at the thought of that tree. It *took* prisoners!

In us all lies a memory of something that triggers fear. We learn to hide it but it remains nonetheless. The Fairy Thorn of Carey scraped at the confidence of every living thing in the land, good or bad. The bony lumps of branches with those razor thorns all along kept most away but here was Nefairious talking about going to it's heart.

"For too long Neroh, who many of you called a friend, has been a captive in the Thorn thanks to the fairies. I must release him for our plan to work. He has magic that we need."

There were mumblings and shiftings in the chairs around and Préak moved to speak but Nefairious cut him off.

"Now before you say anything, no sword we wield will cut it's branches, so how do we get him out you ask? There is one blade in the Hollow which you know will do the job."

"Now just one minute, do you mean what I think you mean?" asked Welset not wanting to believe it.

"You can't be in your right mind, it can't be done," snapped Rant. "We rats know a thing or two about breaking into things and your idea is beyond foolish."

The rat leader shook his head disapprovingly and wriggled his bald pink tail about his back. The voices against the notion began to grow until there was a babble and cackling loud enough to shatter hope itself. Nefairious let them get it off their chest until he could stand no more.

"Enough! ENOUGH!" he yelled and slammed his fist onto the table squashing a piece dead rabbit.

"Did you think it would be easy? Did you think the Greagles and Blalims of the Hollow would welcome you with open wings? Did you see Graneff standing there with tankards of nut ale? This is the Carving Knife of Nut Hollow I'm talking about. The most ancient blade that ever was cast inside the oldest tree I know. The bark itself is stronger than steel!"

He paused for a moment and sipped from his cup. He knew they knew the danger and difficulty of the task but he also knew he could use their fears. It seems that some creatures especially those involved in skulduggery do not often admit that anything or anyone can get the better of them. They'd rather die trying than not try at all or at least that is the impression they give. Usually someone else will die trying while they wait safely in the background. Préak stretched his wings slowly and got up from the table. The others watched and waited.

"The Carving Knife of Nut Hollow you say," said Préak. "Is this not the very same Knife that has you living here in exile in the first place and if I remember right saw you disappearing head first down the throat of one of those cursed buzzards? Surely once bitten should leave you twice as shy . . . hmm?"

The crow left his sentence hanging there, like bait you might say. Nefairious was happy to snap it up.

"Yes my friend," he said, "I almost paid the ultimate price. I have stared down the throat of buzzard justice and seen it's smelly gurgling insides. Yet here I am, ready to try again. My youth has since been tempered and I will not be making the same mistake," he snapped. Rant couldn't resist,

"Oh what *did* happen that day? Did *you* make a mistake?" he asked looking slyly at Préak.

"My only mistake was getting caught," snapped Nefairious.

He didn't tell them that he had been thwarted the first time by his one time teacher, Greagle. They used to practice flying moves together and were as close as could be until that day. At the last moment Greagle saw him fly directly for the Knife. It was the middle of a Ceremony, no one should've been moving but Greagle got a sense of something wrong. The Knife moved out from the inner tree and as the first flyer reached out down flew Nefairious. Only inches between his hands and the Knife when Greagle somehow spun upward hitting Nefairious on the wrist as his fingers grasped the handle. He careered out of control straight into Spindler's web and hung there as guilty as the great sin he had almost accomplished. Justice was swift after that as Nefairious now understood.

The others sensed that Nefairious had suffered for his previous error and were now in no doubt as to the dangers of the attack. However, greed can persuade most to try things they know they shouldn't and control of Nut Hollow and the magic therein was too much to resist.

"I get the Knife, you get the Hollow and my father gets his freedom. The time is at hand."

14

The Secret Stairway

If Katie and Dara could've seen the shadows they would've noticed them stretch long over the ground. In the excitement of the day, time had flowed by like the water in Nut Hollow River. They would perhaps also have noticed the light fading but they did not. Suddenly all they were aware of was another little fairy creature shouting crossly at them flying around above their heads at a furious speed. They looked for some guidance from Clumsill but he was hugging his mother's skirt.

"Get moving. Now! Quickly Silleyn take them inside, lock your door and find somewhere safe," shouted Greagle.

"OK girls just keep your heads down and come on," urged Silleyn.

She opened the door of her house and stood as the three quickly ran past her. She then closed, locked and bolted all her locks and bolts and went to the kitchen.

"Grab whatever you can, this could be all the food you see for a week," she urged.

The girls opened the beautifully carved cupboards and using tea towels filled them up with bread, milk, biscuits, meat and whatever else they could find. With a healthy handful each they followed Silleyn out of the kitchen to the living room where she pulled back her white rabbit tail rug. Beneath it they saw a wooden trap door with a keyhole placed below a black metal handle. Silleyn quickly took off a little gold chain from her neck. It held the key to the trapdoor and she stooped to place it in the lock. One turn to the left and it was done. She grabbed the handle and pulled. Up came the door to reveal a black space. As their eyes got used to the darkness they could see the first of many steps leading downwards.

"This stairway is dangerous and only used in emergencies, one of which it appears we now have. Hold onto each other as you go. Dara hold this," she said.

Silleyn took a long thin object from the top step and handed it to Dara. It looked for all the world like a large upside down ice cream cone. At the top of it were branches and moss and other kindling. Dara held it and was happy that it wasn't too heavy.

"Now Dara, this light will not go out once it's lit because this liquid is crushed nut oil and when you dip your torch in it you'll see what I mean."

She had already gone to the second step and found the oil bucket. It was full to the brim and the oil glooped at the edges as she moved it.

"We have to be careful with this stuff, if it's spilt these steps will become too slippery to walk down, worse than those river stones any day Clumsill eh?"

She smiled at her son as she spoke. This was not how she had hoped to spend her day but a smile here and there always helped to raise the spirits. Clumsill looked back at her with a nervous grin as did Katie who had taken a firm grip of his hand. Dara dipped her torch into the brown liquid and was careful not to spill any over the sides. Silleyn ran her thumb over her four fingers on her left hand and immediately a little flame appeared, flickering and hopping just above the palm of her hand.

"Oh just a little trick I picked up along the way," she said as if to answer the forthcoming questions.

"Doesn't hurt a bit. Now Dara, hold up your torch."

Dara did as she was told and watched as Silleyn blew the flame from her hand. It flew over quickly to the top of the torch and at once it was lit.

"Wow," said Katie and Dara together.

Their sense of wonder was quickly ended by Silleyn.

"I'll lead, Clumsill you hold my hand, Katie you're next and Dara at the back. Remember to pull over the trapdoor as you come down, Dara."

Dara nodded and was about to ask another question but as before Silleyn spoke,

"The door will lock and seal itself when you close it. It will be almost impossible for anyone or anything to open it. We'll be safe in the cave."

Dara and Katie were relieved to hear this but a bit worried at the word 'almost'. They knew nothing about what might be coming after them or where they were going. Even if they did know there was little else they could do about it now anyway. They had to follow this fairy woman down into the darkness and that was that.

The stairway was small and uncomfortable. They all had to stoop to avoid hitting their heads on the rocky ceiling above them. The steps were smooth and grey and just wide enough for them to stand on. It was obvious that they had not been used for some time as there were spider webs sticking to their heads as they descended. Any other day if the two girls had spider webs in their hair they would've been quite annoyed but something told them that was not the worst thing they might expect. On they went with the brilliant light of the torch to show them the way. The shadows leapt all about them and several times Katie thought their own shadows seemed to stop and turn around by themselves. She put it down to a trick of the light and tried to put it out of her mind. Deeper and deeper into the darkness they went. Dara stopped briefly to look back but could only see steps behind her.

"Is everyone ok?" asked Silleyn. "We're nearly there now; I'll tell you all you need to know soon."

Without warning the steps ended and they found themselves at the entrance to a grand underground cave. From where they stood they could make out many other entrances like their own spread out in a large circle at regular intervals. They could see the light flickering in the other entrances as other families descended to join them. They could hear the voices also getting louder and all with worry sewn through them. They walked forward together and soon they found themselves in the middle of the cave with many of the other fairy children and some of the parents.

"Did you ever see the likes of this Dara?" asked Katie. "Granny will never believe it."

"Well I hope we get the chance to tell her. Those fairies do not look too happy. It's time we found out what is going on".

Silleyn had gone to talk with some of her neighbours leaving the three of them standing holding each others' hands.

Still they came. The cave now filled with all manner of fairy, each carrying a small pack of something. Katie and Dara noticed that the clammer and chat was dying down. There must have been seventy or eighty fairy folk in the cave now.

"Someone must be going to say something," said Clumsill. "I've heard stories about this place but never thought I'd have to come down. It must be serious up in the Hollow."

As he spoke Silleyn returned with a stern face. They gathered round her and hoped for some information.

"My dears, don't think of any questions for a moment. We all must listen. A dark day has come."

Then the crowd fell silent. A well dressed fairy woman flew to a ledge above them all. She had blond hair, plaited down her back behind her wings. Her gown flowed down from her shoulders to her knees with every colour of the rainbow sparkling therein. She had multi coloured finger nails and toe nails too. Katie and Dara were amazed at the colours she wore and noticed the gold rings on all her fingers. Around her neck hung a white amulet on a gold chain which she held in her hands and began to speak.

15

Shadows and Splashes

Afternoon yielded to evening on the mountain top. There were many things for this collection of crafty creatures to make ready. Each group spent the daylight hours finalising plans and attack strategies. There were competitions going on about how many fairies the rats could kill and eat compared to the weasels. Some of them even started to fight amongst themselves as they teased and snapped at each other. The slugs had arranged lifts on the talons of the crows. They were so keen to acquire a life in the Hollow that the likelihood of becoming a snack seemed not to bother them. The wasps were sharpening their stings and getting the weasels to chew at the thickest of the thistles that grew about the top of Knock Layde. These would be used as swords and clubs to knock any fairy that approached them out of the sky. The air was thick with cruel chatter and cackling laughter. The horde was confident that a small collection of gentle fairies were no match in spite of anything that Nefairious had said.

Nefairious, Préak, Welset, Rant and their aids came out of the house. They weren't to know but it was around the same time as two little girls were running down to Nut Hollow to splash in the river.

"Evening is upon us," began Nefairious, "and this evening will lead to *a very black night.*" A huge roar went up as he spoke.

"Yes, this at last is our moment. I ask for your blood and life if it is needed, for your reward will be all the sweeter. He raised his arms and his cloak fell back about his elbows,

"AWAY, FLY TO THE HOLLOW, AWAY AND LEAVE NOTHING HERE BUT YOUR BAD DREAMS."

His command to fly temporarily gave all the earth bound creatures the ability to do just that. All of course except himself. His wings had gone with the softening and he had one way only to get them back. He summoned Préak's deputy, Scris and climbed onto his back. Those that weren't sure of their new skill hung on to the other crows and jackdaws.

Almost as one the heaving crowd began to take to the sky. It was like a terrible shadow leaving the earth. The sky darkened immediately and the sun bowed it's head. The fog that sat on the mountain top made way for the swarm.

Down the slope the shadow was cast. All creatures ran for any cover they could find. Woe found any living thing in their path. Rabbits were grabbed and robins stabbed out of the sky. Butterflies were swallowed whole and thrushes and starlings received worse ends than they ever deserved. The inhabitants of Knock Layde which included humans of course took different views on the moving greyness.

Human people it is often said would hardly notice if they had an elephant in their kitchen. They appear to have lost all sense of time in that they never seem to have any even though they are surrounded by it. In this hurried state they miss most things going on in the countryside. Some of them thought it was just a strange sign of bad weather and they went through the usual sentences. You know like,

"The weather doesn't know what to be at" or "Wet again, even when it's dry" and "My washing will be soaked" and "This is some excuse for a summer" and so on.

The fairy families of Tavnaghboy and Craigban went to ground. They too knew the legend of Nefairious and anything that happened out of the ordinary was blamed on him. They were happy to watch the cloud pass by and pitied those who would be receiving it's wrath. Swooping now and growing in numbers all the while the horde now turned to the right and aimed directly for Nut Hollow. Nefairious at the head of all could only see the gleam of the Carving Knife in his mind's eye. He spoke no words and even Préak who was himself a swift flier struggled to keep up with him as he pushed Scris for all he was worth. On now he flew, possessed in his rage and soon they were over Two Hour Wood.

*   *   *

The fairy children playing in the wood at the time were lucky the cloud did not see them. Their names were Cul and Amad and it was only their second time so far from the Hollow. As they looked up the glint of knives stung their eyes, the squawks of the crows terrified their ears and the screeches of the rats tightened their hearts in their chests. They hid under the stones at which they were collecting empty snail shells. Snail shells of course make great fancy tankards for Nut Beer but that was the least of their concerns. From beneath the rocks they could hear what sounded like a strange dark song being chanted by the floating mob. Amad thought the words went something like,

> "See the shadow fall, feel the shadow grow
> Revenge will come to all, who stay instead of go
> Keep clear the path, of where the shadow flies
> Or know then the wrath, of Nefairious the Wise!"

The chanting grew louder and faster as they passed over head. Amad was sure that one of the rats would swoop down and find them. They huddled closer together as a robin crashed into the ground just beyond their feet. Cul noticed that the robin was still breathing but only just. He daren't move to help as it would be certain death for him and his friend. The robin had only enough breath left in him for one final sentence,

"This is the day we thought would we would never see . . . *Nefairious is back!*"

With a brief flutter of his chest feathers he exhaled one last time and was dead. On went the shadow leaving the two fairy children in a terrible state. They knew that there was only one place it could be going and that was their home, Nut Hollow. How could they warn them there that Nefairious was once more on the move?

Amad had also been to the story telling nights in Sherene's and had often been frightened so much he thought he might have a heart attack but this was an altogether new fear. They too had been told bedtime stories about Nefairious coming to get them if they were bold and were at an age to regard them as nothing more than simple stories. Now with their own ears a terrible reality had been sung out loudly before them.

"I think they've gone," said Amad, "we must do something, *anything.*"

"Are you sure?" asked Cul, "that song nearly froze my heart."

He shook his head to rouse himself.

"You're right but what can we do from here. By the time we get to the Hollow they'll be in the middle of destroying it."

Amad nodded in agreement but he could not stop himself thinking.

"I know we can't fly as fast as them even if we had all Greagle's skills but there must be something."

As he said the words he kicked a stone into the nearby river in frustration. As it splashed and skimmed he froze and turned quickly to Cul.

"Hey, what about the old salmon in the river? This leads directly into the Hollow. If we could somehow get their attention we could swim and warn them . . . it would be better than nothing."

"You're right. Quickly, jump in and start splashing."

The salmon that swam in the river around those parts were well known as the fastest swimmers that had ever been. Every year they swam in from the great sea of Moyle right up past the Hollow and back to the place they were born. Although this was a journey that signalled the end of their lives there was always a feeling of celebration that they had returned even though it was tinged with sorrow. This being the case there were always a few exceptional salmon left behind to tend for different parts of the river and keep an eye on things.

One such was Saroist and he did not take kindly to small impertinent fairies splashing in his river messing everything up. Almost before their feet were wet he glided up with a stern face on him. In fact he was so cross he headed straight for Cul's ankle and gave him a nip.

"Ow!" shrieked the fairy but his work had been done.

Saroist lifted his head out of the water to scold but never got the chance. Amad started immediately,

"Oh thank you Saroist and we are sorry for the commotion but we have the most terrible emergency. You see, the day that we thought would never come is upon us and you must swim to the Hollow and warn them."

"Now just one moment there are procedures," started the fish but again he was interrupted.

"Procedures my behind," shouted Amad.

Saroist would've raised his eyebrows at this retort if he had had any. Instead he pursed his lips together even tighter.

"We must warn the people, Nefairious is back and on his way to destroy Nut Hollow!" pleaded Cul.

At the mention of that name Saroist's demeanour changed. He knew the story of the bad fairy. He also had been around long enough to have known his father. This was not good news and the thought of Neroh and Nefairious together again would be a disaster.

Neroh had previously complained that the salmon were given to much respect while passing by the Hollow and had wondered if they wouldn't prefer a different river to return too. Of course he had made his arguments in such a friendly fashion that no one guessed all he wanted to do with a salmon was to eat it.

"Young ones, this is serious indeed. I must do what I can. Quickly now onto my back the pair of you".

With a flick of his great tail he sped down the river narrowly avoiding the boulders all about. The two young fairies wouldn't forget this ride in a hurry and were doing all they could just to hold on. Saroist had to swim just below the surface but even this couldn't prevent the water splashing up into their faces. Still, a little water was no concern to them. The wind roared in their ears as they whizzed down the river. Having made the return journey some years previously the waterfall at Coolaveely was the last great challenge the salmon had to overcome. However, going the other way was the greatest thrill that Saroist would know and later report to his grandchildren. He broke the surface knowing that it lay ahead.

"Hold on to that fin for all you're worth, your lives depend on it," he shouted.

The two gave each other a look and a nod. They had often played at the foot of the waterfall and never thought they would be in this position.

Saroist put in a extra burst of speed, it was all or nothing now. Ten feet to go and his tail thrashed the water like a great oar. Five feet . . . four . . . three . . .

"NOW!" yelled the fairies.

With one last mighty swish the fish pushed himself and his passengers out of the water and into thin air. Out they flew almost six feet and immediately downward. A stone in the ridge in the middle of the waterfall clipped Saroist's tail but it made no difference. All the fairies could do was squeal the loudest 'Yahoo' you could imagine. Then in the blink of an eye they landed with an almighty splash some fifteen feet lower. Down they sunk until they thought drowning was all they had left but the old fish wasn't finished and guided them back to the surface where all paused briefly to catch their wits.

"Everyone OK?" asked the salmon.

"Yes," was the wet and relieved reply.

They didn't wait a moment longer and away down the river they went. As it happened Greagle was out flying at that moment and saw the fish land with an almighty splash. He flew down to see if all was well and met them just as they turned the last corner of the river before Nut Hollow. The two little fairies were by now quite exhausted with their adventures and had hardly the sense left to tell the great fairy their story. They both began together shouting and coughing and splashing. Saroist was too tired to speak. Suddenly Greagle leaned back and hit the water impatiently with his wings.

"What is all this about? Tell me one of you and stop with all this nonsense".

"It's Nefairious," they said together, "he's here!"

Greagle looked up and to his horror saw the shadow no more than a few hundred yards away. He picked up the two fairies and flew as fast as he could to warn the others.

16

The Battle for Nut Hollow

The shadow swooped through the trees cracking off branches and leaves as it's terrible anger pushed forward. The river could not help but to reflect this foul throng as it now engulfed Nut Hollow. Greagle's warnings thanks to Cul and Amad had just given the residents time to get the children and elderly fairies down to the great underground hall. However, those that turned round to do battle were hopelessly unprepared, all those except Blalim of course who had always said to be ready for anything.

The temporary spells that Nefairious gave to all had now no further use and the rats and weasels began to land. Some managed this quite well while others made a complete mess of it and were nearly drowned. Some even got their teeth knocked out on the stones in the river. However such was their eagerness to do no good they enjoyed the taste of their own blood.

The crows followed Préak through the branches and picked off the first of the fairy guards with their talons and beaks. Their attack was so fast these poor fairies did not even have time to utter the few magic words which would have protected them.

This was truly the worst start to a battle that Greagle could remember. He had been in a few but never from such a position of weakness. He did not let this stop him though and was quickly at Spindler's side.

"Old friend if ever we needed one of your webs it's now," he gasped. "We have but seconds to get some sort of a foothold or we are all lost."

Before he had even finished his last word the great spider had shot a line of web across the river to one of the nut trees. With help from Greagle's vast spell collection the web suddenly filled out and become a massive silky barrier to our foes. This was perfectly timed as into it flew almost all the wasps and blue bottles with their thistle swords. They had never been entangled so well before and try as they might they could not escape. Spindler licked his lips and hoped he would have the chance to enjoy them.

It also caught a few of the over eager crows but it wouldn't hold them long. It billowed in the wind as the crows thrashed about and squawked their defiance at this temporary bond. Immediately Greagle headed back and now was hovering just above the boulders that gave Hollow River her sound. He noticed many of the fairies at their front doors turning keys and trying to fix their leather armour.

No time, thought Greagle, *no time for armour . . . c'mon!*

Within a second or two, three of his most trusted friends were hovering by his side.

"Good of you to join us at last," said Greagle to an out of breath Blalim.

"Oh you know me I had to wake these two up," he replied, pointing to Brógun and Graunad.

"Looks like our old friend means business this time," said Graunad, "we should have never let him out of our sight."

As they spoke Spindler fired his web with great accuracy taking down several more crows. They made a welcome thud into the ground. Unfortunately the crows were but one of their many problems. Rant had moved his rats quickly through the long grass and each of the doors of Nut Hollow now had the most unwelcome of visitors. Rant issued his orders within earshot of the four fairies on the other side of the web.

"Eat through the doors and whatever you find on the other side . . . eat it too," he said and smiled the foulest big buck toothed smile you could imagine up at Greagle.

The other creatures that had been part of the swarm now all began to wreak havoc as they entered the Hollow. The web which had given the fairies a brief moment to catch their thoughts had now the unwanted side effect of acting as a barrier to fighting back. As strong as they were, the four would be no match for the invaders. Soon though more of the younger fairies flew up alongside them of which I was one. We numbered thirty and it was time we let Nefairious know there was a price to be paid for such cruelty.

We hadn't much time to act. The web had almost been breached. The beaks of the crows had torn large gaps in it so that they were almost able to fly through. The weasels had lined each side of the river bank hoping to find any fairies who hadn't made it underground. Thankfully their hunts proved fruitless. However, they were in a position of victory. We quickly scattered ourselves into six smaller groups of five in each. I had remembered some of Greagle's stories from times previous when he would tell of battles with the wasp clans.

"Spread out, avoid their sting and let them feel real fairy magic," he would say. Soon enough he was saying it again.

Our first priority was the rats. Our doors were strong but not strong enough to hold those vile, pointed teeth back indefinitely. Greagle, Graunad, Brógun and Blalim suddenly flew their groups high and left over the web through the branches and toward the rats and weasels on the left bank. Each fairy quickly pulled their ash bows from where they hung over their shoulder. The first of the magic began with the spell for a quiver full of arrows. A glance between the four leaders and their two new generals, Laijir and Tridge was shared. Greagle began to speak as the wind rushed by his ears and branches reached and scraped at his clothes.

> "In this Hollow's defence, arrows so true
> For pain makes good sense to enemies of you
> Fill up each quiver, and let them fly straight
> That the cruel shall shiver before it's too late."

Immediately each of the fairies felt the bulge of fresh arrows against their backs. They all quickly reached round and removed their first. Their aims were hampered as they flew under the canopy of the nut trees but soon the yelps and squeals of the rats and weasels could be heard.

I flew as close as I could behind Greagle. If he was as old as they said you would not have thought it. The first wave of arrows had given him cause to fire me a quick smile but there was more to be done. The other five groups had now taken on a pentagonal pattern and we all flew directly at the great crow. He was squawking orders to all about him.

"Quickly you fools, *attack*! Sharpen your talons on their heads!"

His white eye rolled frantically around in it's massive socket. He swooped directly at Brógun's group and scattered them out of the sky. The arrows they fired bounced off his hard black feathers and he turned to attack again. I saw four of the fairies hit the water hard. The river that had sustained them all their lives now proved their downfall. It's powerful current swept them away towards the boulders and beyond. Brógun just managed to drag himself out of the water having landed close to the edge but he was terribly wounded and could move no further. I felt sick to see friends just disappear before my eyes. I flew alongside Greagle,

"We must get the crow, he has protection from the arrows and is too big to fight with our hands. We need more magic," I yelled.

I needn't have spoken. Greagle knew all about this crow and his look told me as much. I kept firing my arrows as quickly as I could. Their tips sparkled like drops of sunlight as they flew and many found rest in the hearts of the rats. Préak landed quickly on one of the large smooth boulders that traversed the river. He was eager to finish his argument with Greagle and was preparing himself for the duel ahead.

All the while the arrows rained down and the invaders wrecked gardens, walls and stole anything of value. We were unable to gain any advantage and were just about holding our ground.

This was the situation that Nefairious had been hoping for. Like many tacticians in battle he had waited for the most favourable conditions. The four remaining groups could not break away from their individual scraps for fear of leaving the others to be overrun. Nefairious steered Scris slowly above the main battle toward the Learning Tree.

He knew we could not stop him. He dismounted the crow and ushered him off into the battle.

"Do your worst crow," he shouted.

From his dark green cloak he had removed a small leather bag bound at the top with the preserved tongue of a rabbit he had eaten years before. He landed at the seat of the First Flyer and began to rub the powder within the bag on the very spot where the Carving Knife had appeared so many times before. A blue smoke began to drift upwards through the branches. I could hardly keep my eyes on him for firing arrows and wrestling with the dagger toed legs of the crows. Suddenly Greagle whizzed past my right shoulder directly at Préak. I had an impossible choice. Did I help Greagle against the crow or stop Nefairious from getting our sacred blade?

17

The Banshee

"My friends I am sorry indeed to have to speak to you here and in these circumstances," began the lady.

She stood above the crowd in the great underground hall and all faces looked at her.

"This is the moment when we need unusual things to happen. I will do all I can but some of you standing here will face the most terrible and frightening journeys. Above us as we speak the battle for the Hollow has begun. I wish I had the power to sway fate but I do not."

As she spoke her amulet swayed slowly like a pendulum in front of her gown which was the colour of the red evening sun and was made from a material that if they could've touched would have reminded Katie and Dara of their favourite soft toys. It would've felt warm too as it was made from the silk of fire spiders.

"Wow, she is beautiful," whispered Dara, "like a ghost or something. Did Granda ever tell you of the Banshees?"

"Yes I think so though but I don't really remember the stories. My other Granda did tell me that if ever you heard a Banshee it was a sign of bad news," answered Katie.

"That's what I think she is," continued Dara, "this can't be good at all."

"Well maybe the bad luck only effects humans, she seems to be very fond of the fairies," replied Katie.

"Yes that's because she *is* a fairy and a very special one at that. The Banshees are very mysterious and you'd both do well to listen to what she has to say," said Silleyn sternly.

The two girls stopped talking and returned their attentions to the lady. Her blond hair touched her shoulders and disappeared behind her back and the girls noticed she held a golden comb in her hand.

"Katie," whispered Dara, "look at the comb, it's beautiful."

"I wish I had one," replied Katie.

Before they could continue another loud 'Shush' came from one of the other older fairies and that was the end of that conversation. (Have you noticed it does sometimes take a couple of goes to get children to listen)?

Clumsill had just about regained his breath after the journey down the stairway and had moved just behind the two girls. As his eyes became used to the flame light he could see all the other younger fairies of the neighbourhood. Like him they were not too far away from their mothers' skirts. He could see Pog and Fer standing behind Gráinne. He often played with them and wondered what they thought of the whole situation.

He gently tugged on Dara's skirt and without a sound tilted his head in the direction he wanted her to follow. Dara took Katie's hand and they slipped gently away from Silleyn's side. The Banshee began to speak and her words rained down on them like good wishes. As the three pushed through the crowd they felt safety in her voice. Perhaps her words were too long or just too important because they didn't really listen to what she was saying.

On they went past the round bottoms of the mummy fairies, trying to avoid their wings which was tricky enough considering how closely together they all stood. Soon enough they had reached Pog and Fer who greeted them all with a smile, the sort of smile you use when you aren't altogether sure of what will happen next. This wasn't the time for introductions and the smile would have to do for now.

Gráinne couldn't help but notice the hustle behind her and gave them all a 'parent look' that says 'be quiet and listen' (you know the one)!

"I have learned that we have two visitors to our family. It would appear they have picked a dangerous day to come to Nut Hollow. However, things rarely happen for no reason and I believe they can help. Please . . . step forward," said the Banshee.

Dara and Katie looked at each other in surprise. How could she know?

Pog, Fer and Clumsill slowly ushered them forward until they stood alone at the front of the crowd with their heads down. They both felt a bit scared and neither could speak a word. Katie suddenly took a hold of Dara's hand and Dara gave it a reassuring squeeze,

"We'll be OK," whispered Dara.

They walked closer to the Banshee as if in a trance. They could not have stopped even if they had wanted too. The whispers of the other fairies now died away and only silence remained. The flickering torches made the Banshee's robe dance with a thousand colours and they made the girls feel less afraid.

They had heard stories of Banshees and they were rarely good but here underneath the ground surrounded by nervous fairies it seemed perfectly logical to approach her. After a few steps they stood in front of her and both had their heads bowed. They toed the ground with their feet and held their hands behind their backs a little in the manner of children who know they are about to be scolded for eating sweets before dinner.

"Children, please look up into my eyes," she began, "I promise I will do you no harm."

Slowly the two girls raised their eyes and took her gaze. They immediately noticed that her eyes were not normal Irish colours like green, grey and blue but instead they were the colour of rubies. The darkest red you could get and inside the pupils were as black as coals. She looked down on them and smiled which put them further at their ease.

"My name is Sheana, and I'm a guardian of the fairies of these parts. Humans know my kind as Banshees, perhaps you are aware of that term?"

"Well to tell you the truth we do know it and have only heard bad stories about . . . you know . . . Banshees. Are you going to cry for us?" asked Dara.

Sheana smiled once more and slowly shook her head.

"Indeed folklore is a wonderful thing. One of the qualities we share with humans is the ability to tell stories. No, there will be no crying today but there will be sadness. Many hundreds of years ago we were closer to our human neighbours than we are now and in times of death we would sing for the spirits of our deceased friends. Sadly time has carved lines between our cultures so that what was once a song of affection and remembrance is now something that humans dread to hear."

"But why do you still sing for us, I mean if no one wants to hear your songs?" asked Katie.

"A good question young one. You never know when human ears will once again hear harmonious sounds in the land about them. We haven't given up on you yet."

Katie and Dara felt more relaxed in her company and she had a wonderful and gentle way with her. She bent down onto her knees and was looking at them directly, eye to eye.

"Do you know what is going on today?" she asked.

The girls shook their heads. Their day had started off normally enough running about the glen and here they now found themselves talking to a Banshee.

"No not really," said Dara, "we were playing at the river, then talking to fairies, then getting shrunk and then running as fast as we could away from somebody called 'Nefreus' or something."

Katie saw her chance to add to the story,

"Yes all that and we got soaked in the river thanks very much and I lost my Wellie boot!"

Sheana smiled again and thought to herself if getting wet was all that befell them they would do well. However, she felt that events above ground would take some sorting out.

"Katie and Dara you will have many more adventures before today is out. For many hundreds of years a story of cooperation between fairy kind and human folk was told around fires and celebrations. We often wondered the origin of this tale and why we all knew about it but it seems that it was more of a premonition of dark times ahead. Those dark times have arrived all of a sudden and it will be important that you play your part in the story. Will you help us?"

Well this seemed a strange question indeed. The girls wondered if a Banshee had any need to ask permission for anything much less the help of two little girls. They both looked into her wonderful eyes and nodded.

"Yes, we will help but what can we do against magic and fairy fights? I mean, all we have is a pair of Wellie boots—"

One Wellie in your case I'm afraid, thought Dara.

"—and these coats," answered Katie.

Dara was also perplexed at the question.

"Of course we will help. But help with what exactly? And who is the Nefreus anyway?"

Sheana didn't answer the questions but gave the girls a look as if to say thank you. She stood up and took the girls by the hand and was between them. She turned towards the other fairies who were also a little bemused as to all the whispering.

"Today we must fight against our own fears and those that would take what is dear to us. I want you all to come to me and listen. Time is often plentiful but not anymore."

She gently ushered the two girls back to where they came from in the crowd. The smaller fairies where already asking questions as to the nature of their conversation. Fairy children rarely got to see Banshees. They inherently had a deep respect for them bordering on fear. Clumsill, Pog, Fer, Cul and Amad also knew things must be serious. Banshees and humans talking together, battles in the Hollow . . . whatever next?

18
Hanging in the Balance

The yellow topped whins sat easily in the glens. They had invaded our senses with their wonderful colours since time itself began. Beneath their soft and shocking yellow lay the barbs of it's branches; a beautiful bush with danger just below the surface.

As I raced towards Nefairious I admired their abstinence from battle. They were having important conversations with sycamore and rowanberry trees. Too important to notice the secret shenanigans of the residents and invaders of Nut Hollow. In my heart of hearts I knew that Greagle would want to face Préak alone. Their feud demanded it. My conscience was clear as I spied the rogue fairy himself slowly breaking through the bark of the Learning Tree.

What magic must he possess? No one dares to touch that bark. Well my old friend it's time we renewed our acquaintance.

I aimed straight for him and beat my wings as never before. The wind began to whisp through my hair and my eyes watered. A tear drop rolled down my cheek and was blown off behind me. I was nearing him with every second and luckily it seemed his attentions were now solely on opening the bark for he did not move or prepare to face me. On and on I flew.

Now, if I can hit him right in the face it would do as an introduction he'll not likely forget.

With less than a mole's whisker between him and I, I raised my feet to strike and flew at him. I braced myself for impact and was quite prepared to take the pain of such a crash landing. However that pain I expected did not come. Instead I was halted in mid flight and walloped violently on my right side. The pain was terrible but what had hit me. I was falling from the sky in a complete daze. I could see Nefairious smile and return to his work. What was happening?

I hit the water just below the first flyers stone at a great speed. I felt sure my wings would be broken. I had no time to think because I had gone so far underwater that the stones at the bottom of Hollow River were all about me. Their edges harboured the menace of the muddy depths where I now found myself. By pure luck I hit the mud in between two such boulders but any wind I had in my lungs was quickly expelled. My head was slowly clearing but my air supply was gone. I had already taken in a mouthful of silt and mud.

Think, keep calm, and get out of here, I thought.

The pain in my side was increasing all the while and I hadn't much time.

Get out of here! was all I could hear in my head.

I forced myself up through the river's flow and broke the surface with the last drop of strength I could muster. Back to the river's edge I crawled and dragged myself out through the cold wet mud.

What in the name of Odhran had happened?

I would have to answer that later. A pair of gleaming talons was now heading directly for my throat. It was all I could do roll to the left just in time. The crow landed heavily where I had been a second earlier. Too heavily for him as it happened. As tired as I was I realised this black feathered fiend was stuck and flapping his wings wildly with no effect. Time for some magic.

You will wish you had never heard of Nut Hollow friend, I thought.

The source of all fairy strength and magic lies in our wings. We generate power with each flap and store it in our finger tips accordingly. I quickly shook off the mud and gave them a couple of quick beats. Immediately I could feel my strength returning. My fingers began to tingle and I had a spell in my head.

> "Black feather, cruel beak
> Sharp talon, hear me speak
> Take your bile, turn it round
> Think a while, on the ground
> Stone encased, fly no more
> Err in haste, cold and sore."

The spark at my finger tip grew quickly to a clear circle of sparkling magic, we call it the Draykt. Like an arrow it sped out and hit the crow between the eyes. An instant later I saw a perfect stone statue ankle deep in the soft muddy ground. A few beats of the wings and I was airborne again. I could see that we were beginning to come to terms with the first wave of attackers. Many of my friends had thought of the same spell and the lifeless stone shapes of the invaders littered the Hollow. Many others were in the grasp of their own private battles, wrestling with rats and dodging weasels.

Greagle!

I saw him on the far side of the river hovering above Préak who was wheeling round again ready to do his worst. I had to hope Greagle would prevail, the Learning Tree had to be protected. I headed back toward the tree just ducking in time to avoid one of Spindler's shots, which true as ever pierced a weasel's eye.

There was Nefairious still but now the hole in the bark was wider and the swirl of the inner white wood could clearly be seen.

"What divilment is this, to get into the Learning Tree itself?" I wondered.

Several of my companions had shaken off their attackers to realise that indeed this was the most disastrous turn of events. If he got the Knife, how could we stop him?

Tridge flew up to my right. He was bleeding and the blood dripped slowly off the ends of his fingers.

"You're wounded," I said, "how bad?"

"Oh I'll be fine. It'll take more than the nip of a crow to stop me. Besides that rascal has nearly got inside the Learning Tree by the looks of things and that my friend will not do."

Without any warning he set off directly at Nefairious just as I had done a few moments before.

"Stop Tridge," I called but he was set fair on his course.

He was about to do what had nearly cost me my life. Once again as he was approached Nefairious barely moved. I couldn't understand it, he's bound to see that he's in for a wallop. However, it was Tridge who would rue his actions. He stretched out his hands at Nefairious's neck and got ready to grab when he bounced off what seemed like an invisible barrier around the rogue fairy. His speed and direction were now transformed into a heap of legs, arms and wings in a confused bundle which rather ungracefully ended upside down in a clump of thistles just behind the Learning Tree. Those of us that witnessed this were now in a state of shock. It seemed that Nefairious was impervious to attack. Had he already harnessed the power of the Learning Tree? Had he one hand on the sacred blade? What was this magic that he wielded? As if to answer our questions he shifted his stance at the Tree, reached deep inside and out in his hand came the Carving Knife.

*　　*　　*

The power of it shot through Nefairious like a lightning bolt and immediately his wishes were realised. A fairy without wings is no fairy at all and because the Carving Knife is the very celebration of flight itself its magic rushed through him to the two stumps of flesh on his back from where his wings had been clipped. The flesh began to redden and grow and the new wings spread themselves slowly down his back under his cloak. However, they would not be ready to use for some time. Nefairious knew this of course but so far his plan had worked well. All he had to do was survive the battle and get the package he had left in Sherene's so many years before.

*　　*　　*

How it gleamed in his darkness. All about us now the animals of the invasion seemed to grow in stature, they too had witnessed the events in the midst of their battles and to see the Carving Knife of Nut Hollow in the hands of their leader must have been wonderful. Now their attacks became even more venomous. All thoughts turned to Greagle. The last I had seen was him dodging Préak with all his skill and bringing down his own blade across the crow's back with each pass. One more such blow would prove a mortal wound for the Crow but that blow would not come. Instead of heading back to his doom Préak called out to Nefairious,

"Quickly use the power of the Knife, Greagle awaits his end."

Nefairious raised the Knife and pointed it at Greagle who although in a position of advantage over the crow was tired and growing weaker. The setting sun had turned into a silent ball of intense golden heat as if it meant to melt the Hollow itself. Nefairious tilted the blade until it caught the last of the sunrays and directed them at Greagle. Instantaneously the great warrior fairy lurched backwards. He began to fall from the sky and was clutching his eyes. He fell slowly at first as he struggled desperately to regain control. However, such was the power of the Knife now in the wrong hands aligned to the power of the sun that Greagle's strength quickly began to fade and he hit the water's edge. He was face down in the mud hardly able to move. Préak headed directly for his old foe.

"No, No, **No**," I heard myself shout.

I had to intercept without getting caught in by Préak's talons and avoiding the deadly beams from the Knife. If I could get to Greagle before Préak there would be a chance that we could get to Fween Talav, our underground hall, and regroup. All around the battle raged and although it was against my very essence to do it I removed the Carey Shell from my belt and sounded the retreat. It's call filled the Hollow just as the great waves of the Moyle Sea from whence it came fill the air.

I reached Greagle just in time. By good luck he was still conscious and had enough left in him to move with me as I lifted him.

"C'mon old friend," I gasped, "you will not die in the mud today."

"Go," he snapped, "I'm done. Save yourself the future lies with you."

"No way old man, shut up and listen. You and Blalim will have another day but now you're coming with me."

I hadn't moved a few inches when from above the flaps of Préak's wings could be heard along with that rasping shriek all crows are cursed with.

"No escape today Greagle, not until I have my revenge . . ."

His talons now were a few inches above my head and I feared the end. I bowed and braced myself for the worst when I heard the soft thud of arrow on flesh and felt the water splash over me as Préak hit the river. We both looked to see the crow float silently over the great stones but didn't wait for explanations. I picked up Greagle and we flew out of the Hollow followed by as many survivors as were fit to fly. We had lost the Hollow but still had ourselves. Those that looked back saw the horde celebrate and caw and howl in delight. They also saw Spindler smile at the accuracy of his last arrow as it shot into Préak's heart before he too was overcome.

Nefairious looked around him then walked slowly toward Sherene's, it was time to check behind the bathroom cabinet.

19

Underground, Overground, Underground

"I'm sorry to say that I will be composing tonight to honour many brave fairies," said Sheana.

Her face was heavy with sorrow at the thought of her duty. She knew that things had not gone well in the Hollow for the fairy folk. She raised her medallion in her left hand and held it close to her chest.

"What do you mean?" asked Katie, not understanding the weight of the Banshee's message.

"Sure we've only been down here a few hours, is the fighting finished?"

"Ah young one, would that the innocence of youth not disappear with age. In this short time things have changed in the Hollow for the worse and only with great skill, courage and luck will they be corrected. In a short time several of you will embark on a journey beyond your dreams and even nightmares. The answer to the riddle of defeat lies outside the walls of your young minds. But it will take young minds to solve the mysteries ahead. Such purity is the only repost to such evil."

Dara and her new friends did not like the direction this conversation was going. 'Evil, journeys, walls of the mind', this seemed far way from running down stairs out of harms way although that was scary enough.

Dara then began to realise that tea and biscuits up at Granny Mary's might not be happening for a while.

However, being the fullness of seven years of age she felt that if there was any sorting out to be done she should be at the front of the queue. How she arrived at this conclusion may never be known. Why do people or fairies for that matter take brave steps forward into the unknown with no guarantee of safe return? Perhaps her answers lay ahead of her or maybe they were always within waiting a chance to get out.

Katie being slightly younger than her big cousin and the height of five was generally more interested in the number of Jammy Delights she could sneak out of Granda's biscuit tin without getting caught; at least she was until the Banshee had spoken. In a strange way she knew she had to help. Why do people or fairies for that matter know they have to help in situations where there was no guarantee of safe return?

So these thoughts passed through the heads of the small company under the ground in the shadow of a Banshee. They all seemed to know and knowing this calmed them for anyone could've justifiably been panicked by all the commotion of the day.

There were seven listening then, Dara, Katie, Pog, Fer, Clumsill, Amad and Cul. Each would play their own part in the adventures ahead but for the moment at least, they were contented in their new company even though some more formal introductions had yet to take place.

Cul and Amad had not really spent very much time with the other fairies in the group. They were a little older and preferred to spend their time hunting and fishing and playing Hurling. Hurling you'll know of course was invented by the fairies many centuries ago and during friendlier times with humans we explained the rules. Sadly the human form that remains, although exciting, is a pale shadow of fairy hurling, it's probably our ability to fly that makes the difference.

Indeed it's a common enough sight for the teams to be battling it out just above the river, dipping down skimming the surface for a low ball or clipping branches to catch a puck out. You'd hardly believe it but oul' Grochin excelled in goal in his day. Hardly anyone could get the ball past him. Frenel would say he was even miserable in nets.

Some of the language on the sidelines is colourful too, as different local teams play. There isn't a seat on a stone to be had and you can hear Frenel at either end of the river, encouraging and chastising!

Clumsill, Pog and Fer knew each other quite well. They had been through the school under the ivy tree together and would often have sleepovers and midnight feasts. The world to them was slowly unravelling with each passing year and it was wonderful. Sad then that such tyranny should befall them. Would that Nut Hollow be the only place for such ill luck but I have learned that the human world is full of such bother and has been for many years. Strange creatures humans.

Which brings me to the two we met today, Dara and Katie. They didn't see as much of each other as they would like. However, they had learned to make the days they did have together as special as they could. (I don't think though that in their wildest imaginings they could have expected a day like this one).

Sheana stood up and let the seven talk together, which of course they did with great excitement and confusion. She moved amongst the other fairies who now needed some answers themselves. Not many of the fairies had talked to a Banshee and were not exactly sure as to the proper way to address her. Banshees are of the fairy race to be sure but they walk the space between the living world and the living world after death. As such they were well respected but evoked fear in most.

'Your lady' was heard or 'Oh songstress' or 'Your worship' got a turn and even 'Your self!'

To such greetings she would smile and say,

"My name is Sheana, and that's all I need to be called."

Most questions asked 'what would happen next?' To this she would say,

"Patience and courage are what we need?"

She continued about them, calming and bringing reassurance as she went.

*   *   *

Above ground, the flight of the remaining fairy warriors was well and truly on. Those that remained numbered twelve from a starting effort of nearly forty. Our losses had been terrible but if we didn't escape hope would have no business again in Nut Hollow.

"Greagle you're the only one who knows where the secret entrance to Fween Talav is, you must remember," I said.

As secret entrances go this was it. Bad enough to lose the Hollow but if our enemies got into Fween Talav that would be the end.

"My young friend," as Greagle often called me when he thought I was being a little above myself, "I may nearly have died at the feet of that dark devil and almost drowned in the sludge but I still have enough about me to remember things that should not be forgotten. Perhaps some day you might be in a position similar to this abominable one I now find myself and I can tell you the last thing you'll need is some young upstart doubting your faculties!"

Well, I thought, *nothing much wrong with his spirit anyway.*

I was going to offer an apology but thought better of it. No doubt another tirade would have been delivered from his ample verbal quiver.

Luckily Spindler's huge net web across the river had given us an advantage. Our pursuers were some way behind by the time they had finally pulled it down. Such was it's stickiness that many rats, weasels and wasps met their wet doom in the river as it fell. As Greagle lay in my arms I felt privileged to be carrying him but sad that I had the duty at all. To see someone so proud and whom you admire greatly, weakened so was not a sight I would have chosen. However, there was no time for such thoughts.

"Quickly, dive left," shouted Greagle. "Our path lies west."

We made the turn left and down toward the small group of trees that sheltered the path up to Brae Height. The path itself was frequented mostly by sheep and a couple of Clydesdale horses both of whom we had got to know quite well.

"Head for the third tree on the right, do you see it?" asked Greagle.

"Yes," I replied as did several of our group.

"Ok, take me to the fifth branch above that Buzzard's Claw."

The Buzzard's Claw is the name we gave to a group of smaller branches which fall out from a tree in the shape of a buzzard's claw and there as I looked was one such. The sycamore leaves clung onto the ends of the branches and cared little for our plight. They had their own issues to resolve with the sun and the not too distant autumn.

We landed around the strong end of the branch next to the Claw. Laijir looked back in the direction of our foes who were gathering now with intent near the large boulders that straddled the river. Laijir had, like the rest of us, been plucked from his now peaceful life as a nut harvester and what he didn't know about the magic nuts of the Hollow wasn't worth knowing. His youth had seen it's fair share of battles and we were lucky he was still with us.

"Wherever we're going we need to be there quickly, that fat weasel is looking this way and those crows are pretty angry," he said.

"OK," said Greagle and I noticed how difficult it was for him to speak.

I had a terrible feeling his injuries were worse than we had feared. We stood out of eyeshot of our hunters and hoped time would be generous to us.

"Whatever happens my friends I need you to hold onto this secret as long as you live. Sadly I'm breaking the very same promise I made to my own father but needs must as they say."

"Of course," I answered for us all.

"Listen and remember."

He plucked a leaf and began rubbing it slowly in a circular fashion on the tree.

> In each sycamore leaf
> A vein of truth
> Dishonesty and grief
> Must not win
> Dear tree and bark
> Now so smooth
> To light through dark
> Let us come in

The last word was not out his mouth when an arrow landed one fingernail's length away from the end of Ionta's nose. As it vibrated in the tree the piece of bark where Greagle had been rubbing the leaf drew apart just wide enough for a few tired and shocked fairies to squeeze through.

"Quickly, they are almost on us," I urged.

The first arrow was soon followed by many more and as we filed in I feared that one of us would be taken with their fury. We could hear the screams and squawks of the crows who were only a few flaps away swearing revenge for Préak.

All in! A second longer would've been the end as the crows landed in a black pile of anger on the very spot we had been. Amazingly we could still see them but it appeared they could no longer see us.

"The tree heals itself from the outside as soon as the last is in. It can detect good from bad so it seems that we are a decent crew after all. From the outside the bark repairs to it's former state but as you all can see from here we have a clear sight of those blaggards," said Greagle. "Better get ready, that outside light will soon be gone."

"Ready for what?" asked Ionta.

"Just listen," he snapped. His temper hadn't improved despite our escape.

"Each of you get a space around the walls there," he ordered.

Inside the tree was perfectly circular and the floor if you could call it that was very slippery, no doubt from the sap. We all spread out to the edge of the circle with our backs against the bark and could've touched the ends of each other's fingers if we chose to.

Greagle spoke again,

"Thank you friend
For this welcome true
To avoid our end
A favour from you
Open your heart
And clear our way
Time to start
No time to delay."

The tree seemed to groan and I felt I had heard that sound before. It was almost like the one you would hear if you were flying past and the wind nudged a tree to the left or right. Almost the same but not quite, this one was more . . . alive!

"Quickly," snapped Greagle, "start flapping your wings for all you're worth."

There was a sense of urgency in his voice that immediately quelled any questions we had begun to think about asking. We did as we were told, each one of us beating our wings in the near total darkness, waiting and wondering. Suddenly the floor itself seemed to be turning to liquid.

"C'mon," shouted Greagle again, "nearly there."

I could just make out the inner tree floor where we stood, rippling like a small lake a stone had just landed in. The ripples now grew greater and our feet were getting wet as if we were standing ankle deep in water.

"Right, well done."

His voice had lifted and he sounded like an excited schoolboy about to jump into Nut Hollow River.

"Now don't panic, and enjoy the ride."

What was he talking about? We didn't have long to wait. The floor then gave way as if someone had removed the plug from a sink and we were suddenly sliding down the inside of the tree. Oh what a rush of air flew through our nostrils and hair.

"Whaaahooo!"

We slid faster and faster bumping into each other occasionally but never getting hurt. Faster and faster still we went and whoosh we began to turn left then right in total darkness. The old fairy in my arms remained silent but all around the others whooped like first flyers. As the passage became thinner we began to file into an order. I could feel feet near my shoulders and shoulders near my feet. On and on we sped, the longest shortest journey of a lifetime. We were slowing and felt the edges of the tree on our backs. The wind rushed by but not with the gusto of a few moments ago.

"I see a light," shouted Ionta.

"Yes, me too," replied Laijir.

"Nearly there," whispered Greagle in my ear.

Out we came into the light flying through the air to land in a bed of moss, dock leaves, grass and yellow rag weeds. One by one we exited the slide until rather ungraciously we lay together in a happy heap. It took us a few moments to adjust to the light and as we blinked and gathered ourselves I noticed a curious crowd of friendly faces peering down at us.

"I'm glad you could make it," said a voice, "you are most welcome. Ah, my old friend it pleases me no end to see you again, and what of Blalim?"

"Thank you Sheana, thank you indeed," replied Greagle. "Blalim I fear fell in battle, although I can't be sure. I saw him last clutching two crow's feet and smashing their heads off a tree. He may have escaped, only time will tell."

20
Feathered Friends

Nefairious paced quickly toward Sherene's. He cast a lonely fairy figure amidst the squawking, sniffing, crawling shapes of his army. He found the surroundings familiar and yet strange at the same time. This was the first time he had walked through the Hollow in sixty years.

As he looked around it seemed nothing much had changed. The houses were still where they always had been, most of them happy and colourful and welcoming. He walked past his own house. It looked well but it was obvious no one was living there or had lived there for a while.

The brown oak door looked forlornly out onto the river as if hoping for someone to come up and knock it. The windows still had the same curtains of his youth but there was no light from inside. He put his head down and walked on by. The gardens were as neat as ever, at least until dead bodies started to litter them. The stones in the middle of the river were as smooth as he remembered except they were a little more worn than before.

He stepped over them carefully testing his wings gingerly between each stone. They had regained much of their strength and he felt comforted to have them back. However, he knew that he could never reach his full potential without the feather wallet.

Now he was on the other side of the river. He turned briefly to look at the great Learning Tree. It's branches hung heavily over the river. It was as if it's very essence had been removed and it had slowly begun to deflate. Nefairious squeezed his hand around the Carving Knife. It felt very comfortable and he knew exactly on what and who he would use it. It caught the remaining rays of sun as he walked and sparkled brightly.

He arrived at Sherene's door and once again thought of previous visits, visits that had made him smile and warmed his very heart with laughter.

"Ach!" he huffed, "no time for yesterdays."

Yet no matter how he tried to bury any feelings of joy he couldn't quite expel them. He shook his head and opened the gate and walked down the path to the old door he had seen many times before.

Sherene's door, he thought and once again memories of sweets and toffee and soft cushions invaded his head. This door had often led to other worlds where anything and everything happened. Now here he stood again with no inkling of enjoyment about his mission. He put his shoulder to the door. It didn't move.

"This should help," he said.

He raised the Carving Knife up in his right hand until his arm was stretched as far as it could go. He then brought up his left hand until they were both outstretched above his head. The animals around continued to loot and wreck all about them. Some washed off the blood from their injuries in the river and it ran red through the stones.

Nefairious didn't bother with them and for the moment at least they were happy in their victory celebrations.

He retrained his thoughts and swiftly brought the Knife down into the door at his head height just below the mole bone knocker. As he expected it offered little resistance and it felt as if he had plunged it into a loaf of bread. He moved it down through the centre of the door and pieces of the green moss which grew upon it fell silently to the ground. He cut out a hole large enough to let him walk through.

He couldn't but feel invigorated at the power the Knife gave him. It felt as if he had always been holding it so comfortably did it rest in his clenched fist. He crouched slightly to get through the gap and soon was standing in the middle of the living room. Silence filled the space only to be filled by the sound that empty rooms make. The rocking chair was still and the pillows sat awkwardly where they had fallen on the floor. There was a half filled cup of tea and a partially eaten bun beside it. Obviously it's owner had left in a hurry.

The sofa also sat quietly as if waiting to be filled. He walked slowly looking round at the clock on the mantelpiece. It ticked steadily and it's pendulum briefly caught his attention as it moved ever back and forth.

Soon enough the business at hand called to him again and he stepped from the living room to the bathroom. He felt his breath quicken.

Could it still be here? he thought.

If not, his plans would be severely restricted. He retraced his steps of that evening many years before and now found himself looking into the very same mirrored cabinet. He did not dwell on the reflection. Perhaps not in distaste at what he saw but more in fear of what he didn't see. He dismissed the thought as quickly as he could and felt his heart pound in his chest.

He raised his hands to the cabinet. It's frame bore the signs of age but he felt it had not moved since he moved it himself. He could bear the suspense no longer and lifted it from the faithful nail which now sat exposed. There it was, exactly as he had left it. The little purse had waited patiently and now almost begged him to pick it up. He lifted it gently from it's hiding place and drew back the string bound opening. The feathers were intact and now ready for his uses. He poured them out into his palm then stroked them carefully and examined each of them.

They were perfect. Back into the purse they went and into his inside coat pocket.

"Thank you indeed, father, you knew they would be safe here. Old Sherene was not as curious as that cat she often talked about in her stories."

He smiled happily to himself and replaced the cabinet.

Now why did I do that? he wondered. *'Tis not as if she is going to back any time soon.*

He searched no further for an answer.

Time to put this Knife into a worthy scabbard for the time being at least, he thought.

As he walked back through the house his cruelty appeared to have replenished to overflowing. Any doubts and second thoughts were banished and he stood again in the living room.

"You will do the job," he said.

His gaze fell upon the old cushion beside the rocking chair.

"The softest most comfortable thing I ever sat on will make the perfect host for the perfect blade."

In a moment the cushion was stabbed and gutted. It's soft padding fell to the floor without a sound. He quickly cut the length required and sewed it together in the shape needed to hold the Knife. He attached it then to his black leather belt and let it fall against the top of his leg with the handle sitting out just touching his palm. He walked quickly from the house and down the path into the late evening.

Crows had set up look outs on the four corners of the highest trees on either end of the Hollow. Black sentries ready to squawk an alert if needed. The weasels had begun to patrol the sides of the river. Each of the banks seemed to slither along with their stealth. The slugs had made it to the tops of the beautiful flowers and were slowly dissolving their bright petals.

The darkness in the sky was well matched by the new mood of the Hollow. The light was almost gone and would not be welcome back if this gathering had anything to do with it. Nefairious glanced around and was content but his journey was not complete. He could hear the rats and the weasels quarrel about which houses they would live in. The crows were pinching at each other the way crows do.

They were oblivious to the fairy with the Knife as he walked away from the river and the Hollow up into the long grass. His wings could now lift him for a longer time than the time before. The brown hoof marked soil passed beneath him as he climbed up the stone ditch that bordered one field from another. The moss on the well placed stones sat soft and green as he passed and the tips of the rushes nipped at his legs as attempts at flight became stronger still. In this fashion he left the scene of the battle behind and soon enough was within reach and the reaches of the Carey Fairy Thorn.

21

Thorn

None of the Nut Hollow fairies were quite sure who planted the Fairy Thorn of Carey. For as long as they had crawled, walked and flew about the place the Thorn had been there , just there . . . waiting and watching. It's not that it looked particularly frightening, far from it. It just looked like a gnarled old thorn bush whose temper would never be better than foul.

The twisted branches didn't help though. They looked as if they wanted to grab the nearest thing and pull it inside, inside into the darkness of the smooth green leaves and the brown shadow that was the deeply grooved bark itself. The fairies did know that Fairy Thorns were not exclusive to them. Reports would occasionally drift back from all over of unfortunate events caused by unnecessary tampering, mostly by humans of course. The general rule was not to bother a Thorn and it wouldn't bother you. But was it alive or was it a refuge for some cruel spirit stuck between two worlds? Hard to say really, best just to avoid them.

These and many other thoughts passed through the turbulent mind of Nefairious as he approached. He had forgotten fear in the years of his anger. It was an emotion lost to days of over imagination and tellings off. Fear does not disappear completely though. It is the subtlest of feelings that will patiently wait on you to come calling and if necessary call on you when you least expect it. This was such a time and Nefairious did not like it.

"Ach, you fool. Old wives' tales and nonsense," he snapped in a harsh whisper.

But he knew better. The heart can't fool the head forever. He was approaching his father's arboreal captor. What sort of creature or plant or thing must it be to hold Neroh?

Then he saw it, not a half a field away against the orange purple sky of summer dusk, as if it were expecting him. It's leaves swayed gently on the branches as the wind filtered through and to the untrained eye nothing could seem more serene. However, his sense of fear and anticipation grew but was twinned and soon locked in battle with his determination to free his father.

Thorn, you have held my father too long. Tonight you will feel the severity of my blade.

He reached down and put his right hand on the handle of the Carving Knife. As before the power of it filled his heart with strength and a confidence he did not have moments before. Too many nights on Knock Layde preparing for this moment tempered his enthusiasm.

Now my boy, nothing too rash. Time neither waits nor rushes and can be freely taken, so help yourself to it.

He would have to let the tree take him and after his captivity the thought of entering willingly into bondage did not please him. There was hardly any light left in the day. Dusk replaced brightness and so sounds replaced dusk. The sounds of the scene were now all too clear.

How loud grass can be, he thought.

The wind gathered itself in rushes every few moments and blew with enough strength to move his long coat about his knees. The creaking of the surrounding trees and bushes filled his ears.

"Enough!" he snapped.

He refocused on the night and his sight was restored. Darkness holds few mysteries for fairies. He picked his steps carefully now. He was well aware that the grass held the treacherous Thorn runners. These slightest of threads sense the area around the Thorn for movement and pass back information as to the position of the unfortunate intruder. One of the benefits of this fairy night vision was that colours changed. Green trees become a light blue and brown bark goes sort of red haired red. Flowers like daffodils turn light purple and daisies head off into turquoise. Many fairies suffer from shock and a sore head the first few times they go out in the dark. As it happened the air that surrounded Nefairious was now a hazy yellow and he could see each different plant individually. He could also see the runners just a few footsteps away.

"Hmm! Thorn runners. Good try but you'll need to do better."

He began to negotiate the remaining space between himself and the Thorn. He had to do it on foot for two reasons. For one, flying into a Fairy Thorn is about the stupidest thing any sort of creature could do and secondly, his wings were still not repaired although the feathers did give him the means to fly a little had he chosen. Not many venture willingly into the realm of a fairy thorn and as he approached, the darkness of it all made him pause.

Too many nights on that mountain to stop now. On you go but carefully mind.

Suddenly his head was alive with thoughts,

What are you doing, you fool, you've gained the Hollow, take it easy forget Neroh.

Then,

Show them all your power, why risk it here, c'mon back to the feast that awaits . . .

Such thoughts continued to question his actions and he fought to quash their rebellion.

On he edged and was now at the very base just among the great roots that stretched in all directions from the Thorn itself. In some ways getting this close was the easy part. He now had to both find his father and release him without them both getting taken forever. He gave his wings another try and they felt stronger again. They would be ready soon. He put his hand into his coat pocket and gripped the feather purse. This comforted him and gave him the boost he needed to go on. His other hand gripped the Carving Knife. The sharpest of all blades that ever was forged and he had it to wield as he would.

Such power in your hands, you'd never lose the Hollow. Just leave old Neroh, his mind was at it again.

However, his resolve was at it's keenest and he brushed the thoughts aside.

Will have to be careful here, he thought, *will have to let theses barbs take me in, this is it.*

The convincing was done and he placed his left boot onto the very last of one of the runners. He didn't have long to wait. Within a breath the tree seemed to wake. Slithering through the grass toward him came the heavier vines. He felt them wrap round the foot that had awoken them.

Just keep calm, you knew this would happen.

Ha! You're done for now and it serves you right. You and Neroh bound for a thousand years.

That's it let them take you in, you have a surprise after all, his mind argued with itself.

In another moment the left foot had been gripped and with a violent tug he found himself being dragged rather unceremoniously through the grass to the blackness of the Thorn. (Just to let you know Fairy thorns are *not* to be tampered with, there is always a particularly potent bunch of nettles round their base).

This was an oversight that Nefairious wouldn't be forgetting anyway soon as they reached out and stung his face repeatedly. Notwithstanding this painful inconvenience his plan was going well.

Not long now.

Other vines now reached around him and raised him into a standing position with his nose to the bark. He looked a little like a mummy as he was now almost completely engulfed by the tree. He then felt the pressure build on his back and his face was now squashing itself slowly onto the bark. The pain of it was intense and Nefairious thought for a moment that this was the end.

You fool, you silly old fool. Tthis Thorn has the measure of you my boy. You're going to be squeezed until the juices all run out.

No, wait. Father said that a Thorn will pull you inside. C'mon now just stick it out. You knew it wasn't going to be any fun.

The pain increased again and he thought that indeed his brain would be coming out through his eyeballs but just as he felt he was about to pass out the bark yielded and he was dragged through the tiny opening. The runners loosened their grip and he fell in a badly stung heap in the darkness.

22

Next Steps

The commotion after our spectacular arrival had died down somewhat. Several of the fairy women had taken Greagle away to be tended to. His injuries were severe but we got the feeling he was far from finished. After relieved greetings from neighbours and loved ones and explanations as to the course of the battle we found ourselves round the Grand Ash Table.

This table had been designed many years before for important discussions. You may know that for an important discussion to be truly important the participants need a good solid table with sturdy seats and plenty of elbow room. Fairies encourage elbows on tables and leaning back on chairs. It clears a space in front, a space behind and therefore a space in the head. In fact the more swinging of the legs as they lean back in the chair the better, something to do with momentum and all that.

Each of us had taken a place, with the Banshee at the head, and were whispering to each other and trying to think of how to survive the day. On the left hand side sat Katie, Dara, Clumsill and me. On the right sat Laijir, Tridge, Ionta and Síoda. Sheana called us to order.

"Friends, we are here because the Nut Hollow that we have known and loved for generations has been invaded and lost. It is up to us all to help get it back," she said and there was steel in her voice.

"Whatever dangers we have faced today will be only a taste of what lies ahead and some of you may not return . . ."

She let these words float slowly over the company. It really was as serious as that. Katie and Dara were waiting to be told that they could go home because they were only little and of course Granny would be worrying and there would be tea and biscuits and . . .

"I'm afraid you will have to wait for your tea girls," said Sheana. "You will have your own part to play in this tale. I am sure you would not want to let us down."

Oh great, thought Dara, *bribery!*

But she knew it wasn't the same sort of thing as when a parent asks you to do pick up your dirty socks for a sweet. This was something entirely different. Being the older cousin Dara looked at Katie and noticed she looked a little tired now and lost. She gave her a big hug and whispered,

"It'll be OK."

Sometimes a hug is the best cure of all.

Katie nodded slowly in agreement and asked,

"Is their any food? I'm starving."

Within reach was a bowl of toffee and they grabbed some of it.

The others round the table slowly let their chairs fall back into the correct positions. One by one the air borne legs of each chair stamped onto the ground like a giant clock ticking down. There they sat and Sheana began again,

"Our best hope lies on the Island, or rather underneath it. You all know of whom I speak. You will need the salmon."

"I agree," said Laijir, "we must get to Rachary and hope he's of a mind to help."

Then Ionta herself spoke,

"Yes it would seem the only way and if that is the case then our difficulties have just begun. However, it must be so. The Hollow was not made for such cruelty and needs us more than ever."

"I agree," said Síoda, placing her blood stained knife down on the table.

She was one of our finest warriors and a woman of few words. She had fought bravely above and had taken down at least three crows with her arrows. Many of the younger fairies looked on her as a hero. She excelled at hurling and was well known to be game for anything.

Tridge and Laijir nodded in slow approval of the fledgling plan. Katie and Dara had been chewing on the toffee and felt their strength returning. With it covering just about every space in their mouths, Katie and Dara said,

"OK!" although it sounded more like "Ogh Kaych."

However their meaning was clear enough and Sheana spoke once more,

"There are eight of you here and on either side of me two spaces are left. One for Greagle who we hope will be returned to health soon. The other is for Blalim. Until we know better we must trust in his skills and that he is alive. When this table is filled again we will be in a healthier position than this one now. Get yourselves ready. Clumsill, come here please?"

Clumsill unbound himself from his mother's embrace with a struggle. She didn't want to let him go into harm's way again. He walked forward, much to Silleyn's annoyance, and knelt before her. Sheana leaned over and spoke softly in his ear,

"My brave young fairy you have made new friends today and have forged strong links in the eye of this storm. It is not for me to break these new bonds. Please accompany Katie and Dara, they will need you before long."

Clumsill nodded and Silleyn knew well her son wouldn't be in bed early tonight. With that the Banshee pushed back her chair, stood up and flew upwards to the ledge from whence she had introduced herself some time before. She gazed down on us all, grabbed her cloak and turned away into the darkness.

The company broke up and the elder fairies gathered together. There was unease among the warriors,

"Why would she include children in this mission?" asked Tridge. "I mean it's too dangerous."

"I think so too," said Ionta. "Is there any way they could survive the trip to Rachary?"

I felt that I had to say something,

"Agreed, 'tis a strange addition to the company and what lies ahead but she is one of the Ban She and I trust her judgement. Perhaps youth and innocence are qualities that we ignore at our peril and besides I do not want to incur her wrath. The young ones may be of more help than we can see now."

There was a reluctant silence which was slowly broken with dubious nods, questioning 'Hmmms' and such like.

Tridge turned to us all and tightened his sword in it's scabbard. He pushed his knife deeper down into it's sheath and then bent down to fix the straps on his boots.

"Right, we're all in this together. The young ones will look out for themselves I'm sure. There is work to be done and it grows impatient at us chattering here like magpies. Graneff, you have the ear of the old brothers and it would seem a good head on your shoulders. I take my own lead on most occasions as you know but if you need council I offer you my wisdom for what it is and my sword."

Ionta stood beside him and nodded at me as if to agree and second Tridge. Laijir and Síoda looked at me directly in the eye and gave me the slightest of bows. So the quickest election of a leader you ever saw concluded with me at the head of us all.

"Works for me," added Dara.

"Anymore toffee?" asked Katie.

I thought a few words would be in order,

"There are no leaders here among friends but if that's what my role is to be I'll accept your offer and all council will be happily received. We are together or nothing at all. Let us call on Rachary."

Katie, Dara and Clumsill munched contentedly on their toffee.

"Katie, you can borrow these," said Fer suddenly, who ran up to the table with her own leather boots.

"They should fit you ok," she smiled and I was a proud dad at my now bare footed daughter's sudden generosity.

"I'll bring them back," answered Katie putting them on. "Promise!"

Goodbyes were waved and the eight of us in various states of mind and dress had to rouse ourselves again. We had to arrange a lift with Saroist which Tridge and I would do together. Of the few advantages we had left our ability to contact that old salmon was surely the best. As far as we knew the underwater world was still untainted, at least we had to hope this was the case.

23
Ordering the Ferry

Saroist was in a bit of a state and was frowning. In his mind he felt quite happy to have played a part in the warning to Nut Hollow with Cul and Amad. The excitement of it made him forget his advancing years for a little while but as the buzz of that huge jump wore off and he was alone again in the water he began to consider how he might reclimb the waterfall of Coolaveely. After all he had retired from all this uphill swimming business years ago and was happy just tending the riverbed.

"Well you old ejit, here you are at the bottom of the waterfall . . . again!" he scolded himself. "What in the name of Ishke were you thinking?"

He knew there was no answer. He had done the right thing. Sometimes doing the right thing doesn't offer up obvious rewards.

As he chastised himself he saw the first of the bubbles, floating the wrong way upstream.

What in the world? he thought.

He didn't have time for further musings as the bubbles then surrounded him and carried him to the surface. As his dorsal fin broke the water the bubbles popped and the sound of a voice exploded from within.

"Saroist, oh great sage of the water . . ."

He was flattered by this title and allowed himself a modest smile.

"Mighty guardian of Hollow River hear us."

I'm sure I recognise that voice. I'm sure it's Graneff, but what sort of magic is this? How can voices be in the water?

Soon enough more bubbles surrounded him and as before they carried the fairy voice.

"We need your help as a matter of the greatest urgency. Everything we hold dear depends on you! Please come to the door under the river."

After a moment or two Saroist gathered his thoughts and reminded himself on the titles he had heard. With his ego suitably massaged he considered the words.

"Well, it would seem my work is not done this day. If I can help the fairy folk then let there be no delay. C'mon you old sea dog, away."

With a swish of his mighty tail he set off down the river.

*   *   *

I signalled Tridge to pull me back from the water's edge. We hadn't used water magic for a long time and I hoped I had got it right. Fween Talav had one direct link to the river. A long thin tunnel climbed slowly upwards to arrive at a tiny door, small even by fairy standards. This door sat underneath the roots of the Learning Tree and from such a position was invisible to anyone peering into the water.

It was by now nearly as dark outside in the sky as it had been in our hearts, we needed this chance to lighten our hopes. As for the bubbles, they were an altogether trickier item but all fairies have the charm. Most have just forgotten some of their older skills. The door is below the surface and you might think impossible to open without flooding the great hall but I remembered the spell and Tridge provided the strength required. Tridge would act to divert the river briefly while I pushed my head in and shouted my message for all I was worth. I hoped I would get it right and began,

> "Moisture of Ishke's unending flow
> Allow this chance to send a note
> Take these words I ask to go
> In bubbled safety let them float
> Far above the water white
> Swims a salmon true indeed
> He must hear our sorry plight
> Please guide my words at best speed."

With that the door was opened and Tridge immediately stood in the doorway and raised his cloak over his outstretched elbow. The mixture of the spell and one as strong as he gave me the chance I needed. I put my head into the icy river and guldered. The words came out in a long gurgle but each one was captured and headed in the direction I had hoped. Of course I felt as I had swallowed half the water that ever flowed on a rock but the job had been done.

We closed the door together and collapsed side by side in the darkness. The river went on about it's business with the power of two suns.

*　　*　　*

Saroist headed down river. Most of his swimming was done well above Nut Hollow around Two Hour Wood. He had been aware since the episode with the two young fairies that things were not well. He knew of Nefairious and was smart enough to know that bigger fish can be fried just as easily as little ones. Caution would be his guide on this journey.

He glided in and out of the stones that speckled the river enjoying the speed the flow gave him. Not since he was very young had he swam at such a rate. He whizzed under roots and through overhanging grasses and even jumped a little before scolding himself once more,

"Now, hold on you old fin tickler, what happened the last time you jumped? Settle yourself. You're not the sprightly young thing you once were!"

For any salmon the freedom of fast swimming is just about as good as it can get. Add to that a few lazy and negligent midges flying near the surface and you are in salmon heaven. So it was no surprise the old boy had an odd jump as he swam. The words were busy asserting their importance in his mind and he had no trouble getting their message. However how would he reply and let them know he had gotten word of their predicament?

"Hmmm, 'tis been a while since I was down around these parts," he thought. "It seems that nothing and everything has changed all at once."

On he went. Down through the curves of the river and the tips of the leaves tickled his back as he swam. On both sides great clumps of soggy grass dipped their feet in the river, the rushes headed sunwards and the branches on the trees drooped in lazy happiness. This was what he felt but there was a shadow on these happy thoughts and he was fast approaching it.

He turned the final corner above Nut Hollow and slowed until he was barely moving. He floated gently to the surface and had a look downstream. All along what he had known as the home of the fairies, were flickering torches placed at intervals on the riverbanks. They shed light on a changed scene indeed.

Each of the perfectly kept fairy houses were badly battered with doors and gates hanging sadly at unnatural angles. Flowers were strewn all about and hedges that had been clipped occasionally with scissors for neatness had huge gouges in them. The din of squawking crows and squealing rats and weasels was deafening. They were no doubt celebrating their victory and the eviction of the fairies.

Perhaps these foul revellers will be a little the worse for wear to notice an old salmon after all, he thought.

On down river he went staying near the shadows of the stones and relying on the near night sky for cover. The first of the Nut Hollow houses was just ahead and he noticed a few sleeping crows with flagons of empty rowanberry ale scattered at their wings. Slugs and worms and beetles were chomping at the garden vegetables and the moths were burning their tails on the torch flames. He didn't cause a ripple and crept further down.

The Learning Tree, he thought as he glanced up at it.

Graneff's house is just below but sadly he'll not be by the fire tonight.

No indeed, for from deep inside he could hear the cold grunts of battle happy creatures laughing and cawing in the bliss of victory.

Luck, if indeed there is such a thing, was with him. The army had relaxed to the point of slumber and his passage was unhindered. He dived.

If memory serves, this fairy door should be just about . . . here.

He swam to the door side and swished his great tail against it.

*   *   *

"He's here," I gasped.

"By all the old magic. Greagle would, I believe, give you a hearty slap on the back. Well done," exclaimed Tridge

We had waited for some time in the damp darkness with no real hope but that dull thud could only be one thing . . . Saroist had heard our call and was waiting.

"Right Tridge, let's get the others, our travels are about to begin."

PART the SECOND

24

From Darkness to Light

Nefairious took a few moments to gather his thoughts. He found himself in complete darkness, badly stung and not a little squashed.

"Well, it's not as bad as the Softening at least," he mused.

"Now Father where are you?"

It was the blackest place he had ever been in for not even his fairy night vision worked here. It would be a matter of waiting to see if light was forthcoming or if he would have to grope his way through the Thorn.

He gripped the Carving Knife and again it reassured him. So far nothing had attacked him. If that were to change he knew he could do serious damage.

Perhaps the Thorn knows what I possess . . . he thought, *and wants it! Time for caution.*

He stood up and stretched his arms in front of him and to the side. His back was to the wall of the Thorn and his arms hit the sides. The inner bark was smooth to the touch.

He took a step forward and then another as tentatively as he could manage. As he had never been inside a Thorn before he knew not if there were traps waiting for him in the silence. He stepped on again and there saw the first of the sap streaks.

What is that? he wondered.

Suddenly another bright blue flash shot up the wall opposite like a fluorescent blue vein.

Another step forward and another streak up the wall. The briefest flicker of light was enough for him to get a bearing on his position. He stood in the middle of an empty room, a perfect circle with nothing in it but himself. The next flash told him no doors were evident. Slowly the veins stayed lit and his room slowly brightened to a dawn like azure.

The perfect jail. How many have you taken and kept here? Not much chance of escape either. How would you know where to begin? Very clever indeed. Yes Thorn very clever but you could not have foreseen this!

He took out the Carving Knife and held it in front of him and began to move it as if to show his invisible captor what he had. He could contain his thoughts no longer and let his voice take over.

"I hold the Carving Knife of Nut Hollow, the sharpest and most potent blade in all these lands. If you do not want to feel it's edge take me to the one you hold here."

The streaks had all stopped as if to gaze upon the prize in the room. A thousand tiny veins giving off one light slowly began to move again. They melted together as in a smith's crucible and formed a circle that closed in on itself as if trying to hypnotise him. His eyes were transfixed but his mind was clear and every few seconds he waved the Knife menacingly. The circle was spinning and gradually a doorway was appearing just in front of him. The whole room seemed to part of this moving light and he struggled to keep his balance. As quickly as they had appeared the lights disappeared leaving the doorway in their wake, a doorway that was shrinking quickly in their absence.

Move, he thought and ran through to a larger area, an area that held a familiar face.

"Father," he cried and ran over to where Neroh was.

He approached the figure in a shocked silence for here lay but the remnants of the father in his memories. Neroh was barely skin and bones and could only just lift his head. When he did manage to look at his visitor no recognition lit his face as Nefairious had so badly hoped. He gasped out a word or two but they were so quiet Nefairious had to step up until he was nearly nose to nose.

"What did you say?" he asked.

"Father, do you not recognise your own and only son? It's me, Nefairious."

The old man made another attempt at speech but in truth it was like a wisp of wind past Nefairious's ear.

This is not the place for you, he thought and made to put his arms around him.

However, Neroh in rags and bare feet shrunk away and curled into a ball on the ground. Nefairious had come too far to stand on ceremony and as much as he loved and respected his father he was not going to spend a second longer in this dark hell than he had to. He picked up the old man and carried him like a babe in arms back towards the opening from whence he came.

By now it was too small to let them pass through and he thought on letting the Knife test it's blade on the Thorn's inner bark. He needn't have worried because once again the blue streaks began circling around the two of them and another doorway formed just to their left. Nefairious could see the grass and felt the cool night air glide over him. He immediately pushed through and in the effort lost his footing and fell head long into another bunch of nettles.

"Oh very funny, Thorn," he snapped.

Neroh could only groan a weak outrage at this latest infliction.

Nefairious had now to act quickly. He feared the shock of release might prove too much for his father. He must get him to the moon beams while there was still time. He knew the replenishing powers associated with them could restore anyone or anything to their former selves. He placed his father down gently in the soft grass out of reach of the Thorn runners and took out the purse with the feathers inside.

I'll never make it without these.

He put his hand in his pocket.

Time to test the old spells again.

He stretched out his wings behind him. They felt good and he began to move them up and down.

It's like my first flight all over again, he thought.

As the momentum increased he poured the feathers out into the palm of his hand and replaced the purse. They tickled his palm slightly but in an instant he brought down his other palm on top of them and began to grind. Gradually they merged together in a sweaty, feathery goo. He rubbed and pressed as hard as he could and began to speak,

"The time for flight is here
Your strength I now release
I know my way is clear
My desires will never cease
Crushed I will consume
The power of winged ones
None can dare presume
What their way will come."

He put the feathers into his mouth and swallowed them immediately. He felt them slide down his throat and they burned as if he had swallowed a nettle but the power built within him immediately. He knew that this power was temporary, Neroh told him so, but he hoped long enough for him to complete his task. He picked up Neroh who seemed to have regained a little colour and took off into the night sky. The ground shrunk behind him as he stretched his wings and took off straight at the moon.

A flicker of a smile from his father encouraged him and he built up speed, the wind rushing through his hair and clothes. He didn't need to touch the moon of course but fairies, even bad ones, know that there is a certain point in the sky where the beams still hold some of the energy and magic that got them all the way from the moon in the first place. This point is known as the Line of Remnants and Nefairious was just about there. It lies just above the top of your last breath. The higher one goes the colder it gets and at the point where you can hardly move you must exhale and quickly ascend to the top of that breath. The breath will attach onto the moon beam and the breather must quickly bathe in that light. This is what Nefairious did for Neroh. The moon beam he had caught stretched away into the nightness of space. To anyone looking into the sky then it would've reminded them of a spider's web reaching away out into the night. He held Neroh in the light and let it wash over him. The risk of death to his father by freezing had crossed his mind but he decided it was worth it.

Sure enough Neroh began to breathe with more purpose; deeper and stronger. He then began to make a kind of humming sound with each exhale as if to signify the sound of returning power. He opened his eyes and looked at his son and mustered a few words,

"It would seem I have been freed and clinging onto a moon beam for dear life."

"Yes, Father, that is indeed where we are. It had to be done, you were so nearly dead."

"Death will not see me for a long time now. I feel my old energy returning but I will need some time to recover, after all being the unwilling guest of a Thorn is not to be recommended. Take me down."

"Happily, and tonight you will sleep in the Mayor's bed," replied Nefairious.

The Line of Remnants had also help fully repair his wings. He flew masterfully again in the darkness.

25

On the Tip of a Tongue

The crew, if we could indeed be called that were ready to go at my return. All had said whatever goodbyes they had and given the fondest farewells they could muster. This revolved mostly around Clumsill and his mother, Silleyn. She was not well used to such public intimacies and yet the thought of her boy heading away into danger brought her through her awkwardness. She held him and stroked his hair.

Clumsill was at a bit of a loss with this emotional outburst and looked rather like he was being hugged to death. To be honest I don't really think the enormity of the day had hit him and seeing his mother in this new vulnerable light was another experience he would filter later on. As children do he pushed her off tenderly, gave her a kiss and stood proudly beside Katie and Dara. I walked over to Gráinne, Pog and Fer and for the life of me could not say goodbye.

It's too final, I thought, *like the end of something . . .*

We gathered ourselves together and had a big family hug. To those watching it must have seemed as if we were preparing for the second half of a hurling match (against the wind!) as we huddled. I felt safe in there amongst those arms and kisses and brave too.

"OK, I have to go for a while and you have to keep an eye on things here, I'm relying on you three."

I thought some words pertaining to duty might deflect the sadness of parting but Gráinne squeezed my hand and smiled and I knew I had all the strength I needed. Pog and Fer slowly let go and returned to the crowd. They were worried for me but appeared to be calm almost as if they knew their work lay here. Their eyes met mine and we smiled together. I turned to the others,

"Time is calling and Saroist will not wait too long for tearful fairies, let's go!"

We walked abreast of each other until we reached the entrance of the tunnel that lead to the river door. I went in first with Ionta behind me. Then Katie, Dara and Clumsill followed by Tridge, Síoda and Laijir. Each of the adult fairies held a torch to light the way. We were soon at the little door again.

It had been hewn from bog oak some three hundred years before and was sticking it well. Only bog oak was any good at keeping out water. We had a final check on what we were carrying. Each of us had a sword which we kept in the sheath attached to our belts and a shield which we carried on our backs. Tridge, Ionta, Síoda and Laijir had a host of smaller, deadlier weapons including human tooth tipped arrows and penknives. (For many years we have harvested human children's teeth and used them in various ways. Some teeth being better than others of course and to the owners of the better ones we leave a small financial reward in the currency of the day).

We all wore beetle leather boots. The warrior fairies always wore their great long coats which were sewn from ragweed roots which was a laborious process right enough but it yielded the strongest of thread. The human girls still wore their red and black dotted garments which I hoped would be strong enough for the journey.

"When I knock the door, Saroist will reply. We have about fifteen seconds to climb into his mouth."

His what? thought Katie. *Don't we eat fish?*

"We will be safe there until we reach the surface where he will spit us out onto the river bank downstream a bit. Once we are on the riverbank we will climb onto his back and hold onto the dorsal fin . . . and each other. Is that clear?"

Ionta, Laijir, Síoda and Tridge didn't respond being almost insulted at being told the plan that they had helped formulate.

"Do you think I'll get to make a first flight?" asked Clumsill.

He was quite anxious now and afraid.

"My brave young fellow your first flight will be the talk of Nut Hollow for many years and we may even allow your dad to do the sandwiches," answered Tridge.

He smiled a little smile and recalled stories of his dad's famous error.

"Katie and Dara, any questions?" I asked.

"Ummm, just one," said Dara. "Were there any fairy dinosaurs?"

To be honest I wasn't expecting that and was momentarily stuck for words.

"Erm, why yes of course, I'll show you some fossils when we get back."

Tridge let go a smile and looked to the heavens as if to say, "Children!"

"Cool," said Dara.

Katie nodded in agreement.

I was impressed indeed with her calmness, either that or she was in such a state of fear she had gone mad. I decided that she was far from mad.

I made a fist and banged three times on the door. Almost immediately we heard the three thuds of Saroist's response.

"Ok Tridge, can you do the same as before," I asked.

"Of course."

I said the spell again and opened the door. Tridge immediately held off the water. In front of us was the black tongue of the great salmon. We climbed inside as quickly as possible. Finally, Tridge pulled back his coat and pulled the door closed and clambered into the mouth dangerously close to the darkness at the opening to the throat. Saroist closed his mouth and we were away.

It was extremely cramped in there and none of us could move. Thankfully a matter of moments later we were at the bank and Saroist hummed at us to prepare ourselves. The children went first to the tip of his tongue and with a grand spit out they flew and landed safely in the long grass at the river's edge out of sight of the invaders. The rest of us were also allowed to prepare ourselves by standing crouched on Saroist's tongue and leaning forward. Without much warning we were then projected out like orange pips. Having the benefit of fully functional wings did help us to break the fall and land with a little style. We gathered ourselves up and checked that all of us were still intact which we were. Saroist was licking awkwardly at his cheeks as if to recover the shape of his mouth.

"Thank you fairies but you won't mind if we don't attempt that again. It was all I could do not to swallow you all and then where would we be?"

"No we don't mind at all," replied Tridge. "The thought of ending up in your stomach I do not find appealing."

"Indeed," I added, "but we have no time to lose. A more conventional position I suggest this time."

"Yes, that'll do," answered Saroist, who despite himself was getting quite a thrill with the excitement of it all.

"Everybody on," I ordered.

This time we placed ourselves in order along his back and held on to ridges of his dorsal fin which now also doubled as a not too uncomfortable seat. We dug our feet in under his scales for extra grip. Katie, Clumsill and then Ionta followed by Dara, Tridge, Síoda, myself and Laijir.

"If you are ready? asked Saroist.

"Yes. Please try to keep near to the surface or we'll drown for sure."

"Honestly, my good fairy, do you think I would forget?" replied the indignant salmon.

With a couple of great thrusts of his tail we were underway. Negotiating the stones was the first and most difficult task. However, Saroist had been swimming in the river for a long time and with wonderful agility and no little skill he avoided the dangerous edges and a couple of jumps later we were through. The jumps gave us a good chance to test our gripping skills and thankfully there were no further soakings.

Down through Stony Banks under cover of darkness into the dawn we sailed. I felt guilty as we left the Hollow to those devils but knew this was the only way. It's quite a distance down to the sea of Moyle and we took the time to get comfortable and get a firm hold. Occasionally our feet trailed in the water and we must have been a curiosity for any onlookers. Down through the townlands we went gathering speed, to Ballynagard where we passed the Temple of Magherin, then through Carey Mill and passed the houses there and under the bridge. On the slopes above us we could make out the old Friary against the new day sky and finally Saroist pushed on until we were at the end of the Margy River looking into the open ocean. The salmon swam slowly through the whitening foam.

"Where the two waters meet," said Saroist slowly, "I didn't think I'd ever see it again."

"Sorry," replied Laijir, "but we can reminisce another day. We have a long way to go."

"I know, fairy, but these waters hold many memories for me and my kind. You would do well to take an occasional rest in your reflections and I don't mean those in a mirror."

"Ok you two," I said. "Laijir, give him a moment, eh?"

Laijir didn't reply and tightened his belt and fussed over his knives, pushing and settling them in their secret places.

"Whoohoo!" said Katie. "That was great, can we do it again?"

"Yeaaa," said Dara and Clumsill together, "Pleeeassse!"

In their excitement I suddenly saw one of the reasons Sheana had insisted on their presence. Here in the very face of danger their innocence took the good out of the situation so much so that I too thought briefly about asking Saroist to head back up the river for a second run.

"This is no game children," I answered instead. "As much fun as that was we have work to do and that begins with us all surviving the next part of the morning."

My tone was a bit sterner than really was required but I felt that it was good for them to be a little afraid. We sailed on Saroist's back under the second bridge of the day and noticed in the early blue morning light the sand on either side of us.

"Katie would you like to make a sand castle?" whispered Dara. "We're down at the beach."

"Aye but I don't think this old fish is for stopping. We can come down later maybe."

"I hope so, but for now just hold on for all you're worth and don't let the water splashing in your face worry you."

"You ok there Clumsill?" asked Dara taking her big cousin role very seriously.

"Well I think so. I mean I'm sitting on a giant fish surrounded by humans and adult fairies that normally never talk to me and I'm heading out into the sea of Moyle. Also my feet have never been this wet and I don't suppose they'll be dry anytime soon . . . but apart from that I've made new friends and won't have to do the washing up in my mum's today. So I suppose I'm ok for now," he smiled.

The motion of the water beneath us changed suddenly, from the smooth ripplings of the river to the tidal swings and bumps of the sea. We were on our way to Rachary.

26

Pog and Fer

"Well what are we going to do, just sit here?" asked Fer. "Those thieves are not going to steal our Hollow and that is that."

"You're on, what's the plan?" replied Pog.

The children of Graneff and Gráinne felt at a loose end. Their father had been instructed to take others with him and they weren't about to do nothing about it. They had moved to a quiet part of the hall and began discussing a counter attack.

"Well that oul Nefairious can't be that fast, I mean he's been Softened and lived up on Knock Layde for ages. He couldn't handle two determined and clever fairies. No, he'll be expecting some form of attack but I doubt it would be from us," continued Fer.

She was quite willing to go and start a fight right then.

"Right this is all very well plotting to take on the dastardliest villain ever to have flown but what do we do? I mean this is Nefairious after all and he has just driven us all down here and goodness knows where else," said Pog thinking of his father.

"Well you didn't really think I just meant me and you? There is one here who will only be too willing to help and you know who I mean."

"You don't mean Greagle do you?" gasped Pog.

"Of course," replied Fer smiling excitedly. "Who else?"

"But he'll never listen to us, sure he'd hardly listen to the Banshee herself!" said Pog somewhat shocked.

"Oh, I think he'll listen alright especially when this could be his chance for revenge on that foul rogue."

"Oh Fer, I always thought you were a bit crazy but now I know it. What is this great idea then? I mean you do realise the Hollow is full of all the sneakiest vilest brigands you'll ever see . . . crows . . . rats . . . weasels and those slugs."

"Yeah of course but it's extremely hard to catch something you can't see or smell," she answered.

"Aye but we don't have magic enough to be invisible . . . but I know who does," said Pog.

His voice became more excited by the minute.

"Now you've got it," replied Fer.

"All we have to do is convince Greagle that we are the best fairies for his plan."

"But it's your . . . *our* plan," answered Pog.

"I know that and you know that but we could perhaps let Greagle think it was his plan you see?"

Pog did see of course but wasn't sure a fairy as great as Greagle would be easily persuaded.

"But wait this is Greagle. You know . . . *Greagle!*"

"Now Pog I need you to get your thinking cap on. You're one of the cleverest children I know, I mean you're nearly as clever as me," said Fer goading him ever so slightly.

"We're the best team in the Hollow. Now are you ready or not?"

Pog didn't think twice,

"Let's go."

The hullabaloo in the great hall meant that these two young planners were not seen heading for the door that lead to Greagle's room. Everyone had settled into family groups or groups of friends or whatever group felt good at the time. The chatter bounced around the hall like the shadows around the flickering lanterns that lit the walls.

Gráinne being Gráinne though did have a mother's eye and noticed her children deep in conversation. However, she put it down to children just sharing stories and reassuring each other. She headed into the crowd and began to comfort her neighbours telling them it would be alright and not to worry too much. Some people do this job but get little thanks for it but the people who hear those kind words don't quickly forget them.

"Right," said Fer, "we have to get to Greagle without being seen. He's in the room over there behind the great table."

The room she referred to was no more than a cutting into the wall of the great hall but it had had a door attached and did now as a place of rest. They headed nice and slowly in that general direction just trying to avoid the light and staying close to the wall.

"Not too far now," whispered Pog. "Did the nurses come out?"

"Yes just a few moments ago," answered his sister.

"That just leaves Greagle in there."

"Ok," answered Pog again, "how do you propose we get in without them seeing us?"

"Oh you're always asking silly questions. Trust me and get ready to run on my word. I will apologise to everyone for this another day."

"Apologise . . ." wondered Pog, "for what?"

"This!"

With that she jumped up and grabbed one of the flickering torches off the wall and threw as hard as she could over the heads of the crowd against the opposite wall where it smashed in a hail of sparks. As it hit the wall she roared at the top of her voice,

"Nefairious, he's here! Run! Run!"

Well if there wasn't a complete panic all about them. Children started crying, women were guldering and yelling and the whole place was in uproar. Several of the older ladies fainted and old Grochin was last seen heading for the toilet.

"Oh my goodness," gasped Pog, "we are in so much trouble after this."

"Trouble my toe," answered Fer. "We'll be heroes and eating toffee for a year. Now quick, c'mon."

They ran as quick as the flick of a lamb's tail to the door, pushed it open, ran in and closed it after them. All done in a second or two and on the other side of the door the commotion continued to the sound of

'Oh my goodnesses' and 'we're doomedses' and 'it's the endses' and frankly much worse language I shall not record here.

The only light to break the darkness came from a small candle on a little wooden table with one drawer. The weak yellow glow revealed the top of a bed and a figure rousing from slumber.

"What in the name of Odhran?" barked Greagle. "C'mon Neroh if you'll attack me as I lie here don't think you're in for an easy fight!"

He started to push himself onto his elbows and made to throw his leg out the side of the bed.

"Sir . . . sir . . . please it's ok. It's ok please don't get up. It's alright," pleaded Fer.

"What? Who? What divilment is this Neroh? You would take on the form of a child? Have you no shame?"

By now he had one bare leg approaching the floor and the other following quickly behind.

"No sir, it's ok, it's us Pog and Fer. You know Graneff and Gráinne's two," said Pog nervously.

"P . . . Pog and Fer, of the Hollow.? Of the house under the Learning Tree? What nonsense is this?"

Clearly the old fairy was not himself and just as well, for had he been the two little fairy heads that had dreamed up this plan and looked so nice on their necks, would be rolling around the room at a distance from the rest of their bodies.

"Explain yourselves, and quickly. This is no day for games," growled Greagle, his mood worsening with the shock and the pain of his injuries returning.

Fer held her nerve and spoke first and as she did Greagle eased himself gently back under the covers and under the light of the candle.

"Well, sir, Greagle sir."

"Oh Greagle will do," he snapped.

"Well, we knew you were injured and the others have left under instruction from the Banshee—"

"Left! Without me?"

"—Yes, they're away to Rachary to get help and I was thinking that we had to do something you know, to fight back."

"Hmm, fighting back is it?" he asked quietly. "And you propose to do this how?"

"Well Greagle sir," began Pog, not wishing to be left out, "we thought that because you are one of the few fairies with the power of invisibility that . . . well we could . . . well you could . . ."

"Oh you have a voice too young one," he said pushing himself up onto his elbows again.

"Yes sir."

"Now listen you two scrubs, this is no game of hide and seek you're playing. This is life and death, probably yours by the way you are talking but life and death all the same. You thought you could come in here and get me out of bed with some half brained notion of fighting Nefairious and reclaiming the Hollow just as easy as one, two, three?"

He fairly barked out these last three words.

Suddenly Pog and Fer felt like this had been the worst plan since ever there was a plan concocted. Add to this the commotion outside which was dying down and the words

"Who did that? Wait 'til I get my hands on them," started to filter into the half lit chamber.

The children looked at each other then at the ground knowing that they were in deep, deep trouble and they prepared for the telling off of their lives. But then the most peculiar thing.

"Great idea!" said Greagle excitedly. "Now help me out of this damn bed, we have work to do."

27

A Dark Gathering

Nefairious was tiring quickly. The flight to the Line of Remnants had taken it out of him even with the magic of the feather spell.

Not too far, he thought.

He was over Stony Banks and well on his way back to the foot of the Learning Tree.

"Where are we son?" asked Neroh.

He was looking up at the night sky trying to negotiate the stars to get his bearings.

"Father it gives me great pleasure to tell you that we are back where we belong," he replied proudly.

Nefairious had always been in awe of his father and now here he was restoring him, caring for him and leading the way.

"You will sleep well tonight in the softest fairy mattress and tomorrow we will strengthen our grip on the Hollow."

"Sleep, indeed to sleep would be a wonderful thing and in fairy quilts too but son I have wasted enough time in darkness. I will waste no more."

"But Father you are in no state to do anything else, you must rest."

"Nonsense I have all the strength I need from the Line of Remnants, which I must say son was very good thinking. Now listen."

Nefairious was within a few wing beats of the bottom of the Learning Tree. The invaders he had left previously were in various states of disrepair and celebration. Winning had come with a cost and the rats and weasels who had survived were busy drowning their sorrows with the finest fairy beverages that could be found. The flickering embers of their torches guided him in closer and closer.

Their rippled reflection mirrored them in the river as they flew. He landed at what had previously been Graneff's front door and pushed it open. He found his generals awaiting him round the kitchen table.

"Ah the great warrior returns, and what's this, another victim?" snarled Rant.

"Looks just like an old dead moth," growled Welset, licking his wounds.

"So you avoided being turned to stone, a fair day's work indeed," replied Nefairious. "Perhaps your manners would be better improved with a lick of this Knife about your shoulder blades."

"Oh no need for that," said Welset dropping his nastiness a little. "I think we have seen enough of blades for one day. Now who or what are you carrying?"

Nefairious approached the couch in the adjoining room and removed his cloak from his father. He placed him carefully on the couch propping him up with pillows so that he could see about him.

"Of all the kingdoms!" gasped Rant.

"It . . . it can't be," stuttered Welset.

They were amazed to the point of shock and together they dropped their tankards to the floor.

"Gentlemen, might I reintroduce the Lord of the Hollow," said Nefairious in a grand manner. This was working itself into a wonderful moment. Not only did he command these two sly generals but here was his ace in the pack, something to reinforce the power he held over them and anyone else who would venture his way.

On hearing his cue, Neroh, also no stranger to theatrics used the flickering shadow light to increase the impact of his return. He slowly pushed himself up onto the pillows until he was almost in a sitting position. He then reached over and lifted one of the candles that sat in a small, exquisitely carved nut shell holder. He moved the candle slowly from his left until was just under his chin and used the light to reveal his face. As he did this he spoke,

"You villainous rogues, never have I seen two more foul creatures in my life and to tell you the truth it warms my heart to see you."

There was an evil glint in his eye.

"Now approach. Together we must ensure that the work done here today is not just as quickly undone. The fairies you have evicted will not take such action kindly. We need to be ready for them, for they will be back."

He let the candle throw shadows about a little while just to highlight the point and Nefairious admired his command of the moment. However, he was tweaked with the need to be the next to speak. This was his plan after all and as glad as he was to have Neroh back he was not about to yield the run of things to him just yet.

"Now friends we have cause for double celebration. The Hollow is ours and we would do well to lay off the hard stuff. A clouded head never helped a clear idea. Now pull up your seats and let us council," he said.

Welset and Rant pulled up their chairs and with Nefairious they sat beside the couch and bade their greeting and joys to the old fairy saying how glad they were to see him. Nefairious listened intently knowing all the while that given the chance either of them would as quickly cut off his head with the Carving Knife. Loyalty is thin on the ground in gatherings of this sort.

Welset had had a moment or two now and was settling into the conversation. He did have one question that nagged him though.

"Neroh and Nefairious, would you ever have thought it?" he said, finishing off his drink before his spoke again.

"The Carving Knife you hold there Nefairious, might I ask in the interests of our mutual well being of course, how you came by it so . . . well . . . so easily? I mean on the mountain top you made much of it's difficulty and many of my weasels are in stone or worse but here you are without a scratch wielding the fairy blade. I expect you must have magic that you are not willing to share. Of course to have some would be in all our benefits you know, to protect things."

His words were heavy with jealousy and desire.

"Glad you asked. It was far from easy," began Nefairious.

Rant flicked his tail about waspishly from side to side.

Neroh smiled at his son's sharpness and at his own strength returning.

"How much did I want that Knife? I asked myself that question every other moment on the mountain top. I wanted it more than life itself and when I had made up my mind I bartered my Cree against the old magic of that tree. The Cree is a powerful thing and rarely will a fairy risk it's safety for we need it to enter the next world. A heavy price but one worth paying. So don't doubt me friend, I will do what I need to. For I am no ordinary fairy likewise my father before me. From my very essence I conjured up my Cree, my source of self if you will. Of course it can't be seen but it's darkness will overshadow the light, even of the Learning Tree. It gave me a shield to fend off attacks of which I recall a couple but really it enabled me to pierce the bark and with that achieved it was a matter of time before I grasped the handle and withdrew the Knife."

"You fairies and your magic," remarked Welset, "hardly seems fair, but I suppose we creatures of the land and sky have strengths in other areas," he said looking at Rant.

Neroh had heard enough,

"Friends we digress away from the real issue. To protect what we have gained today will need all our skills. If the fairies were to capture us and the Hollow, death would be a sweet relief from what they would do to us. We have a little time before sunrise. We will let your men sleep but on my mark you will wake them all for tomorrow another battle awaits and I——".

"Are you being a little over dramatic?" interrupted Rant. "I mean the fairies are scattered to the four winds, their finest warriors disappeared into the river, the so called Hollow and it's treasures are ours. These nuts we have heard of sit waiting just begging to be picked off the trees. Once we have harnessed their potency we need fear no one, no one I tell you."

"You need fear me," boomed Nefairious and as quick as a click he leapt at Rant, grabbed his tongue and stuck it to the table with the Knife.

The pinned rat squealed in agony knocking chairs and tankards everywhere.

"Have *you* anything to say?" grunted Nefairious staring into Welset's eyes.

He removed the blade and watched Rant scurry in agony to the corner.

"No, no not a word, let us plan," replied the weasel nervously.

28

Across Yonder Blue

We set out into the deeper water leaving the bubbling meeting point of river and sea behind. I was surprised at how deep it got so quickly after leaving the shallows near the buttery coloured sands. Our situation demanded we stay near the surface. Saroist swam quite slowly at first giving us time to get a good grip on him. We were all wet after the river run and there was no choice but get wetter and push on.

The day continued to move the clouds from dark greyness into a hint of lighter grey and almost white. The coast line began to remould itself in this light as if it was the first time it had ever been seen. Dark greens mixed with the craggy greys and almost blacks of the rocks. The white horses butted against the dark brown sandstone that had hosted the feet of thousands of inquisitive children and where no obstacles lay, they laid a foamy siege to the shore.

"How long will our journey take?" asked Katie smiling. "This is great craic!"

"I never thought I'd be heading out into the open sea on a salmon," added Clumsill.

"Yes I know, it is amazing but you better hold on tight," said Dara just tempering their excitement.

"A good question," said Tridge. "I would imagine the sun will break the horizon before we are there."

As he spoke he again fussed at his knives and blades. He looked out over the sea and the wind lifted his long brown hair about his shoulders.

"I have a question too," said Ionta who had held her silence until now.

"We are heading to meet with Rachary right?"

"Yes," I replied

"Well has anyone ever met with Rachary without arrangement?"

Laijir now took it upon himself to speak,

"I have heard stories of Rachary and to be honest it's hard to say whether he is friend or foe. His temper is extremely short and his teeth sharp and long. I'm sure your father would have tucked you in at night with tales of his fierceness, eh Graneff?"

"Aye indeed he did. There wasn't a fairy in the glen who hadn't heard of him. Strange to think that here we are going to ask him for help."

"Oh I don't think we need worry too much," said Laijir. "I mean the Banshee would not have sent us knowingly into harm's warm way would she?"

The sound of the waves lapping around our ankles was the only sound he got for an answer. Everyone trusted the Banshee but that was the thing, she was very mysterious and in touch with all sorts of spirits and magics we know very little about.

"I heard one time that to arrive unannounced is a terrible thing," added Clumsill.

"That's not really helping," answered Dara. "I reckon if we explain our predicament to him he will help. I mean he's no friend of Nefairious is he?"

"No he is no friend of cruelty as far as we know," I said. "It will be up to us to make a good case and await his judgement."

"Well I hope for all our sakes his mood is gentle then," said Tridge sharpening his knife. "I really do not want to start fighting again, but if needs must," he concluded and raised his knife for us all to see as if to say he was ready for anything.

On further out into the sea of Moyle we went rising and falling with the gentle rolling of the water. The white horses that live near to the shore slowly became fewer and fewer and we were alone, well alone as eight can be. Saroist popped his head above the water and gave us a look that suggested all was not well.

"What's the matter, Saroist," asked Laijir. "Surely you're not tired already?"

"I may have expected such a question from you," he scowled back, "but the fact is this water is hard enough to negotiate on your own never mind with a group of ungrateful fairies on your back. Plus I'm getting no younger and really I should be enjoying my retirement far from this sort of carry on."

He put his head back beneath the waves leaving us to ponder his words.

"Does that mean we'll have to swim?" asked Katie. "Because I'm a very good swimmer you know and all I need are my armbands."

"Yes Katie, you're dead right. I've been learning to surf recently and if I could just get my hands on a surf board we'd be set," said Dara.

"I'm not sure what devices you two are talking about," said Clumsill, "but I'm not a bad swimmer either. You know I'm not allowed to fly just yet but there's no rules saying you can't use your wings in the water."

Ha! Water wings, thought Katie.

"Well three fine swimmers we have by the sounds of things," said Laijir, "but this is no river or pond we are dealing with here. Your swimming aids and even your wings young one would not get you all the way across. I'd say a large wave would be the end of the lot of you. No this calls for another plan."

As he spoke his great wings started to flicker as if he was getting ready to take off.

"Are you feeling strong, Ionta?" he asked.

"Always," was her terse reply.

"Why do you ask?"

"Well Graneff, I trust you're in good shape?" he asked again.

"Yes not bad. I suppose I should really lay off the toffee biscuits but you know with a cup of tea they're hard to deny," I answered patting my tummy.

"Ahem, why do you ask?" asked Tridge this time.

"Well it would appear that the old fish needs a bit of help to complete this journey. He's been our saviour so far and we are indebted to him no doubt. I suggest that each of us who can fly gives him a hand."

He's not getting my hand, thought Clumsill nervously.

"Go on," I said.

"Ok, we should be able to lift the fish clean out of the water, two at the head and three at the tail, and fly for all we're worth to Rachary or at least as far as we can."

"And the children?" asked Ionta. "Do we lift them too?"

"I didn't say it would be easy," answered Laijir, "but they're not that heavy I'm sure."

In the distance I could see several dark shapes in the air heading our way.

"It would appear that we have no choice, look," I said pointing in the direction of the cliffs on the island ahead.

"Oh great," said Ionta. "That's all we need."

"Excuse me," asked Dara, "but what are you talking about?"

"Puffins," answered Tridge.

"Cool," said Katie. "Sure they're lovely birds. Have you ever seen their beaks, they're like rainbows."

"Indeed they are," replied Tridge, "and those same beaks will be happy to swallow you whole. To them we look like little fish just nice and close the surface, easy pickings you might say."

"No time to waste," I said. "Children whatever happens hold on."

The five of us immediately took off and headed for either end of Saroist. Tridge and Laijir went to the head and waited. Ionta, Síoda and I went to the tail.

"What's going on?" Saroist popped his head out of the water again to inquire at the sudden loss of weight but he barely got the words out.

Tridge and Laijir dived into the water just in front of his nose. Ionta, Síoda and I performed the same manoeuvre at his tail. We were all below him now and began to flap our wings with all the power we had. Tridge and Laijir came up together just behind his great lower jaw. Ionta and I were at the joint of his tail fin and his body and Síoda held the top of his tail fin. We began to pull together.

Saroist's eyes opened wide in amazement and I'm sure I heard some form of foul fish curse as he slowly became airborne. We broke the surface and I heard the children screaming nervously in excitement and dread all mixed together.

"Hold on children," I yelled.

"Whoohoo!"

Thankfully Saroist, although heavy indeed, was within our limits and we started to pick up speed. We kept him just above the water so that he was able to lower his head just deep enough into the sea to catch his breath. As he did this Tridge and Laijir moved up his jaw enough to stay dry and when he came up again they returned to their original position. Our trouble was that we were flying almost directly toward our potential eaters.

The puffins were approaching from the north west of the island ahead. I had heard rumours that they had a stronghold there and could now say the rumours were true.

This is going to be tight, I thought.

As we flew on the island became clearer and we could see the gashes and grooves on it's white stoned flanks. I had just enough spare air in me to enquire after the children.

"Everyone ok up there?"

What with the wind and spray no words could be heard but I took their enthusiastic nods as a positive response.

On we flew clipping the wave tops and letting the old fish get a gulp of air to keep him right. On another day this would have been a complete wonder but this was not another day. We were now in sight of the island's large harbour. The hulls of the human boats began to loom large. Unfortunately, the calls of the puffins grew loud in our ears and they were upon us. The first of them barely missed Katie's head and I knew we were only moments from disaster. In came another aiming his colourful beak at Tridge. No time for bravery or battle.

"Dive! Dive! Take him down," I yelled to the others.

"Children, hold on we are going under. Take a big deep breath, NOWWWW!"

I saw the children hugging the fin and hoped their grips were strong. Into the sea we went.

29

Now You See Them

The candle light inflated momentarily as if filled with air. The shadows jumped to chaotic attention on the walls and wax broke free of the wick and trickled down the side of the candle itself. As the wax cooled it's rivulet slowed to a stop and waited reinforcements. The pale yellow light resumed it's consistency as quickly after and there was silence.

"Well I must say I never thought I'd see this day. Here am I lying in bed licking my wounds only to be disturbed by two young upstarts. 'Tis like something I'd have done myself," he said with a smile.

As he spoke he slowly brought his other leg round and down beside the first one. The first one as now feeling a little cold and Greagle quickly pulled the blanket over his knees.

"Pog, will you pass me my boots, there under the wee table?"

Pog did as he was bid and got an approving nod from Fer. He placed the black beetle leather boots at Greagle's feet. Fairy shoes of course being warm enough on their own, socks were something of a curiosity to fairies who had noticed generations of humans wearing them.

"Ok Fer I'll be needing my britches."

"No problem," she replied and lifted them from where they hung on the end of his bed.

"Now turn around, thank you."

Pog and Fer giggled at each other but turned around and let him get dressed. There were a few 'tuts' and other 'humphs' as his pains expressed themselves but soon enough Greagle looked as he always did. His green jumper which had been knitted from Nut tree moss completed his attire except for the light brown jacket which also lay on the wooden rail at the end of his bed. He stretched down for his jacket held it in the crook of his left arm while using his right arm to push himself up so that he was standing beside the bed. He looked fairly unsteady and in a flash had fallen back onto the bed again.

"Are you OK?" asked Fer, the previous light heartedness now gone.

"Mmm," answered Greagle, "could be that old crow got a better swipe at me than I thought. I'll need a moment children."

He sat for a little while on the edge of the bed. His head was looking downward and he was far removed from the great Greagle in whom all had placed great trust and respect.

"What do you think he's doing?" whispered Pog, not so sure of their plan.

"Perhaps we should have let sleeping moles lie," answered Fer, now also doubting her wisdom.

The two of them stood side by side at the bottom of the bed near the door just far enough to be out earshot.

"One of your friends has recently had his First Flight, if this sleeping mole is not mistaken?" said Greagle suddenly.

Nothing wrong with his ears then, thought Fer.

"Yes sir, Druhin just celebrated the day before yesterday. They say he has the making's of a great flyer," she answered feeling a bit guilty for calling him a mole.

"Well as you noticed I'm not just at the peak of my powers and if this plan is to work we will need fresh wings. I see you two are not ready for flight just yet."

"Just two more years," blurted out Pog.

"Don't interrupt!" said Fer and Greagle together.

"Well that's no good, we need wings now. I need you to go and get Druhin. Tell him I'm feeling better and would like to offer some advice on the best way to fly fast. That should gain his attention. But get him only, the last thing we need is a gang of young hot heads rushing about Fween Talav."

There is a funny thing that occurs with young fairies sometimes. When one acquires his wings so to speak he briefly leaves his peers behind. Simply put, he can fly and they can't, until their time comes of course. His circle of friends now includes others like him and he is more inclined to seek out their company so much so that those who do not share his new skills are regarded in a lesser light. I think it's a mixture of pride and arrogance and it can be an uncommon nuisance among friends. Fer had felt this from Druhin ever since his first flight and was not looking forward to asking him for help. However, Greagle had spoken and neither she nor Pog were going to disobey.

"You must go back out quietly and tell Druhin to come to me," said Greagle again.

"But they'll all hang us up by our ears after scaring them all senseless," said Pog quite worriedly.

"Aye and they'd be right too. I'm sure oul Grochin won't be the better of it for a while. Still, it shows me you are a resourceful pair and that is what we need in times like these. There's no law to say you can't make things easier for yourself. You know some of the older ones still think that hard work is the only way. Any shortcuts are for rogues they reckon but not me. As much as they're my friends, times are changing and this fairy will not deny himself a less troublesome road."

As he spoke he reached up to his neck and pulled a small gold necklace over his head. He lowered it slowly into the centre of his left hand. It was as pure gold of course and as thin as the hair on your head. It twinkled in his hand like the eye of a newborn kitten. He lifted it again and as it unfurled they both noticed a tiny nut shaped locket hanging gently in the middle of the chain.

"There are as many types of magic as stars in the sky and depending on the state of the sky you see different stars every night. Magic is a little like those stars you know," began Greagle.

His voice was low but steady and he had their complete attention.

"Each of us may gaze upon the same thing and see something different therein. Contained on this wisp of gold chain here is a kind of magic peculiar to me. You see we all have our own personal magic as well as the stuff everyone knows. My little piece of the sky if you know what I mean is here, on this chain. It was passed down through the generations as is our way and if we ever survive this predicament you two will one day receive your own special magic."

He breathed deeply.

"But that is neither here nor there and here's the thing. If you put this on and open the locket you will release a hundred years of energy. It's the stuff that makes seeds grow and birds sing and stars shine. It will envelop you and anyone touching you at the time and you will become invisible."

He let his words hang in the air for a moment to increase their importance. He moved the chain from hand to hand as if reluctant to give it away.

"Now you two must go and get Druhin," he said and as he spoke gave the chain to Fer.

She let the chain fall into the centre of her right hand. She pushed at it gently with her left hand as it she was waking a tiny creature from a deep sleep. In a way she was awakening the magic within for the chain began to glow ever so slightly on her palm.

"Em, excuse me but what's it doing?" asked Fer nervously, she was not expecting the glowing at all.

"Ah my dear," said Greagle reassuringly, "that is the sign of an honest heart. A scamp you may be but an honest scamp for all that. The chain knows it's powers are needed and before you ask I don't know how it works. Some things are best left unknown."

"Ok, well if you're sure it's safe."

"I am."

"Well, here goes."

She lifted the chain and opened it wide enough that it would go over her head. She fixed it around her neck so that the tiny locket rested in the centre of her chest.

"When does she open it and how long will it take to be invisible?" asked Pog, who was getting quite excited.

"Don't worry about that," answered Greagle, "the effect is instantaneous. Now remember your vision will not change. I will not be able to see you. You may touch me or whisper to me. I recommend whispering to Druhin too, a voice from the blue can lead to great shock."

Pog held on to Fer's arm as she opened the little locket on the chain. He noticed that he could suddenly see right through his sister and would not have been able to see her at all but for the glow around her. It was the same glow as they had noticed earlier on the chain itself.

"Wow, can you see me?" he asked.

"Well, yes sort of. You're glowing!"

"Yes, you too," he replied.

"Ah the magic, amazing," sighed Greagle. "Now you two, on you go and don't let go of each other. Bring back Druhin immediately."

30
The Root of all Evil

"Oh stop your yelping and come here to me," snapped Neroh at a whimpering Rant who approached as he was bid. The pain of his stabbed tongue was overwhelming and his moaning and groaning was now incessant. The blood dripped off his teeth.

"Son, while I admit I'm glad to see you're not one to suffer fools it may serve you better to use your blade with a little more thought. This old rat is no threat to you and indeed has proved a worthy comrade today. We will need the likes of him before long I assure you."

Now here was something Nefairious hadn't experienced for years, a telling off. He said nothing and watched his father click his fingers over the tongue of the rat. The yelping stopped and Rant licked his lips and touched his still tender tongue with his paw as if to make sure the hole in it had been fixed.

"Hmmm," began Nefairious, "perhaps I was a little hasty but a lot has happened today and you could say I was a little on edge. My apologies to you Rant. I hope we can put this behind us?"

The rat threw Nefairious a foul glance indeed but nodded his head slightly to acknowledge the apology. It wasn't clear if he accepted it or not.

"Now then, to more pressing matters," said Nefairious eager to reclaim control of the situation.

"You will be aware that several of the fairies escaped to Fween Talav. We could mount an assault there but honestly it is so difficult to reach and as it was designed for fairies only it would prove too much of a task for even Neroh and I against the angry horde that waits there. Our best plan is to prepare ourselves and the Hollow for their counter attack. We have the upper hand here and enough men left to consolidate our victory."

"How long until they return?" asked Welset.

He had refilled his tankard and was about to refill it again after a large gulp. His nerves needed calming after the incident with Rant's tongue.

"Not long," answered Neroh.

His strength was returning with every breath and he felt the authority of fatherhood begin to influence his thoughts. Images of Nefairious as a young lad tripping after him now began to argue with the warrior before him giving orders. He thought he would listen a little longer before letting everyone know just who really was in charge.

"Not long indeed," said Nefairious, "they will have received council from the Banshee. She will also try to inform the buzzards and there will be hell to pay if we are not ready if they return too."

"So we have angry fairies, Banshees and buzzards against us!" asked a high pitched Rant.

"Glad to see you've found your tongue again," quipped Nefairious. "Yes all of those but please do not be overly concerned for we have our own strengths and strength enough to hold on."

"Son, you know we will need the help of every weed that resides in this vicinity," said Neroh.

"Yes father and that is where your skills are needed. You alone among us can control the weeds and thistles and ragweeds and any number of deep rooted malevolences."

"Indeed I can. Me alone, holding our aces as it were. From here on in you would do well to take my council before making any further decisions, don't you think?" he asked mischievously, sensing that here indeed was the moment he'd been waiting for.

"Father . . ." began Nefairious, he had to think quickly.

He had set his father up as the one with the real power to sway the balance and one wrong word here and his authority would be gone. He noticed Rant prick up his ears and Welset put down his tankard in mid gulp. They were aware what was going on between father and son. Neroh and Nefairious had loyalty to each other but self interest was their true master.

"Father, you know the fate that awaits us if we fail. You will be back in the Thorn with me for company. The Thorn will show us less mercy than the fairies. Now I feel it would be unwise to tire yourself with strategy. You are still weak and not as young as perhaps you feel and besides . . . I have this."

He removed the Knife from it's sheath. Rant bolted again for the corner. Welset dared not move.

"The Knife, Father, is mine and in a way I am yours but I control the Knife. You do not control me."

Enough said. Neroh relaxed into his cushion, smiling both in pride and anger. The other creatures understood how the land now lay.

"Ah yes you're right son, I'd best wait for my strength to return, yes," he leaned back further into the cushion and into his thoughts.

Well done boy, enjoy the moment. It won't last long.

A moment or two of awkward silence followed. Nefairious began again,

"Father, I need you to perform the spell of the weeds. We need to make sure every living thing can help us against them," he said in a friendlier tone.

(It's no easy thing to tell your father what to do I'm sure). Easy or not he needed Neroh and they both knew it.

"Ok son," said Neroh calmly, "let us proceed with this, forewarned is forearmed as they say. Now help me up."

The three immediately rushed to his side. Rant took an arm as did Welset and they began to pull him gently into his standing. Nefairious stood in front of Neroh guiding the three as best he could to the blood soaked table. Neroh half sat and half slumped into the chair, clearly a little way to go as regards his strength. He leaned forward on his elbows briefly before pushing himself upright. He looked a picture of illness with his bedraggled clothes hanging off his thin body.

"Rant, go outside with Welset and bring back the roots of any weed you can see. Be quick mind, I'm tired still. Now go."

Away out the pair went knocking cutlery off the fine wooden sideboard made by Grast as a wedding present for Gráinne and Graneff. Neroh straightened himself up. He was a good bit stronger than he let on.

"Right Nefairious you can have your way and I'll help, for now, but remember this," he breathed deeply and clearly as he spoke filling his lungs with all the air he could.

"I will rule the Hollow for as long as there is life left in me and you will inherit all that I leave behind. It is the way of things and it is the way things will remain. We are stronger together than divided, give me my day and revel in memories as you rule yourself, agreed?"

"Father I have always followed you, followed you away from friends and a peaceful life. You made me what I am and I would wager that you were not altogether surprised that I stood up for myself. You have seen that I am worthy of your respect and if you can respect me then so be it, you will have the Hollow to rule as you wish. We will have enemies enough without making enemies of each other."

Neroh smiled and offered his hand to his son who shook it warmly.

"How sweet," said Welset coldly as he returned, "now where do you want these roots?"

"Here. Rant chew these roots until they are truly crushed then spit them out into that pool of blood there," ordered Neroh.

Rant did what he did best and chewed and gnawed his way through the large bunch of roots spitting out and refilling his gob as quickly as you ever saw. The pile of green mush grew until it covered the blood spatter on the table.

"Enough," said Neroh. "Stand back you two. Nefairious come here. Take out the Knife."

Nefairious removed the Knife from it's sheath and stood ready.

"You know what is required son. Do it quickly."

Nefairious raised the Knife above his head with both hands, the tip pointing to the ground , Neroh began to chant . . .

"Oh sweet soil giver of life . . ."

He mixed in some of the soil that had fallen off the roots.

"Oh humble weed in eyes ignored
Blood of foul and cruel beast
Now I'll mix upon this board
No firmer hold in nature's chest
Than your crawling pallid roots
Spread your forceful silent words
On all those coloured florid shoots
Seize the ground wherein you dwell
Distinguish all such fairy light
And grip to choke our enemies
To suffer each a horrid plight."

As he spoke the last of the words he grabbed a handful of the mixture then turned upward his open palm.

"Now Nefairious, now!"

Nefairious brought the Knife down through Neroh's palm and stuck it in the table in the middle of all the crushed green root soup. The blood gushed out and mixed with the handful he had before turning it into a pungent red green dust.

"Quickly," he struggled to speak, "spread it. Spread it."

Nefairious withdrew the Knife and left Neroh to his pain in the good understanding he would be able to cure himself. With Rant and Welset he went outside and they began to sprinkle the dust amongst the grasses and weeds that grew about.

31
Rachary

The sharp pang of cold water jabbed at my skin when it soaked in through my clothes. I turned myself as quickly as possible but the foam of our entrance mixed with the bubbles to obscure my view. It quickly cleared and I was both relieved and horrified at the same time. Relieved to see all hands still holding grimly onto Saroist and horrified at our predicament. I knew that our kind could hold our breath under water for a reasonable time. Reasonable enough anyway to get a bearing on things but what of the two human children?

Humans and the sea have enjoyed a very turbulent relationship over the centuries and I did not want the waves to claim two more lives. The puffins were breaking the surface and snapping down at us all the while but Saroist had taken us down out of their reach.

Saroist! I thought suddenly, *that's it!*

I manoeuvred myself along his slippery flank until I could see his eye. Thankfully my companions had the same idea and had grabbed Katie and Dara and were holding them on the other side of his mouth. We had stopped our descent and I gestured to him that we put the children back into his mouth only this time he would keep it shut. I hoped he would get that point. The pressure of the water and the lack of oxygen was beginning to press heavily on the children who must have thought they had come to watery end.

The great fish opened his giant gently hooked jaws and we pushed Katie and Dara in. He closed his mouth and we could see him expel the water therein. I looked at him as if to say,

"Now don't swallow whatever you do."

He looked back as if to say, "Wise up fairy!"

I should have expected that.

Young Clumsill was hanging on to the fin but in relative comfort considering all that had happened. We held our noses and blew to ease the pressure on our heads and took hold of Saroist's fins again. We had to trust the fish's sense of direction. Downward into the darkness he went his tail swishing through the murky blue of the depths. Further into the now almost black water and I hoped that we would arrive at our destination soon. My lungs were letting me know that oxygen was in urgent need.

Then in the distance a light. A light under the sea! It glowed weakly through the gloom but it might as well have been the sun. I felt Saroist push on with renewed gusto. I had to trust Laijir, Tridge, Ionta and Síoda had made it this far. The light grew in strength with every swish of that tail and I felt my stomach tighten anxiously. We had reached the kingdom of Rachary, the seal.

Many legends surrounded him. Some said he had lived among the humans for a time as one of them and even fallen in love with a maiden but had fallen out with them because of their pillage of the sea. He had tried to make them see that a balance is needed between what is taken and replaced but ultimately he was swimming against a tide of greed and desire. Some say that the humans took him off the island in a boat several miles out and suggest he swim to another shore. Others say he walked into the sea in front of the locals and never returned. They presumed him drowned and mourned his loss thinking that was the end of him.

Whatever the case might be, he resumed his seal form and swore never to have anything to do with humans nor touch the island again. He had then ordered all other seals to desist from changing to human form and vowed to kill any seal that dared disobey him. Many of the seals disagreed but would not anger him further. They did reach a compromise of sorts in that he lets them lie out on the shore and they may even approach any human if they desire, in most cases just to get fed but that's it. In the years since he lived in this underground hall from which flickered our light.

We did not have time to announce our arrival and I hoped this was not taken as an insult. Suddenly from the darkness we saw two streamlined shapes swimming straight for us. Two large grey seals went to either side of us and motioned that we follow them. I was happy to comply and we followed their hind flippers to a circular entrance which had been carved from the surrounding rock. We entered a long tunnel which began to move upward. In the distance I noticed that there were now many lights just a short distance away. We broke the surface to find ourselves in the great hall of Rachary.

"Is everyone ok?" I asked.

All those on the outside of the fish confirmed their health but no sound from within.

"Quickly Saroist, could you open your mouth?"

"Well if I must," he mumbled as if chewing marbles.

He opened his jaws to reveal the girls. They were still alive but wet and miserable.

"Oh thank goodness," exclaimed Dara. "Can we get out of here?"

"Please," said Katie. "I don't think I'll ever eat another Fish Finger as long as I live."

I supposed old Saroist's breath would not have been too pleasant but we had all made it thanks to him. Saroist guided us to the water's edge and we jumped off onto the smooth rocks.

"I'd rather this be done as soon as possible," said the salmon. "You are aware that seals are partial to . . . well . . . me and my sort for dinner."

"Fear not, Saroist, you will not be dined upon, today at least. Who and what have you brought before me?" boomed Rachary, his voice echoing all about the hall.

"I have brought you people in their greatest need on orders from the Banshee."

"I see. The Banshee herself, eh? 'Tis long and many's a tide since I've seen her. And is there one among you who can speak or shall we leave it to the fish?"

The eight of us stood in a line before him and I took a second to gaze at him before replying. He was obviously not short of food. He lay kinglike on his bloated belly. His two fore fins propping him up. His fur was the grey of winter morning skies but dappled all over with small black patches. His eyes were the darkest of browns and stared at us intently. His nose sniffed the air and his long black whiskers twitched as he did so. You could not help but notice his teeth. They were pure white and the two big canines on each of his jaws as long as any of us. He licked his lips which didn't help my nerves.

"Rachary, my name is Graneff, of Nut Hollow and I come to you for help. I have with me companions from the Hollow and two human girls."

Rachary sniffed haughtily and tutted on hearing the word 'human'. He squinted his eyes at Katie and Dara.

"We have been exiled from our homes by Nefarious and his minions. We have no doubt he will try and most likely succeed to release his father Neroh from his well earned imprisonment. He was banished from the Hollow many years ago but has come back and wreaked his revenge. In the Hollow lies the great power with which he will cause much suffering to any that oppose him. He will not stop at Nut Hollow either. There are fairy villages scattered secretly in every part of the countryside and he will try for them all if his strength grows unchecked."

Rachary raised his left flipper, a signal that he had heard enough for the moment.

"This is serious indeed. I have heard rumours of this Nefairious and Neroh. A fine pair indeed to be loose. If what I have heard is correct they will have bought or bribed the help of crows and weasels and the like. It would be considerably worse of course if he has somehow managed to obtain the Carving Knife . . ." he paused and looked at us all.

Like naughty school children we all looked to the ground avoiding his stare.

"Oh I see, he has the Knife too," he said in a very unimpressed tone.

The other seals around him began to push themselves awkwardly toward the water again, they had heard enough. In their on land clumsiness Katie, Dara and Clumsill saw a moment of humour.

"That one looks like a hairy water balloon," giggled Katie.

They sniggered together with their hands over their mouths to avoid detection but nothing escaped Rachary.

"Ah so you find something funny do you?"

"You two." Katie and Dara pointed at themselves and looked at him.

"Yes you, humans. Come here to me."

The two girls moved out of the line and walked slowly forward until they stood a few inches from his well whiskered nose. They were tiny before him and he could have snapped them up right there like a couple of sardines.

"I haven't seen a human girl for a long time and I didn't think I'd ever see one let alone two again. Now you are a touch smaller than I remember, fairy magic I suppose?"

The girls nodded and he looked at me. I looked at the ground again smiling awkwardly.

"Yes, fairies indeed. 'Tis rarely though that humans and fairies mix so your situation must be precarious, especially as none other than the Banshee herself has sent you here. An event as you have described if not nipped in the bud can easily blossom into complete carnage."

His thoughts took him out to the open sea of his youth as he spoke and he remembered the hordes of fish swimming and the puffins and other wild fowl circling above.

"Yes, carnage and lack of thought for the future. Terrible things can happen right under your nose. Not so many puffins now (I was going to disagree but thought better of it) or fish for that matter," he stopped and barked something in seal language to one his companions.

"Come and rest yourselves for a moment, we can prepare food and get warm clothes for you all."

We sat in a semi circle in front of him as the seals brought out bits of crab and seaweed for us to eat. The younger ones looked at each other as if to say 'where's the pizza?' but knew that this would be all the food they would see for a while and we ate all we could. They quickly fashioned 'clothes' for us from their old fur piles and it felt good to be warm again. We piled our wet clothes on the stones which were warm underneath the seals. The steam soon started rising and they would dry quickly. Our meal was soon finished and he began again.

"Graneff, I will help as best I can. I will transfer you back to the water's edge from whence you came. From there you must proceed to the Vanishing Lake. Once there you must collect the last droplet of that lake before it disappears and keep it here," he pointed to his eye.

"One of you not given to crying would be the safest choice. Keep the droplet there in your eye it is vital," he looked at Clumsill as he spoke.

"You will see the Towers of Loughareema but more of them later. From the Vanishing Lake go to the Everlit Turf Mountain and collect a few of it's red embers, keep them here," he lifted his flipper to reveal a tiny glass jar.

"You!" he said looking at Ionta. "Take it."

Ionta walked forward and put it under her arm.

"Your final task awaits you on the top of Knock Layde, the Stone of Pity to be precise. Some of you with strength enough must chip out a piece of the stone," he looked at Laijir and I as he spoke.

He turned his eyes on the three youngsters,

"Children should not know of such dangers but our world is imperfect. To help mend it you will need to bring all of your courage. You will need it before your journey's end."

Dara, Katie and Clumsill were getting used to this sort of request now but again knew him to be right.

"And Graneff, you will need to combine these needs in such a way as to help you reclaim the Carving Knife. Would that I could tell you what it should be but I cannot. There is another who knows better than I. Now let us go, the sea beckons."

32

Druhin's Task

"They should have taken us too. Sure what use will those youngsters be, they can't even fly!" exclaimed Druhin to his friend (the fact that he had only started to fly the day before yesterday didn't seem to bother him).

There were four of them, Druhin, Deagoir, Milte and her brother Trailte. They had gathered themselves in the corner of Fween Talav nearest the entrance where Greagle and company had landed unceremoniously some time ago.

"Is there nothing we could do?" wondered Milte.

She had been flying for a year or so now and was quite good. She did have some issues with taking orders though and her parents, Mildred and Teal had often fretted over her rebellious nature. Deagoir offered his thoughts,

"Exactly. We know enough magic to help out. Why would the Banshee ignore us?"

"I haven't a clue what she was thinking, sending that brat Clumsill is even worse than sending those two humans," said Milte.

There was general huffing and puffing in the corner and they were considering different plans and theories to enable them to fight Nefairious. Pog and Fer slowly opened Greagle's door and quickly closed it after them. To anyone watching at the time it would've appeared the door had suddenly blown open and closed.

"So far so good," whispered Fer, "I don't think they noticed."

By now most of the fairies in the hall had settled into family groups and were comforting each other with songs and stories. It is the way of fairies in times of sorrow, or happiness for that matter, to gather together and support one another. This was such a time.

"Do you see him anywhere?" asked Pog, still amazed that no one could see them.

They walked forward carefully through the crowd being careful not touch anyone.

"He's over there," said Fer suddenly.

"Oh he's with Milte and Trailte. They'll be giving out about something I'm sure," said Pog.

They tiptoed over closer and closer and were troubled with the worried tone of the conversations they couldn't help but over hear. Within a few moments they were right behind the gang of five. They could hear their whispered intentions to take on Nefairious, to break out of Fween Talav and other lofty plans.

"Hey Fer," whispered Pog, "have you thought about how we're gonna do this? I mean without the others hearing?"

Fer gave him that older sister look that younger brothers really hate. The one that would just like him to be quiet and leave things to her.

"Whatever you do don't let go of my arm or else we'll really be in it," she answered. "Now watch and learn."

She reached into her pocket and took out a tiny feather, most likely one from a swallow's tail.

"I didn't know you had one of those," whispered Pog.

"Sshhh!"

She moved as close as she dared until she stood directly behind Druhin. She raised her feather carrying hand and slowly drew it across the back of his neck. He immediately lifted his arm to itch the spot and she managed to remove her hand just in time. After a moment or two she repeated this procedure and once again Druhin quickly slapped his hand on his neck. This time he turned round and looked for the fly or midgy or whatever it was.

Well that's got him thinking there's a fly after him, thought Fer.

She now moved in front of Druhin and knelt before him. Pog tiptoed around so that he stood behind her with his hands on her shoulders. She raised her hand up and quickly tickled his nose careful not to touch him with her hand.

"What the . . . ? What is that?" asked Druhin.

His friends looked at him in bemusement.

"Are you ok?" asked Milte.

"Aye sure, there's something buzzing about and it's taken a shine to me."

"Probably after those rowanberry pies you were eating earlier," joked Trailte.

Pog beckoned Fer to come out of the circle and they moved a few yards away.

"So what was that? Are you going to tickle him all day? Great plan! We are in a hurry here you know. Here, grab that clay pot there and throw it just behind them. As soon as they turn around grab a hold of Druhin. I'm sure that gang of geniuses will get over it. We haven't time for tickling," he said crossly.

"Hang on short stuff . . ." she began but it was too late.

Pog's patience had run out. He grabbed the pot himself and launched it against the wall behind the gang. It smashed with a loud bang and all heads went for cover. The clay pieces flew spectacularly all over them.

As soon as the heads were suitably in hands Fer did as she was told for a change and grabbed Druhin. He did not have a clue what was going on and struggled to break her hold.

"Don't fight me," she whispered. "It's me Fer, just come on and please be quiet."

"But . . ." started Druhin.

This time Pog put his free hand over his mouth.

"Sshhh!"

He quite enjoyed saying that.

Druhin watched his friends pick pieces of clay out of their hair and begin to ask each other where he was. He began to realise that he could hear Pog and Fer and see them . . . well sort of see them. As he thought, he found himself being dragged away from his confused companions by these two glowing fairies.

"What is going on?" he asked.

He was strong enough to pull away out of their grasp but the urgency in Pog's voice told him he shouldn't. They moved awkwardly along in the direction of Greagle's room. As they went it was impossible not to hit a few bums and ankles with their feet and hands and those that saw various bits and pieces disappear briefly had to rub their eyes in amazement.

Soon enough they had reached Greagle's door and once again they managed to get in without causing a fuss. Most of the fairies were too preoccupied listening to the excited rantings of those young friends of Druhin going on about his sudden disappearance.

Once inside they approached Greagle but stood a few feet away not wanting to frighten him. Druhin had stopped struggling and stood quietly to see what was going to happen next. Greagle of course had noticed the door,

"I trust you are all here?" he asked.

Fer moved her hand to the necklace and slipped it over her head. In an instant they were visible again. Druhin rubbed his eyes as if someone had just turned on a bright light.

"Ah my good man," began Greagle, "might I apologise for the necessary dramatics but you'll appreciate that today we do not need any more mishaps."

"Em, Ok sir but what do you want me for?"

"You have very recently got your wings, am I right?"

"Yes just the day before yesterday," he replied and gave them the briefest of flutters as he answered.

"Good, and would you say you can fly?"

"Yes sir I can fly alright. To be honest I've been practising for a while you know . . . secretly. You won't tell my parents will you?"

Greagle smiled and shook his head,

"Of course not. I don't think there's a fairy in the glen who hasn't pulled that one. Now I saw your first flight and it wasn't half bad; nothing that a little tuition couldn't cure anyway."

Druhin was all ears now, to be taught by Greagle was . . . well it didn't get any better.

"I need you to go out into the Hollow and fly to the bat tree and ask for Strelle, lord of the bats."

"Bats!" gasped Druhin. "But they don't really get on with us, do they? Only last week they knocked Shest and Lirna half way into next week. They were going out for a flight at dusk and all of a sudden they found themselves bounced out of the air onto their ars . . . em . . . behinds."

"Ach sure it did them no harm, all that lovey-dovey carry on," replied Greagle who these days didn't have much time for romance.

"It is fair enough to say though that our two cultures haven't always seen wing to wing but we go back a long way together and sometimes your so called enemies can be your friends. Or to be quite frank, if they don't help us we'll be seeing more of Nefairious than we would like."

"What do I say to him? I mean would it not be better if you went?" asked Druhin.

"No. You may have noticed I'm not in prime condition here."

"Can we go too?" asked Pog who felt ready for anything.

"Not this time," said Greagle, "wings required for this one."

The four of them took a space on the bed as Greagle told Druhin of the doorway into the river and the necklace. Druhin would use the necklace once above ground and go straight to Strelle's tree. Greagle felt he had enough magic to get him out safely into the river and told him how to get back in at the buzzard's claw. He must have talked for a half hour explaining exactly what he wanted Druhin to do. He also turned his attentions to Pog and Fer and told them their work was far from over.

"Can you do this Druhin?" he asked gravely. "This is no easy task but I wouldn't have asked if I hadn't seen something in your first flight that doesn't present itself very often. You have all the magic and power you need within. Can you do it?"

"No choice have I?" answered Druhin. "But yes, I can do it."

33
Decisions, decisions

The beauties of Nut Hollow and many places like it are obvious enough if you care to notice them. I have heard though that humans are generally too busy to notice anything but the things they wish they didn't have to see! They will often pursue activities that destroy the very thing that sustains them, that being their environment and yet there are still a few who treasure the land. Sadly it appears this group are not in any position to affect the wreckers. The peculiarities and contradictions of humanity have often been discussed over a warm fire and a glass of rowanberry juice. How could any living creature be so perfectly contradictory?

In some ways the image of the three scoundrels running round the glen spreading the foul dust would also have raised an interesting discussion or two. Their actions were reckless and done only to suit their own ends without a thought for the future of the Hollow. Perhaps humanity's destructive influence was stronger than we thought for here was a fairy doing the very same thing. He should have known better. At least the rat and weasel had an excuse. Their kind was never known for such wanton vandalism and these two representatives were acting under threat of certain death. Perhaps that's not even an excuse.

Nefairious had flown almost half way up Brae Height sprinkling the dust over the already healthy population of thistles. Thistles as you well know are the unfriendliest weeds that ever grew. They are notoriously deep-rooted, foul tempered, trouser catching, itch inducing annoyances. The dust had barely touched their hairy leaves when the already clinging thin white roots began to push further into the soil. They fastened themselves around nearby rocks and tree roots in a manner that suggested they were not for moving. Nefairious was warming to his task.

Nut Hollow, he thought, the wind curving around his body as he flew, *I never thought you would be mine to wander through so freely. Look now . . . where are your precious guardians? Hmmm? No answer? Nothing to say? Shall I tell you? Yes I think I will . . .*

Rant and Welset looked up at him enviously, oh what would it be to fly?

They are scattered to the four winds, that's where. Oh I suppose they may try to reclaim you but you will have a few surprises in store. Oh what was that? You would never hurt anything you say. Ha! We'll see soon enough just what a little twisted nature can bring.

He smiled to himself and for a while was lost in the pure divilment of it all. But there suddenly in front of him was the Seating Stone. He hadn't seen it for years.

My first flight, he thought.

Pictures of that day flooded into his mind.

There was cheering, smiling and . . . Mum. She stood with a tear in her eye and could hardly speak for joy and pride. No sign of Neroh that day. No, he was debating with the Thorn at the time. No hugs from him were there Nefairious?

He landed awkwardly on the grand stone, his head spinning.

"Ah none of that nonsense," he shouted loudly at himself.

So loudly in fact that Rant and Welset stopped what they were doing and looked over at him.

"I tell you Rant," started Welset, "something's not right with that young upstart."

"Oh, and what makes you say that?"

His tongue was still quite sore and he licked his lips tenderly.

"Well he seems to be fighting with himself as much as anyone else."

"Do you think? I didn't really notice but now you mention it he did spend a long time amongst them after Neroh was caught, perhaps he's having second thoughts about the whole thing. Then there's the whole business with his mother," answered Rant.

"Oh yea? You seem to be well versed in fairy goings on," said Welset raising his eyebrows.

"Yes we rats keep our ears to the ground you might say, nothing happens that we don't know about."

"And what about the mother, I mean she reared him alone didn't she and couldn't control him was what I heard. He needed the father about to rein him in but the mother couldn't do it . . . too soft I heard."

"Yes she was a gentle creature, not sure how she ended up with Neroh," laughed Rant, "opposites attract eh?"

"Aye maybe so, but her heart was broken. What with Neroh in the Thorn and Nefairious turning to the bad, the shame and heartbreak of it all proved too much. She threw herself off the old log bridge that traversed the river. She chose not to fly and was swept away to her doom."

"Hmmm I wonder is he a bit soft after all? Quick, back to work, he's coming!" snapped Rant.

Nefairious had gained control of his thoughts again and flew over to his two colleagues who had quickly reverted to their chore. Nefairious circled above them,

"You've done enough, nothing will be able to sneak through on the ground and anyone who tries will be sore and sorry they did. Rant gather up whatever of your mob are fit to walk and start gathering nuts. You'll find what's left of them all along the stretch of nut trees on either side of the river. There may not be too many by now but every one you find will help. Might I also suggest that you do not try any."

"Why not, we're in this together aren't we?" huffed Rant.

"Don't try any for your own good, that goes for you too Welset. If you eat a wrong one it will kill you," said Nefairious coldly.

Rant shook his head not believing his bad luck.

"No one mentioned 'wrong' nuts," he moaned quietly.

"Welset, I have another task for you. Meet me back at the Learning Tree," said Nefairious and flew off in the direction of the tree.

"Better do as he says," said Welset and made to walk away.

"Yes I think we'd better . . . at least for now," agreed Rant, "but keep an eye out, you never know how this will all end and I want to make sure it ends well for us."

They sprinkled whatever dust they had left and it was all they could do to get back inside the circle of thistles so fast did they grow. Rant rounded up his men waking them with whips of his long pink tail over their sleepy heads.

Welset watched about ten big grey rats head down to the waters edge. Once there they split into two groups, one half swimming swiftly across the river where they began searching out the nuts of Nut Hollow.

As he looked at them Welset wondered what task lay ahead of him. He didn't have long as suddenly from behind Nefairious tapped him on the shoulder giving him a start. The cunning little fairy's wings slowed behind him until they were still.

"Welset, the difference between weasels and rats is simple; weasels are infinitely more selective in their choice of prey."

Welset felt his shoulders tighten immediately, he had learned to be wary of anyone handing out compliments for no good reason. However, he did nod slightly in passing approval of the statement.

"You know yourself that rats will eat just about whatever they can to sate that eternal appetite of theirs. On the other hand weasels are particularly fond of cute and fluffy bunny rabbits if I'm not mistaken. Indeed Neroh brought me along once or twice to watch you hunt. You wouldn't have seen me of course but I saw you . . . and your ruthlessness inspired me even then. You were not one to let appearance or emotion cloud your judgement on what had to be done."

Welset continued to stare at him not exactly sure where he was going with such praise.

"Here's the thing, when the battle begins again I have no doubt we will win . . . again and when we do there will be a place for a loyal general to stand beside me and my father."

He looked Welset dead in the eye.

"Someone who will be able to follow orders precisely without having to be lead around by the nose. That someone will be well rewarded in the Hollow and enjoy luxuries beyond all reckoning. That someone, it has been decided, will be you."

Welset held his silence, Nefairious hadn't finished.

"If you decide you will take the post and I strongly advise that you do, you have only to rid yourself of the one person who threatens your future happiness," he paused a moment. "Rant."

The old weasel walked a step or two back. What sort of a mad day was this at all? He had survived a long time on his wits and intended to be around for another while. He breathed deeply.

"A tempting offer young one, you are quite the dealer. You would have me do away with my old friend and all to service you and your father. That being done I and any who would listen to me would enjoy the fruits of the Hollow."

He breathed deeply again.

"Tempting, but do I have a choice in this or is a matter of pick any answer as long as it's yes?"

"Indeed, you do have a choice, you can either do as I ask or the offer will be made to your 'old friend' as you so sweetly put it. I don't think the rat will have such difficulty choosing . . . do you?"

34

On the Turning Tide

Rachary and four of his seals lined up along the water's edge. We quickly finished whatever we were eating and prepared ourselves for the sea. Thankfully our clothes were dry again and we redressed ourselves quickly. I noticed Saroist looking rather anxious but Rachary spoke,

"Don't worry salmon," he began, "you have well and truly risen to your task and will not have such a mouthful this time. I do need you though. Are you ready to finish what you have started here today with your new companions?"

Saroist didn't say anything. He was not altogether happy about being so close to so many seal mouths in spite of Rachary's assurances.

"I do not take orders from seals you know, but this task is bigger than any reservations I may hold for you and your sort. One of you probably gave me this hole in my tail!" he said and raised his nibbled tail in the air. One of the seals looked guiltily over his shoulder.

"But to answer your question, yes. I will do whatever I can to rid the Hollow of it's current foul landlords."

"Glad to hear it," replied Rachary. "I may change my opinion on you salmon after all. Now, Graneff and the three young ones will come with me . . . in my mouth."

Oh great, thought Katie, *more fish breath*.

"Laijir and Síoda will go with Phoca, Tridge and Ionta will go with Grypus and you Saroist will swim behind and you will be able to keep up I trust?"

Seals! thought Saroist and fired over as dirty a look as he could.

We took our places in the various mouths and it felt strangely safe and dangerous at the same time. We had to trust none of them felt the urge to swallow.

"To the sea friends, to the sea and what fate holds . . ." shouted Rachary and we slid under water again in an instant.

There was enough room in Rachary's mouth for us all to be fairly comfortable and although it was dark we did not feel afraid. We sat on his tongue which was all soft and wet with our backs to his back teeth. We could hear the whoosh of the water go past us on the other side of his cheeks.

"Graneff, what is the Vanishing Lake?" asked Dara.

"What are the Towers of Lucky Ream Boat?" asked Katie.

"Well Dara the Vanishing Lake is a curious affair indeed. It is the only one of it's kind that we know about. It does what the name suggests and no one knows why. It was a place for all sorts of magic for many's an age. They built towers in the middle of it and had all sorts of rituals there. Some say there was dark magic at a time but that was in the days when the sun was young. Magic still had to learn about the people who used it. You might think it still has a lot to learn judging on recent events," I said and snapped my fingers as I did. A wee trick I picked up at the Learning Tree and we had a little light in the palm of my hand.

"I'm pretty sure that there is something in one of those towers that will help us and Rachary knows which one."

"My Dad told me that no fairy that went into one of those towers ever came out," said a worried Clumsill. "Do you think it's safe?"

"Hmmm at a time your Dad was probably right, it certainly is a mysterious place. We should be ok though. There hasn't been a fairy, good or bad, there for a long time," I replied, hoping to reassure him.

Suddenly we felt Rachary move upward in the water at speed. We then heard him blow the stale air out through his nose and the new fresh sea air rushed in around us. I wondered how many breaths he would need before we reached the far shore.

"When we get to the other side will Saroist take us back up the river? I mean he's bound to be tired," asked Katie.

"I'm not sure he'll be able to," I answered, "but we have friends who will help."

"Who?" asked Dara.

"Oh you'll see and you won't be disappointed."

Three children in the middle of all this made me wonder again at the Banshee's wisdom but I let that thought go for fear more like it might come along. We fell silent for a little while as our thoughts swam around in our heads. Katie and Dara sat together with their legs crossed in front of them. They were looking at the roof of Rachary's mouth and at the back of his teeth.

"Here's a fish bone," said Katie. "I wonder is it a salmon's?"

"I hope not, Saroist would not be impressed," said Dara

"Can I have it?" asked Clumsill. "I like collecting strange things and a salmon bone from a seal's mouth is quite strange I'd say."

"Yea, here you go," said Katie and handed the bone to Clumsill.

"Cool."

"Are you all ok?" I asked.

"Yes, I suppose," said Dara, "just wondering what will happen next. It's been quite a couple of days."

As soon as she'd said that I felt that we had stopped. An instant later Rachary opened his mouth and we saw hands reaching in to help us out.

Laijir, Tridge, Ionta and Síoda had made it safely across and were now lifting each of the children onto the beach between them.

"This isn't the place we left from," said Dara.

"Quite observant for a human aren't you?" said Rachary. "You are right though. Half way over Saroist pulled up along side to remind me that the tide was on it's way out. We would have been too far away from the mouth of the river. Here at least we are closer but another problem has arisen. The Lake and Towers of Loughareema are too far for us seals to make by land and with the tide out we can't swim there either."

"I know how we can get there?" I said.

"Oh yes, please tell me," replied Rachary.

"Yes I was wondering that too," added Dara.

"Yes, and me," said Saroist.

He was circling just at the water's edge. "I don't think I could swim up that river again with you lot hanging on to me and frankly I am not too comfortable swimming here with these seals, no matter what Rachary says."

"The Children will take us?" I said.

"But how can we take you?" asked Katie.

"Not you my dear, the Children of Lir."

"But they aren't real," said Clumsill. "I mean there just in a story aren't they?"

"Oh I wouldn't be so sure about that, my good young fairy. You know some humans don't believe that we exist. Look behind you," I said.

The three children looked behind them to see four white swans approaching. They were flying in their familiar one side of a 'V' formation and were soon skimming the water as they landed.

"Everybody bow . . . quickly!" I urged.

Each of us in the company bowed our heads low. Even Rachary lowered his head a little.

"Greetings your highnesses," he said.

"Greetings to you all," said one of the swans.

Each of them wore a small intricately decorated silver crown.

"We are the swans of Lir, charged by the Children of Lir to protect and help those in trouble on the Moyle Sea. When the Children themselves were released from their imprisonment it was agreed that there would always be four swans to continue their kind work. We are friends of travellers and guardians of the tides.

In honour of the Children we use their names. I am Conn, these are my brothers, Fiachra and Aodh and this is our sister Fionnuala."

"How did you know we were here I mean we didn't tell anyone?" asked Clumsill, now quite convinced that they were real.

"Nothing happens on this sea that we don't know about. We saw you travel over on the salmon's back. Such a strange sight demands an explanation and we kept an eye out for you to return. Now here you all are and in the company of Rachary no less. Good to see you old friend," said Aodh.

"And you," replied the seal.

"If I may tell you what is happening?" I said.

"By all means," said Fiachra who flapped his wings and made himself comfortable on the waves.

I quickly recounted as much as I could about what had happened. The swans listened intently, slowly shaking their heads in dismay. The morning light gained in strength as I spoke. The darkness of my tale against it made for conflicting emotions among my listeners.

"The return of Nefairious indeed, and in all probability his father Neroh. It's hard to think of a worse thing you could you have told us. Such evil needs to be countered," said Fionnuala.

"I suggest you take them to the Towers of Loughareema," said Rachary.

"A good idea," said Conn. "Can you take the children Fionnuala?"
She nodded yes.

"Aodh can you take Laijir and Tridge?" He nodded also.

"Good. I will take Graneff and Ionta."

"If I may be so bold Conn, but they need to hear the secrets of the Towers. They are dangerous places but contain answers. You just need to know the right questions," said Rachary.

"We need to take Saroist home too," said Síoda. "He can't swim back up against the current. He's too old and should be taken back above the waterfall."

They were the first words she had said for some time and the message in her voice was clear. Saroist *had* to get back with us. I wondered why she had chosen this moment to speak. I also fully expected Saroist to protest his age and fitness but he didn't. If we didn't take him with us he would die far from the place of his birth, a terrible fate for any salmon.

"I agree, we need Saroist," I said.

"He can come with me," said Fiachra.

"In the interests of speed you'll need to leap on to my back as I fly past you. From here to the Towers will take your longest breath and my fastest flight and even that may not be enough. Will you be ready Saroist?" asked Fiachra.

"Saroist will be ready," he answered.

Fiachra stretched his wings and the momentum quickly built. He began to move forward and upward on the water. His black legs appeared and he was quickly running on top of the waves. Five, six, seven steps, his long elegant neck stretched out in front, eight, nine, ten and he was airborne flapping strongly and gaining height. The rest of us watched as he flew just over our heads.

"We're going on ahead. I have the best chance with Saroist. We'll meet at the Vanishing Lake, ok?"

Then he circled and headed back toward us. Immediately Saroist dived deep down. His tail thumped from side to side.

Who'd have thought, me at the Vanishing Lake on the back of a swan, if they could see me now he thought and turned upward.

The light at the surface became brighter as he rose. Fiachra was with within striking distance about a foot above the water.

Any time now salmon, thought Fiachra, flying at top speed.

If there is one thing a salmon can do it is leap. They have the strongest tail of all fish and can judge distances wonderfully. Saroist broke the water just ahead of Fiachra. I thought he was going to hit him on the neck but no. He jumped straight over the top of Fiachra's head just missing his crown and landed safely on the broad of the swan's wide back. Fiachra slumped immediately, loosing altitude.

"C'mon, Fiachra push," shouted Síoda and took off after them.

She was going to help get Saroist to the Vanishing Lake and no mistake. She caught them up but before doing so I noticed her collect sea water in her shield. In a moment Fiachra began to climb again, they were quickly disappearing over the rocky ground and soon were out of sight.

"Now listen," said Rachary, "fate will carry them over . . . or not. We can do no more but to help yourselves you must hear this. I will tell you the secret of the Towers and what lies within but listen carefully, each of you is vital."

35

To the Creaking Tree

Druhin's head was alive with thoughts. He had been given a very specific task and was left in no doubt as to it's importance. He removed the locket from his neck and held it in his hand as they walked slowly down the tunnel that led to the door into the river. They were now out of sight of the others and needed to be in sight of each other. Greagle walked slowly behind, his injured leg hadn't the strength to carry him and he limped badly. Druhin offered him his shoulder to lean on, which he accepted. Pog and Fer were a little further back, side by side.

"Do you think Druhin can get to the bat tree without getting eaten or pulled to bits or - ?" Pog started but was interrupted.

"Enough. Of course he can. He's one of the best flyers ever and he's strong and brave and he has the locket. He can do it no problem," answered Fer.

Her feelings on the matter were a little confused all of a sudden. She felt terribly worried for Druhin but was not altogether sure why.

I mean, it's not as if we're best friends or anything. Sure he's hardly looked at me for ages, she thought.

"You like him don't you?" whispered Pog teasingly.

"Of course, so do you," snapped Fer a little too hastily.

"Yea I like him but not like you, ha you're in love! You should go and give him a kiss, you know for good luck. I'll ask him if you want," said Pog enjoying his sister's awkwardness.

"If you ever want to fly or see tomorrow for that matter you'd better keep your mouth shut!" she whispered loudly.

Loud enough for Greagle to hear.

"Quiet you two, I'm thinking," he snapped.

The little door was waiting, the only thing between them and the might of the river.

"You do remember what I told you?" said Greagle, looking at Druhin.

"I do and I'm ready."

Greagle walked up and put his hand on the door. A fairy of his age accumulates a wealth of magic and spells over the years. In normal circumstances he would have no trouble holding off the water to allow Druhin to get into the river and keep Fween Talav dry. These were not normal circumstances.

In the name of Odhran, give me strength, he thought.

He began to flap his wings and immediately felt the old power within albeit weakened. Faster and faster they went, a blur to the eye and their wind blowing the hair of the three young fairies. Greagle's face was set in complete concentration. He knew this was an extremely difficult spell for him to be risking in his current state. But he had no option. The young fairy had to alert the bats and that was all there was to it. Whatever the price, he would pay it.

He opened his eyes and put his right hand on the door, palm up to the wood. His left hand he rested just under his neck. His wings were at full speed and his three companions watched on in silence.

It was the second in as many days time the river would listen to fairy magic . . .

"Moisture of Ishke your unending flow

Hear this from an honest friend

Gravity denied, as you must know

Can save us from a fluid end

Your guardians true upon you ask

A favour in our darkest hour

Hold your water please to task

A sign of your eternal power."

Greagle's last words trailed off and it was difficult for the others to hear them. They wondered if the old fairy truly had what it took to hold off the river.

"We're going to get drowned," groaned Fer.

"Or worse," sighed Pog.

Their youthful doubts in the face of adversity and a good drenching had resurfaced.

"Ssshh!" snapped Druhin.

Greagle moved his left hand to the door handle very slowly. Once there he took a firm grip and before another moment had passed he pulled the door open.

"Oh my . . ." started Fer

"We're drowned, we're drowned," squeaked Pog.

But they weren't drowned at all. The doorway was open and they could clearly see the river flowing past them. They looked up through it and could see the roots of the Learning Tree and noticed the just awoken light of early morning filling the sky.

"He did it!" said Fer.

Pog couldn't speak such was his awe at what he was witnessing.

"Quickly," gasped Greagle, "get into the water Druhin. I cannot hold this much longer. Put the locket on now and let the water take you. You must use the roots there to climb out or else the current will sweep you away. Good luck."

Druhin did as he was asked and slipped the locket over his head.

"He's gone," sighed Fer.

"No look," replied Pog.

They noticed a disturbance in the smooth river surface just in front of them. As quickly as it had come it was gone.

"Greagle slammed the door shut with all his might and collapsed in a heap at the feet of the two remaining youngsters.

"Get me back. Get me back quickly. I must see the Banshee," they were his last words before he fainted.

*   *   *

The water Druhin had entered was cold indeed, cold enough to cause serious trouble if he had to stay in it for any length of time. However, Greagle's instructions were alive in his head and he grabbed hold of the first Learning Tree root he saw. Of course he was now holding on for dear life with both hands but his grip was strong.

The current forced his body longways so that to any fish passing at that moment it would've appeared that he was flying underwater. He pulled himself forward against the current hand over hand. The root thickened as he moved along it. Although this was tiring work he felt secure enough in his own strength. He pulled onward again and soon enough was able to take his first breath of air.

He had remembered to break the surface gently for fear of unfriendly eyes checking the water. He raised himself out of the river onto the lower end of the long brown tree root and rested for a moment. All about he too saw the signs of war and destruction. There were bodies of the enemy lying here and there. Their black dead eyes were as empty as the Hollow was of happiness at that moment. Suddenly he heard the unmistakable coarse caws of crows over head.

They can see me, he thought, *the locket doesn't work!*

His panic was short lived as the crows flew straight past him on their patrol path.

Odhran's claws! They can't see me after all.

His spirits were lifted no end as this reality settled on him.

Right, Druhin, no good sitting here.

He shook himself off and took off immediately. Up through the thick branches of the Learning Tree he went. The same branches he had flown through on his First Flight. That wonderful feeling was now replaced with urgency and caution.

He looked out over Nut Hollow and Stony Banks and up the large lower part of Glenmak Mountain and saw his destination in the distance among the five great Sycamore trees. Side by side they had stood and had housed bats and birds for decades. Their branches had allowed for human children's hands and remnants of blue rope swings hung there forlornly waiting to be filled again.

Druhin surveyed the ground as he flew over it. The steep green slopes were lined with the ancient tracks of passing sheep and cattle. Their paths had cut steps into the hillside and were often used by weary humans as they laboured over the braes in their wake. Long rushes grew down near the river in the marshes. The humans had left their mark on the land too. Large rutted tracks from their machines had been carved from their stony house down to the river.

I'm surprised it's taken them this long to meet us, thought Druhin.

He approached the sycamore line, noticing the small pine copse that swayed in the wind. He remembered what Greagle had said,

"Strelle's tree is in the middle of the line. It is the biggest of them all and two great branches fork out from the base. The other trees house bats also of course but Strelle is still their leader. Do not take up with other offers, deal only with him."

He took off the locket and was visible again, only to the bats he hoped. Nefairious had not recruited them and he wondered why. Why for that matter should they bother with fairies? His question was answered almost before he thought it. He suddenly heard a high pitched squeak and the flutter of wings past his face.

Then there was another squeak and another and suddenly he found himself to be surrounded by these highly skilled dark flyers. On their next pass he heard,

"To the fork," as one flew by. Then again, "To the fork," and again, "To the fork, fairy!"

They must mean the tree with the forked base. Huh! That's were I was going anyway, he thought.

He watched the three small black bats whiz and dive and dip around him. They couldn't hover like him but by now he was getting fed up with their sonic bleeps which rattled the edges of his eardrums. He headed over to large centre tree and landed on the flat space between the two upward branches where he was bid. Then the three bats whizzed past him again,

"Just," "Wait," "There!" Each of them said one word and dodged away between the star green leaves.

Ah they're just showing off now.

He was right. Bats had a reputation in the Hollow for showing off their undoubted flying skills. Flight was their way of testing each other and their neighbours. They had little regard for any other winged creature because, as they were quick to point out, they were almost blind. Many had argued that this sonic sight they had was even better than ordinary vision but they chose to ignore that. If given the chance they liked to encourage the myth that they could not see at all but they could.

Druhin settled himself again. Those bats had given him a start. He had never been this close to them before and their manner was quite distant and unfriendly. He ran his fingers along the bumps and grooves of the old bark that covered the tree. It was rough to the touch but he found that it calmed him.

"And who might you be?" came a voice.

Druhin nearly fell on his backside in shock. He spun around to see the broad, flat, dark furry head of another bat looking right at him from above. He was slightly ungainly attached to the tree with his almost see through brown/grey wings spread open and using the claws attached for grip.

"My . . . my name is Druhin of . . . of Nut Hollow and I'm here to see Strelle, Lord of the Bats. Are you him, I mean Strelle?"

"Strelle indeed? And who are you to ask for the company of Strelle? Are you a king or a prince perhaps? At least some manner of royal?"

"My mother told me once not to speak to someone unless you know their name," replied Druhin, who surprised himself at his boldness.

"A wise fairy woman, indeed," replied the bat. "I see you have just got your wings. They look strong and you seem to be able to use them well enough."

Druhin remained silent and stared at the bat, who spoke again,

"Hmmm, you seem pleasant if a little rough round the edges. My name is Tragus. Now what's your errand here? I'm sure I can help."

"Thank you Tragus but I bring a message from Greagle himself for Strelle's ears only. Now please in the name of Odhran will you bring me to him?"

Druhin's fear had now turned to impatience and he was sorry if he sounded cheeky but frankly, time was short and he had no time for games with this bat.

"OK young one, your situation must be precarious indeed. You have turned down a good offer but no doubt Strelle will listen. Whether he helps after that is another question. I will inform him that you are here."

Tragus shuffled awkwardly back into the hole from which he appeared.

Druhin could see the top of it from where he stood. Almost immediately Tragus returned.

"Follow me," he said urgently.

Druhin climbed up the short distance to the hole and crawled inside. He had to hold on tightly to the inside of the tree and steadily lower himself down. It was then the noise started. Gently at first but the further down he climbed the louder it grew. It sounded like the tree was creaking and groaning as if in a fierce north coast storm but Druhin remembered no significant wind during his conversation with Tragus. Louder and louder and now his ears were beginning to hurt.

What is that noise?

He didn't have too long to wait to discover it's peculiar source.

36

Backstabs and Double-crosses

Neroh sat alone in the house of his enemy. He was growing stronger by the minute but knew he had a way to go. He pulled the many coloured, hand crocheted, quilted blanket that lay on him up over his chest and patted it's many delicately designed holes into place.

Patience, he thought.

If anything was learned in the Thorn it was patience. Little did I think I'd be here again in such circumstances . . . such finery, such delicate, breakable things all over the house. You seem to be a fair craftsman Graneff, as your father was before you.

He picked up a small wooden cup that sat near him noticing it's wondrously intricate engravings.

I'd even suggest Aoibheen spent a day or two here by the shape of things, Graneff. Your mother was a fine fairy, perhaps had things been different, he sighed, remembering. *No she was too kind to fall for my charms.*

He smiled to himself, an opportunity missed perhaps.

He lay back into his soft buttercup yellow cushions and looked up at the roof. The circular white ceiling was split by almost orange oak beams, which followed the round groove down to the floor.

Fine house, fine house indeed, he thought. *I do believe I'll live here after the battle. Perhaps Graneff will be my slave. Now that would be fun . . . his wife and children too. How would you like that Graunad, your son and grandchildren running around at my beck and call? Yes, I think that would work out very well.*

His thoughts continued to paint his desired future; his former friends would crawl before him. Those that had stood and did nothing to help him as he was locked away. It had been a dark time in the Thorn and he had cultivated many black ideas there. At last here and now was a chance to watch these thoughts grow and ripen.

Whatever goodness there ever was within him he had left in that dark cell. The Thorn had soaked him in it's malevolence and he thought of happiness for no one but himself.

Nefairious, my boy, walking around the Hollow as if you owned it. You have come a long way from the crying whelp I left behind his mother's skirts.

He was in a tricky position but was happy for the time being to go along with his son's plan, he had agreed after all. So in a brief moment of contentment at his situation he closed his eyes. He breathed deeply again and most likely would have drifted over to sleep had it not been for the out of breath gasps of Rant.

"Must get a drink," wheezed the rat. "Must get a wee drink . . ."

His humped furry form squeezed awkwardly through the fairy house. He was just a little too big to fit in there comfortably but when did a rat care for fitting in? The rooms were big enough for him as far as he was concerned.

Neroh tutted as he heard glasses fall. He knew those glasses would've have been of the finest quality.

"Would you please be careful you big fool. This house is a work of art and doesn't need you stomping through it like one of those great clumsy cows the humans are so fond of."

Rant held his silence; he was not about to risk another sore tongue for the sake of a rash reply. He waited a moment or two before saying anything. He found a small bottle of what he thought water and took a swig. He sighed in contentment and his thirst was satisfied for the time being.

"Woh! That's the stuff, Neroh. You'll have missed that in your time away," he said.

"Yes the finest, the fairies are well known for their distilling skills. How goes it outside? I trust the mixture I gave you did the trick?"

"Oh yes no bother, thanks. I remember you, you know," began Rant again, his confidence growing. "You were a hero to us all. It was a dark day when they took you away. I remember your speeches, inspirational stuff. Especially as none of the precious Hollow folk even knew about your meetings with us. Funny how things turn out, eh? I never thought I'd be here with you in Graneff's house. I mean, Graneff the mayor of the Hollow! What would old what do you call him think?"

"Who do you mean?" replied Neroh, not exactly sure what the rat was up to.

"Graunad."

"Ah yes, Graunad. The instigator of my incarceration," hissed Neroh.

"I would happily pull him limb from limb for you, him and his heirs, the whole righteous bunch of them," offered Rant finishing the last of the bottle. He wiped the drops off his whiskers with his paw and waited.

"All in good time. Nefairious has things in hand, wouldn't you agree?" asked Neroh deliberately tempting an answer from Rant.

"Yes he has things in hand alright, Neroh, but if I may be so bold I believe you could do a better job. You'll have you're strength back in no time and then . . . well you'll be back in charge where you belong."

"Oh now Rant, 'tis quite the silver tongue you have there. Why would I betray my son's trust?"

Rant twitched his whiskers and licked his still healing tongue. He would have to be careful here as to come between a father and son is an extremely dangerous game. He did know that they had been apart for many years and perhaps Neroh's feelings on his son were a little confused. He knew the Neroh he remembered and admired had a ruthless streak that could cut through any family tie. All he had to do was to reignite it.

He was also a survivor and would try to load the scales of fate in his favour. After all Nefairious had just shown that he had no respect for him, he was a means to an end and that was all. He felt that his best road lay with gaining the favour of the old fairy.

"Well, he is still young and much less experienced than you. He has spent too long alone on top of Knock Layde with no one for council. Of course he has done a splendid job to this point but we both know that the fairies are not finished. They will return with all their swords gleaming. No doubt they will wield their magic masterly and we need to be ready. The crows have lost their leader. Will they look to Nefairious or maybe they would feel more secure with a wiser head at the helm, hmmm?"

"Rant, you do indeed speak wisely . . ."

This sounds promising, thought Rant.

"The crows will be arousing themselves very soon and their generals will be asking for the next step. They will want revenge for Préak and who can blame them—?" said Neroh.

He stopped in mid sentence as the door of Graneff's house swung open. It was Nefairious and behind him Welset and two crows.

"Father, the crows have asked for a meeting, what say you? Are you up to it?"

Neroh shot a glance at Rant as if to say 'we'll continue this later'. He looked at the small gathering at the doorway, which had now moved into the room beside them. He nodded slowly at his son,

"Let them speak."

The crows struggled for space in the restricted confines of Graneff's front room. They were two huge black beasts and their talons glinted menacingly in the candlelight. They had broad grey backs and their beaks were like black daggers. If they had opened their wings no doubt they would have wrecked everything around them.

"I am Borb," said the first crow, "General of the Lower Glenmak crows and this is Grod, leader and General of the Upper Glen. We answered to Préak but in his absence answer only to ourselves but offer our strength to you now. We would like to make sure we finish this."

His voice was harsh and cruel. The curse of crow kind had not been lost on him. Grod did not speak any words they could understand but let forth the most horrendous cawing forcing the others in the room to cover their ears.

"Enough," shouted Nefairious, "ENOUGH! There will be no more of that thank you or you will lose a wing friend," he snapped and flashed the Carving Knife in front of the crow.

Rant immediately put his paw over his mouth.

"Now now son," began Neroh, "the crow was only thinking out loud, so to speak. We will hear worse before long I am sure. I would implore you though to refrain from such outbursts, not good for the old ears."

Neroh looked at Grod as he spoke and the crow acknowledged him. The little hint of humour offered in the sentence proved to lighten the mood.

"Save your energy, Grod," said Nefairious, resheathing the Carving Knife, "a voice like that would scare even old Greagle perhaps . . . and if it doesn't you might use your beak for more lethal purposes, eh?"

Grod nodded and said nothing. His silence worried Rant somewhat. The rat felt the crow was pushing his luck not replying to Nefairious but he said nothing and watched the scene unfold. They stared at each other in silence.

The crows gazed with their black eyes at Nefairious. He in turn looked at Neroh. Neroh glanced over at Rant who looked at Welset only to see the weasel staring right back at him.

"There is not enough room in here and I am weary of this fairy neatness," cawed Borb. "Come Grod we will await our company outside."

"I agree," said Neroh, "the day is almost fully reborn. Let us go and indulge ourselves in the sunlight. Rant will you help me please?"

He felt stronger still and could have probably stood without aid but in deciding to ask Rant for help and not Nefairious, he planned to keep his son guessing as to his thoughts. Rant's flattery perhaps had more effect than he wished to admit.

"Welset," snapped Nefairious, "you will help Rant with my father."

"Oh I'm sure we'll manage, son, the rat will do on his own," replied Neroh.

"Ach whatever! Out . . . all of you."

There was much to organise.

37

To Seal Our Fate

Rachary cleared his throat as if to call us to order. He was used to being listened to and we were not about to disappoint him.

"Friends, the Towers of Loughareema are what remain of the oldest civilisation that ever there was. It existed before the mountains were born and had great influence in all the surrounding areas from naming the hills and fields, the animals and plants and even our customs and beliefs. These people were friends of the sea and the land, the forests and the skies. Many of their rituals have shaped all our ancestors' behaviour ever since.

They lived together in harmony with each other and the land that supported them. Their society was made up of all members of the animal and fairy kingdom and as far as I know no particular species sought dominance over the other. The source of this harmony is said to have emanated from the Towers, which as you may or may not know are located in the centre of the Vanishing Lake," he said, and would've continued but for a small voice. It was Katie.

"I have heard of the Vanishing Lake."

"Excuse me young lady, but it would serve you well to listen," he snapped but Katie went on.

"Yes I know but that's just round the road from our house. Some people have even seen ghosts there," she said excitedly.

"Oh give me strength. I admire your spirit young one but please listen."

Katie smiled and nodded her head. The thought of ghosts and the Vanishing Lake had taken her away on a brief daydream. Dara smiled at her too to make sure she was ok.

"If I may, Rachary," interrupted Tridge, "we fairies have also heard of the Vanishing Lake and more importantly not to go near it. It is said to be cursed and any fairy who touches the water there will drown where they stand."

In short, the Vanishing Lake was not a place any fairy would bother with given the choice.

"Yes Tridge, I appreciate your fears but if you would let me finish I'll explain," answered Rachary now losing his famously short amount of patience.

He cleared his throat again but this time we got the message he did not want to be interrupted.

"Every creature that I have ever met or heard about has similar doubts and worries about the Lake. Birds will not fly over it, hedgehogs will not swim in or drink from it and as you have heard the humans have their stories too. However, it is no coincidence that fear surrounds it. Our ancestors left it that way because of the terrible fate that befell them-"

Katie couldn't help herself.

"You mean there were seals there too?"

"What on earth . . . who? Katie! I might have guessed."

After another stern look he continued,

"Seals spent time at the Lake. The land wasn't always shaped the way it is today. At that time there was a river down to the sea but sadly it too has been eroded. In fact the track of that old river will be your safest guide from the air. You will see it easily enough from above.

"What happened to them?" it was Dara's turn this time.

Rachary smiled and shook his head, realising that youthful curiosity was very hard to curb.

"Well, we don't talk of it much to be honest. Talk of that nature brings bad luck. Suffice to say that all that remains are the Towers themselves. In these Towers lie the remnants of their old magic but you need be very careful. Each of the three remaining Towers contains a line of a spell you will able to use when the time is right. But they will not yield up their prize easily. There are tests for you to complete. Many have tried to get this spell over the centuries but all failed and no one has made an attempt for a long, long time. However, it is vital you do succeed. The spell will not only help you defeat Neroh and his son but with any luck you will also be able to design a suitable punishment. Well, it may prove a little more difficult than that but you get the idea?"

We nodded and hummed together, rapt in the tale. Who were the citizens of this wonderful society? Where had they gone? How could an ancient spell help us now, today?

*   *   *

"You know this is a wonderful sensation. I mean how many salmon can say they have flown on the back of a swan? But honestly dear one I can't hold my breath much longer and I fear we have a long way to go to the Vanishing Lake," gasped Saroist.

He feared his end was near.

"Don't worry Saroist," said Síoda. "I will take care of you."

"But how? We can't land anywhere, there's no water in mid air and by the time I'm finished speaking my breath will have run out and this old fish will be no more than a bunch of dry scales."

Síoda sat beside Saroist with her shield on her legs which were bent beneath her. She put her hands into the shield and began to stir the seawater within. The salty clear liquid dripped in tiny droplets off her fingers as she raised and replaced her hands into the water. Saroist strained to see what she was up to. He reckoned he had perhaps a minute left before he drowned.

What is she doing? he wondered.

The wind blew through her hair and cloak and they billowed out behind her. The swan was flying as fast as she had ever felt anything fly and it was difficult for her to continue her spell but she was determined. She began the word music and as she spoke poured the water over Saroist's large gills.

"Spirit of Ishke, hear me now
Every drop reveals your might
Snow, frost and ice you know how
But water here is what is right
Spread about this noble one
That he may find the air he needs
And cover with the rising sun
Rainbow's light, your fairest deeds . . ."

She stood as high as she dared and reached over the top of Saroist's head and poured the water over his other gill. The fairy drew back her hand and the skin of a bubble came with it. She moved her hand slowly over the top of the salmon's head and watched the bubble grow. The sunlight now began to catch it and she could see the rainbow colours swimming on it's slippery surface.

"Careful fairy," she said to herself.

"Hurry up fairy," gasped Saroist.

"Nearly there . . . nearly," whispered Síoda as the wind growled loudly around her ears. In another moment the bubble was joined and began to fill with the water she was hoping for in the spell. It filled from bottom up and she could see the relief in Saroist's eyes as he began to breathe again.

He looked like he had a piece of the Moyle Sea on his head like some exotic liquid hat. Síoda sat back down on her hunkers again hoping that the Vanishing Lake would soon come into view.

"How much further?" she shouted to Fiachra.

The swan turned his long neck and head toward her,

"Not long, how is the salmon?"

Síoda gave him a nod as if to say he was ok but would like to get back to the water soon. Sometimes you can squeeze quite a lot into a look! Saroist felt able to speak again,

"Thank you Síoda, you have saved my life for sure but at great risk to yourself. I don't know if I deserve it. I mean . . . why? You seemed so determined to help me, as if we were old friends but we've never met before today have we?" he asked feeling very humble and just a little confused.

"You're right Saroist, we have never met as such but I know of you. I know how you tend the river and I have heard many stories of your kindness to fairies. Do you remember saving a young couple who were swimming too close to the waterfall at Coolaveely?"

Saroist looked at her and slowly nodded his head.

"Yes I do and I gave them a right good telling off," he answered. "Why do you ask and how did you know about that?"

"Well those two fairies were my parents Símse and Darbh and not too long after that they were married and not too long after that they had me. They would've drowned but for you. So in a way you helped me to be born. They often talked about the cross salmon with the kind heart and here I am returning the favour."

"Well I never," exclaimed Saroist. "Those two young whippersnappers… your parents eh? Indeed it looks like you've inherited their sense of adventure."

Síoda smiled and looked at Saroist. He was happy to see her smile, it didn't happen very often. Their gaze was suddenly broken by yet another lunge forward by Fiachra. Síoda looked over her shoulder and saw the Towers of Loughareema slowly rise up in the distance. They began to descend and Síoda could see the brown and barren land that defined the countryside around them. They could now see the ripples on the lake itself and could feel the wind that made them. Fiachra lowered his feet and they slid to a spectacular halt. Saroist rolled off the swan's back and with a flick of his tail was back in the familiar environs of deep water. Síoda flew to the base of the first tower and waited.

*   *   *

Rachary said no more. His silence was heavy on us. The interruptions of the little human girls were mildly irritating but they served to break the seriousness of what Rachary was telling us. Now that he had finished we were in no doubt that certain danger lay ahead. However, certain danger now lay behind and we were determined to go on.

"My friends, I hope that what I have told you will be of benefit to you later on. It is with great regret that my friends and I must take our leave of you. We have our own battles to attend to and must return to the island. I hope that your journey ends the way we would all wish. Are you ready?"

He looked at the other seals. They nodded and slowly clambered back into the tide. Rachary himself began to shift his great bulk and was consumed by the waves. We watched them all slowly disappear into the grey green waters of the Moyle Sea. Before he went completely out of our view Rachary turned toward us,

"Remember, keep a clear head. The Towers will give you your answers . . . just ask the right questions, fare well."

"But what are the right questions?" asked Dara, unimpressed with all this riddling business.

"Perhaps he has told you already. In the meantime we can hope that Fiachra has delivered his passengers," said Conn. "We will find out soon enough. Now I would kindly ask your company to climb aboard."

"I need no lift," snapped Laijir. "Greagle would be insulted if you offered him such a service."

"Please Laijir," said Conn, "no one here doubts your flying skills but if we are to believe Rachary all your strength will be needed before long. Please accept the lift as a gift from the Children of Lir. It will be our honour to carry you."

"He's right," said Katie, "you would be tired out if you flew and then no good to any one."

Only one so innocent would have survived that sort of statement.

"Humph! Children," grunted Laijir and with a flick of his broad wings he flew onto Aodh's back.

Katie, Dara and Clumsill all walked to the water's edge and climbed onto Fionnuala's soft feathers. Tridge joined Laijir on Aodh and Ionta and I climbed onto Conn. The three swans swam out onto the sea and one by one began to flap their great wings and take off. The wind they created ruffled our hair and capes. The sea disappeared slowly behind us, it's great expanse yawning at our adventures. Beneath us the dry riverbed pointed the way to Loughareema as Rachary had said it would.

38

Strelle's Test

There is a weird thing that happens when you leave light in exchange for darkness. It's as if the light surrounds you and pleads with you not to leave. It will reach with you as far as it can until you take that last step or turn that corner which surrounds you in pitch dark. As you enter into the gloom you yearn for the comfort and sanctuary of the light, your imaginings take on a life of their own and you wonder are you mad in the head altogether.

These were some of the struggles that were going on in young Druhin's mind. As he climbed lower into the tree the noise now became almost unbearable.

What is going on? he wondered.

He would have covered his ears but it would have meant him falling off the inside of the tree into the unknown. There wasn't really room for him to fly or lower himself down in a hover so he continued his slow descent. Just when he thought his ears were about to burst his foot hit a solid bottom and the noise stopped. A yellow hint of a flickering light now appeared in the distance and he moved toward it.

The bats were a strange enough sort. He had grown up hearing that they were friendly in their own way toward fairies but there was something about them . . . they weren't to be trusted. In fact a conversation he'd had with old Grochin now bubbled to the surface,

"If any of you young brats are within a hound's gowl of a bat do not be a bit surprised if you get a handshake with one hand and a slap on the face with the other."

Druhin himself was going to answer back about bats having wings but thought better of it.

"I never met a bat I liked yet."

"How many have you met?" asked Druhin.

"Two! And it was two too many!"

Hmm I think I understand what he meant now, he thought.

However, he was under strict instruction from Greagle and he was going to do his best. The yellow glow grew ever brighter and he turned round an inner corner. The light revealed a clear standing area but there were no signs of anything to sit on. He certainly could have done with a couch or one of Sherene's cushions.

Suddenly the noise started again but now it was directly above him. He covered his ears as quickly as he could hoping it would soon stop. As he stood with his hands over his ears he again felt the disturbed air around his head and the flick of bat wings all about him. He also felt a sharp tug around his neck, which knocked him off balance, and he fell on his knees.

"What is your business here?" came the voice.

Druhin removed his hands from his ears; the sudden silence was almost as shocking as the din he had just been surrounded by. He was still a little confused and disoriented but heard the voice and looked up in the direction whence it came.

"What is your business here?" it said again only this time with more anger and urgency. Druhin saw a host of bat heads all with their eyes on him. He noticed also that they were all upside down, hanging on by their pink five fingered claws to the inner bark of the tree. There must have been fifty or sixty bats all regarding him with a mixture of curiosity and contempt. The largest of these was directly above him and he didn't know how best to look or speak back. He quickly decided to stand his ground and pulled up his shoulders to make him look as big as he could. He took a deep breath and answered,

"I come with a message from Greagle of Nut Hollow, for the ears of Strelle, Lord of the Bats."

The bats hanging around him flicked their wings and wriggled about tutting and complaining. He heard a few unpleasant words about fairies but soon silence prevailed.

"I am Strelle. I have been informed of your request for council and will let you speak. Make haste young one my patience has worn thin with fairy folk," said the great bat who spun slowly this way and that as he spoke.

His movement above caused Druhin to turn with him to maintain eye contact. This had a dizzying effect and he stopped before he fell over.

"I bring news of a terrible attack on Nut Hollow by none other than Nefairious himself. He has over run our defences and has taken the Hollow as his own. He has been helped by rats and weasels and all other foul manner of thing that runs, crawls or flies. Greagle himself was badly wounded in the battle but we survive still in safety, at least for a while, in our underground sanctuary. Greagle used the very last of whatever strength he had in him to help me get to you for he is of the notion that you could and would help and that as annoying as you find fairies, (*though why I'm not sure*, he thought into himself) you would prefer to deal with us than to have Nefairious as a neighbour," he hardly took a breath as he spoke so keen was he to get everything said.

Now that he had stopped he inhaled deeply and waited. The curious creaking noise from before now began again. It was the bats themselves as they began to send out their sonic beeps and flap their wings, but what did it mean?

Strelle gazed directly at the young fairy who felt his eyes burn into the top of his head. Druhin looked up again and held his ears. To be this close to the noise was terrible. Suddenly Strelle opened out his large wings and the noise ceased.

"This is not the news I was expecting at all young one. You have risked a lot to come and see me and that sort of courage is not to be ignored. 'Tis long and many's the dark night since I heard Greagle's name spoken. I thought that old rogue had long since passed away but it would appear he is fighting still, just as I remember him," he began, breathing slowly between his sentences.

"Now you tell me Nefairious is back. I thought the judgement of the buzzards would have been the end of him but it seems not. Any word of his father, Neroh?"

"To be honest, Greagle did not mention him. He has been captive in the Fairy Thorn this many a long year and it's thought impossible to get out of a thorn. I mean no one would go near one," answered Druhin, feeling a little less dizzy.

"It's Nefairious we are talking about and I would put nothing past that villain. I think it's fair to assume that if he could indeed defeat the fairy defence, Greagle and Blalim and all, he has gone after his father and in all likelihood freed him. This is trouble and no mistake."

Druhin noticed his eyes close and he was deep in thought. There were more whispers amongst the upside down crowd, mini conversations and shaking of heads.

"We all have our own particular skills and talents, young one. Most animals are happy enough with their natural strengths and even weaknesses can be improved on but you fairy folk seem to delight in the use and abuse of magic. Magic nuts, spells and potions and all sorts of nonsense and now at last it all has come back to cast you from your precious Nut Hollow. The Banshee should have known better but she's as bad if not worse than you, scaring those big, disastrous humans half to death with her songs. Be that as it may, we are neighbours and although you are a wonderfully annoying lot you have always shown great respect for the land and have never harmed anything or at least anything that didn't deserve it," he paused for a moment and opened out his wings to their very tips.

He inhaled again and drew his wings in around himself once more.

"Druhin, we will do what we can to help you but in return you must share with us a few secrets of Fairy magic, even though it is entirely the biggest waste of time there could ever be."

"But, I don't understand. You want to learn fairy magic even though you don't really approve of it?" asked Druhin who felt his neck now was stuck looking up.

Grochin's words came back to him again,

"Always saying one thing and doing the other. Sure did you ever look at them flying? Jigging about without rhyme or reason. Aye, they're a strange lot and no mistake."

Clearly old Grochin had little time for his mysterious neighbours but Druhin preferred to trust Greagle's opinions. He must have good reason to ask him to call on Strelle even though he did decline to mention a certain eccentric quality.

"Yes, of course I want to learn fairy magic, who wouldn't? Just because someone wants something does not mean they like it or agree with it. I mean fairy magic is of little value to a bat but a bat would be a bit better off with a bat . . . ahem . . . excuse me . . . with a bit, of course. Now, how does this little trinket work?"

He slowly lowered Druhin's necklace down in front of him but high enough that he couldn't leap up and snatch it back. Instinctively Druhin drew his hand up to his neck but there was nothing there and he remembered the nudge he had felt earlier.

"How did you get that?" he asked angrily. "It's not mine and you'd better give it back right now."

The hanging audience now laughed scornfully at him and he felt the atmosphere change suddenly for the worse. They began to raise their sonic beeps around him and the noise of earlier came back slowly but growing with every second. Druhin now was terribly worried. He had heard that bats had attacked and even eaten the odd fairy and now here he was looking up at a lot of mouths full of sharp white teeth.

"Enough, enough," shouted Strelle. "How can he answer me with all that racket? Eh, well? Now my young fellow what of this?" he asked again and his voice was friendly too, adding to Druhin's confusions.

"That was given to me by Greagle, to help me get to you. I need it to get back. I am dead without it."

"Hmm that is an answer and yet no answer at all. I take it that if Greagle himself gave you this it has magic of some sort. No doubt it protects the wearer in some way . . . but how? Come here," he shouted at Tragus.

Tragus wriggled free from his place among the crowd and climbed over to Strelle. He then lowered himself down so that he was almost nose-to-nose with his leader. He stared down at Druhin with a look that said 'you should have listened to me earlier.'

"Now Tragus, this little amulet contains a little of the magic we have heard so much about and I want you to try it on."

"Wait!" said Druhin. "You're right to say it's fairy magic but if a non fairy wears this necklace they will die unless you get the spell changed. Now I am nowhere near strong enough to do that and you may have already guessed that there are only a few who are. You will kill your friend if he puts it on. If you help me I will get the magic for you. Greagle himself will give it to you."

Strelle's face changed slowly again, this time into a warm smile and he returned the amulet to him. Tragus winked down at him then clambered back to his spot on the wall.

"You have proved your intentions young one and have shown me you care for your Hollow and those who share it with you. I am aware of the dangers associated with your magic. Inspite of your questioning here you acted to save Tragus. I apologise if we scared you but these days we have to be careful. Your heart is indeed true and it will be the honour and duty of the bats to help you. Let us hope your friends can hold out until darkness falls."

39

Spreading the Net

The six walked outside to the front of Graneff's house. The daylight had now lit the glen and revealed it in all it's glory. Solas lua (early light) the fairies call it. With such light hope comes and a promise of new things but the planners of this particular meeting did not care to nurture hope. They had an end in mind, an end to the fairies of Nut Hollow.

"What do you foresee as our best defence?" cawed Borb. "These fairies are no fools. We have lost Préak to their skills and I do not plan to be next."

Grod nodded slowly in agreement and paced forward and back. He scraped his talons against a nearby stone just to keep them sharp. The noise was something like dragging a fork across a plate and too much for Welset.

"Oh if you don't stop that I'll eat your leg off."

That was too much like a challenge for Grod who immediately ran towards him cawing wildly. Welset opened his mouth wide and stood up on his hind legs ready to sink his teeth into whatever part of the crow he could. Simultaneously Rant grabbed a hold of Welset and Borb moved swiftly in front of the on rushing Grod. Grod did not want to harm his fellow crow and bumped into him without malice. Borb opened out his wings to stop him progressing any further. Rant had a struggle to contain Welset's anger and they were a bit like two footballers after a bad tackle being held apart by their team-mates. Nefairious took upon himself the role of referee.

"Enough! I would ask that you keep your fury for the fairies. Injuring each other by fighting now will not help!" he said firmly.

Ha! That's good coming from you, thought Rant licking his lips.

"I am well aware that feelings are running high but we must all keep a cool head."

The two calmed enough for those holding them apart to let them go.

Neroh tutted disapprovingly and surveyed the Hollow. He stood at the door and looked up through the trees of Brae Height then let his eyes follow the natural curve of the Hollow until he now viewed Glenmak Mountain.

"Friends, our enemies have a variety of ways to attack us but something tells me they will choose the least obvious. If Greagle and Blalim are still alive we may prepare for a full on bloody charge. Those two are like bulls on a chain when it comes to battle. You might say we have the brains and they have the brawn but they are cute enough for most. Borb can you and your companion be sure to guard any advance from the trees there?" he pointed up toward the small copse into which the fairies had disappeared into Fween Talav earlier.

"Nothing would give me greater pleasure," cawed the gravel voiced Borb. "Nothing will get in . . . or out! Come Grod we must get the men ready."

Grod nodded once more and the two of them flapped their great black wings and were airborne in a moment. They both released grotesque and loud caws to their fellows in the surrounding fields. The waiting crows bounced along on great brooding steps balancing against the wind until almost as one they took to the air like black shadows. Nefairious watched them fly to the trees and one by one they disappeared into the deep foliage. It wasn't long before they were seen diving down to the ground and dodging branches as they collected twigs and bits and pieces. Crows are master builders and they were preparing something special.

"I can only trust that those two crows are half the warriors that Préak was," said Neroh. "Otherwise Greagle will make short work of them."

"What is it with you and Greagle father?" asked Nefairious, knowing that Greagle had been injured in the battle.

"To be sure he was the strongest warrior in the Hollow and the best flyer, at least until I came along but time waits for no one and still you mention his name with such . . . reverence."

Neroh stared into the Hollow for a moment then at the river before replying.

"I admire him son."

It is a trait amongst warriors of any kind that in a minute they would kill the other on the battlefield but afterwards with reflection they see so much of themselves in their opponents that it is hard to deny admiration.

So was the case with Neroh. Even though he lived a double life for many years he had had many conversations and experiences with the Greagles and Blalims and even Grochins of Nut Hollow. These experiences although locked away in a dark corner of his heart had not vanished completely. He knew the stuff these fairies were made of and he respected it. That is not to say he liked it and it is not to say he was fearless in front of it. How could he not know? In spite of everything both he and Nefairious were fairies too although none would again see them as such.

"If we have a victory at all today it will only be secure when Greagle's head is on the mantelpiece. Don't mistake admiration for weakness son."

"If we might step out of memory lane and back to today," offered Rant in what he hoped was the right tone, "where would you like me to place my men?"

He looked across the river at several of them who were still after the nuts. Many more still lay about the place. Before Nefairious could answer Neroh spoke.

"Nefairious, if it can be managed I would keep Rant and his men around the base of the Learning Tree. I don't fancy our enemies will relish the teeth and fighting qualities they possess. Perhaps Welset can take the weasels and place them somewhere. No doubt you will have the ideal location already picked?" he said mischievously.

Very good old boy, thought Rant. *Get him to do what you want and let him think he thought of it himself.*

"Well father as it happens the rats would provide an excellent last line of defence. However I don't intend to let things get so bad that we rely on them to save our skins . . . with all due respect of course, Rant. No offence."

"None taken of course," said Rant. (*You cheeky imp*, he thought.)

"OK father you can sort your grey horde as you wish. The weasels are with me. Welset get your men ready."

"As you wish," replied Welset quietly.

He had things on his mind and decided that he could clear his head away from prying eyes. The weasels had had their celebration along the edge of the river underneath the overhanging branches. The ivy leaves that were in abundance on the ground had been shaped into pillows and moulded together into makeshift quilts. Weasels are as partial to celebration as any other creature and most had consumed their share of rowanberry ale. Welset walked amongst them quietly for a moment. He felt a good bit safer amongst his own kind than anywhere else but knew that this feeling would vanish as soon as he woke them up. Once awake they would be bound for battle again, bound to do to death the fairies of Nut Hollow who had never been of much consequence to weasels.

Then there was the whole affair of Nefairious's offer; well offer was a nice way to put it. An offer hints at some sort of choice but he did not feel as though he had any. As ever the river washed over the stones and Welset watched it flow.

Living water, he thought. *Nothing to do but . . . be.*

He wondered if jumping in would be an easier option.

"Ach! You have work to do Welset," he said to himself.

"Your friends will help and perhaps the rewards will make it worthwhile. A life supply of food, a good safe house, no more worries about scraping a living. Maybe the fairy has some wisdom after all."

His confidence was growing, as was his greed. He could picture himself enjoying the fruits of Nut Hollow and living with Neroh and his son might be no bad thing.

"Get up you lazy dogs, c'mon shake yourselves. We have a war to finish," he shouted and reached into the water and threw what he could over his sleeping companions.

"C'mon, move yourselves."

There were a plenty of reluctant murmurs and stretches. Eyes opened and he received looks that contained words far too rude to repeat here. Their slender bodies that had mostly been curled up or strewn about in various shapes now took on their familiar sleek appearance. Their fur was divided perfectly between snow white on their necks and bellies and a very subtle light brown all along their backs. They were the colour of glens and gorse bushes, a mixture of night and day and elegant ruthless killers one and all right down to the black tips of their long tails.

After a time there stood before Welset his weasel brigade. They walked behind him then stopped just at the water's edge near the Learning Tree and drank.

"Good," said Nefairious, "we have a climb ahead."

"Might I ask where we are to be placed?" asked Welset, not wishing to lose face in front of his men.

"We are going to the bend in the river. I want you and your men to check every rabbit hole, every hare's lair, every otter's holt and seal them all. There must be no way in, do you understand?"

"I do."

He turned and barked his own instructions. Nefairious took off and the line of weasels followed him through the leaves and mossy grass.

"I'll be back shortly father," he said.

"Yes that'll do son, that'll do," hissed Neroh under his breath.

40

The Towers of Loughareema

Our journey over the countryside was breathtaking. Never in my reckoning had anyone from Nut Hollow traversed this route to the mysterious Vanishing Lake. Beneath us the fields showed off their fine stone walls (an acceptable human addition, for once!), which divided them up into neighbours of different sizes, shapes and colours.

It seemed the whin bushes had been placed in corners and along edges just to brighten things up a bit. The humans had also the habit of fencing along the edges too, to keep their sheep and cows from escaping. Of course this doesn't always work and when we're feeling a bit down a sure fire laugh is to watch the farmers chase the runaway sheep around the place. Sheep know full well their meanderings annoy the humans but considering where the sheep end up you might say it was a reasonable revenge.

There were trees of all sorts, ash, oak, chestnut, most of which were preparing to lose their leaves but they stood strong and firmly rooted in the land. Like our own in the Hollow they were silent guards against wind, rain, snow or sun. We flew below the tops of the taller trees to reduce any possible wind interference. Being so close to the shore the wind was still strong enough to wreak havoc on the beautiful and strong Children of Lir with us weighing them down. Beneath were old stone ruins that had housed human families for a hundred years but now lay sad and empty. It is possible to listen to the stones and what wonderful stories they tell.

The sun moved slowly towards it's great midday throne and the day was almost at it's brightest. The noise of the wind made speech difficult and to be honest each of us had plenty to think about for talking. However, just at the nape of a swan's neck there is a wee place that is quiet enough for a sentence or two. I beckoned Ionta over to join me. She was one of the finest fairies I ever knew. She was a master of all things stone, as was her father, Greanta, before her. The fact that she was a girl didn't raise any eyebrows amongst us, talent we'll encourage no matter what.

She sculpted wonderful statues and shapes for her neighbours. Fairies have a bit of a thing for nice stonework around their houses. Ionta was the woman who had done most of the ones in Nut Hollow. She was a woman of select sentences not given to whimsical outbursts you might say. Her hands were like something she had carved out from one of her many boulders. They were chipped and rough but strong and skilled. She had the appearance of outside and the wind about her. She looked at me and raised her eyebrows slightly to acknowledge my request then pulled herself over on her belly using her knees to push herself along.

"I've seen a few things in my day, but to see the world from here is truly amazing. That being said and as good as this is, what in the name of Odhran is the world coming to?" she asked looking totally at a loss for any logic in this situation.

"You know as much as me and more than you think."

"Well maybe not as much as you but whatever the answer is I think we're supposed to find it there," she raised her arm and pointed just to the left of Conn's long straight neck.

I turned away from her and followed her finger to see in the distance the midday sunlight dancing on the Vanishing Lake.

"Wow, it's beautiful."

"Yes beautiful indeed but I wonder what dangers lie behind it's pretty face?" she answered.

The Lake was crucial to our journey and of course it housed the Towers themselves. Our questions would only begin when we reached them. We flew along and again the swans were flying in their diagonal line, Conn at the front, then Fionnuala, Fiachra and finally Aodh. I looked round and got enthusiastic waves from the children. They were clearly loving every minute of this flight. Laijir and Tridge raised their hands to suggest all was well. Conn arced his head around,

"We're heading down, hold on."

I felt him descend and watched the others mirror our path perfectly. The lake now grew with every beat of his wings and the Towers rose before our very eyes. It was as if invisible hands were constructing them again before us. Conn lowered his legs and we felt the bump as he slid across the top of the water.

In a few moments the swans had gathered together and we could see a delighted Síoda standing on the small island on which the Towers stood. The swans swam over and she raised her arm in greeting.

"What of Saroist?" shouted Laijir.

"Behind you," she smiled.

We all turned around to see the salmon exit the water in a wonderful leap and come splashing down only a sling shot away. The splash he created ended up giving us a good wetting.

"You old goat!" snapped Tridge. "I ought to pull your tail off for that."

"Oh don't be a spoilsport," shouted Katie

"Coooool," laughed Dara.

"Why thank you," said a very happy Saroist. "I'm glad to see someone respects my skills," he sparkled his eye at the children (this is a salmon form of winking).

"Humph!" grumbled Tridge.

Saroist disappeared once more leaving a large wake on the top of the lake. On his way down he suddenly realised that there were no other fish anywhere to be seen.

Now did you ever think you would have the run of such a beautiful lake all to yourself? No, I didn't think so and to be honest there is something not quite right about all this, he thought.

Another peculiar characteristic of the lake was just how clear it was. Saroist was well used to the mud and plant life of the river and such clarity was strange to him.

Well if I can see everything and anything there's more than a good chance that everything and whatever else can see me.

He flicked his tail a couple of times and headed for the company of his new friends he had grown quite fond of. He broke the surface just where the loose stones that had lost their grip sat half way out of the water. Those that remained dry formed the foundations for the Towers, and on those foundations in front of the first Tower the group had regathered. The swans were whispering quietly to each other. Saroist felt they were eager to get back to the Sea of Moyle.

"Friends," began Conn, "it has also been our honour to help you this day. Sadly we are bound to the sea and it is there we must return."

The other three swans bowed before the company but did not speak. Conn spoke for them all.

"Our thoughts are with you and we wish you luck. Let us hope your task is successful for there is no joy to be had when evil prevails. Fare well."

The four separated slowly on the lake and took off one by one. We watched them quickly disappear beyond the brown hills. Saroist now wondered how he would get back to the Hollow.

"Right, what next?" said Tridge, who was not one for dramatic silences.

"Well," I began, "Rachary said the answers lie in the Towers, so let's go. Everyone ok?"

There were nods and silent looks but no words.

"Enough silence! C'mon, the Towers are this way and somebody say something," said Tridge again.

"What do you call a deer with no eyes?" asked Katie suddenly and looked at Clumsill.

He thought for a moment and everyone waited for the answer. Dara looked as if she knew the answer and smiled.

"Don't know," said Clumsill and shrugged his shoulders.

"No eyed deer!" laughed Katie.

"What? You don't know either?" said Clumsill, a little confused.

"No, that's the answer. No eyed deer," said Dara, relieving us all truth be told.

"Oh," said Clumsill. "Funny . . . I think."

Clumsill smiled and didn't care if he didn't get the joke. He was among friends and he felt safe. The little bit of childish nonsense had once again proved a pleasant distraction and in the few moments it lasted we had covered the ground to the doorway of the first tower. We looked up. The Tower stretched up into the sunlight forcing us to cover our eyes. Then it stopped quite abruptly and we could see that the top of the tower was missing. It was uneven and there were blocks in disrepair leaving us to wonder just how high it had once reached.

"How does anyone reckon we get through the door?" asked Tridge.

"Couldn't we just fly in through the roof or should I say where the roof was?" asked Ionta and took off. We had our answer in a moment when he returned.

"Well?" asked Tridge impatiently.

"No chance. There are old rafters running across the middle and they're just waiting to collapse. I'd say if we brushed it with a wing the whole lot could come down. That would not be good."

We nodded in agreement. The old oak door stood closed before us. It was still very solid looking and arched up into the stonework above. There were two massive golden handles on each door but to reach them those of us with wings would have had to fly up to do so. The handles were about five times as high as Dara's head.

"This may take some strong magic," offered Laijir, and he began to flutter his wings.

He began to chant and suddenly let forth a flash of Draykt from his hands. It bounced off the handles and splashed into the water not too far from a shocked Saroist.

"Hey! Watch it," shouted the salmon.

Laijir muttered something that gave Dara a start.

"I didn't know fairies had bad words too," she whispered to Katie, who nodded in agreement.

He tried again only this time it was a much larger flash but it brought the same result. The beam bounced off the door, skimmed the top of the water and smashed a rock on the far shore into smithereens.

"Hold on, hold on," I said. "Laijir wait a minute."

He was all revved up and ready to go again but he might have tried all day for all the good it would have done.

"Well, you have a go," he snapped and walked away from the door in a bit of a huff.

Síoda and Ionta came over and stood with their hands on the door.

"Laijir, come here please and you too Graneff. Tridge we'll be needing you as well. Clumsill come on," said Síoda.

"What do you think?" I asked.

"Between us we should have enough power to open it."

"I have an idea," said Katie.

"Thanks Katie but this is fairy business," replied Laijir.

I hoped she wouldn't be put off by Laijir's sharp answer but she didn't seem bothered. We stood side by side with our hands on the door. Síoda began to move her wings and we followed her lead. Within a moment or two all our wings were buzzing and the power was in our hands. We all pushed together and the large dark wooden door budged a little but almost immediately budged right back again.

Again we pushed and our wings flapped and our hands glowed with the magic, but still nothing. After another huge effort we broke our line and slumped to the ground. The door had beaten us. This was a disaster, how could we get the spell if we couldn't even open the first door?

"Em! Can you not just knock the door?" asked Katie.

Her question was greeted with scornful laughs and groans.

"Yea I agree," added Dara.

"Me too," chipped in Clumsill.

"I mean look at those two handles, perfect for knocking, wouldn't you say?"

This was a tricky one to answer. Here we were the grown ups and supposedly wiser of the company being asked a question the answer to which seemed to make perfect sense. I looked around at the others. They all said nothing and looked up at the handles.

"Well now that you come to mention it," said Tridge. "They are quite well made and seem capable of being used without falling off and killing someone."

"I would have to agree there," said Síoda. "Perhaps there is a spell on this door that we would never break."

"Aye, the youngsters do have a point, annoying as it is," said Laijir.

"Yes children, well done. Sometimes the obvious answer is the best," I said trying to regain a little authority.

"Oh don't mention it," said Katie cheekily.

"Happy to help the wise old fairies," laughed Dara.

"Don't push it!" snapped Laijir although I did see a hint of a smile before he turned his head away.

"That settles it," I said. "This is going to take the five of us. Tridge, Ionta and Laijir will you take the one on the left? There's a bit of rust there and it could be tough to move. Síoda the other one is clear enough and we should be able for it. OK?"

Without another word each of us flew up and took a grip on our handles and flew backward. As expected ours was easily moved but the other one took all the strength of the three. However, with some pulling and tugging and toing and froing it was moved out into place.

"OK, after three. One, two, three!" I yelled.

We flew the handles toward the door letting go just in time. BANG! They sounded as one and we thought the door would crack.

41
Saivir

We waited a few moments and then a few more but to our great disappointment there was no answer. Nothing. The golden handles sat as they had done and the only sound was the wind blowing off the lake. I would have to say this was the lowest moment since losing the Hollow. Any hopes we had of facing Nefairious seemed to stand silently behind that door unwilling to come out. We stood around looking at the handles hoping they might yet reveal something or suddenly open the door but they too remained silent, probably happy to be back against the door.

"Friends there must be another way," I said trying to revive our spirits.

"Ionta do you think you could make it through those rafters?"

I was loathe to ask her, knowing the dangers, but it felt as there was no other way as she was a little smaller than the rest of us.

"I'll try Graneff but I could do more harm than good. Maybe Laijir and Tridge could help to hold the beams."

"Aye anything we can do Ionta," answered Tridge.

This was a terrible twist. In order to go forward we were risking everything knowing full well our chances we very slim. The three shook hands and prepared to fly. We stood close together hoping they would be successful and knowing that if the tower did come down we would all be crushed.

"Did you hear that?" Clumsill asked Síoda who stood beside him.

"Hear anything?" answered Síoda. "No, did you?"

"Yes I think . . . well it sounded like a splash," he said meekly.

"A splash?" snapped Laijir. "Sure that's old trout face jumping about like a young 'un."

"But he's here," said Clumsill pointing to an unimpressed Saroist who was just at the water's edge beside them.

"For your information Laijir, I haven't left the water for some time and I'm much better looking than a trout," replied Saroist with a sniff.

"Well if it wasn't you," started Clumsill again, "who or what was it?"

"Ok, quiet, please everyone . . . listen," I said.

This time there was no mistaking it. There was splashing coming from the other side of the tower.

"Saroist, you're the quickest, can you go round and see what it is?" asked Síoda.

"Oh if I must?"

"You must!" demanded Tridge.

No sooner had the salmon slipped under water when the splashing stopped. Saroist returned a moment later.

"I'm afraid I didn't see anything except the back of the towers."

Then it came. The noise we had feared since we were young fairies, the cruel hard caw of the largest blackest crow we had seen. It rose above the top of the tower and was now falling, screeching and squawking towards us.

"Run, jump, swim get out of here!" I yelled. "Préak has found us."

All I could think of was to protect the children but it was too late the crow was right on them. Surely this was the end.

But why had he not pecked their heads off? Why was he standing with his wings spread wide? Why was he . . . changing shape? The four other fairies had drawn their swords and spears and were ready to fight to the death but our foe was a crow no longer. Before our eyes he had shrunk and looked for all the world like one of us!

"What divilment is this?" roared Tridge and readied his knife.

"Explain yourself," cried Laijir, "or I will surely carry your head off your shoulders."

The crow or fairy took a step back so that his back was to the large oak door.

"Sorry for the dramatic arrival but you did knock."

"Knock? But you attacked us, we thought you were Préak himself," yelled Ionta.

The children had regained their wits sufficiently to let go of my cloak. They peered round my legs at the little fairy or whatever it was. Tridge raised his spear,

"Whatever you are you'd best explain yourself or else," he said as he motioned to throw.

"Ah yes," said the creature, "a fine spear."

He snapped his fingers and in a second the spear flew from Tridge's hand and landed in the ground at his feet. He picked it up, examining it for balance and looking at the tip.

"Hmm, fine work indeed. Looks like the hands of a master craftsman made this. 'Tis very similar to the original design we used."

"Original design?" snapped Tridge.

"Look, just who or what are you? If you wanted to harm us you would've done it already. What are you waiting for?"

"I mean you no harm at all and if I frightened you earlier I apologise. My name is Saivir, Keeper of the Towers."

"Do you mean you live here?" asked Katie.

"But you were a crow a minute ago," said Dara

"And a fish before that," added Clumsill. "How?"

"One at a time young ones. "I could answer here but would you not rather come in?"

We nodded enthusiastically. Our luck definitely seemed to have turned for the better. Saivir put his hand on the door and pushed. It was as if he was pushing a door made of paper so easily did it open for him.

"How on earth?" gasped Ionta.

We followed him in expecting to see barren and empty stone spaces but instead all was perfect. There were torches on the walls to light our way. Everything was as if it had been made that day. A spiral wooden staircase reached up in to the darkness. There were tables laden with food, chairs with red cushions, and a large grandfather clock, ticking steadily. There was a beautiful soft maroon rug on the hearth before the most ornate of mantelpieces. To say we were stunned would be about right.

"How can this be?" asked Síoda.

"Appearances can be deceptive," answered our host, "as you saw with me."

"Yes I was wondering about that myself," I said, looking at him.

He had peculiar eyes, brown one minute, then green, then grey.

"An old trick, one which we Léargas—"

"Léargas?" interrupted Tridge.

"—all would do for fun and to protect ourselves. To know your enemy is one thing, to look like him quite another. When I heard the door being knocked so loudly I thought for sure those crows had come back. They have tried several times to get at the secrets the Towers hold before they ran out of patience. When I heard that bang it woke me up straight away and normally I can sleep for years," he said ignoring Laijir's curiosity.

"My mum says I can do that to," chirped Clumsill.

"Anyhow I headed out the back door and into the lake and had a wee look around. The first creature I saw was this noble salmon and I knew that unless things have dramatically changed that salmon do not get out of water to knock doors."

Aye but they do answer, I thought and smiled to myself.

"Well I briefly took on salmon form but got out of the water thinking that it was surely those crows. I did notice some newly damaged rock over on the far shore and thought they must have been sharpening their claws to get in. That was why I landed in from above looking like a crow. Then when I saw the creatures that actually made the noise I felt a little safer and now took the form you see. It is hard to know but I do think I look quite like a fairy."

He certainly did but his eyes were the main difference. The clothes and shoes and the cloak could all have been made in Nut Hollow but his eyes were made of different stuff altogether.

"Do you have your own shape?" asked Katie.

"We do indeed but it is not one you would recognise for we never stay in one shape too long. Our natural condition would be almost liquid but you know how liquid can quickly change . . . water, ice, snow, frost, fog, sleet. We can be all those things if necessary."

"Where are your people?" asked Tridge.

"That's a question, young fellow, indeed it is," he replied. "We are here and there and everywhere, all at once and all at nonce."

"Nonce!" exclaimed Dara. "Never heard that one before."

"Yes it means never but at the same time, if you know what I mean," he replied winking at her.

"Now you've lost me altogether. Is it your nature to be so vague?" asked Laijir a little impatiently.

Time was marching on and we still had much to do.

"Vague? Why we are perfectly clear and perfectly here until we are perfectly gone and then we come back . . . perfectly."

"Might I ask you a question?" I asked

"Sure you just have and you didn't ask to ask me that one."

It seemed he was warming to this. A bit of a 'know all' my father would say. Still he was all we had. I tried again.

"I have heard that there is a part of a spell in each of the three Towers and that if you can put them together it will help you when in need."

His eyes flashed green, red and sky blue and he stared right at me.

"I say, you have been well informed friend. Knowledge like that is hard to come by and well guarded. You may also know that each part of the spell is locked within an answer. You have to ask me the correct question and the spell is yours, simple. I'm afraid it is forbidden to just give you the lines, 'tis all to do with getting something for nothing and treating that something as nothing, sorry about that. Now who will ask me the first question?"

We looked at each other in silence.

42

Question Time

"Woh! Woh! Now just a minute," shouted Tridge, shaking his head, his red curls jumping about his shoulders.

"What do you mean three questions? I mean was that one? Which would make two?"

"Three actually," said Dara.

Tridge stared angrily at the Léargas. He didn't mind quizzes and indeed was a good addition to any quiz team but this was different.

"Ah now don't worry yourself. We haven't started yet. You'll know when we do."

"And just how will we know?" fumed Tridge who now would've liked nothing more than to fling this little fellow headlong into the lake.

"Well I'll tell you of course," he quipped. "Now follow me."

We gathered ourselves behind him and waited. He pottered about for a minute at a desk and blew out a candle.

"Now why did I do that? Sure won't I be needing a light?"

He relit the candle with another breath and walked briskly up the wooden stairs.

"C'mon then, the first of your answers lies at the top, do hurry."

We followed him up. The children went first then me, Ionta, Síoda, Tridge and finally Laijir. Each of them loosened the buckle on their sheaths and moved their hands a little closer to their knives just in case.

The stairs were the colour of good tea, not your oul' weak stuff either. These were a beautiful rich brown, deep and mysterious. The spindles themselves were each covered with carved curling shapes like snakes. The hand rail was smooth but gnarled and bumpy. It looked for all the world like a long sinewy arm.

On up into the darkness we went, the light from the candle bouncing happily atop the candle. Our host stopped beside a wooden door also with the curling carvings and from his pocket removed a bunch of golden keys. He fingered through them until he was content with his choice. Into the hole, a quick click of an agreeing lock and the door opened.

"In you go, you'll notice that we are in the library. Here as you see no doubt are many, many books. Please fell free to open a few but careful mind, they're extremely old."

"Yes there are many answers in here, but not so many questions. Your question will be the next thing you say. Now I'll be back in a moment. Please be ready when I return, thank you," he said, closing the door.

"But!" snapped Ionta.

It was too late, he was gone.

"Oh this is just great," began Tridge, "what are we meant to ask him?"

After a moment of silence Clumsill spoke,

"I think we should ask him for help."

"Oh brilliant," moaned Tridge. "Why the Banshee said you could come I'll never know!"

The rest of us said nothing.

"No wait," said Dara, "we haven't asked him for help. We woke him and told him our business but did anyone actually ask him for help? I mean it's just good manners."

"You know I think you might be right," said Síoda. "No one asked for help at all. What do you think Graneff?"

"Well I . . . ehm . . . perhaps . . . maybe . . . er," I mumbled. (Some leader I was).

"I think Clumsill is right," said Katie. "It's just good manners really."

We had barely finished when the door opened and in he came.

"Now, has anyone got anything they'd like to ask me?"

A moment of silence can be a long time but the moment between two words even longer. Clumsill just popped out with it.

"Will you . . ." he paused taking a deep breath, ". . . help us, please?"

No one moved or said a word, the wrong question and who knew where we'd be.

The Léargas looked directly and coldly at Clumsill for what felt like a lifetime. His wrinkles furrowed and his hairy eyebrows moved up and down on his brow. His eyes opened wide then scrunched until you could hardly see them. His nose wriggled and he sucked in his lips. Then suddenly,

"Ha, ha! Of course I will. Sure all you had to was ask," he shouted, his face breaking into a wide smile.

We sighed together relieved that we still had a chance of getting the rest of the spell.

"I suppose after all that you would like the first line?" he said as his eyes danced and changed colours.

"You could say that," growled Tridge.

"The spell lives in an old language that not many will understand, that's just the way of it. It can be translated but for it to work best it must be spoken in it's original form."

Oh no, I thought, *some ancient tongue we'll never unravel.*

But he began with sounds I found familiar or at least they felt familiar.

"Thig leis an croí macánta an scian is ribeanta a mhaolú!"

(Hig lesh un kree makkanta an skin is ribbinta a whale-oo)

My mind was in a state of confusion. Here was the first line and for the life of me I couldn't understand it. I looked at my colleagues only to see shaking heads and glum, puzzled faces. They each had flashes of recognition but they quickly faded as knowledge of this tongue eluded them.

For my part I felt a mixture of frustration and guilt. I knew this language. I had heard of it in stories from Greagle and Blalim and my own parents. It had been the language of the fairies for generations but it had been let slip away over time. I regarded it as a memory or a notion of the past but here it was again now, today and we needed to know what he meant. The words were like echoes in a small room we could not open.

"I know that!" said Katie suddenly. "That's easy."

"Aye, me too," nodded Dara, "simple."

Clumsill wondered what they meant as did we all.

"You understand the line?" he asked.

The girls nodded with an

"Umm Hmm!"

"If you would be so kind," said Tridge, not really enjoying this curvy thinking. (He preferred straight lines where thoughts were concerned).

Saivir raised his eyebrows. Could the humans have relearned this language? He knew that centuries ago it was the language common to all creatures but over time new languages had arisen to replace it. Nowadays everyone had their own language with hints of the original scattered about them.

"It means 'an honest heart can blunt the sharpest knife'," said Dara.

The rest of us thought on possible uses for the sentence and knew the Carving Knife must be the knife in question.

"Yep, that's it," agreed Katie. "Easy."

"Why, wonders will never cease," smiled Saivir. "Well done my young friends. The language lives and so does your quest. This is most unexpected and wonderful all at once. I never thought it would be heard again, especially amongst the humans, come."

As we followed Clumsill's curiosity could no longer be contained.

"But how do you two know?" exclaimed the small fairy, stunned by the latest of the day's surprises.

"Time for questions later, and now," laughed Saivir. "The next line awaits."

We went back down the stairs together in a state of happy amazement. Clumsill was not to be denied,

"How do you know fairy language?" he whispered to the girls. "I mean most of the fairies don't even know it."

"Oh we learn it at school, our name for it is Irish or Gaelic. I didn't know it came from the fairies," replied Katie.

"Hmmm it seems it's even older than fairies but none of us have looked after it too well," said Clumsill.

"Yea well, we can do our best for it from now on. All of us," said Dara.

"Ar fheabhas!" said Katie

(Air owas!)

"Cool!" said Clumsill.

"Exactly!" smiled Dara. "See, you're learning already."

We went back out through the great door where we had entered some moments before and immediately saw the ruins again.

"I'm glad to see you all," gasped Saroist. "It's the lake . . . it's running out!"

We surveyed the waters and there was no doubting the level had dropped significantly. Síoda stared straight at me as if to say 'Get a move on', (a skill she shares with Gráinne, perhaps it's a woman thing). Well if we weren't under enough pressure already here was another worry.

"We'll be as fast as we can," I shouted to him.

He gave me an unconvinced look at with a flick of his tail swam under the water again. We had no such difficulties getting into the second tower. Saivir pushed it's great door which was very similar to the first, and we were in. Once more the inside was a view of exceptional craftsmanship, belying the run down outer walls. Statues of every kind of animal sat out on specially designed plinths attached to the walls. Eagles, buzzards, bears, cats, wolves, dogs the list was endless. This time there were no stairs.

"Follow me," said Saivir, whose voice broke us free from the beauty of the statues. He stopped suddenly and bent over to raise the corner of a grass green rug that lay in welcome in the hallway. There beneath were two doors carved together in such a way that their edges curved alongside each other leaving what looked like a very thin black snake between them. I marvelled at the craft of it all.

43

Making Arrangements

The next question was now in our thoughts. The children had come up with the first one but I doubted if we would be so fortunate this time. We descended together, Saivir leading the way down a gentle slope. We followed in silence, watching his candle as it did its best to light the way. He stopped and turned to face us.

"Time for the next question," he said quickly and as quickly turned his back to us again.

In a few steps he was at another smaller wooden door. He put his shoulder to it, lowered the handle and pushed. Nothing. The door did not move. He tried again only to get a tiny budge out of it.

"There is something blocking it," whispered Katie.

"Eh! What was that? Someone say something?" he asked distractedly, his back still to us.

"No, no," replied Ionta suddenly, "just thinking out loud. Isn't that right Katie?"

Katie shrugged her shoulders.

"I suppose."

Saivir put his shoulder to the door again. He pushed and shoved and groaned and moaned. It seemed to occur to us all at the same time, well it occurred to Katie first,

"Can we help you?" she asked.

Saivir turned around slowly to face us with another wide grin.

"Ha! I thought you'd never ask!" he said.

"Was that the second question?" asked Ionta worriedly.

"It was and what a fine question it was too," he replied.

Laijir, Tridge, Ionta and I put our shoulders to the door. Katie, Dara and Clumsill moved behind us and put their backs to the backs of our legs and we all heaved together. After brief resistance the door yielded to our combined might and opened reluctantly.

The blockage we could now see were hundreds of books of all shapes and sizes now scattered in a heap of pages, covers, words and pictures. We walked through the doorway trying to avoid standing on the books beneath our feet and found ourselves in a small round room. A torch flickered on the wall in front of us throwing out warm orange and yellow light. From the light we could see a three legged wooden table in the centre of the stone floored room, atop of which sat a number of envelopes.

"Well there you go. The second line is there, a word for each of you in those envelopes, which I made myself by the way," said Saivir proudly. "You just have to arrange them correctly."

We each moved to the table and picked up an envelope. They were made from a sort of purple paper but felt like silk to the touch. On opening we found a tiny piece of flat ash bark with a word burned onto it. As before the words were in the old language and all eyes drifted toward Dara and Katie for help.

"Ok," said Dara, "can each of us read out their word? I'll start."

Nods of agreement and worries about pronunciation followed.

"Chomh!" she said. (Ko)

"Obair!" said Katie. (Ubar)

"Níl!" said Tridge (Kneel)

"Furasta!" said Síoda. (Furista)

"Crua!" said Laijir. (Krooa)

"Sin!" I said. (Shin)

"Cinnte!" said Ionta. (Kinnche)

"An!" said Clumsill. (Un)

As we spoke we replaced our words on the table, where they now sat in no particular order.

"Right," said Dara confidently, "if we put that one there . . . and this one . . ."

"This one here," added Katie.

"Yep, and that over . . . there. That's it I think."

"Well clever clogs what does it say?" asked Tridge, jittering his wings impatiently.

His impatience I shared because I felt I knew what they meant but just couldn't get it.

"Well in this language it says,

'Cinnte, níl an obair crua chomh furasta sin' or 'To be sure, hard work isn't easy.'

"Hard work isn't easy?" snapped Tridge. "Sure I know that already!"

"Hey, pull your wings in," said Síoda.

"The obvious passes us by every day, its no harm to stop and think about it now and again. This tells me our work today is worth all this no matter how difficult or frustrating."

"Ok Saivir, on to the next Tower," she finished determinedly.

"As you wish fair lady."

We left the room and went back up the slope. Saivir closed the trap doors and replaced the rug. The statues of the animals stared down at us as we exited through the grand door again. The drop in the lake was now very obvious so much so that we could see the top of Saroist's dorsal fin just breaking the surface. We did not have much time and no one dared ask how we were to get him back to Nut Hollow even though it was on all our minds. The sight of the lake was enough for Síoda. Suddenly she took off and headed in the direction of the setting sun.

"I'll be back soon, promise."

We watched her go, hoping she would be ok and wondering where she was off to. Saivir walked into the third tower.

"I think I know the last question," whispered Ionta to me.

"I have a fair idea myself," I answered.

Saivir stopped in the middle of the grand room that sat behind the front door and was in keeping with the grand furnishings of the other towers. He walked over to a red leather seat and sat down. He looked directly at me this time. I think he knew we knew the question.

"Go on then, trust your instincts," he said. "Have you something to ask me?"

"Yes I believe I have."

I got approving nods from the company as I checked that I could indeed speak for us all. I took a breath,

"Can we help each other?" I asked tentatively.

"There you go," he said and again a wide grin, his eyes glowing purple and blue and turquoise.

"Clever bunch you fairies. Yes indeed we can help each other but first this."

He spoke in the old language himself this time.

"Go ndéanfaidh seo maith daoibh."

(Gu nyanni shuh my deev)

The third sentence. We turned to the children again.

"That this may do you some good," they said together.

I began to put the translated sentences together in my head.

—'An honest heart can blunt the sharpest Knife.'

—'Sure, hard work isn't easy.'

—'That this may do you some good.'

"Now my friends I urge caution. These sentences are powerful in their own right and contain the magic of the Towers. They must be used carefully. The time and place for that is up to you," he said then turned toward the lake.

"You have what you came for and may leave with my best wishes but before you do I would ask for your help now to complete our bargain as it were."

"You have our strength and whatever else we can offer," said Laijir who had perked up rightly now that the riddles had finished.

"Well, the lake is my home. My people are there and it's there I must return. For me to do this I need a little something from you. I gave up something of myself in order to take on these forms you have seen and for me to be complete again I need a single male fairy tear drop, nothing more nothing less. 'Tis the hardest form of water to acquire. Would any of you be so good as to give me one?"

Now here was a thing. We all dearly wanted to help him but getting male fairies (or male anythings I suspect) to cry is a tricky business. Uncomfortable shufflings from Laijir, Tridge and myself began. I looked guiltily down at young Clumsill hoping he could help. I am really a terrible one at the crying and try to avoid it if at all possible. Gráinne has often scolded me about that.

"I think I could do it ok," said Clumsill, much to my relief.

"Katie will you stand on my toe?" he asked.

"Do I have to?" she said giving me a look.

I nodded.

"I don't want to hurt you, you know."

"Its ok, I'll be fine."

Katie walked over to him as he removed his small leather boot. He wriggled his toes on the grass and closed his eyes.

"Can you think of something nice, like whin bush ice cream," I offered, trying to allay my guilt.

Well before he could answer Katie brought her borrowed shoe down plum atop his big toe.

"Owwweee!"

"Sorry," said Katie worriedly.

"There it is," exclaimed Saivir excitedly as a single tear rolled slowly from the corner of Clumsill's left eye. He ran over to him and took out a tiny glass jar, not dissimilar to the one Rachary had given Ionta earlier. He waited for the tear to fall from Clumsill's cheek and caught it safely in the jar.

"Thank you! Thank you indeed."

He turned quickly and added one or two pieces of what looked like salt granules from his pocket, gave it a shake and drank the mixture.

"Mmm, lovely. Now this shouldn't take too long. I do hope your toe gets better quickly."

"You're welcome, I'll be fine," replied Clumsill who was now sitting down caressing his swollen digit.

This seemed a reasonable outcome but with a splash my mind was quickly brought back to Saroist's plight. As I thought of what to do next I heard a mass fluttering of wings and a chirping chorus. We looked up to see, with Síoda at the head of them, a flock of robin redbreasts. They landed as one just beside us on the small island. Síoda and two of the robins approached us.

"You know Rithacus and Rua," she said.

I nodded and thought to myself what a remarkable fairy Síoda was. Only she could've flown as quickly to the robin tree of Culnagobbit.

"They've kindly agreed to help us carry Saroist back to the river."

"Hello again Rithacus, it's been a while."

"Aye it has Graneff. Síoda has told us of your journey and we are happy to help. We have lost friends today to Nefairious and his crew."

"And Rua, you're as red and as beautiful as ever, great to see you old friend."

"And you Graneff. Do I see a few grey hairs there?"

"Ha, that's the least of my worries."

"We will need a harness," said Rithacus. He hopped busily about then turned to the other robins.

"Quickly, collect those rushes there, they'll do the job."

Saroist popped his head out of the lake,

"Oh that's all I need, more flying!"

The entire flock took off spreading out around the lake and began diving into clumps of rushes that sat up like spiky hair all round us. We collected what we could and it wasn't long, perhaps a half hour, before thousands of long, thin, green strands sat piled. With these the robins began to weave rush ropes.

They had to be strong to carry the salmon yet flexible enough to reach round underneath him. I wished there was a spell I could use to hurry things along but I didn't have one. As we wove the sun began to head downward toward the horizon. It would be dark before very long and we still had to get to the Everlit Turf Mountain. The robins twisted and chirped and whistled and wove as the harness took shape. With some final nips and tucks and pulls and pecks it was ready. The robins regrouped behind Rithacus.

A green bed of weaved rushes to fit the salmon's belly and maybe fifty smaller ropes of varying lengths designed to take the strain. The red breasted troop flew the harness into position and Saroist had just enough water beneath him to move gently on top of it.

"I do trust this is a strong enough device," he asked, not altogether convinced of its merits.

"Don't worry," said Rua, "we've carried bigger and plumper creatures than you before."

"Although not many," laughed Rithacus.

Saroist gave them his best and haughtiest look.

Humph! Never been fitter, he thought.

As the robins each took hold on one of the smaller ropes Síoda flew quickly up to me.

"Graneff, I must go with Saroist. I should be able maintain his air supply as I did before. I also know a secret way back up to the river, hopefully out of the gaze of Nefairious. I will wait for you up near the cross trees at Two Hour wood for as long as I can. Please take care of yourselves."

She walked over and kissed the youngsters each on the forehead.

"I'll see you soon. Now listen to Graneff and the others and we'll be together again before you know it."

She smiled as she spoke but the sorrow in the children's faces was easy to see. Still they gave her a loud send off shouting "Goodbyes and good lucks' for all they were worth. Now with everyone in position the robins took the strain.

"Pull now," shouted Rithacus,

"Fly like you never have before," shouted Rua.

Slowly the great fish left his watery home and was raised skyward leaving a cascade of drips to splash on the lake's surface. Síoda was immediately busy with her water spell and as they flew into the soft, late evening sunlight the completed bubble glistened around Saroist's head. Suddenly Laijir spoke.

"Graneff, don't you remember what Rachary said about the last drop from the Vanishing Lake? We need it and quick."

I turned to face Saivir again and left the others to get ready. The children each climbed onto the backs of Laijir, Tridge and Ionta and waited.

"Saivir, what did you mean when you said your people were living in the lake?" I asked.

"Oh had you more time I could give you a fuller explanation but for now believe me when I say we *are* the lake. It has long been thus and will long continue to be our duty to protect the towers and their contents from harm, hence their unseemly appearance from without."

"If you are the lake why do you leave at all?"

"To replenish our strength in the Moyle Sea. We are never too far away that we can't protect them but we are subject to the tides and time itself."

I thought of Rachary's words about the dry river bed, the one we had followed.

Did the Léargas use it still? It would never be wet long enough if they used it only occasionally and so appear dry of course. I longed to hear more but for now had one last request of him.

"Rachary told us that if we are to succeed today we need the last drop from the Vanishing Lake and it is to be kept in one of our eyes and cried out when needed."

He smiled.

"I know and what better person to give a drop of the lake to than the one who gave me one himself. Could you come here a moment Clumsill?" he asked.

Clumsill climbed off Ionta's back and walked over to us. The lake bed was plainly visible and the stones that live there were now exposed. There was but the smallest of trickles left. I feared he would be too late and urged him to hurry but Saivir tapped me on the shoulder, his eyes now the darkest of blues.

"It's ok. You will get the last drop from the lake," he said. As he spoke he began to return to his liquid form, melting away in front of our eyes.

"Your tear was all I needed, thank you Clumsill. I am happy for you to have one of mine in return," he said as the tiny droplet rolled down his cheek.

Clumsill let it sit on the end of his finger before tilting his head up and letting it fall into his left eye.

"Good luck and if chance allows come back some day."

With that last whisper he was gone.

"I always knew there was something funny about that lake," said Ionta.

Good luck in your guardianship, I thought. *What secrets must those books hold? Here's to meeting again in more agreeable circumstances.*

In spite of the answers we got there were far more questions left to unravel, another time perhaps. We took off with the children, leaving the dry lake bed beneath us and headed for the Everlit Turf Mountain. We hadn't much daylight left and needed to make the most of it.

PART the THIRD

44

Under the Radar

The trees around heralded the onset of late evening with a rustling of their banquet of leaves courtesy of the impatient and often ill tempered north wind. Strelle had climbed down and propped himself up on his wings in order to talk with Druhin.

"I don't do this for many you know but I'm quite sure your neck was getting sore looking up at us all."

"Aye it was, thanks."

"Are you sure you know how to get back to Fween Talav?"

"Yes," replied Druhin hoping he could find the buzzard's claw so late in the day.

"Good, for this battle will not be a place for youth, although it is my sad experience to have seen many perish who were not near grown. It is important we get some idea of what is going on in the Hollow. We have nests down there and I'm sure you've seen us in the evenings getting our dinner."

Indeed he had and every fairy knew that flying when the bats were eating was asking for trouble. There had been incidents in the past that had left ill feeling. Mostly inexperienced younger fairies flying at dusk of course. Quite a few had returned with badly damaged wings and legs, occasionally even worse.

"I'll take a gang down shortly and hopefully the crows will think we are just out for the evening meal as usual. You will have to stay invisible for if any crow or whatever creature Nefairious has working for him were to see you our element of surprise would be gone."

"I agree sir, but if I am invisible how do you propose to keep an eye on me?"

"Well I'm glad to see you still have your wits about you anyway," said Strelle. "You will use this."

From underneath his wing he produced a small hollow pipe.

"A whistle!" exclaimed Druhin, who suddenly remembered that he had neglected to practice his music these last few weeks.

"I use one just like that in my lessons."

"Well not just like this one I suspect. We do not share your musical abilities, a bit of a waste of time if you ask me. We use sound for more important tasks. This whistle as you call it is designed to play notes that sound like our own. If you blow on this we can locate you instantly."

"Wow, so I'll sound just like a bat?"

"Aye, to everything other than us bats," replied Strelle a little sarcastically.

Strelle handed Druhin the whistle and gave a click on his tongue. This was the command for those who were on the scouting mission to get ready. They slowly moved themselves onto the branches outside until each of the groups were in position. Below them in the late evening blue, crows patrolled down near the river in twos and threes. The sound of their harsh voices sent a shiver through Druhin. He had heard many tales of crow cruelty and now here he was about to fly into their midst.

Like the rest of the young fairies of the Hollow he had been reared on tales of the battles between crows and fairies. Blalim's and Greagle's skirmishes with Préak kept him dreaming through many's a night. In recent times crow contact had been minimal and reduced to receiving caws and curses.

The night was busy chasing whatever was left of the day out of the Hollow. It made itself comfortable in the spaces underneath branches and at rabbit burrows, underneath hedges and wherever leaves congregated. The embroidery attaching darkness to evening is seamless and now darkness was almost upon them. But for now darkness did not prevail entirely. The moon had little or no cloud to worry about and was well on its way across the sky. It shone brightly, revealing its many grey indentations.

"Put on your amulet," said Strelle suddenly, bringing Druhin back to his wits.

"Fly carefully and quickly and you'll be ok."

"But what will you do? I mean the crows are so many and so strong," asked Druhin, anxious as to the bats' welfare.

"True, they are that, but they are strangers to the night and I can promise you they will be sick of darkness before the dawn."

With another click they began to fall from the branches and into their eccentric flight. It seemed to Druhin they flew as if scribbling their path before them without a care. Their wings fluttered like mad giant eyelids as they appeared to bounce off invisible sky cushions to turn themselves. He had to fly hard to keep up. The bats flew at a higher speed than he expected. However, he was young and had just acquired his wings so to speak and he aimed after Strelle. He decided to test the whistle before they got too near the Hollow. To his relief when he blew each of the bat heads turned to look for him. He caught up with Strelle and flew just off his right wing tip. He gave another blow to alert the great bat.

"Good lad," replied Strelle. "Now stay close."

Once again he clicked his tongue and immediately the five groups of three all split as if scattered by a gust of wind.

"The others will scoot round amongst the trees as they do every evening and hopefully the crows will not notice us few landing. Now

when you locate the Buzzard's claw blow on your whistle and we'll see
you safely inside."

"Ok," replied Druhin and flew just ahead of the bat.

He had never flown back into the Hollow from this direction before
and what you'd think would be familiar surroundings did seem a bit
strange to him. He got his bearings from the grey bridge and it wasn't
long until he spied the special branch that Greagle had told him about.
He had to climb high into the evening air to avoid the deadly crochet
the crows had made.

"How could they have done it so fast?" he wondered.

It spread all round the trees from base to branches and was expertly
crafted from sticks, twigs, grass, rushes, thistles and rag weeds. No doubt
it would trap any unsuspecting creature capable of flight.

By now the other bats were wheeling amongst the leaves like the expert
flyers they were. Several of them came perilously close to getting entangled
in the crow mesh but just managed to avoid it. Their daring enabled them
to buzz right by the crows who barely gave them a glance, bats were not
their concern this night. Strelle followed the sound of Druhin's sonic
whistle and they landed safely together. The two other bats in Strelle's
group zipped off to pull unwitting moths out of the twilight.

"We have a little time left but we need you to be quick. Once you
return inform Greagle and any other fairy who can fight that the bats
are ready. We will gather and wait for your signal in the trees around.
Sound your whistle four times and we'll be a wing beat away. Then we'll
see what Nefairious is made of!"

"It will be an honour to fight with you, sir," answered Druhin.

"Ach, 'sir' my wing tips! My name is Strelle, no other. Farewell young
one we have our own work to do," he smiled, and as suddenly was gone.

Druhin dared not remove the amulet for fear of catching a crow's
gaze. He turned to the tree and hoped that the words Greagle had told

him would now come to him. He was just about to speak when a light shone.

Oh no, he thought, *I'm caught*.

But his fears passed as the light moved on through the branches.

"Nothing there. Next tree," cawed the crow.

"You sure?" said the other. "I thought I heard voices."

"Ach, your head's soft with the ale," cackled the first.

Druhin's heart nearly came out of his backside. He had never had such a shock and was sure he was done for. He touched the amulet as a thank you. He whispered the spell words and rubbed the leaf on the bark as he had been told. In a moment or two he had squeezed himself into the bark of the tree and could see the crow's light filter through the far branches. The bark had healed itself as the light passed by where he had just been. He leaned up against the wall as he had been told to do and sure enough part the floor on which he stood melted away and he flapped his wings to hover. With another deep breath, he stopped and was soon hurtling through the tree tunnels. In the darkness he had one thought,

"The fightback has begun."

45

On a Knife Edge

Since he had brandished the Knife in the thorn, Nefairious had found himself too busy to experiment further with it. Granted he had stuck it through Rant's tongue but really he could have done that with any old blade. He felt now was the time just to see what he had risked so much for. From a little way back he watched Welset rouse his troops. Quickly they began to get to work filling in any gaps as he had demanded. For a moment he thought that never again would he be amongst his own kind, certainly not in any friendly capacity anyway. He had forsaken the luxury of kinship for what he now held in his hand.

The white wooden handle seemed to have changed just to fit his grip. He couldn't remember ever having grasped something so comfortable. The handle was indeed wood of some description but not even the white wood of saplings when stripped of their bark could compare. It was smooth in his hand but there was no way it would fall from him. He felt the only way to remove it from him would be to take arm and all. No, this was a living thing he held. He felt connected to it somehow, as if it had become a part of him.

In some ways it was already. After all he had bartered his Cree to release it. He was never so alive and yet it was a precarious path he was on. Should anything happen to the Knife, well suffice to say that would not be good for him. He cared not to dwell on such a consequence and instead delighted just in holding it. It was this exchange that would shape the Knife's actions. It did not differentiate between good and evil. It did as it was told to do. Since it was placed in the Learning Tree by the Léargas the fairies had used it for their ceremonies. They adored it and cared for it and it in turn yielded up magic and wonder. It had become the Carving Knife of Nut Hollow and young fairies marvelled when they held it.

Nefairious remembered well his first brief encounter with it. His impatience and petulant raid came just after his official First Flight.

Hmm, funny how things work out, he thought as he skimmed his finger along one side of the blade.

And what a blade. None of your run of the mill tempered steel here. No this was gold. The gold of sun rises and star bursts and stronger than all. It was cold to touch and yet not like the harsh chill of metal. It ran down toward a tip as fine as any fairy needle. Nefairious gazed along the edge of the blade and wondered should he dare run his finger along it.

No I don't think so, he smiled to himself.

He was not about to rise to that challenge.

My fingers will do nicely where they are! Ah, you'll do.

He pulled down a couple of thinnish branches that drooped down from the nut trees above him. They were flexible but thick enough to give a normal blade a bit of a sweat in their cutting. He raised the Knife from below and pushed upward. It may as well have been mole butter so easily did it pass through.

"Indeed the old Thorn had good reason to worry when it saw you," he whispered to himself.

He whisked it through the air a few times in front of him listening to the swish it made.

"Hey Welset," he called gruffly. "Tell your men to break off as many branches as they can. We are going to need spears and these nut trees will provide good strong ones I'm sure."

Welset turned and nodded, this was an easy enough task for a creature with perhaps the sharpest teeth in the country. As soon as the particular hole they were working on was closed up each of the weasels set to gnaw off the branches. If they were too high they scurried up the tree and started from there, careful of course not to stand on the one they were chewing. The pile of branches soon grew until Nefairious was satisfied.

"That'll do, now come and watch."

The weasels gathered round in a circle about him. He was completely surrounded and not for the first time did the thought flick through Welset's mind,

What if we all just jumped on the little devil?

The reason why it stayed just a thought was quickly revealed. Nefairious picked up one of the freshly shorn branches in his right hand. In his left hand he held the Knife.

"Time to sharpen up on a few things you might say," he said and ran the Knife down the length of the branch.

He only had to it once as it peeled off the remaining bark and sharpened itself to a fine point. There was an audible intake of breath from the spectators. Suffice to say they would not be messing with any creature in control of that blade.

Nefairious quickly repeated this procedure and in no time had perhaps one hundred deadly spears and arrows.

"Take a handful each of you. Anything you see that even remotely looks like one of those fairy dogs be sure and introduce these to them."

The weasels gathered as many as they could and returned to their tasks. As Welset left Nefairious called him back,

"I strongly suggest you get your men to armour up."

"Armour? Where will I get armour here?"

"Improvise! The fairies have a store of points and blades that will make short work of your fur. Haven't you ever wondered why we collect young human teeth?"

"We?"

"Eh? Oh 'they' of course," replied Nefairious quickly.

"Well it had crossed my mind," said the weasel.

"Those young teeth have the hardest edge that you can get. For centuries they have been shaped into knives, arrow heads, axes you name it. Be sure that a store of them is well and truly exhausted now and ready for the likes of you and me should we be that unfortunate."

"I see," replied Welset. "I'll think of something."

"Aye see that you do. Oh and if you forget to mention that to the rat or my father for that matter, well . . . I won't be overly worried."

Welset went back to his task.

Now Nefairious, would you have this weasel kill your own father?

The thought loomed loud in his head and took him by surprise.

Well would you? You risked it all to release him and now here you are plotting with this root rodent.

Nefairious breathed deeply. Here was the crux of the whole affair. On the one hand he admired and loved his father. He had been robbed of his company for such a long time and now here was the opportunity to get to know him again. On the other hand he didn't trust him one bit. He had seen the look in his eyes, he remembered him on the day of his arrest. He would have killed those children and no mistake. It is a strange thing to want the things you can not have. He wanted a good relationship with his father, a normal desire to be sure but in his heart he knew Neroh was power hungry and would not take orders from him for very long. His quandary was lightened somewhat in the knowledge that the Knife itself meant he was virtually untouchable from his enemies.

He resheathed it carefully and buttoned the little handle strap. It was secure again.

The weasels had soon finished their work and there was hardly a gap to be seen anywhere. The rabbit holes had been filled in with blackthorn branches, birds nests were emptied and filled with whin bush barbs. Thistles sat menacingly in wait in the long grass as did nettles and ragweeds. Nefairious turned and looked across the river at the crows. The spaces in between the branches of the taller trees had been filled in. He listened as they continued to caw and curse at each other, it was the crow way.

The larger crows bullied the rooks and ravens, the lower orders if you will. They in turn squabbled amongst themselves. The Hollow was suddenly a very unwelcoming place and Nefairious smiled at the thought of it.

"I want you Welset to stay up here and keep your men on their toes. If you see or hear anything and I mean anything suspicious let me know immediately. I am heading back to the Learning Tree. I have one or two things to attend to. Remember your reward will be great after the storm."

Welset nodded, letting a grin turn up the edges of his mouth a touch. Nothing would get through if he had anything to do with it. Nefairious took off, his wings felt strong. His skills were ready and waiting. He was well aware that in spite of all the magic he possessed and even with the Carving Knife he would be sorely tested before long. He knew of Fween Talav, though had never been there.

They'll be hard at it, preparing and planning. Sure I'd do the same myself, who wouldn't fight for Nut Hollow?

Then another rogue thought out of the blue. His mother appeared in his mind and for once he didn't have the shield of anger about him.

"What are you doing Nefairious?" it said in her voice, at least the voice he remembered.

"Doesn't matter to you, you're dead. Dead and gone."

"Son, if I was still alive would I too not be in Fween Talav? Under the ground and frightened at this madness. Did I not always do my best for you?"

Ha! Wasn't very good was it?. I mean look at me. Lamenting my mother and plotting to kill my father, you must be so proud.

Nefairious shook his head, trying to shake the argument out of his mind.

This is no good. You'll be comparing flowers with her next. What are you going to do, overcome Greagle with a bunch of bluebells?

The wretched bark of one the crows pulled Nefairious back from his thoughts.

"I'd say we're ready for your kin," teased Grod. "Are you?"

Nefairious looked him straight in the eye,

"I am," he replied coldly. "I am."

46

Footing the Turf

The setting sun around the lands that include Glenmak Mountain, Brea Height and Nut Hollow itself is a sight to behold. Due to the nature of weather in these parts it is difficult to predict if the sky will be cloudy, rainy, blue or a mixture of all three. Mostly it is a mixture. This means that the sun may be flame red or almost white, or shimmering orange or pure yellow as it sinks into the Moyle Sea.

Tonight we watched the tip of its fireball costume away in the distance. The sky was streaked with orange and the far away clouds seemed on fire. We have often wondered at the relationship between the sky and the sun, not to mention the moon and stars. It seems to us that each has its own personality and they get on well enough. Of course the clouds are the jokers in all this and helped by the wind they can cause havoc for those of us on the ground or with wings. Tonight the clouds and wind were whipping up mischief somewhere else for they surely were not here. Our flight from Loughareema was unhindered by gust or gale.

"Are you ok?" I shouted to Katie.

She was holding onto Tridge's back. Her arms were round his neck and there was just enough room for his wings to beat.

"Yes thanks, I feel a bit tired. Are we there yet?"

I couldn't help but smile, I had heard that question once or twice before.

"Not too far now," I said and she smiled back at me.

Both Dara and Clumsill were holding on to their pilots and each gave me a grin.

Beneath us the leaves of the trees knitted together into a verdant quilt, perfectly still. Night was almost upon us. We flew a few feet above the tallest trees hoping not to attract unwanted attention. The land dipped and peaked and suddenly before us now was the Everlit Turf Mountain.

The top of it was as I had always heard, covered in wisps of mist and mystery. As we approached, the sides of the mountain vented so much steam that it looked like a volcano ready to explode. It has ever been thus.

"Well, well," said Laijir, "the Everlit Turf Mountain. It's long and many's the day since I was here."

"You were here before?" asked Ionta.

"Indeed I was, years and years ago with my father."

I had heard about that journey but we really didn't have time for one of Laijir's yarns. He was known for rattling on a bit and as much as he was a good story teller now was not the time.

"Yes it was a fresh winter's morning when my father, Halai, woke me—"

"We'll land there," I interrupted.

"Good idea," said Tridge with a wink.

"But the story," asked Laijir all hurt. I almost felt sorry for him.

"Later," I promised.

There was a clearing about three quarters the way up the mountain. Some cow or horse must have been asleep there and had flattened grass, thistles and weeds. Laijir, Ionta and Tridge carefully touched down and their tired passengers slid off their backs.

"What do we do now?" asked Katie, with a stretch. "Will we have to wait 'til morning? It's too dark to see anything."

"Too dark?" said Clumsill. "It's perfect. Can't you see the colours?"

"Humans you know. Like you know!" said Dara, pointing at herself and Katie.

"Oh yeah, of course. You don't have the night sight," said Clumsill, happy to have one up on somebody at last. Of course he didn't say his night sight was still developing.

No they certainly didn't have that fairy gift and we would have to be careful with them. The Everlit Turf Mountain as the name might suggest was not to be fallen into. The orange red glow of the turf could now just be seen underneath the grass in the darkness.

Laijir, Tridge and Ionta came over to me and we watched the three children settle down in the grass.

"Three of us can go and get what we need from the mountain, one can stay here with them," said Tridge, who clearly was not going to be babysitting.

"Agreed. Ionta, will you stay?" I asked.

"Aye I will but not because I'm afraid of the mountain mind."

"No doubt about that Ionta, but the children will feel happier with you than these two charmers," I said smiling.

Laijir and Tridge walked on ahead. Before I followed I called the children.

"Clumsill, Katie and Dara, could you come here for a moment?"

They walked slowly toward me. The day was catching up on them and they were obviously getting tired.

"We have a little work to do and the safest thing for you is to stay here. This mountain is treacherous if you don't know where you're going. I suggest you try to get some sleep for we have a long night still ahead. Ionta has kindly agreed to keep an eye on you, what do you say?"

Dara answered first.

"I think we should stay here until you come back. Of course if you don't come back we shall have to rescue you and we don't want to be too tired for that. Aye a bit of sleep will help."

"Good idea," agreed Katie.

Children, I thought. *Wonderful creatures.*

"Oh and don't forget this," said Ionta, taking from beneath her coat the glass jar that Rachary had given her in his cave.

"Thank you Ionta," I said putting it in my pocket. "Time to get the embers."

I quickly caught up with Laijir and Tridge.

"We'd be better off flying up here," said Laijir. "I for one am not going to step on a stray sod tonight."

(Stray sods of course were planted by mischievous ground dwellers many centuries ago; we believe you know them as leprechauns. They are few and far between now but are curious beings that live at the end of rainbows with a thing for gold. Should you ever meet one you'll see what I mean. They did this to confuse humans and it always worked. The moment you step on a stray sod which looks like every other sod your mind clouds over and you can wander for hours in a circle until someone sings you out of the trance. Mostly such sods had been found and marked but there are still plenty left scattered all over the countryside. Just be careful of them is all I'd say).

We took off together heading up the side of the mountain.

"How will we know which embers to take?" I wondered.

"Well if you are quite ready to listen I'd be happy to tell you," said Laijir.

I had hoped he had taken the hint but obviously not, although his story would turn out to prove very useful. We nodded, it was a good five minute flight to the top of the mountain and there were worse things to listen to than Laijir.

"As I was saying . . ." he began and cleared his throat. "Halai gave me a shout and told me to come on. I was in bed instead of school that day but not sick enough that I couldn't go with him. He knew I'd be up for it in spite of my mother's tuts. I threw on the first jumper and trousers I could find and in no time we were away with me on his back, leaving the Hollow trees swaying behind us.

"Now son, I need you to watch carefully when we get to the mountain. There are ways into it alright but they are well hidden."

"Ok but what are we getting, father?"

"We need fuel for the Hollow. Winter is coming and we need turf of course."

"Oh I see."

"This is a singular honour you know. The turf from this mountain burns for ages and only every fifty years or so do we need to replenish our supplies. This year it's my turn to do it, with your help."

"Well sure I felt about as tall as a dandelion." (Very tall for a fairy you understand).

Laijir smiled as he recalled the story. As we ascended the orange glow became more intense.

"Now we reached the bottom of the mountain, just a bit lower than where the others are now and my father said,

"Right son, the turf we need is just beneath the surface. There are several different types as you go up the mountain and they say the one at the very top lasts forever. The higher you go the stronger it burns you see. It is the best turf in Ireland, everlit and glowing, but you need to handle it with care otherwise you'll get scorched. For our purposes though the lower stuff does the job. Use these," and he hands me a pair of foxglove leaf gloves knitted by my mum and put on his own.

"They'll protect your fingers."

"So we just dig it up?" says I.

"Dig?" he says. "Dig? Are you kidding? There's a very good chance the mountain would swallow you whole if you dared dig into it."

"Well how do you know where to get it then?"

"There are five entrances to the mountain for the five types of turf. They are easy to spot but you—

"Have to know what you're looking for," says I, finishing the sentence with him.

"What are we looking for?"

"Good lad?" he answers and then points straight ahead.

"Do you see the plants there?"

"Yes."

"Notice anything peculiar about them?"

"Not really. Well . . . are they in a circle?"

"Indeed they are son, well spotted."

Laijir broke from the story and had a look down, then continued,

"Well," says Halai, "there you go," and he lowered me into the middle of the circle.

"Sure my feet weren't a second on the ground when the plants . . . there was a daisy, a rush, a bluebell, a crocus, a dandelion and a snowdrop all leaned outwards and pulled the ground apart. I fell into the hole and on top of a pile of lovely warm soft brown turf."

"But it was winter wasn't it? There's not many plants that flower in winter, how did you know which was what?" said Tridge loftily.

"Ach Tridge, magic. The plants weren't in flower but I knew which was which when I saw them in the circle and my boy if you look straight ahead now I'd suggest that even you could tell what they are."

Laijir headed downwards immediately. We were almost at the very top of the mountain and could feel the heat under our boots.

"We can't be long here," said Laijir. "I've never been up this high but when I fell into the hole my Dad flew up and grabbed an armful of turf and then grabbed me. He just had me out in time before the hole closed over again."

On seeing the circle Tridge was surprised as he realised what Laijir had predicted was true. He knew the name of the flowers no problem. Of course at this time of the year they were in bloom but even so he had never been one for gardening.

"Well if we land in the centre of the circle the land should open up, right?" I asked.

Laijir nodded a yes.

"Ok how do we lift the hot stuff?" asked Tridge.

"Not with our hands anyway. Use your knives and hope they were well made for they reckon this high up stuff can melt steel," said Laijir.

"But not glass," I said in hope.

"We'll soon see if Rachary's gift works," said Laijir.

I took out the glass jar. It was the shape of a pear and had a glass lid that fitted snugly on the top. It was easy to remove and held fast with the help of some seaweed which had been ingeniously engraved into it.

"Ok each of us stab a piece of turf and fly straight up and out, we'll get it into the jar somewhere a little cooler," I suggested.

We hovered above the flower circle and with a look to say we were all ready we flew straight for the centre. It happened as Laijir had described moments previously. The flowers drew up to their full height and slowly began to lean away from us until they almost reached the ground. Suddenly the ground opened and a blast of hot air nearly scorched off our eyebrows. The glow of the turf was an intense orange/red/yellow mix and the smell of turf normally so friendly now seemed hostile and hungry.

"Quick," urged Laijir, "get what you can and get out."

We flew as close as we dared and I thought my wings would surely melt. Each of us took a turn to poke in our knives and thankfully we each withdrew some of the radiant embers. Upwards then as quickly as we could but not quickly enough. As we flew up the earth whipped closed trapping Tridge by the boot just at the ankle.

Laijir and I flew back, knives in one hand and with the other grabbed hold of Tridge. I had to throw the jar from me onto the grass hoping it would land safely. We pulled for all we were worth. Tridge grimaced in pain. His feet were surely roasted and his arms almost out of their sockets. However, he managed to hold onto his knife and we got him out at the cost of his boot which was swiftly consumed. We flew him over to the jar and as quickly as we could put the turf inside, closed the lid and collapsed in a heap together.

The pain was obvious despite this proud fairy's best efforts to conceal it. His face was crunched up and his eyes tight closed. He breathed in deeply over his clenched teeth.

"Are you ok?" I asked and as I did wondered at the wisdom of that question in such circumstances.

"I trust we got what we came for?" he winced.

I nodded and we raised our eyes to see the glass jar on the grass and in it glowing strongly was the everlit turf.

"Well now Tridge I suppose you'll be wanting a new pair of boots!" quipped Laijir.

"Oh very funny."

His voice contained an element of mirth that relieved me no end. He was hurt but it would take more than a scorched toe or two to stop him.

"Can we get off this not so friendly furnace? I would really like a word with Nefairious," he said flatly.

Laijir and I looked at each other then at him caressing his foot.

"Aye," we said, "join the queue."

47

The Music of Healing

Gráinne could hardly believe her eyes. She sat in amazement as she saw Pog and Fer walking up form the tunnel to the river with Greagle between them resting on their shoulders. He looked half dead. She got up immediately and ran towards them being joined by several other fairy women. They had been busily readying spears and arrows and sharpening teeth tips. She put her shoulder underneath the exhausted Greagle much to the relief of Pog. Sherene took hold of the other shoulder.

"Quickly lie him down. Over there," she urged.

They threw blankets and coats and whatever else was at hand on the floor near the fire.

"You old gilloot," she said crossly. "What on earth is going on? Fer and Pog what are you doing with Greagle?" she didn't give herself time for an answer. Sometimes parents are a bit like that.

"I thought you two were over near the table playing and here you are with Greagle no less and him not fit to stand up. What is going on here?"

"Mum we need your help. Greagle has to talk to the Banshee *now*," said Fer, ignoring the request for answers.

"Talk to the Banshee? Sure he's not even conscious," she gasped.

"Oh Gráinne," said Greagle suddenly, his eyes still shut, "just get her."

Gráinne was surprised to hear him but relieved. Any chance of reclaiming the Hollow would rely heavily on Greagle. Even if he was not able to fight himself his clever mind could still help to plan.

"For goodness sake, you should know better at your age," she scolded, but was not in the least surprised at him.

He had been in more scraps and scrapes than any other fairy of her considerable acquaintance. Her dilemma was much more obvious. It's rare indeed to call on a Banshee and it really wasn't the done thing. Gráinne knew this and thoughts of bad luck stories came to her of those that had not waited for the Banshee to come to them.

"Oh! In the name of Odhran, to thistles with it. I'll go and get her. Right you two don't move. You keep an eye on Greagle and tend to him. Sherene will tell you what to do. I'll be back with Herself soon. I trust she won't be too angry with me."

"Ok mummy."

"Do you know where she is?" asked Silleyn.

"Yes I have a fair idea."

The Banshee had the welcome of the whole countryside and had places to stay among all the fairy communities. Because Fween Talav was so rarely used by the Hollow folk, she had taken to staying there of late. She had manufactured for herself a small room just above the great hall where the survivors now waited. She returned to her thoughts after her earlier speech. Banshees spend most of their time alone. They are constantly urged to compose songs for the fallen, songs for the risen, songs to make you rise and songs to make you fall.

Now if you have ever known creatures who are composing in any way, be it with words or pictures, or music or sculpture or whatever then you will find that they are best approached with caution. Gráinne did not

fear for her life, far from it. It was more the bad mood of the disturbed
thinker that perturbed her. She gave her wings a couple of trial beats.

It's been a while, she thought.

Up she went. On landing she could see the Banshee sitting at her
table staring into the candle which sat in its centre. It would be harder
for Gráinne if the lady was in a trance. She walked slowly along the low
hallway. The bottoms of grass roots were peeping through the soil, thin
and wispy white. There were several stone parts jutting out here and
there and branch bits. Closer now until she was only a few feet from
the Banshee.

"My Lady . . ."

No reply.

Oh great, she's away in the song world.

She breathed in deeply and tried again, a little louder this time.

"My Lady . . ."

The Banshee slowly lowered her head, breaking her gaze with the
flame.

"I knew it would be you," she answered.

"You knew?"

"Yes Gráinne, you have uncommon kindness even amongst your
wonderful people. Greagle needs my help again no doubt."

Gráinne was about to utter a sentence with that exact message.

"My song is ready but for it to work it will need you all."

"Of course, my lady, if I can be of any help. But how?"

"Just clear your throat and bring your voice with you."

She stood up away from the table and took Gráinne by the hand.
They walked to the ledge and flew down to where Greagle lay. Their short
flight accompanied by 'There she is' and 'she's coming, be quiet', 'look
at those eyes' and other half sentences of that nature.

"He hasn't moved or spoken a word since," said Sherene worriedly.

The Banshee walked up to him and bent down onto her knees. Those that could, stood and watched. The rest of the fairies gathered as close in as they dared. In the silence that followed the Banshee made herself comfortable and lifted Greagle's hands in hers.

"Friends, you are well skilled in music. Any of you that was able to rescue an instrument, please get it now."

Most of the fairies were sad to recall that their instruments now most likely lay in pieces under some drunken crow or worse . . . in some rat's gut. However, some were able to reach them in time and after a few moments returned with what they had. Pog and Fer and some of the other children took out their whistles from their inner pockets. They had been doing lessons together for a good while but I doubt if they thought this would be their first performance.

"Which tune shall we play?" asked Fer excitedly.

"I know three you know!" added Pog.

His enthusiasm led him to blow a few random notes without thinking. The Banshee quickly scolded him.

"Young one," she said sharply. "Please wait. Notes without any rhythm or reason are no help."

Pog quickly removed his whistle and felt suitably chastised. Some of the other children who'd had a mind to do the same thing now withdrew the whistles without delay.

"Songs and music together, that is what we need here."

"Your instruments are ready now I hope?" she said and winked at Pog, who immediately felt a lot better.

"Everyone . . ."

The fairies put whistles and flutes in mouths, fiddles under chins, banjos on knees and wherever whatever other way their instrument demanded.

"When I give you the signal, play. Is that understood?"

The impromptu orchestra nodded 'yes' although most thought that it would be a horrendous mish mash of erratic musical notes crashing about.

The Banshee raised her left hand, while still cradling Greagle's hands with the other. The silence was gently ushered away as her voice began to sing,

> "Music of the streams, music of the trees
> Music of the winds, come to us please
> Music of the voices singing in this hall
> Music of the instruments, played by one and all . . ."

The melody she used to carry these words now began to filter into the heads of those listening. Her hand came down slowly and with a click of her fingers she instructed all those to join in. The youngsters blew their whistles, and the older ones pushed their bows across fiddle strings. A set of pipes (sadly without the drones which were lost to the raiders) and a guitar were heard. There were a couple of flutes too and even Grochin with his old accordion and amazingly all seemed to be playing the very same melody as the one she was using. Pog and Fer didn't even know the tune and yet their fingers lifted and lowered covering the holes on their whistles as their breath released the notes. Grochin had never really mastered the accordion but here he was playing beautifully,

"If only it was as easy as this all the time," he mumbled.

Slowly the music began to fill the space between the floor and the ceiling. The musicians and listeners felt it surround them, move them and warm their hearts. On with the music and rhythm of her song,

> "You're welcome here dear friend, with your passion and your play
> We need you to raise the spirit of the wounded on this day

Let your strength invade his heart that he may stand again
And face the foe that injured him, to give them back such pain . . ."

She returned to the words she began with, 'Music of the streams . . ."
gesturing for help. Those without an instrument sang with her; her song
now filling their heads and gaining in volume. As they sang they felt
bonded in a way only music and singing can unite. Up went their voices
to another level and in behind, the musicians and the music. She smiled
and stood up urging everyone to continue but a little lower just so she
could hear herself. The voices now provided a steady chant which she
used as a base for her own lines. She then began to step around Greagle
and dance,

"Let not our friend and warrior, quietly slip away
Replenish him with your will that we might have our say
Let his body dance again to your rhythms true
That we can call on you forever as all musicians do . . ."

Greagle's left eye opened very slowly and as quickly flickered shut. It
was enough to give the Banshee encouragement. The power of her music
was not as often used as she would like but now there was a sign that it was
working. She raked her hands through her long hair. Her deep ruby eyes
now afire in her head, back she went to the 'Music of the Streams . . .' but
no need this time to ask for help. Up came the volume and voices again.
The entire hall was alive with waves of sound. The energy from the voices
and instruments was now bouncing off the walls. The flames on the torches
seemed to be flickering in time and once more the Banshee began,

"Take the tiredness from his eyes, that he might see us all
Take the deafness from his ears that he might hear us call

Make his ailments turn away and ply their trade elsewhere
And let him lead the heartfelt cry that his enemies should beware."

Her steps were now faster and faster around Greagle. The crowd of fairies sang and played with all they had and watched for more signs of recovery. As the chorus began again Greagle opened his other eye and kept it open. Then the first opened again. He moved his head from side to side to the delight of the singers and the Banshee. He wasn't finished yet though and he raised his hand to his brow. His hair carried hints of winter white about it but he didn't appear old at all. In fact in another moment he sat straight upright, to a loud cheer. Then he bent his legs at the knee and pulled them into him and stretched again. As quick as you like he was up on his feet, the music as loud as was ever heard in Fween Talav. He had a grin on his face like a child who had just found a bowl full of toffee and the next thing you knew he was dancing. Dancing alongside the Banshee! The two of them bouncing about like a couple of youngsters. Grochin's fingers were dancing merrily on his accordion too and he even had time to notice the dancers,

Well I've seen it all now, he thought.

Head down again and away with the music he went.

The pair of them then slowed down and as they did the Banshee conducted her musicians to do the same. The music began to dim and soften but the music magic had worked. As they finished off together each fairy felt they could walk through a stone wall without any problem. Greagle looked like he had been hit by a lightning bolt.

"Well, well," he grinned. "Thank you again, Sheana. I think that instead of improving its better you're getting at the magic."

She smiled back at him, catching her breath. Greagle had more to say,

"C'mon, it's time we took back Nut Hollow."

As they smiled and hugged each other there was a sudden whoosh and a soft thud behind them. They turned quickly, ready with whistles and various other instruments to attack the invader. As it was, a rather bedraggled Druhin pushed the moss and various leaves that cushioned his landing off his shoulders and hair.

"Druhin my boy," exclaimed Greagle. "You made it! Come tell us what news, what news?"

Fer's heart missed a beat and she couldn't help but smile widely at seeing Druhin again.

48
Ogham

"Can you hear that?" asked Rant.

"Hear what?" answered a distracted Neroh.

"Listen. It sounds like . . . well . . . singing!" replied the rat, not liking this one bit.

Neroh put down the blade he was sharpening and listened. There just above the sound of the river, he could hear it too. The faint and distant sound of a hundred voices. It was as if the very river itself had begun to sing.

"What divilment is this?" demanded Rant, now quite concerned.

The thought of the river coming to life filled him with dread.

"Hmmm," answered Neroh.

He knew exactly what it was. Some one was getting a song of healing.

Would that I were on better terms with the Banshee, he thought.

He could've been doing with a song himself, although the Line of Remnants did almost as good a job.

"It would appear the Banshee has been busy. One of those fairies is getting a song, and not just any fairy gets a song. There's a good chance its one of the elders. Tell me did you hear of any injuries to the fairies? Nefairious would've surely noticed. Did he say anything?"

"Not anything obvious anyway," replied Rant. "But I do remember seeing a bit of the fight between Préak and a dangerous looking wee buck. It was pretty rough and I think they carried him away in the end."

Yes, only one of them would dare take on the old crow . . . Greagle.

"I'd be surprised if the song wasn't for Greagle. Blalim is dead," he mumbled. "If he now has the song strength about him he'll be even harder to stop this time. Get two of your men immediately. Put them here as my personal guard."

The thought of Greagle coming for him was not a happy one.

For too long have I waited to come back to the Hollow. Too long in that thorny cell, too long for any fairy to stop me.

"Rant," he called, drawing himself up, "come with me."

Rant was happy to be in league with him. The great rat snapped out orders to the other rats to 'keep an eye out' and 'make weapons' and that sort of thing. If he was to be number two he wanted them all to know it. The pair of them set out from the Learning Tree.

"Quickly, get down," urged Neroh in a rough whisper.

They both crouched down behind the wide leaf of a docken plant. Nefairious approached and Neroh did not want him to see them. Nefairious walked deliberately, watching his step and looking behind him every few feet. Such were his preoccupations he did not notice the slight bulge in the leaves as he passed. He reached the door of Graneff's house,

"Father. Father. Rant," he shouted and on getting no reply walked inside.

"Quickly, follow me," said Neroh.

He led the rat along the water's edge up past the front doors of the fairy houses. They were very close to the river and could have reached over and dipped in their toes if they'd wanted to. Rant was struggling to keep up. Neroh had flicked his wings a couple of times and found they responded well. One or two more flicks and he jumped and landed a little further away. Further each time until he found himself flying just above the damp ground.

That feels good.

Rant's breathing was getting deeper and deeper and his face was now quite red. He was out of shape and no mistake.

"Where are we going anyway?" he gasped.

"Not far. Not far at all," replied Neroh, flying a bit higher and faster.

Each wing beat felt like a gust of wind behind him. He felt the electric tickle of the Draykt build in his finger tips. He had almost fully recovered and he knew it. He also knew what age takes away cannot be reclaimed. They had covered perhaps fifty feet and suddenly Neroh landed. Rant bounded up a moment later, looking quite ill. They stood at a dry stone wall that was the friendly border between two gardens. The rat was quite capable of wrecking it of course but a look from Neroh told him that was not required.

"I can safely say that life has led me on a merry peregrination," began Neroh softly. "Who'd have thought I'd be scurrying about with a rat in my own Hollow eh?"

"Er . . . who indeed?" Rant muttered indignantly, once again the recipient of a less than complimentary remark.

"Well certainly not me but here we are nonetheless."

As he spoke he bent down at the base of the wall and began to hack away at a clump of nettle stalks with his knife. When he had cut them away he began to loosen a couple of stones just about half way down the wall. He pushed and shoved and small pieces of moss that had been asleep for many years fell silently to the grass.

"Never . . . know," he puffed and pushed at the stones, ". . . where the . . . wind will blow you?"

Rant agreed with a look that said 'Aye hard to know at all'.

"Ah!" said Neroh. "There you are."

He removed two perfectly round stones about the size of a rowanberry. The rest of the moss was brushed off to reveal two solid spheres. His fingers sparked blue in excitement.

"What have you got there?" asked Rant, now intrigued.

"What indeed? Would you like to see?"

Again a look but more eager this time.

Neroh opened his hands to reveal the stones, one in each. They were the equivalent size of a human holding an orange. The moonlight showed them deep and dark blue for the most part with veins of green and red running through them. Each contained a very specific engraving which looked like a capital letter 'L' in human writing. This was joined at the bottom to another upside down capital 'L' by a little line one third the length of the long side of the 'L'. It signified the Rowan Ogham stone. These stones were common all over many years ago and are believed to be the script used by the Léargas. Each symbol took its power from the tree it was named after. Sadly they are scattered now and only a very select few know where to get one.

"These are Ogham stones and more specifically Rowan Ogham stones given to me . . . well taken by me truth be told, from a well meaning old fairy long before your time. It was sad he died so suddenly. Bit of a mystery really, no one knew why . . ."

His deliberate pause told Rant exactly who had killed the old fairy.

"Few can use these stones now but fortunately I am one such."

He placed the stones carefully into the pockets on either side of his coat.

"Now back to the house quickly before Nefairious comes looking for us."

"But what do they do?" asked Rant, his curiosity now afire.

"Well, they are protection from enchantment. Should the Banshee try anything she'll find me a difficult subject. If he asks we were checking security arrangements with the crows."

He chuckled coldly. They returned quickly and were just back at the door to see Nefairious coming out.

"Where were you? Didn't you hear me call?"

"We were up with Grod, he wanted some advice," answered Rant again fairly out of breath.

"From *you*?"

"He came to keep an eye on me son, just in case. Oh I need a seat . . . I feel dizzy. I shouldn't have gone."

Oh very good, thought Rant. *Clever old dog, not a thing wrong with him.*

Nefairious went to his side quickly and helped him inside. His natural instincts told him to help his ailing father. He sat him down on the couch and cushions once more. Rant flicked his tail from side to side and waited at the front door.

"Father, if they come and you're in this state you'll have no chance. We should arrange passage to safer place until the battle is over."

"Rubbish boy," snapped Neroh, forgetting himself briefly. "Rant has provided me with two bodyguards. They'll be here shortly. I had a light head for a moment. I'll be fine."

He pushed on quickly.

"Are the defences ready?"

"They are," answered Nefairious.

"Good, let us wait on our guests."

"Yes, father, let them come."

49

A Split in the Camp

Our efforts in and out of the Everlit Turf hole had taken a little longer than planned. The injury to Tridge was more severe than we had hoped. In spite of his protestations to the contrary we had to stop to heal him. Thankfully there was an abundance of docken plants, the leaves of which would do the job.

"Look I'm telling you I'll be ok, now c'mon," said Tridge.

Typically he was getting on with it but it was obvious that he needed a little help.

"We will soon enough but you're no good to us with only one leg," I said.

"Foot," he quipped. "There's nothing wrong with my leg."

"You know what I mean."

"There's what we need," said Laijir.

A few feet from where we stood there was a healthy collection of docken plants. Their wide and slightly wrinkled red veined leaves sat loosely on the grass. Laijir and I removed our knives and quickly cut one off. We cut it into manageable strips and piled it up. Then using two flat stones we crushed the leaf and collected the juice in a buttercup. Very handy plants these dockens. We use them for stings and itches and burns of course. Tridge sat on the damp grass, gliding his shoeless toes along it to keep them cool.

"Foot up," I said to him.

"Oh do I have to?"

He raised his foot and I held it still while Laijir applied the juice. I had to hold tight too because as you might know, anything rubbed on the soles of your feet is very tickly. This big fellow surely had the most ticklish feet in Ireland such were his wrigglings.

"Ah would you stop," he said, half laughing and half wincing.

We got as much on as we could. It was like wrestling a snake and a good strong snake at that.

"Goodness man, we're trying to help, would you sit at peace," snapped Laijir.

Before long though it was done and immediately the effects could be seen. The red burned skin began to return to its natural healthy pink. We headed back down the mountain and were happy to see the children all sleeping soundly as Ionta kept an eye out.

"Any bother?" I asked her.

"Not a sound. I've never heard the countryside so quiet."

"We may be thankful for small mercies," said Laijir.

Ionta noticed Tridge limp slightly and he quickly informed her what had happened.

We whispered to each other so as to prolong the children's sleep.

"Ok," I began, "we have the lines of the spell and we have the embers. Rachary said that we had to get to Knock Layde and the Stone of Pity."

"He did indeed," said Laijir, after a silence. "I suggest that you and I go, Graneff."

"Now hang on," began an indignant Tridge, "just because I hurt my foot a bit you don't think you're going without me."

"I'm saying exactly that, Tridge. Who knows what devil we may encounter up there. I'd be surprised if Nefairious didn't leave something nasty as a guard dog. You, dear friend have had a lucky escape and are injured. Not badly by your terms but bad enough to slow you down and make you vulnerable. I do not want to lose you if we can avoid it and by you staying here we can avoid it."

Tridge was bubbling with anger. He would never admit to being anything less than fully fighting fit but we, and he knew different.

"I'm sorry Tridge," I added, "but you have other duties now and they're asleep around you."

"What? Me? A . . . a babysitter? Of all the nonsense in the world."

"Hey big fellow," said Ionta, "we can do this together. I'll be glad of the company."

Laijir was right, we had to get to Knock Layde without delay. We gave Tridge a minute. Such silences can often make the most persuasive arguments. Occasionally words get in the way. There was a little wind and it blew the grass to one side. As it swayed back Tridge sighed deeply,

"Ah this is a proper set up. Curses on those embers. But by all the bee stings you are right. We have to get to Two Hour Wood with these youngsters. I'm sure Clumser would never speak to me again if he knew . . . and besides Ionta can't carry them all."

Ionta walked over and sat down beside him. There had been a time when they were said to be more than friends but nothing had come of it.

"You are a good man Tridge and all your strength will be needed one way or another before long. I am happier that I don't have to take them alone."

She smiled warmly at him. He wasn't just ready for smiling yet but looked at her and enough was said.

"Oh if ever Greagle hears that I was babysitting he'll never let me hear the end of it, and me with only one boot," he moaned, removing the other one.

"Hopefully we can tell him the full story before long," said Ionta.

I gave a few quick beats of my wings and tightened my sword and knives about me. Laijir did the same.

"Wait for us at Two Hour Wood. With any luck Síoda and Saroist will be there. We'll be back as soon as we can. By the way, you can babysit this too," I said and handed him the jar with the glowing embers inside.

"You've earned these."

We took off together and hoped no harm would befall them. I wondered should I have said goodbye to the children but I knew they were in the best of care. We left them behind in the darkness.

*   *   *

The sound of the discussion had roused Dara from her sleep. She crawled over and nudged Katie gently.

"Hey Katie, wake up."

"No . . . its not a school day. I can sleep in . . ." came her slightly slumbered response.

"No its not a school day but c'mon," said Dara again and gave her a push.

Katie opened her eyes and realised where she was.

"Oh I thought I was at home," she said a little sadly.

"I dreamt about seals and swans," came Clumsill's voice suddenly. "Weird too as the seals had wings."

Clumsill's images made Katie smile and she felt better. They woke up slowly and had a stretch.

"Ok you three," said Ionta, "time to go."

"Go where?" asked Dara.

"We have to get to Two Hour Wood. It's our best hope for now. Laijir and Graneff have gone up to Knock Layde and will meet us later. Graneff said to give you all a big hug when you woke up." She proceeded to get them all together and hug them.

"Aren't you going to hug us too?" Katie asked Tridge mischievously.

"You never know young lady, I just might and then where would you be?" he replied and it was as near to a joke as Tridge could manage.

He was not the most gifted around children and felt a little uncomfortable but whatever it was about the last while he was certainly warming to his new charges, all be it slowly. He walked over to them and ruffled each of their heads.

"Right Dara, you're the biggest but as big as you are I'm sure Ionta can carry you," he began and Ionta smiled in agreement.

"You other two are about the same size and will come with me, one at the front and one at the back."

Katie and Clumsill shared a little look. They had never been carried in this way before. Could Tridge manage the two of them?

"Can I be at the back?" asked Katie.

"Yes, and I'll go to the front," said Clumsill.

"That was easy enough," sighed a relieved Tridge, who wasn't in the mood for potential bickering as to who should go where.

"Have we got everything?" asked Ionta.

"Yes . . . but I'll have to leave the boot, can't just wear one boot."

He quickly flew down and lodged the boot into the wall that surrounded the field.

It'll do no harm there, he thought.

They each had a look around to make sure they left the mountain as they found it and quickly satisfied this was the case, they nodded.

"What's our path, Tridge? You know these parts better than I," asked Ionta.

As she asked Dara jumped up onto her back and held on tight.

"If I remember rightly we head down through Altifirnan Glen to the White Rock at Killuca Bridge. From there we follow the river which flows through the wood and with any luck we should find old fish face there with Síoda."

Clumsill and Katie climbed up onto him. Katie put her hands round his neck while Tridge lifted Clumsill up in his arms.

"Now you two, whatever happens don't let go," he said seriously.

Katie winked over at Dara, whom she could just about make out in the gloom, while Clumsill gulped at the thought of it all. After a couple of wing beats he was up quickly followed by Ionta and Dara. The human girls were now at a distinct disadvantage in that they could see very little now below or above or anywhere else.

This is like Blind Man's Bluff, thought Katie, as the wind rushed by her ears.

She could feel Clumsill's arms on top of hers. He was just busy holding on and hoping this would all end quite soon.

The two flyers stayed as low to the ground as long as they could. It would take approximately an hour as far as Tridge could remember. Below them the countryside seemed to be holding it's breath such was the silence. The night vision of the fairies yielded up no movement below or above them apart from the gentle swaying of grass and tree tops. On and on they flew gaining speed and rushing over the speckled fields below.

After a while Tridge began to feel the pinch of carrying two passengers and they grew heavy on him.

"Hi, Ionta." he called. "I'm going to take a break, just five minutes or so. These two are a little heavier than I thought. Too much toffee perhaps?"

He flew down toward the ground again and as gracefully as you like landed on a mossy stone that lay close to one of the many hedges of Altifirnan Glen.

"Phew," he said, as his passengers climbed down.

"How are we getting on would you say?" asked Ionta.

She had never been up this far from Nut Hollow before and wanted to get her bearings.

"Pretty well," answered Tridge. "Another ten minutes or so should get us to the White Rock. Once there we can follow the stream down. Is everyone alright?"

Apart from a little cramp, there were no complaints from the children. They were all just tripping over the other end of tiredness in spite of their brief rest at the Turf Mountain.

"Here, take some of this," said Ionta, digging her hand into her pocket.

From it she withdrew more of the toffee that had given them such a boost earlier.

"Now not too much you two," she smiled at Katie and Clumsill, "don't want to give your old pilot a heart attack, do we?"

"Oh very funny," sniffed Tridge, who was a tad sensitive about his fitness.

Katie, Dara and Clumsill got a hold of a good lump of toffee each and began to chew. In a moment or two they felt awake again and ready.

"Ok, let's go then," said Katie eagerly.

"Thanks a bunch," replied Tridge looking at Ionta.

"Here, this works on adults too," she smiled.

He broke off a square and ate it quickly. Soon enough they remounted and were flying again. The grasses, plants and bushes passed below them, the trees watched them go by in silence. In the blackness a hazy whiteness began to appear. It was bright enough even for human eyes to notice.

"Hey, look," said Dara. "What's that?"

"That my dear is the Carraig Bán, we are nearly there," answered Ionta and pushed on with her wings.

Tridge speeded up along side and pointed down as if to say 'we'll land right on it'. He received a nod and in no time they were on the White Rock itself.

*   *   *

Laijir and I flew upwards over the low fields that skirted the base of Knock Layde. The land rose quickly after that and we found the air getting colder as we ascended.

"You ever been to the Stone of Pity before?" I asked.

"Never. Never thought I would be either."

"No nor me."

We flew onwards and upwards until the land began to flatten out again. Knock Layde had long cast its imposing shadow over these lands. Magnificent and silent it was visible from as far away as any fairy could fly in a week. We gazed on it like an old friend whom we knew without visiting. It was always there, always in our minds surrounding us in the stories and legends of our growing up.

"I heard my Da talk about this place once or twice and on each occasion he didn't know I was listening," I said.

"Yes, I know what you mean. It's not the sort of place you would just . . . visit."

"I have heard it's one of the Places of Sadness, a lamenting ground if you like. One of the few places we shared with the humans, at least until it all went awkward between us. Buried here you'll find kings, queens, princes and princesses of all types; human, fairy you name it. There are names carved on the stones there that form the circle."

We were fast approaching the circle Laijir referred to. I saw them there, fifty hexagonal stones of varying sizes all laid out to form a circle at the bottom of the mound. The mound itself sloped upwards to maybe six or eight good wing beats or 'feet' as humans would call such a distance. We landed on one such stone and noticed that the engravings were now almost completely worn away, never again to reveal who lay beneath them.

How long they must have been here? I thought.

We settled ourselves for a moment and our gaze was quickly drawn upward. The Stone of Pity itself sat quietly on top of the mound. It was a perfect cube only for a general softening of the edges thanks to wind and weather and what not. Each of its exposed sides were now smooth. No engravings had been left.

"I'm not altogether comfortable about chipping into that stone," said Laijir. "I mean it hasn't been touched by anyone since the day it was laid, which must be a thousand years ago."

"No, nor me," I replied honestly.

This went against all that we held dear. To damage something as old and as important as this felt completely wrong.

"Graneff," began Laijir after a moment, "I don't have to tell you what's at stake here and if this was a normal visit we would not go near it. However, that stone or parts of it at least are vital to help us reclaim the Hollow. That being the case we have to do the right thing, even if it's the wrong thing."

I let his words settle. He had only said what I would've said myself.

"Aye, I know Laijir. C'mon."

We flew up and landed beside the stone. It towered above us, the keeper of memories that it was.

"We'll strike it together." I said. "If there's any price to be paid for this at least we'll both pay it."

From our belts we both took off our hammers. Not hammers as humans would know them, great heavy clunking things, no, these were blackthorn hammers. All male fairies of a certain age carry one. Indeed the design can be seen on the shillelagh. I've heard humans have made them on a grander scale and generally for bashing each other over the head. These blackthorn hammers can crack anything.

"After three," I said. "One, two, THREE!"

We brought them down together along the upright edge of the stone. The vibrations of the blow shot back up through our arms and forced us to drop the hammers. They did not fall alone. A chunk of the great stone fell down with them and lay on the grass. I quickly chipped off the smaller pieces that were loosened with the blow, leaving the wound as neat as possible. If we got the chance we would return with Ionta and repair it as best we could. We bent down quickly and pocketed the pieces, two for me and two for Laijir.

I was half expecting the tenants under the stones to rise up in protest but no, no complaints were heard. The wind whisked around amongst the rushes and one clump in particular struck me as odd. The rushes in it did not yield to the breeze. It sat not far from where we stood, perhaps one hundred good wing beats. I had made my mind up to get away off the mountain top as quickly as possible but that clump had aroused my curiosity.

"Follow me." I said quickly and took off.

"What? Where? Of all the . . . ? Where are we going now?" asked Laijir. "We must get back!"

"In a minute."

In no time we were there and this was no ordinary rasp of rushes.

"Someone lived here," I said slowly, noticing the rough stone shell of a house.

"Yes and I think we know who," replied Laijir, his tone uneasy and telling me to hurry.

"We should go in. He may have left something here we could use against him," I said, surprised by my own curiosity.

"Sure look at it, it's a wreck! Any wonder he wanted to get back to the Hollow."

"Two minutes and we're done."

"Or done for."

We both withdrew our knives and approached the door. Any creature that was left to guard it would surely make its move now. We stood ready but no sound. The door itself was fashioned from rushes with bits of twig to strengthen it. It sat lazily on its hinges and opened without argument.

"Phew! What is that smell?" gasped Laijir.

I had no idea except that it was foul. I then noticed the collection of bones scattered about and several half eaten rabbits and moles.

In the name of Odhran, I thought. *What kind of creature has Nefairious become?*

We walked around slowly and carefully but such was the state of the house and its appalling furniture that we were quickly finished with our investigation.

"Right, time's up," said Laijir. "I'm going now."

"OK. OK, you're right, there's noth . . ."

There *was* something. Just behind the front door. I walked over as quickly as I could and bent down. Beneath a smooth stone I could see part of a small chain. I lifted the stone to reveal the rest of the chain, which seemed to be made of silver. On it was attached a small silver medal with the letter 'V' carved neatly into the centre.

"What is it?" asked Laijir turning to me.

"Here look," I began, offering it to him to see. "It's a silver necklace. Homemade by the looks of it, though well made at that."

"Do you reckon *he* made it? Is that a 'V' on there?" asked Laijir peering closely at the medal. "Why a 'V'?"

"I'm sure it is. V . . . V . . . Vifell! That's it, his mother!" I exclaimed.

"Well well, perhaps old Nefairious has a heart after all," said Laijir, not too sure if this was a good development or not. "Anyway, time we weren't here."

I quickly put the chain into my inner coat pocket, hoping it would be of some use. Then we were off, heading for Two Hour Wood as fast as our wings could carry us.

50
Many Happy Returns

Suerna would not be denied. She trampled through the throng of well wishers and almost knocked down her son on seeing him. She made several attempts at words in between the hugs but all that could be deciphered was a short sequence of 'Eeeks' and 'Ooohs.' She kissed him, petted him and stroked his hair until the poor lad looked like he'd been caught in a whirlwind. With care and a little embarrassment he gently untangled himself from the delirious, teary old fairy that loved him so much. He stood to face us, smiling.

"You're back!" gasped Suerna suddenly.

"You're safe and you're not a bit dead!" she wheezed out as if it was her last breath.

Aldarn came up to join in the reunion. His limp and bloody complexion was forgotten. He had sustained injuries in the rush down to Fween Talav but they were suddenly of little concern now that his son had returned. Greagle gave them a moment then asked again,

"Well my lad, what news?"

Knowing he had a further part to play his parents stepped back and gave him air to speak. They stood shoulder to shoulder behind him.

"I bring news from Strelle himself."

The hall fell silent, only the soft murmuring of the flames round the walls could be heard.

"The bats are with us—"

Wonders will never cease, thought Grochin.

"—Strelle has his men ready and waiting on our signal. They have seen the crow mesh and have determined to drive them mad in the darkness. We will hopefully reap much benefit from this on our counter attack."

Druhin stopped for a breath, then briefly explained how the mesh sat net like all around Nut Hollow. He felt a little odd too for it's a rare enough thing for a youngster to have his heroes hang on his every word.

"I have heard no word from Graneff and the others, but it seems as if Nefairious is concentrating all his efforts in and about the Hollow. Neroh has been released."

On hearing this the hall sighed as one and there was a real sense of dread. Neroh's actions had cut deep scars in their memories. With his information spent, Druhin paused and Greagle, now back at himself, stepped in to fill the gap.

"Well done Druhin, well done indeed," he said shaking his hand.

He turned to face the crowd.

"Friends, we have a chance, slim though it may be, to reclaim what was wrongfully taken from us."

The Banshee moved beside him.

"It will not be easy but we have help now we did not have before. If we can use all that we have to our best abilities we will give those villains a fight they will not forget."

There was anticipation in the air and in the crowd listening. Their spirits were down after their exile but here was hope. Those that were injured suddenly felt as if they could fare out again. The stock pile of weapons had been finished and a formidable bundle of tooth tipped daggers, swords and spears lay ready. Then a voice from the back of the crowd, it was Grochin.

"Greagle you've known me a long time and you know I don't mince my words."

"Aye, true enough."

"Well, it has been a while since I fired an arrow from a bow or threw a spear. I suppose that says more for the peaceful times I've enjoyed. I'm keen to renew those old skills this day but how do we, and I mean all of us, get out of Fween Talav? Sure we got in by the skin our teeth and those blaggards will be guarding the doors. 'Tis one thing to know they can't get in but quite another to know we can't get out."

Frenel came up behind him and squeezed his hand. She had no desire to see her favourite sparring partner die today but his death and most likely her own were a real possibility.

"How could I ever take on one of those crows or weasels?" she asked worriedly.

"I'm as close to three hundred as I'll ever be and I just wouldn't be up to it. I'm sorry Greagle but I doubt I'd only be holding you back."

She finished with her head down and Greagle noticed several other elder fairies nod and tut and wonder.

"Rubbish woman," said Greagle straight back at her and with such gusto old Grochin wished he had said it like that to her more often.

"Absolute dung . . . beetles! You two are two of our oldest and most respected residents and I agree that perhaps you are not as strong as you were but do not look to your weaknesses. Do not look to what you can not do. Look at those wings on your back. You have all the strength you need there. C'mon, any of you who can flap a wing at all do it now and you *will* remember," he urged.

He was aware that pessimism and despair can spread like wildfire and was determined it would not spread here. Slowly the elders began to move their wings and many now heard Blalim's words in their minds.

'You have to look after the wings, you never now the minute you would need them'.

Very few if any had heeded him and now most flapped very stiffly and awkwardly. Then an 'Odhran preserve us' and a 'Fry me freckles' and a 'Jeepers'. The Draykt was returning to them, down from their rusty wings to their finger tips.

"I feel it! I feel it!" yelled Frenel, who looked at Grochin.

"Well you old goat, anything?"

"Now you ask fish face I'm getting tinglings in places I haven't had tinglings in for years," he quipped back, smiling.

Frenel's face broke into a cheeky grin and only for the youngsters within earshot she would've answered him with a quip of her own. As it was the mood had lifted again and the blue crackles of the Draykt could be seen and heard all over the hall. Greagle called order but this time it was the Banshee who spoke.

"My dear friends, young and younger, strong and stronger I am with you in this fight. You have all the power literally at your fingertips but let there be no mistake, this is no easy task. Neroh and Nefairious are both strong but will not be expecting such spirit and belief. Nor will their minions know what has hit them when you release such vintage Draykt upon them. But we must wait, timing now is the key. Please be patient for we must plan our next step with great care."

Pog and Fer desperately wished they too could summon the Draykt but they were still too young. However, they had realised that everyone could and would have to help and so were ready for whatever the plan would demand of them. Greagle, Gráinne, Druhin, Aldarn and the Banshee all walked to the great table. Pog and Fer walked round behind their mother and stood behind her as she sat down. They were soon joined by the other fairy children whom they had frightened earlier. Everyone was ready to help in whatever way they could. The Banshee stood up.

"There are three empty chairs. Who will fill them?"

"Get in there beetle bum," urged Frenel with a smile and for once Grochin yielded to her wishes without protest.

He sat down beside Gráinne. From someway back in the crowd someone was pushing forward. A small and delicate fairy made her way to the front.

"I will join you if I may," she said almost in a whisper.

There was silence in the hall and sorrow in her voice.

"My husband Shesk has not returned from battle and I am lost without him but I know he would have me join you."

No one said a word. Lirna had shown amazing courage in her hour of grief. The Banshee walked over to her and hugged her warmly. One seat left.

"I am aware that the remaining seat belonged to my brother and your friend, Blalim. I am against admitting it, but it seems he has fallen. Therefore . . ."

That last word had just left Greagle's tongue when all eyes turned quickly to the exit of the sycamore slide and a voice,

"Oh I just wouldn't be too sure about that brother."

It was a battered, bruised and blood covered Blalim, but Blalim nonetheless.

51

Blalim's Tale

"Blalim! But how? I . . . I was sure I saw the end of you," stammered Greagle.

The others rushed to him. The Banshee was sure another song of healing would be required.

"Ah friends, I'm ok. I don't feel near as bad as I look," he said and walked strongly between the caring hands to his seat.

The hall was silent once again waiting in disbelief for news of his return. Now Blalim had an eye for drama you might say and was a fine storyteller, well able to hold his audience enthralled. He didn't say a word and waited until the place was about to burst with curiosity.

"Well," he began as eager eyes stared at him, "you'll be wondering what happened no doubt?"

Greagle shot his brother a quick glance to say 'alright get on with it'. Blalim smiled and took the hint. Greagle was relieved that he hadn't lost his sense of occasion and humour in spite of all.

"Ok, ok," he began as Suerna brought him over a drink of Rowanberry juice which he quickly gulped down.

"Now, ah yes, if you remember Greagle, I had a fair good grip on the legs of those two crows."

"I do."

"Well, I had just begun to spin them to crack their heads on one of the nut trees. Indeed I did get one of their heads open but the other one was a bit stronger than I gave him credit for. On seeing his comrade's demise he must've got the life scared out of him for he pulled himself up through the canopy. I've never seen a crow do it before and it was all I could do to hang on to the cur. Up through the branches he went taking leaves and twigs and all sorts with him until we were suddenly above the battle with only ourselves to worry about. He soon regained his wits and I found that my belt had become entangled around his left foot. He quickly realised this and must have thought to take me back to dangle me up for one of his kin to peck me to death. Well says I to meself 'no thanks' and I persuaded him to land with this."

He tapped the handle of his knife.

"Most of the blood you see on me is not mine but his I'm happy to say."

"So what's with the bruises?" asked Gráinne.

"In my eagerness to free myself of the crow I didn't think of the consequences of my action. I found myself plummeting earthward with this black feathered dead weight I could not shake off. If he didn't hit one branch he hit them all I'd say on the way down, hence the black and blue version you see of me."

He paused for breath and a mouthful of mole milk cheese, his favourite. After a couple of healthy chomps he continued,

"Ummm, now where was I? Aye, well I suppose luck was on my side after that for my landing went unnoticed in the melee, just another dead crow. However I had landed on the wrong side of Spindler's great web, a fair bit on the wrong side. If I were to move then I would've been overcome by any number of brigands so I tucked myself under his wing, lay in wait and watched. I was heartily relieved to see you make to the Buzzard's claw Greagle, good to know that your memory is still intact at least."

Greagle gave him a quick smile.

"I knew then we had lost many friends and the Hollow too for that matter. As darkness fell their soldiers celebrated but there were still enough eyes looking out to remain careful. I made my way through the grass to keep out of sight. It was a hard road and one I would not choose again. It seemed Nefairious had turned everything against us even the very grass itself. It was like green quicksand and I was plagued by flies trying to flatten me and worms trying to squeeze me. My knife was never busier and the blade will no doubt need resharpened but I'm glad I had it.

As night came this very evening I wasn't too far away when I saw more commotion at the Buzzard's claw. I'm sure it was Strelle himself, though it's a while since I saw him. I couldn't imagine how he knew about the entrance and feared he had teamed up with Nefairious. But it happened that the tree opened and he remained outside. I wondered what on earth was going on then it struck me and I thought of you and your amulet Greagle. So I awaited my opportunity and came in that way myself, down the great passage and here I am, home and happy for it."

He finished and pushed himself back in his chair raising the two front legs off the floor. It was all the crowd of listeners could do not to applaud. The Banshee decided she would say a word,

"How your parents ever put up with you two I'll never know," she began gazing firstly at Blalim and then at Greagle, "but no doubt they did some job. Luck would seem to have smiled on us and no mistake. We have a full table and surely a full belly will help."

She closed her eyes and said a few words in the old language which had earlier delighted and frustrated those at the Towers of Loughareema.

"Go mbeidh bia againn uilig!"
(Guh mayee beea uging illig!")

In a moment the table was full of food. There was a fine selection to rival that of Clumsill's at the Ceremony, indeed Clumsill on witnessing the spell wished he could've have done it so easily. The thought of the cow pat still bothered him.

"Plans are better made when the table's laid," she said smiling and inviting all to come and pick whatever caught their eye.

The crowd lined up and walked slowly along using lady bird shell plates complete with red and black patterns picking out Rowan berries, mole steaks, daisy pie for the vegetarians, fruig juice, nettle salad for those who liked hot food to name but a few of the delicacies. There was a myriad of colours and tastes which were heartily enjoyed. Grochin was particularly happy to see such a spread, his rations were just about done and he did not relish the thought of another night nibbling on hard bread.

As they ate their spirits lifted and their tummies filled but there was work still to be done. The Banshee gave Greagle a look and he knew what she meant by it.

"My friends, I trust you are feeling better for that. I would ask you all to finish off and join us round this table. Our plans will need as many heads as possible and anyone with an idea that might help will certainly be given an audience."

The crowd set down their plates and drained their glasses. Each of them nudged in tight beside the other forming a circle around the eight who took their seats once again.

52

Remembering and Forgetting

Neroh, Nefairious, Rant and Welset sat in awkward silence in Graneff's kitchen. As far as was possible the Hollow was ready to repel visitors but none of them seemed particularly pleased about it.

"Those that escaped are now in Fween Talav," said Neroh quietly.

The others pricked up their ears to listen.

"It would appear on the surface we have them cornered," smiled Rant. Welset nodded in agreement.

This could be easier than they are making out, thought the weasel.

"Yes on the surface," said Neroh, "but nothing can be taken for granted. Not where Greagle is concerned. No doubt he will have them ready to fight."

"But they're mostly older fairies anyway aren't they?" said Rant again.

A picture of Sherene flashed into Nefairious's mind and he suddenly had the taste of toffee on his tongue.

Get out of my head woman, he thought and fidgeted uncomfortably for a moment on his chair.

"Age is nothing!" he snapped, out loud this time. "Would you say my father is an easy adversary?"

Rant looked down immediately. His thoughts had been running away with him and he needed to rein them in, for his own sake.

"No, he certainly is not that," replied the chastened rat.

"No indeed," reinforced Nefairious.

Things were not going as he thought they would. It was a curious predicament for him. He had the upper hand in that he was in a very secure Nut Hollow. He had the Knife. He had a strong army of rats and weasels and goodness knows what else at his beck and call and yet the one thing he needed to feel safe eluded him. He could not trust Neroh. He stood up and left the others in silence and went to the front door. From there all looked as he had wanted and even the river appeared to flow uneasily. "I'll be back in a while. I have to go out."

The others looked at him and said nothing. He left them there and pulled the door behind him. It was in his mind to fly straight to the Seating Stone but he walked up instead. He cut a lonely figure. There was no gathering of friends, relations and neighbours. There were no proud and excited parents this time. There was no feeling of magic or of being special. He was alone. He climbed up over the roots and through the grass, his long cloak falling and rising to the shapes of his body as he ascended. On reaching the Seating Stone he pulled himself up onto it and walked slowly to the First Flyer's spot.

Well mother, if you could see me now, he thought. He knew she would never see him, never talk to him again.

A gentle breeze skidded up through the Hollow ruffling his black hair as his cloak lapped gently at his heels.

"Do you claim first Flight?" he said to himself, looking around to make sure no one was listening.

"I do claim First Flight," he answered and began to beat his wings.

Closing his eyes he imagined a hundred shining happy faces urging him on. But there were no friends left for Nefairious. Just himself on the stone, the Learning Tree silent beside him and the river rolling relentlessly onward.

"Ach!" he said suddenly and was back in reality again.

He flew down to Graneff's door.

"First flyers be damned."

As he landed he heard the last few words of a conversation between Welset and Neroh.

"Ok, ok," said the weasel, "leave it to me."

"Yes and make sure you do," snapped Neroh.

Nefairious walked in watching their faces for clues as spoke, he wondered just what they were on about.

"Do what father?"

Neroh turned slowly to face his son; there wasn't a shred of guilt or surprise anywhere to be seen.

Perhaps he was just throwing his weight about, thought Nefairious, also not wishing to give anything away.

"To make sure he does all he can to provide us with the right outcome. I've noticed some of his weasels not exactly breaking their backs you might say."

This was not what Nefairious wanted to hear. He looked quickly at Welset who immediately looked to the ground. He had made a deal with this weasel and was hoping his loyalty would come without question. However, he was aware that in his brief absence his father could have applied an even worse threat to the Welset than he had. He would have to act quickly to clear up any confusion.

"Father, I'm satisfied with his efforts and have seen at first hand his men at work. I assure you they have done an excellent job."

"We'll see," replied Neroh coldly.

"Time to give the men a boost," said Nefairious quickly, happier that he had re-established the order of things.

"Rant and Welset, get your men up and out front. It's time we shared a little magic with you all."

"Oh and just what do you mean?" asked Rant suspiciously.

"This place is called Nut Hollow for a reason which I'm sure even you have worked out."

Rant gave him a look to say that he had, trying desperately not to give him a look that said 'I'm gonna pull your wings off and eat you.'

"The nuts that grow here will give you such a tonic the likes of which you never will have felt before. But they must be taken with caution and that will be our job."

Neroh shifted a little uneasily in his chair. He did not have good memories of these nuts.

"Fair enough. Let's hope we manage to avoid the Fairy Thorn this time."

Rant and Welset took their leave and soon could be heard barking orders at their men. This was the moment they had been waiting for. They headed outside and Rant wasn't at all sure how he should approach the weasel. He had an idea but a dangerous one at that. It had been in his mind to kill Nefairious whenever he could especially after the incident with the Knife and his tongue, which he now rubbed against the back of his teeth. He didn't know of course that Nefairious had struck a deal with Welset the outcome of which would be his own death. However, a rat is many things but utmost of these is an opportunist. His gut was telling him that an opportunity had just arisen. He didn't have long as the troops were tidying up work areas and slowly heading their direction.

"Hold an a second, Welset."

The weasel stopped and turned to face him. They stood on the slightly damp soil not far from the edge of the river.

"What is it?" snapped the weasel. "We haven't much time and I do not want to get on the wrong side of those two in there."

"Well, that's exactly it," began Rant. "I'm pretty fed up with the whole deal."

There, he had said it but he hoped in such a way he could retract it should Welset's reaction prove awkward.

Welset didn't answer for a moment and instead quickly turned to check where everyone else was. He could see his men heading toward them, perhaps now just ten seconds away. Had he held his silence that would've been the end of it. However, it would be fair to say he too had been having similar thoughts. Weasels are a ruthless breed and being ordered around by a couple of fairies, no matter how powerful they were did not sit easily with him. But he had gone this far and the end was in sight.

"Hmm," he began, "they are a scheming pair alright, mostly against each other as far as I can gather."

He hoped his answer could be construed as more of a gripe, in case this was some sort of trick by Rant, instead of potential treason.

"Well I feel that those of our sort should stick together when the battle is over and relieve them of their duties, if you know what I mean?" said the rat.

"Oh I know what you mean but they have so many other creatures in their service, do you mean to do away with them too?"

"I should think we wouldn't have to worry there. Whoever was seen to be more powerful than Nefairious and Neroh should hold their loyalty I'd say."

"And you have it all worked out I suppose?" asked Welset, now realising another deal was presenting itself, "you know, to actually do it?"

"Well now there's the thing. We rats are more getting into places types, the getting out bit isn't always our forte," he replied with a look that implied he would be needing help with the plan.

Before Welset could answer the first of the troops were presenting themselves and from behind they could hear the father and son fluttering down. It was all that Welset could do to fire a 'leave it with me look' back at Rant who quickly straightened up as Neroh walked over to him. The weasel and rat horde formed into four sharp toothed rodent platoons, about twenty in each. The platoons were not mixed. The nuts they had gathered previously were in piles at the foot of the trees from whence they came.

"Let's see how the magic is," said Neroh.

He threw off his blanket and gave a couple of flaps of his wings. Almost immediately he felt his hands and fingers tingle and the magic sparked blue around his finger tips. He increased the momentum of his wings even though they were still a little stiff. Nefairious couldn't but notice how quickly the Draykt had returned to him. Neroh closed his eyes and raised his arms. The blue sparks stretched now between both his hands. Suddenly he clicked both thumbs with his fingers beginning with the little finger right up to the index finger. As soon as he had done this a single nut appeared at the feet of each of the animals in platoon. The remainder disappeared to where no one knew, except Neroh of course.

"Might I suggest," he began, "that you all eat quickly and the more you crunch the better."

They did not have to be asked twice. There wasn't one among them who hadn't been dying to try the nuts of Nut Hollow. Never before had their kind been permitted to eat them and now here was their opportunity. Welset lowered his head and soon had the nut between his teeth.

Now, there is a peculiar and delicious sweetness that accompanies the first crunch and this is spread over the tongue as the nut disintegrates.

Hmmm wonderful, thought Welset.

He continued to munch, his short strong teeth perfect for the job. The bits now spread from his tongue to all parts of his mouth finding brief refuge in the gaps in his teeth. They didn't last long there though and in a moment or two the whole nut was en route to his tummy. It is here that the magic takes place, for as the nut dissolves it releases its secrets.

And so it was with Rant. He immediately began to feel a rush of energy run through him from head to toe. It was as if he had been plugged in to Hollow River itself. His claws felt as if they could cut through steel and his mind was alert and ready.

Wow!

He looked around quickly and could see the other animals display similar wonder. He noticed some of the younger rats and weasels pushing against each other in trials of strength and flexing their muscles.

"I trust you all enjoyed that?" asked Neroh.

Nods and grins were his answer. They were now ready for anything. Rant and Welset suddenly felt all the bother of the previous days well worth it. An endless supply of magic nuts would be prize enough to be sure. Nefairious was happier too. The troops whom he had mustered now had a taste of what they might inherit and should be easier manipulated. He meant to ram home this advantage immediately, though he was slightly troubled as to the whereabouts of the remainder of the nuts. If necessary he would 'ask' Neroh later.

"Retake your positions," yelled Nefairious suddenly.

As requested the animals dispersed back into order. The four of them were left once more. Neroh fluttered his wings and delighted in how good it felt. Fairies enjoyed the nuts to be sure but they were strong enough without them. They had power enough in the Draykt. Being surrounded by nuts all the time meant they didn't often use them for power although some of the older ones did if they were feeling a bit tired. The quartet walked back towards Graneff's house and slowly split into two pairs. Neroh and Nefairious eased ahead leaving Rant and Welset behind. Immediately Rant looked over at Welset as if to say, 'Well, what do you reckon? Should we go for it?'

He wasn't sure at all, a wrong step now and all those wonderful nuts would be lost to him. He winked back as if to say 'you're on' but his heart told him something else. His heart told him that given the opportunity he would kill the rat. Rant was contented no end that the weasel seemed happy with his plan. The nuts had also changed his mind. His heart told him that given the opportunity he would kill the weasel.

53

The White Rock

The warm white glow of the Carraig Ban was a welcome sight for the flyers. Though he would never have admitted it, Tridge was finding it hard going carrying his passengers. Of course Katie was having a fabulous time. Flying in the dark is perhaps the most exciting thing a young human can do. Dara was also enjoying the sensations of the wind and flying at such speed through the night sky. They just wished they had wings themselves.

"Ok, get ready," said Tridge rather breathlessly.

He headed downward.

Thank goodness, thought Clumsill, *my arms are aching.*

Tridge touched down. Katie and Clumsill let go from around his neck and sat down on the cool white stone. Ionta followed and in no time they were in a wee circle.

"Now then," began Tridge, "we are nearly at Two hour Wood, another twenty minutes should do it."

"Do you think they made it?" asked Ionta.

The children listened intently.

"Aye of course, I have no doubts where Síoda is concerned."

"Neither do we," said Dara, speaking for the youngsters who smiled in agreement.

"Should we wait here for the others?" asked Katie.

"Hmmm I was thinking that that might be a good idea. The White Rock is on the way to the wood if you were coming from Knock Layde. Graneff and Laijir will fly right over us all being well," answered Tridge.

Ionta smiled to herself. Here was Tridge chatting away to the children without any of his usual nonsense.

Well, there is hope for him, she thought and if the truth be known she was warming to the old fairy by the minute.

"Does anyone have anything to eat? I'm hungry," said Clumsill.

The boost from the toffee had worn off and his tummy was beginning to rumble. Katie was also getting peckish and could've been doing with a warm sausage roll with red sauce all over it, her favourite. As her parents often said 'sweets'll never fill ye.' Here for once she thought they might actually be right about something.

"Aye me too," she said.

"And me," added Dara.

A Marguerita pizza was filling her mind but sadly not her tummy.

"Hmm, warm melty cheese on my chin," she mumbled out loud.

Clumsill wondered why she said 'chin' but didn't know that she sometimes got as much food on her as in her.

"What was that?" asked Tridge. "You are no doubt going on about some weird human food."

"'Tis not a bit weird at all," replied Dara sharply. "It's delicious."

She quickly explained the ingredients to them and Katie could've eaten her own fingers as she listened to the tasty descriptions. Poor Clumsill was beside himself. He had never seen a pizza but he knew about cheese and tomatoes and the sound of all that on a piece of special round bread was driving him crazy.

"Oh I would really love some of that pista."

Dara and Katie laughed at each other.

"Close enough," they said together.

"Well children as much as I'd like to I can't conjure up an oven for your pizza or whatever you call it," said Ionta. "However, this will do the job I'm sure."

She reached into her pockets again, first the inside ones then the outside.

"Oh where did I put it? I know I put a couple in here . . . somewhere. Ah, there you are."

"What is it?" asked Katie excitedly.

Ionta opened her hand to reveal a juicy nut.

"A nut!" exclaimed Dara. "But it's a nut. Not a pizza! We've eaten a gazillion nuts from there and I don't remember any being magic. Do you Katie? I mean they're sweet and lovely and all but . . . well . . . they're just nuts."

She couldn't conceal her disappointment.

"They are also hard to open. I have to get my Granda to do it only that's no good 'cos he keeps eating them himself," added Katie.

Ionta smiled widely and looked at Clumsill. His silence hinted at a treat indeed. It would give him a boost alright but not to the same degree as it would give the girls.

"Just try them," said Ionta again, "and make sure you crunch."

She broke the nut into three segments and from the palm of her hand offered them to the children.

"Well I suppose it's better than nothing," said Dara, who was still really wishing she could have a pizza.

She swallowed her bit after a crunch or two.

"Yes I suppose," added Katie, also munching down on the nut but really wishing for a sausage roll.

Clumsill ate his without a word.

As with other creatures not too far away the nuts began to release their magic in the tummies of the girls. Both their eyes opened wide and they looked like they had just swallowed a big mouthful of fizzy juice.

"This feels great," said Dara.

"Wow!" said Katie. "My tummy is doing somersaults."

The nuts filled their arms and legs and heads and eyes and ears and toes and teeth with a great burst of energy. They were positively bouncing as they sat.

"But how come this doesn't work all the time?" asked Dara barely fit to get the words out such was her excitement.

"The nuts only release their magic on order from those who have cared for them," said Ionta.

"We have been able to tap into their power for ages. Now I must say it's a rare treat to be able to share them with humans again. Perhaps someday you may be able to fully enjoy them as you do now, we'll see."

"Who would have thought a wee nut could be so strong?" said Dara.

"That's it," added Katie, "no more for Granda!"

Tridge removed the embers from his coat and set them down on the rock. They burned the brightest orange he had ever seen. He was amazed and relieved that the glass itself was still cool to the touch.

"What do we do with those?" asked Katie.

It was the same question Tridge was asking himself at the time.

"To be quite honest young one I'm not altogether sure but I can only trust they will reveal their uses before too long."

He replaced the glass jar and stood up, listening to the silence.

"Do you hear anything?" asked Ionta.

"Hmmm," he replied, "how those two made it off Knock Layde without being eaten I'll never know but if I'm not mistaken they did and they're not too far away."

The children smiled and the thought of being all together again raised their spirits yet further. They did not have long to wait. As Tridge had predicted the wing beats of the two could be heard gently in the distance.

*   *   *

Then just like that we were back. Laijir and I landed between the visitors on the white rock.

"Well?" asked Tridge.

The children ran to meet me and hugged my waist.

"Hey, what a welcome," I gasped in delight.

Tridge had no time for hugs just then and again asked flatly, "Well?"

Laijir approached him and gestured to him to open his hand. He looked over to me and I nodded. He opened his palm into which Laijir placed the pieces of the Stone of Pity. I walked over and showed him mine.

"Well, I never. The Stone of Pity in the palm of my hand."

"Well bits of it anyway," said Katie.

He didn't scold back but smiled in relief.

"Indeed Katie," he said and examined the fragments carefully.

"It seems friends we have collected all that we need. I suppose you might say that the hard part is going to be to use them correctly."

"And I still have a drop of the Vanishing Lake in my eye," exclaimed Clumsill just so no one would forget.

"Didn't Rachary say there was another who could help?" asked Dara.

"Yes, but who or what has yet to be revealed. I think we should push on to Two Hour Wood and see if Saroist knows anything. He's been around a long time and perhaps something will trigger his memory. We also found this in Nefairious's house," I said and showed them the silver necklace with the little locket.

"You were in Nefairious's house?" gasped Clumsill. "What was it like?"

"About as nasty as I'm sure you have all imagined. It was dark and unwelcoming and there has been no joy there for long and many's the day. I'm just glad to be out of it."

"And no traps or guards?" asked Ionta.

"Not that we could see," answered Laijir, "it seems he doesn't mean to go back."

We gathered ourselves again. This time I took Katie, Laijir took Dara and Tridge took Clumsill. The darkness now was complete around us and we were in the dead hours of night. We took off together in silence. Everyone knew that even greater dangers lay ahead and we had to face them for the sake of Nut Hollow and who knows how many other places just like it. Once more the air rushed past our ears and we flew together, alone in our thoughts.

54

Skin and Stone

The conversation ebbed and flowed. Blalim and Greagle were throwing ideas around the room waiting to see how they would be received. Each of those at the table had their say as to how they might go about contacting the others. As time moved along it was becoming clear that in spite of all their great experience the fairies were finding it hard to see a way out that wouldn't lead to bloodshed. Faces lit up and dulled again as ideas were thought up, considered and rejected.

"This is a right mess," said Greagle, most frustrated of all.

He had just raised up the company's expectations only to be well and truly stumped and stuck in a jail of their own making. Silence began to cover the ground between sentences like clouds on a sunny day.

"Well, if we have to we can go back out the way we came in. Any rat or weasel that awaits will have this to deal with," said Grochin and took out his sword.

"Good man," said Frenel, very proudly indeed.

"Greagle, just say the word and I'm ready," he said, surprising many with his bravery.

Greagle sighed, not at Grochin of course but at the realisation that they may after all have to go back up through the stairway, open their trapdoors and face whatever waited there. It would be terrible and he knew it. He was about to rally them again when the Banshee spoke,

"I will go."

The other voices were silent immediately.

"I will find the others."

There was as much confusion as relief in the room.

"But how? With all respect dear lady, not even one as powerful as you could withstand so many sharp teeth and talons," said Blalim.

He was worried that his friend had volunteered for the impossible.

"Do not worry, I will not be seen by them although there will be a price for it."

"What price?" asked Greagle. "I for one will not have your blood as a cost to free us."

There was a spontaneous burst of 'No, nor mes' and 'no ways' and shaking of heads. The thought of the Banshee coming to harm for their sake just did not sit well with the fairy folk.

"My friends, my very dear friends, such times call for all solutions to be tried. Please do not worry about me. My time amongst you has been the most rewarding of my long life."

"Then what price must you pay?" asked Greagle, not happy with how the conversation was going.

"I still say we gather up the Draykt and let them have it between the eyes," added Blalim.

"Now you two," she said, looking at the brothers. "I will leave and try to find them but you need to come with me back to my room."

The hall was uneasy. She was normally so open with them that the mysterious price for her help just added to their anxiety. She walked through them and they made way for her reluctantly. They did not want her to be hurt.

"You must think of yourselves, I will be fine but your strength is all important."

She took off and landed up on her balcony again.

Blalim and Greagle followed. The hall became a sea of whispered worries and all eyes were on the brothers as they flew. As ever it was Gráinne who spoke.

"Right, let's go. We must ready ourselves."

Gráinne walked around rousing them and hoped the Banshee knew what she was doing.

"Ok my lady," said Blalim, "we've known each other a long time. Now would you mind just telling me what is going on?"

Sheana looked at him and walked to her little table with the candle on it. It glowed tall and yellow in the near darkness.

"I haven't heard of this being done for nearly one hundred years. Not since the days when we used to call on the human folk, long before they got scared of Banshees that is."

She stared into the flame and breathed deeply.

"I would have preferred to stay amongst you as I am for a little longer but maybe this is for the best," she paused for a moment.

"I have work to do."

Blalim and Greagle stood facing her across the small wooden table, a simple item indeed in the middle of all.

"I must leave through soil and rock, there is no other way. The only way I can manage this is with a song."

She cupped her hand around the little flame.

"Before you ask, not a healing song. No this is an altogether different affair. Once I have sung the words you must blow out the candle and blow hard, it does take a bit of wind, which shouldn't be too hard for you two."

She smiled and gave them a wink.

"Then your work really begins after I . . . well you'll see, ok?"

The brothers nodded but had never heard the Banshee talking like this before.

"Please don't be alarmed when it happens. It's all part of the magic.."

She stared into the candle again.

"Oh and there is one more thing."

"Thought there might be," answered Greagle.

"You must sing me back. As soon as I leave until you see me in front of you again do not stop."

They looked at her again and waited for her to say 'only joking' but she didn't say anything.

"Sure I can't sing," protested Greagle.

"Aye you're not wrong there," agreed Blalim.

"Hey what are you on about? Sure you would make a crow sound like a blackbird."

"Gentlemen," interrupted Sheana, "just know that the quality is not important. What matters is that you sing, do you understand?"

"Yes, yes," replied Greagle, "but sing what exactly?"

"Ok, now listen, it isn't hard but it is important you get it right."

She cleared her throat,

"Sail on, sail on in the lines of this song
Sail on, sail on be carried along
Sail on, sail on through the soil and stone
Sail on, sail on you are never alone
Return, return from the darkness therein
Return, return to your friends and your kin
Return, return from the way that is long
Return, return to the lines of this song."

Once she had finished she looked at the brothers,

"For the spell to work it needs at least two voices, if more join all the better but you two must keep going, ok?"

"Aye we'll get it," replied Greagle looking her straight in the eye.

"I know you will," she answered, "now let me begin."

She stared at the candle so intently that her ruby eyes consumed its yellowness. As she stared the little flame slowly became still, not flickering at all . . . it was listening. She spoke again,

> "That soil so soft would welcome me
> To pass right through its very heart
> That stone so hard would not obstruct
> A traveller on her journey's start
> That roots so strong would not ensnare
> My errand in their reaching vines
> That skin and bone would melt away
> Like mist when the warm sun shines
> Now candle light so bright and true
> Take me now in your embrace
> And guide me through the bonded earth
> And return in haste back to this place."

The Banshee looked straight into the flame and this time it did move but not as they expected. Suddenly hundreds of smaller flames flew out from the flame, which stayed alight on the black wick. They scattered like a flock of birds off a branch then settled carefully around her. It was as if she was on fire such was their brightness. The Banshee continued to stare at the little candle through it all.

"Now," was all she said.

The brothers blew hard and the candle went out with a wisp of blue smoke. Immediately the other smaller flames began to disappear one by one, slowly at first then with more speed. As they did they too yielded a puff of blue and so the Banshee began to disappear. As each flame extinguished so a piece of her went out. Flame by flame she disappeared before their very eyes. In another moment she was gone, amulet and all. What remained was the blue smoke which now began to rise slowly toward the roof and there it stopped.

"It didn't work," said Greagle.

"Wait," answered Blalim. "Look!"

The smoke began to filter into the soily ceiling, slowly at first but suddenly quicker and quicker and then it was gone.

"Well," said Greagle, "there's something you don't see everyday."

"Right enough," answered Blalim, "are you ready?"

Well I suppose they wouldn't have won any singing competitions but after a nervous and croaky start they began. The words tripped a bit on their tongues but soon they were running and the brothers sang for her life depended on it.

55

Talk of Buzzards

"I trust we shall have all done and dusted before the buzzards return?" asked Neroh.

Nefairious did not answer him directly. The buzzards had been in the back of his thoughts for some time. He was not really afraid of anything, except them. They were judge, jury and executioner and where possible tried to make sure episodes such as the one Nefairious had pulled did not happen.

This being the case they were away often keeping an eye on things around the country. Inevitably they would be back and would not take the current state of affairs at all well.

"If they see that there is some semblance of hope for the fairies they will kill us all!" added Neroh, who for the first time sounded a little anxious.

In his hurry to re-establish himself amongst his cohorts he had forgotten about the buzzards until now.

"I have tasted buzzard justice," answered Nefairious. "I have no desire to do so again."

"No, nor me. Every moment spent here waiting like this is a moment closer to their return and I do know no one will be spared. They are partial to rats and even weasels."

Rant and Welset drew in a breath. If mad fairies wasn't enough they had the extra delight of being potential dinner for the buzzards.

"Sure you can just use your magic," sniped Rant as his skin shivered down to the tip of his tail.

"Good old Rant, a swish of a fairy wand and all is well?" snapped Nefairious.

"Well no I'm afraid fairy magic does not cut it against these tyrants. They were given protection many centuries ago otherwise their job would be impossible," added Neroh.

The rat and the weasel nodded in agreement, they understood that the buzzards were to be feared and respected.

"But you have the Knife, don't you?" asked Rant.

"I do indeed and I suppose it may injure one of them but the others would overcome us and no mistake. However, they are not due to return for a little while yet and by that time the Hollow will be ours. A quick tidy up and those fairies that are spared will obey us or lose their heads. The buzzards will find nothing to be concerned about."

The others smiled to themselves. If they could help pull off the deception the buzzards would think all was well and fly off again. Of course had Nefairious known the location of the buzzards as he spoke he would not have been so calm.

*   *   *

Their red tinged brown and white feathers rippled on their great wings as the wind rushed over them. With their black hooked blade sharp beaks 'the three judges' as they were known cut through the sky. They had recently settled a major skirmish away in the land of the Narrow Lake and were planning to head their separate ways once again. They only met three times a year and took it in turn to visit each other's territory. However, the exceptional incident at the Narrow Lake had forced them together earlier in the year than expected. It was while they were administering justice that rumours of disquiet about Nut Hollow reached their ears.

"Tell me Brandon, could there be any truth in it?" asked Clav.

"I mean is it at all possible he could have escaped? Did you ever think you would hear the name Nefairious again?"

Clav had been a judge for many years, a finer example of flight and grace you would not see. Add to that a keen mind, a sharp eye and talon and you had the essence of what being a buzzard judge was all about.

"I did not. I don't understand how the rogue could ever have seen the light of day again. But however he did it, he did it and if the rumours are to be believed he's up to more mischief."

From behind, Gearr sailed up on the wind. He presided over the lands to the east, those of rushes and woods.

"We will have to be extremely severe Brandon, there can be no escape for him this time," he warned.

"I agree. I do believe it's your turn to administer the ultimate sentence."

"It is," smiled Gearr and his brown eyes glinted in the moonlight.

"But we have a way to go. It's unlikely we will be there before sunrise at the earliest."

He nosed to the front and the three swept away to the north like brown arrows intent on their target.

*   *   *

"So you are saying that if all seems well the buzzards will just fly away again?" asked Rant somewhat unconvinced.

"Well one thing is for sure, they will be amazed to discover that I have escaped and will want to finish me off," answered Nefairious.

"Still, if we can convince Graneff or Greagle perhaps to say all is well and that I have seen the error of my ways, you know the usual nonsense, they would have no reason to sharpen their talons on me."

Neroh nodded in agreement.

"Good thinking indeed, son."

It wasn't lost on Nefairious that it took the very real threat of death for his father to see merit in his plans.

"Yes, that's all very well," said Welset this time, "but none of you expect any fairy to go along with that. Do you? I mean Greagle will be out to rip our heads off as will the rest of them."

Neroh stared coldly back at him,

"It's all about striking the bargain. If we could get something or someone close to them and use them as a bargaining chip, well there's no telling what they would say to protect them. Now Graneff for example, has such weaknesses I'm sure."

"Oh aye and they are?" asked Rant.

"His children of course. Their time is coming to leave that hiding hole but not all will come believe me. They will not risk the children and there lies our opportunity. I will take the job of going into Fween Talav and snatching the little worms myself," he cackled.

"What and leave us to fight alone?"

"Alone! Sure you have an army of men around you and a one man army too. You might say we are covering all eventualities," he answered patting Nefairious on the shoulder as he spoke.

"Well if you can't beat them, kidnap them," said Welset. "But can you get in? I mean they will do whatever they have to keep the youngsters safe."

"Oh just leave that to me."

This was a cunning development by Neroh. He could now avoid the main battle and head underground. His son would not expect him to fight if he wasn't at full strength. He would not reveal his strength until it suited him. Thrown into the bargain the real likelihood Nefairious could meet his doom . . . well no wonder he was smiling.

This could be a good day, he thought.

56
Reunion

I could see Two Hour wood slowly appear up in the night in front of us. I sincerely hoped that we would meet up with our friends and that they had made it safely back from the Vanishing Lake. We flew high above the wood until we could see the welcome and life giving river flowing on its winding way.

"Down we go," I said.

We were soon jinking through the branches that overhung the river. I could hear the odd 'ow' and 'ouch' as the leaves and things we couldn't avoid clipped and stung our heads. We headed upriver as quickly as possible listening for a friendly shout or a signal from Síoda or a splash from Saroist.

"Do you see anything?" I asked the others as loudly as I dared.

There were just shakes of heads and stern faces looking hard into the night. We were approaching the furthermost part of the wood, after that the river ran in open countryside and that would be no hiding place. I then remembered that Saroist's pool was just up near that exit.

"Hey, Saroist will have probably directed them back to his place, it makes sense. I doubt he'd be able to swim there otherwise, c'mon," I urged and felt a new energy in my wings.

The river curved gently along the ground and we had one more bend ahead. As we flew I kept waiting for a charge from the crows or stings from the wasp armies but they did not come.

We turned the final bend and my heart fairly jumped in my chest for there they were, Saroist, Síoda, the robins all at the water's edge in conversation. And not only robins but now thrushes and starlings too. These tenants of Two Hour Wood were eager to join with Rithacus and Rua after being informed on recent events.

Immediately on hearing us they jumped to arms and would have skewered the lot of us but for Síoda. She saw our relieved and happy faces in the night and smiled widely. We landed on the bank beside them and as many hugs as we could manage were shared out.

"Well, well," began Saroist, "I thought you would never get here."

"Ha, 'tis well for you tentacle teeth, getting carried about the place like a lord," quipped back Tridge.

"Some of us are not so well treated. Still I'm glad you seem to be in one piece."

"Oh yes I'm quite well and happy to be on wet land again."

"What news?" asked Síoda quickly getting back to business.

"We have all that we need, according to Rachary at least," said Tridge.

"And what of Knock Layde?" she asked again.

"Yes we were there and got fragments off the Stone of Pity," I said and removed mine to show her.

"Good. Now how about our young friends?" Síoda walked up to Katie, Dara and Clumsill who had settled themselves on a mossy rock at the water's edge.

"We're ok," answered Dara, "I'm glad you made it safely."

"And I am delighted to see you again," said Saroist from just beyond the stone on which they sat.

"This should wake you up a bit," he said and with that flicked a dollop of chilled mountain river water over their heads with his tail.

"Hey!" gasped the three together and quickly leaned into the water and splashed him right back.

"I suppose you could say you are a flying fish now," laughed Clumsill.

It felt good to see everyone again. A moment's silence followed and then it was Katie's turn to speak,

"Will we be heading down to Nut Hollow now?"

Such an innocent and logical question but how to answer it, I wasn't at all sure.

"We will indeed," said Tridge, saving my blushes somewhat. "Our only problem is how do we contact the others? No point in us going down there all arrows and swords and no one knowing about it."

*   *   *

The blue smoke moved slowly but surely through the soil until at last it made it out above the grass above Fween Talav itself. To any guard looking it appeared like a sudden fog, silent and covering a small area. Sheana surveyed the Hollow.

Listen, she told herself, *listen*.

She was aware of the usual sounds and could hear the voices of those in Graneff's house although not clearly. Her ears strained for more familiar and friendly echoes. She moved up river. She floated easily enough on the light breeze and slowly began to regain her form. On up she floated, past the waterfall at Coolaveely, up through Fernglen, listening all the while. Slowly she transformed back into the lady the fairies so adored. However, she was like an apparition, a see through version of herself. This was the price she had hinted at earlier, and she would never again be the same.

However, she had other things on her mind and as she listened she heard the water splash some way above her.

That's not the ordinary rippling of the river, she thought.

It was the moment that Saroist had splashed the children and they had splashed him back.

Now who would be out and about in the river at this time?

Her gown flowed like mist behind her. Her eyes though still red were not near the same strength as before. She hoped that she wouldn't prove too much of a fright to anyone that saw her.

Not too far now, she thought and then heard the unmistakable sound of children's chatter.

"Well, well, if that's not Katie, Clumsill and Dara giggling I'll be amazed indeed."

On she went and stopped behind one of the many sycamore trees that made up Two Hour Wood. She saw them all, Tridge, Graneff, Síoda, Laijir, Ionta, Katie, Dara and Clumsill. She saw the birds on the branches. She saw their faces and the worry that rested on each one.

Time to say hello again, she thought and moved toward them.

*   *   *

"Look! There!" gasped Síoda grabbing at her sword.

"Quickly, get your bows Neroh has found us," shouted Tridge.

He was as swift at loading a bow as had ever been in the Hollow and had an arrow flying through the air directly at the Banshee. In the flick of a lamb's tail it had passed right through her and sat quivering in the trunk of a tree.

"What divilment is this?" he raged and made to fire again.

This time though his fingers and thumb kept a tight grip on the feathered arrow. He stared again, straining his night vision to the limit to define what approached.

"It can't be," I gasped.

"Oh no!" moaned Tridge. "What have I done?"

57

Spell Bound

Laijir and Ionta by now also had their bows loaded but they too stopped themselves. The apparition came closer still and they could see it was smiling. The children had hidden down underneath the moss on the stone but looked now toward her and she was of such a light that even the humans could clearly see her face. It was the Banshee.

She approached them and was there floating in front of them over the water which reflected back the light blue colour of her form.

"Well that's a nice welcome and no mistake," she said looking at Tridge who was of course in an awful state of regret.

"My lady if . . . if I had known."

"Don't worry, nothing you can fire at me, if that is, you wanted to fire at me again, would do me any harm. I am in another place where matter, doesn't matter, if you know what I mean."

I was immensely relieved to hear this and yet confused. What had happened to her? Why was she here? What had happened to the others? How was the Hollow? I had a million questions to ask but she spoke before I could ask them.

"Friends I am here to help and bring news from Greagle and Blalim."

"Blalim! But I thought . . ." said Ionta.

"Yes Blalim lives and is ready to fight but the Hollow is not as you would remember it. Nefairious and his cronies have sealed it up tight. They mean for nothing to get back in. The crows have been busy building a mesh which stretches from root to tip of the trees and the rats and weasels have filled in each hole in the hedge with whins and thorns and nettles."

This was worse than I feared, how would we even get close to those villains and get a swing at them?

"My lady," began Síoda, "what of the others? Are they still safe in Fween Talav?"

"Indeed they are, Síoda, and therein lies the problem. Greagle is faced with going out through the trap doors but of course they are well guarded and it would be a terribly difficult road."

"I'm sure it must be the only option left to him," said Tridge, "he may be brave but he is not reckless."

"No he is not. And if I have my way he will not go out that way."

"How can you do it? Against those furred freaks even you would be in serious danger," said Ionta again.

She floated toward those of us on dry land. I watched her reflection move in Saroist's dark eyes.

"Might I be of some help in all this?" asked the salmon.

"You!" gasped Laijir. "Would you risk your neck again for the Hollow?"

"I would and will, my friend."

"And here was I thinking you salmon were meant to be wise," replied Laijir and smiled widely. He knew that Saroist was behind them and all the happier for it.

"Can we go down on your back?" asked Dara, remembering the earlier spin to the sea of Moyle.

"You may."

"Ah, my even younger friends," said Sheana. "I am delighted to see you and still ready to help it seems. Would that there was an easier way but you will get your chance soon enough."

"My lady how shall we get word to Greagle?" I asked.

"Gather round and I will tell you."

We got into a circle about her feet, well where her feet should have been at least.

"I will address our feathered friends first, if you don't mind."

"Robins, you have proven your worth already but there is more to do. I will need you all to be ready on my signal and fly at every crow you see. Go in threes and fours at them and use these."

She cupped her hands together and began to blow. The darkness was suddenly lit up with the very flames from the candle she had used earlier. Each tiny flame floated to the branches and stopped just in front of the beaks of the birds.

"Please, do not be alarmed but I need each of you to swallow a flame."

There were quite a few feather rufflings and lots of chatter in bird language which hinted at uncertainty. However, Rithacus called them to order and simply said,

"The lady has spoken."

He opened his beak and swallowed his flame. The others did the same.

"Thank you all," she said, "in the heat of battle, the flame will give you strength. It will also enable you to breath a breath of fire and warm the hide of any attacker. But remember you will have just one flame so use it wisely."

"Now, the rest of you will follow me down stream until we are as close as we dare get to the Hollow. I will go on and treat the trap door guardians to a little of the old magic. They will wish they had never heard of Nut Hollow when I'm done with them. When the doorways are clear,

Greagle and those who are able to fight with him will come up from Fween Talav. I will give him my last flame and when you see it fly up on his arrow you will know they are ready. After that I can do no more. I'm quite sure that Greagle and Blalim will go straight for Nefairious and Neroh and they will need all the help they can get. I trust you have the items from your journey?"

"We do," I answered.

We reached into our pockets and placed the items on the ground in front of her.

"Well done indeed," she exclaimed and her red eyes glowed brightly again. She was the person Rachary had referred to.

"Each of these has its own power and you must use them with caution. Now these embers I will give to you," she said and handed them to Tridge.

"What should I do with them?" he asked, knowing how keenly they had burnt him previously.

"You Tridge have felt their strength. No flesh can withstand them but it is their light that you shall need. It must pierce the darkest of hearts and surely there are none darker than Neroh and Nefairious. If the opportunity should arise and you can hold them up to their eyes then do it quickly. Do not let go if they squeal or beg you to stop for you will be burning away years of cruelty and badness."

Tridge took the embers in their glass jar and put them into the inner pocket of his great coat. He walked back and rejoined the group.

"These shards of the Stone of Pity. Will you Graneff, Síoda, Ionta and Laijir pick them up?"

We walked forward and picked up the pieces between us. They were sharp and cold in our hands.

"They used to mourn the souls of those who rest underneath the Stone of Pity. They would lament their loss and miss the kings and princes, queens and princesses. But death is not the end of life, merely a part. The Stone absorbed all these good wishes and passed them on to those who had left this life for the next. Indeed I will be joining them soon," she said and looked away into the river for a moment.

She picked up her conversation again before any of us could object.

"Pity is a devilishly hard word to describe and an even harder emotion to share but these stone slivers will help. Keep them on your person and when the moment comes you will know it. Search deep in your heart for forgiveness, to do otherwise is to become little more those you fight."

She turned her gaze to the children.

Laijir was about to say 'Pity Nefairious! Are you mad?' but stayed quiet. His thoughts were loud enough in his head.

"You three, come forward."

Katie, Dara and Clumsill edged toward her reluctantly. They were not frightened and instead kept staring at her beautiful ruby eyes dancing in the night.

"My brave young friends, you have seen more today than I think any one child might happily expect to see in a year. You have faced all sorts of dangers and still here you are, close to home but with a long way to go yet-"

"Do we gat a flame too?" asked Katie.

"Sssh!" said Dara suddenly, fearing that interrupting her would be very rude.

"Oh yes please, I'd love one," added Clumsill, who had learned to be a little more daring these last hours.

Of course Dara wanted one too but didn't say anything; she hoped the Banshee would grant their wish.

"Hmm, it's a wonder old Rachary didn't eat you whole for such interruptions. I would be happy to give each of you a flame, to begin with."

She cupped her hands again and blew out three little yellow flames which made their way just underneath their noses.

"Ok, eat them up."

Dara felt like saying that this would be no problem as she loved curry and pepperoni and other spicy stuff but to be honest eating fire was perhaps a little too hot even for her taste buds. (Oh, and never try this without a Banshee present).

"Well here goes."

She stuck out her tongue and pulled in the flame. The other two did the same. Happily for them, all they felt was a quick tingle on the tips of their tongues and a warm feeling going down their throat not unlike good hot tea.

"Now then, you're ready . . . almost. On your travels you will have learned something of the secrets of Loughareema—(The three of them nodded)—Yes? Good. That being the case you will have found the lines of the spell—(more nods)—fine. Now you will have realised that they are not in the normal language of everyday folk and fairies, at least not any more unfortunately—(more nods)—Who can remember what they were?"

"Sure that's handy enough. The first one goes like this,

Thig leis an croí macánta an scian is ribeanta a mhaolú! *(Hig lesh un kree makkanta an skin is ribbinta a whale-oo)* which means 'an honest heart can blunt the sharpest Knife'," said Katie all proud of herself.

"My word, aren't you the clever girl?"

Katie agreed whole heartedly.

"Now do you know what that might mean?"

Instinctively Dara put up her hand as if at school.

"Hold on Dara, I need Katie to have a wee think."

"I suppose it must be something to do with what you feel inside being stronger than knives or swords and arrows and all."

"Go on . . ."

"That's all I can think of really," she answered. "But can a heart really blunt a Knife?"

"That is what we will soon find out. You three children have hearts as honest and as clear as the river water itself. From your honesty you gain courage and from courage you can dull any blade. Remember the sentence Katie and only utter it when you feel you must. Now back you go. Dara come here."

Dara did as she was told and shot a 'well done' glance at Katie.

"Now what was the next line Dara?"

"It went like this, 'Cinnte, níl an obair crua chomh furasta sin' (Kinnche, kneel un ubir krua ko furista shin) or 'Indeed, hard work isn't easy.'"

"Well done, and have you thought on what that might mean?"

"Yes, as my Granda would say 'if its worth doing, its worth doing right no matter how hard."

"Well this Granda of yours sounds like a clever man and you are right. These last days have been hard on you but here you are still going because you know you are doing the right thing. Hold this line on your tongue and speak it when things are tough as they will be before the end. Now Clumsill, over you come."

Poor Clumsill wasn't looking forward to this. He had struggled with the new language since hearing it and doubted whether or not he could manage the remaining line. The lady did not have to ask him as he knew what she wanted to hear.

"Here goes, 'go . . . ndéan . . . fáidh . . . seo . . . maith . . . daoibh' (Gu . . . nyanni . . . shuh . . . my deev) or may this do you some good," he stammered, relieved he had got to the end of it in one piece.

The others gave him a little round of applause as they realised how well he had done. He had started and hadn't given up, not a word was missed.

"My boy, your parents will be proud to hear about this!" smiled the Banshee. "Now what do you think that means?"

"Ehm I suppose it would be that something you give might be useful?" he said quietly.

"Indeed it does and you have done us some good. It also means thank you, and thank you indeed young man. Don't forget to use it when the time is right. Before you go you have something you can give me now."

"What do you mean?"

"I believe you have something in your left eye, hmm?"

The tear!

"Yes I have a drop of the Vanishing Lake here your Lady . . . er . . . my Lady but I need to cry it out," he said fearing for his other big toe.

"Don't worry, just look up."

He looked into her eyes and as he did felt the little tear trickle down his cheek. The Banshee moved her head under his chin and caught the droplet in her eye as it fell.

"Thank you Clumsill, well done indeed. Now back you go."

He returned and stood beside the two girls.

"My lady," asked Tridge, "Saivir said these lines were parts of a spell, are there anymore lines or what other parts do we need?"

"Tridge I'm glad you asked. YOU all are the rest of the spell. Any spell is useless unless it is spoken and you have earned the right to use it. Any of you may say the lines but they are more potent in the original language on the tips of young tongues. I would ask you to resist if possible and trust the children but if you have no choice just make sure you get it right."

My mind flashed back to Clumsill's episode all those years ago.

"Now, we have waited long enough. Saroist will you carry the children—"

"Oh not back in his mouth," groaned Katie.

"—on your back."

"Whoohoo!"

The children climbed aboard again and we flew just above them. Away into the darkness down to reclaim Nut Hollow if we could, the blue light of the Banshee brightening the water and the brown broken bark of the trees.

58

Escape

The sound of the two brothers singing had proved too much for Gráinne. She flew up to the balcony and was quickly joined by Lirna and Grochin. They approached the two of them, listening all the while to their less than harmonious efforts.

"What's going on?" asked Gráinne.

Of course the two dare not stop and could only look at her very seriously in the hope she would realise their song was of the utmost importance.

"I've never heard a worse racket in my whole life," began Grochin but something of the brothers' manner told him this was more than just a song at work.

Greagle motioned with his hands for them to join in.

"You want us to sing too?" asked Gráinne uncertainly.

Blalim nodded heartily.

This surely would help the Banshee find her way back, he thought.

They listened for a moment as the words went round again in their cycle. With each run around the words began to find room in their minds and it was Grochin who suddenly struck up,

"That soil so soft would welcome me

Good man, yourself, thought Greagle and his heart beat in time with
the music.

To pass right through its very heart

Now it was Lirna's turn and in spite of her heartbreak her voice was
clear and sweet.

That stone so hard would not obstruct

Gráinne needed no further encouragement and was beginning to
join in when she suddenly turned and went to the balcony. She waved
at all those that were able to come up quickly and join them. Those that
could not find room would sing where they stood. Back she came with
three then four others and the song now was gaining in energy and they
all felt it.

A traveller on her journey's start

With each word a new voice was added until the voices rang out in
the Banshee's little room.

That roots so strong would not ensnare

But that was not the end of it. Like a musical snake the song weaved
its way down amongst the fairies in the hall. It only took a few seconds
before the words came to them.

My errand in their reaching vines

Now the volume was growing and there was hope again in the room. Greagle and Blalim smiled at each other but not too widely as it's a tricky thing to smile and sing at the same time.

That skin and bone would melt away

And all together

Like mist when the warm sun shines
Now candle light so bright and true
Please take me now in your embrace
And guide me through the bonded earth
And return in haste back to this place."

What a sight and sound they made, standing shoulder to shoulder singing for the Banshee.

*   *   *

She led us on as Saroist swam steadily below. It was a fair distance to get to Nut Hollow or as near as we could without being seen but we flew along and made good time. I felt as if I wanted to say a hundred things to the Banshee but I had no stomach for her answers. She would be gone from us after all and that filled me with sadness. In a way it deflected the impending battle from my thoughts and that would not do.

She stopped briefly and waited on us to catch up. Saroist and the children glided along in silence, their feet in the water creating the slightest of ripples behind him.

"Graneff," she said, "as mayor of the Hollow all eyes will look to you for guidance. You have all the council you need around you but it is important you seek out Greagle and Blalim. They are pure and brave fairies without question but often bravery needs a little guidance especially in the heat of battle, do you understand?"

"Yes, my lady, but the brothers are no novices in a scrap," I replied, feeling uneasy that I would have to somehow dilute their passions.

"This is no scrap. What you will face tonight is a fight for your very soul and all that makes you what you are. Your land, homes and traditions are under threat by those who should know better but they do not care to see. You stand to lose it all for ever."

Her words sat uncomfortably on the night air.

"But I believe that you have the mettle for what lies ahead, Graneff, as I do in each of you."

She stared into my eyes and I resolved to do whatever I needed and deal with my feelings another day. We flew in a line behind her and I noticed her colour becoming less vibrant, almost as if someone was turning down her light. The five of us who had helped Saroist in the Sea of Moyle now lifted him gently over the waterfall of Coolaveely.

"Not long now," she said.

The river gurgled beneath us and the grass seemed to whisper encouragement as we passed over it. The rushes and whins, clover and shamrocks bowed slightly as if they agreed that what we were about to do was right. On we flew until there in the distance we could see the flickering lights of the invaders.

"There is a great boulder just above the Hollow, you know the one?" she asked.

"Yes the Hide and Seek stone you mean?" I answered.

"Indeed, it would seem well named."

It was a great lump of granite rock that had ended up in Nut Hollow and was a favourite for the youngsters to play around hence it's name. We had heard that a giant had left it there after a fight and that was a good enough story for us.

"What about Saroist?" asked Síoda suddenly.

"My dear," he answered as the children got off his back and climbed up onto the dry bank, "I have come this far with you without rack or ruin. It is my wish that we finish this together."

"I'm sorry but its just . . ."

"I know. Now you would do better to listen to the Banshee than me. I will be ok down here."

We flew up together to the great stone and sat on one of its many ledges out of sight. The birds flew silently into the trees and waited.

Laijir, Tridge and Ionta all began tightening belts and bootstraps and knife sheaths and bow strings and arrow quivers and whatever else they would need.

"You have a good view from here," began Sheana. "I haven't much time left but thanks to Greagle and Blalim's singing I've got this far."

Singing? I thought, but would ask later.

"I will go and release them from Fween Talav, watch out for the arrow . . . good bye."

With that she floated silently over the rock into the night, transforming again to her wispy state.

The Banshee approached Nut Hollow and hoped that she would not raise any eyebrows. For all the world she just looked like a piece of lost fog. She saw beneath her the platoons of rats and weasels with the discarded nut shells around their feet. She knew now they would be even stronger than before. Closer and closer now until she was just at the first house on the right hand side, number thirty four which belonged to none other than Grochin and Frenel. As she expected there were several rats on patrol at the gates and at the front door.

There'll be more inside no doubt, she thought.

She subtly changed direction as if the wind had blown her but had they been alert the rats would've noticed the wind blowing the opposite way. As she floated overhead the rats looked up at her thinking it was fog but once they looked up they were transfixed by her two red eyes. She stared at them all and as she floated inside they followed her in like schoolchildren. To any rat watching it would've seemed as if they had just gone indoors for a moment. Had she wanted she could have killed them right there but did not. Instead she began to hum a few notes.

There may have goodness in you at one time and you may find it again, she thought, *but for now all you will hear will be fairy music.*

Now you may think that this was too light a sentence but fairy music to a rat is just about the worst sound there can be. It left them at her will until she released them. They stood in front of her staring blankly unable to move and there they would've remained. However, she told them to go back to their posts so that again, anyone looking up would not see anything wrong.

Each action weakened her further but she had enough left to break the seal on the trap door and floated down through the tunnel into Fween Talav. She could hear the song and the voices ringing out to guide her safely back. Of course all eyes had followed Greagle's and Blalim's and were looking up at the roof through which she had disappeared. She appeared then behind them as a mere shadow of her former self and headed straight for the candle. She floated around it and as if emerging from a seed, a flame began to slowly grow on the wick. They kept singing, she had not said to stop and they didn't want to risk anything going wrong now. She looked at Blalim and Greagle and puffed out her cheeks at them, as if to get them to blow.

Again? thought Greagle and looked at Blalim who must've had a similar thought in his head. He nodded and once again the brothers blew, happier in the knowledge they could stop singing. This flame split up immediately into a hundred tiny versions of itself. Another blow and it began to spiral upwards and surround her. The light from them all was enough for those closest to raise their hands and cover their eyes. The voices now began to fall away until all eyes waited and watched. The swirling light began to fall inward on itself like a circular waterfall and as it emerged at the bottom the Banshee began to regain her form. In a few moments she was back with them again but even weaker than before. Nonetheless there was great relief and joy and they were silent as she made ready to speak.

59

Long Night, Short Tempers

More singing, thought Neroh, *I don't like it? Why would they be singing again? It's not as if they have much to celebrate. No they aren't celebrating. They have already sung a healing song. There is some other trickery at work here and the Banshee has something to do with it or else I'm very badly mistaken.*

He reached into the pockets of his coat and felt for the Ogham stones.

Time you were awoken.

"Nefairious, I need a moment alone. I wish to prepare myself and my magic. It will require a short time of absolute quiet. I do not wish to be disturbed. Take our friends out and I will be with you shortly."

"But father, I do not expect you will need your magic. You will not be fighting if we can avoid it," answered Nefairious, who broke off talking of plans with the rat and weasel.

They had not heard the second song such were there discussions.

"You never can tell son, if I can help with an old spell or two then surely we are better off for that?" he said, as if he was truly thinking of his son's best interests.

"Right, you two, you heard my father. Out."

The three stood up from the table and followed Nefairious to the door and into the darkness. All was quiet again since the singing had stopped.

"All is ready," said Nefairious calmly.

Yes ready for you, thought Rant, eagerly anticipating Nefairious's end.

"How quiet it is," said Welset, "you would hardly think anything had ever happened here."

"Yes indeed, but it has and you will make your own history after today," answered Nefairious.

A history and future without you, thought Welset.

The rat and the weasel now stood behind Nefairious, right behind him. His hands were down at his sides and importantly not on the handle of the Carving Knife. Rant looked keenly at Welset.

"Go on . . ."

Welset wished his eyes had been fit to speak but whatever about his initial doubts here was a real opportunity to rid themselves of one of the fairies they unhappily served. His earlier accord with Nefairious now sneaked away to the corner of his mind. He crouched down low to the ground and made as if to leap. He dug his claws into the soil. His thoughts were on fire alight in his eyes.

Go on, kill him.

Then,

No wait, he can give you the Hollow, don't risk it for the whim of some fat rat.

No! Kill him now and that will be that. We will deal with the rat after.

The power of the nuts was surging through his veins and he felt he could jump across the river if he'd wanted to.

Sure I could have his head off before he would even know. C'mon.

Suddenly just as he was about to press down for the jump a flutter of blackness from above accompanied by the unmistakably blunt caws of the crows. Both Grod and Borb landed in front of Nefairious who was unaware of how close he had come to his demise. The wind of their wings blew against Welset's exposed teeth. He quickly closed his mouth and stood up again in his normal posture. Rant couldn't believe his bad luck. He knew that Welset stood a fair chance of killing Nefairious just then but no doubt he would have got a mortal blow in on the weasel.

Patience, he thought.

The three waited until the crows had settled then Borb spoke,

"My crows grow impatient. Any sign of anything? Where are these cursed kin of yours? Perhaps this is some ruse to gather us here for your amusement, perhaps you made this whole attack up?"

Nefairious held his silence. He could've quickly answered with assurances of their imminent arrival, what strategies they could expect but decided the crows would know all about it soon enough.

"Keep alert, enjoy what little silence remains. They will be here, be sure of it."

Grod suddenly walked up to him until his beak was millimetres from Nefairious's nose. He opened his wings, drew breath and let go the most horrendous caw.

That was enough for Nefairious who had been a little sore from this crow's ill manners at their earlier meetings. Out with the Carving Knife in a golden second and up under Borb's beak. But he did not stop at the chin and instead pushed up until the tip was just cutting into it. The shocked Borb made to fly back and released a very uncrowlike squeak. Nefairious pushed the Knife further into his beak and his wings flashed as he hovered under the great crow's lower jaw.

*   *   *

Neroh stood up as soon as they had left. He knew the rat knew about the Ogham stones but gambled his earlier promises would keep him quiet. To arouse an Ogham stone took knowledge of the old magic, something which Neroh knew well. He placed them on the table so that their symbols were facing him. In the candle light their dark blue was not as mysterious as when in the moon light but their deep green veins held their colour.

Perfect. A protection my lady that even you will not suspect.

He placed his two hands on top of them, covering them and began then to roll them gently on the wooden table. They made a soft grinding, whispering noise as he moved them.

"Time for a song myself," he smiled, "now how does it go?"

It had been a long time since he'd had an Ogham stone near him and he wanted to be sure of the spell. He continued to move them under his hands, waiting. They were beginning to feel warm to the touch and the words came.

> "The present and past and future at last
> Here and entwined all three combined
> In Ogham stones more than skin and bones
> From the mountains mined now here aligned
> With the present and past and future at last."

Neroh took his hands off the stones and waited. After a moment the deep red and green veins began to glow. This new light began to spread quickly round the stones. He put his hands back on them and felt the shock through his body. The energy within transferred to him until he too was surrounded by the same light. He breathed deeply, breathed it in and with each breath the light dimmed as his body soaked it up. The brief ritual was quickly completed and Neroh was ready.

The now dull stones were placed back in his pockets. He got up and walked purposefully outside. He felt strong and able to deal with whatever came his way. The fracas he saw at the front door came as little surprise to him.

How did that boy ever think he could rule the Hollow?

However, he would have to intervene as an injury to one the crows or Nefairious himself would place them all at a disadvantage.

"Enough!"

For a second Nefairious was a youngster again tripping behind his father in the Hollow. That harsh tone he associated with many scoldings and the sting of a cuffed ear. He immediately withdrew the Knife from the crow's beak and flew back down to the ground. Borb, who had been a shock of black feathers and caws also settled himself. He had heard tales of Neroh's temper from Préak and did not wish to see it revealed further.

"Friends. Nefairious. This will not help. A misunderstanding I'm sure on the edge of battle. These things are common enough but they do no good. We need to be united, for their arrival is at hand, I'm sure of it."

He failed to mention hearing the second song and instead gave the impression of having some sort of fairy foresight and so add to his mystery. Grod took off without another word. Borb followed and left only a cold stare for Nefairious.

"Stay alert. You heard Neroh. Get back to your positions," shouteded Nefairious.

Welset and Rant sloped off to their platoons. They were sure they had missed their opportunity. Now they would have to see what way events played out and gamble accordingly.

Curse those crows, thought Rant.

If those crows hadn't come, thought Welset, *I could've been in real trouble. Curse that rat.*

Neroh watched them disperse and Nefairious approach. He stood at Graneff's door with his hands behind his back and rocked slowly forward on his toes. He looked very much at home. The wind suddenly blew up through Nut Hollow. Nefairious walked up to the door and stood shoulder to shoulder with Neroh. For a brief moment he seemed to have achieved all he wanted as they stood there together but he could only think of what lay ahead. He wouldn't have long to wait.

60

And so it Begins

The Banshee looked at them then breathed deeply. The fairy faces were all fixed upon her, a mixture of intrigue, fear, anxiety and hope. Greagle and Blalim watched her carefully. This was not the Banshee of old and they knew it. Just when all was silent a rustle or two in the background and to the front Druhin, Pog and Fer stepped out and stood beside Greagle.

"I have one flame left from my candle and when it flies it will be a signal for the others to come to your help. The doorway back up to the house at the end of the Hollow is free but we must act quickly."

"That's our house!" whispered Frenel.

"There will be a patrol soon enough. You will have no trouble with the rats that you see there. They are awake and asleep all at once. Greagle get your bow. Blalim, all of you, get whatever weapon you can use."

She stopped and almost disappeared completely. Her strength was almost gone but in a moment or two she reappeared.

"Greagle you must fly your arrow with this flame as soon as you get outside. It is the only way the others will know you are free."

"But an arrow my lady in the dead of night, surely all those foul creatures will see it too?"

"Sir," interrupted Druhin, "I must go with you and alert the bats. They are waiting four notes from this whistle. They will keep those rogues busy if Strelle's word is anything to go by."

"I can help you there too." said the Banshee. "Call it my parting gift to you."

"But you said you would be back?" exclaimed Blalim.

"And I will, but not for a while. When I return it will be to a friendlier Hollow than I leave I'm sure."

There was silence until Fer said a simple,

"Yes, the Hollow *will* be a friendly place once again."

They all began to nod and 'yeses' and 'you're right by nettles' and soon 'c'mons' were heard and 'let's get thems'.

"That's the spirit but I must urge caution. I do not wish for the children to be put in such danger and will need them to stay here. I will ask Graneff to seal the door when we leave and that will hold it," she said.

The stronger and fitter fairies immediately headed back down to the hall to collect their swords and assorted weapons. Even Grochin who must've been close to three hundred was getting himself prepared. Frenel did not protest and helped her husband with what he needed.

"I know you'll be alright you old curmudgeon," she smiled, "so I will stay here with the children."

"I'll help you," came a voice. It was Sherene.

"Thank you my dear, these youngsters would be up to their oxsters in danger if we didn't watch them."

Gradually the company got ready with goodbyes and good lucks. And here too a moment that Fer would not forget in a hurry. She had resigned herself to waiting with Pog on her mother's instruction. Gráinne would brave the battle and had to leave Fer in charge of her younger brother. In the rush of it all, the fighting back of tears and hugs and handshakes Fer had missed her chance to wish Druhin good luck. She watched them ascend the stairs behind the Banshee and was completely grumpy at how things had turned out.

"Hey, where's my smile then?"

It was Druhin. He stood in front of her looking quite the young hero with his wings and sword and all. Of course Fer blushed almost crimson but in spite of that she grabbed Druhin's collar and pulled him toward her.

"Here it is!" she said, and planted a big wet kiss right on his lips.

"Woh, woh up there," he stammered but secretly he was perfectly happy.

"I'll see you later on," he smiled and as quickly was gone to the crowd and the unknown. The younger fairies and their guardians now numbered about twenty in all sat around the great table where plans had been drawn up earlier. Fween Talav had never seemed so silent.

*   *   *

We reached the trap door in a few minutes. There was no talk as we climbed the stairway. Around the door we could see the thin strips of light that formed a perfect square above us. The Banshee turned to face us. By now she was almost completely transparent.

"Remember the rats here are under a spell. They will look straight at you and will no doubt like to pull your heads from your shoulders but they will not be able to. Their minds are otherwise occupied you might say."

With a wave of her hand the trap door flew open and they could see the red ceiling of Grochin's kitchen.

"I never liked that colour you know," came his voice from a little way back in the darkness, "and I wouldn't have had it but do you see that woman of mine!"

"Good man Grochin," said Blalim, "never miss an opportunity."

Greagle led us out and we were quickly all in the kitchen but as more of us came out we pushed forward into the living room. As Sheana had fore warned us there were plenty of rats walking slowly and aimlessly around. However, being fore warned is one thing seeing them there with those long, sharp white teeth gave my heart a fair shock, especially as they regarded us all with complete disdain. I felt very vulnerable and uncomfortable being in such close company with them but typically it was Greagle who spoke.

"Ok, you heard what the lady said, think of them as big cuddly toys . . . big ugly cuddly toys."

Blalim pushed his way to the front door and waited for the Banshee there. She joined him and we stood close behind.

"I will go out first," she said, "wait until I say the word, and then fire your arrow."

Greagle prepared his bow and as he pulled an arrow from his quiver Sheana raised her palm up to her mouth and released her last flame. It sat on her hand until she blew upon it gently. It sailed directly to Greagle's arrow blade surrounding it in flame. Out she went and headed skyward and using the power of the Léargas tear droplet, it looked like a sudden heavy fog had descended on that part of the Hollow. This time she climbed higher than the tree tops and we all heard it . . . as if the wind itself had whispered it . . .

"Now!"

Greagle immediately released the arrow on the other side of the fog curtain so that the watchers could not see it. Up it went like a lightning bolt ripping through the darkness like a sword through silk. Slowly the fog began to disappear piece by piece, blown apart by the gentle river breezes.

"Thank you my lady and goodbye," said Greagle.

*   *   *

"Look! Look there," said Ionta.

We all saw it; a brilliant streak of yellow hope warming the night. It reached the height of its glorious arch and soon was earthbound. Its light quickly faded and in another second darkness enveloped us all again. Little did we care for darkness now.

"C'mon," cried Tridge.

"Yessss, c'mon," growled Laijir.

Síoda and Ionta took off immediately with Katie and Dara. I carried Clumsill. We set them down onto Saroist's back.

"Now old friend," I began, "we are heading into dangerous water but I know of no one who could guide these youngsters through it as well as you. Please, if things go badly take them back upstream as far as you can."

"Don't worry, they'll be safe with me," he answered and set off cautiously down river toward the Hollow, gracefully swimming between the large stones therein.

The canopy sliced up the white moon beams so much that they speckled the passengers on Saroist's back. As welcome as the moon light was at times in Nut Hollow, this was really not one of them. At once it made it easier to see and be seen. In the distance I could see the crow mesh that surrounded the Hollow. Thankfully they were unable to cover the river but only a few yards away we could see the curved furry backs of the rat guards whose lives depended on stopping anything the river might deliver. We flew above it using the overhanging branches as best we could to avoid detection and keeping an eye on the children on Saroist's broad back.

"The arrow came from Grochin's garden," I said.

"Indeed," agreed Ionta.

Laijir and Tridge were now a few feet ahead of me and signalled for me to follow them to a branch. We all landed on its moss lumped edge.

"I see them. I can see Greagle and Blalim. Can you see them, there?" asked Tridge urgently.

"Aye, that's them alright. C'mon quickly we have no time to lose," answered Laijir.

"Wait just a second. Look at the rats beside them just standing there. Do you reckon Blalim has put a spell on them?" asked Ionta.

"No I would say it was the Banshee. Clever indeed for I'm sure the rats lower down will think there is nothing wrong," I answered. "We need just be careful. Fly as low to the river as possible."

We descended down through the leaves until our boots were almost in the water. Saroist was only an arm's length ahead and the children watched us as we flew in behind them. In another moment we were at the large stone that sat just at the bottom of Grochin's path. It seemed as if our luck was holding for now. There were no obvious signs we had been seen. The rats now beside us walked around as if in a trance.

"Inside now!" snapped Greagle. "Were you expecting a hug?"

We waited for the children to get off Saroist's back just behind the stone. No chance of anyone seeing them from there. From the other side of the river, we could hear weasel shouts and orders.

"Keep your peepers open and your sniffers. The first one of you to catch a whiff of one of them can eat it!"

They were just up near the Hide and Seek stone. It wouldn't be long before one of them picked up our scent.

"Saroist, we can go no further together. Thank you for all your help. Will you be ok?" I asked, knowing there was no answer to that question.

"Oh I've got a trick or two yet young fellow. I will see you soon."

With that he sunk silently into the river. I hoped it would not be too long before we spoke again.

We ran up the pathway keeping low to the ground and were safely inside the kitchen before another word was spoken.

"Well, well, I thought you were as dead as a winter whisper," said Laijir.

He walked up to Blalim and heartily shook his hand.

"No, not yet at least. It's great to see you all again but our work is far from over."

Druhin, get that whistle of yours. Its time we gave those crows something to think about," said Greagle.

From the crowd out stepped young Druhin. It seemed so long since he took his first flight. I did not know why Greagle had asked him to play his whistle, it hardly seemed an appropriate time but then again this was Greagle. Druhin looked on us all nervously and wished he had time to give us a hug and a handshake. He walked over to the front door, stepping over a big rat's pink tail as he went. He quickly pulled out his whistle and gave four puffs of his cheeks.

"Try again," I said, "your whistle is broken or something."

"It's notes aren't for our ears Graneff," said Greagle. "In a moment or two there is going to be complete mayhem."

I went to the trapdoor and opened it as quickly as possible.

"Ok Dara, I need you to lead the other two to Fween Talav. It's a straight run if a bit dark. Can you do it?"

"Yes."

"Use this," said Ionta and handed Katie one of the torches that flickered on Grochin's wall.

I pulled open the trap door and watched them descend a few steps.

"Go quickly and stay there until we come for you," said Tridge.

"But wait," said Clumsill. "What about the spell, the lines and all?"

"I know I know," I said. "But I can't risk your lives. If the Banshee is right you may well get your chance but for now go, and go quickly."

I closed the trapdoor behind them and put a locking spell on it.

"Now," said Greagle, "it's time we finished this."

61

Flights of Fancy

Strelle's head shot straight up. His large ears twitched and flicked as if they had a mind of their own and were trying to get off his head.

"That's it, that's the signal," he shouted. "Let this be the night crow kind will never forget."

As one they flew from their perches. Perhaps a hundred of the finest flying bats ever to grow wings all spinning and weaving and jittering and dancing their way through the night en route for havoc. They were at their work in no time. They had silently built their numbers on the inside of the mesh and were now zipping among the branches of Nut Hollow in search of crows.

They began to wheel upward to the higher branches where most of the crows sat half asleep. The initial noise of the mass take off had not registered in their black heads as danger, just a gust of wind perhaps.

They had hardly time to open their eyes before the bats were on them. Strelle had ordered at least five bats to attack each crow where possible. Any less than that would be certain suicide. The bats began to choose their victims and soon their razor sharp teeth were finding their way through wing and feather.

Because of their weight the crows were roosting away from the edges of the upper branches close to the centre but this proved to be of little comfort. The bats flew in and landed en masse on the dozing devils.

The first to meet his end was Cawn. He had recently enlisted in the crow army. He thought Préak to be a great leader and that wars were a noble duty. Two bats landed on either wing hampering any attempt he might have made at flight. Two more landed on either side of his neck sinking their teeth into his throat. The last landed fair on the top of his beak so that they were eyeball to eyeball. The bat bit straight down on his black left eye and in a moment had it out of its socket. The other eye rolled furiously in his head such was the pain. The other bats about him quickly broke through his tough skin to reveal his neck and from there he had no hope. Bite after bite went into his neck and the blood began to spit out on either side. He tried desperately to flap his wings but the bats had bitten into the muscles and his wings were useless. Soon enough his other eye was out and he let forth a bloody gurgle before the five of them pushed him off the branch to his end. He bounced very unceremoniously off each branch until he hit the river.

Once the initial shock had worn off, the crows soon began to rouse themselves. They began to swing their sharp beaks ferociously and soon several bats were skewered upon them. Strelle and Tragus flew together. They were on the hunt for Borb and Grod. As is the crow way when trouble is at their door, those that could flew up and out of the trees. Their dark shapes sketched themselves rudely against the brilliant white moon. Borb began to roar his chilling orders,

"Kill them quickly and kill them all!"

No sooner were they above the branches until the bats were after them again. However, it was a far more difficult prospect to get at them as they flew. Still, the bats rallied as best they could and soon their sheer number began to tell. All round the top of the canopy a single crow with at least five bats about was a common sight. Their large slow wings were stark contrast to the industry of the bats.

"Tragus! There, I see the two of them. Yes," urged Strelle who was delighted their surprise attack was wreaking such chaos.

To add to their advantage the moonlight was dimmed suddenly as a large white cloud sailed slowly past it.

"Quickly," said Strelle again, "follow me."

He quickly realised that in the temporary darkness lay their best chance to put an end to the crow threat. This latest inconvenience brought more foul crow curses from Borb but he was not a general for nothing.

"Higher," he squawked. "Higher."

The crows did not need to be told twice. They pushed themselves further into the night sky thus exposing the bats who were much happier darting about amongst the leaves and branches. Strelle quickly realised what was going on but felt he had little choice. Should the crows get a clear run at them they would not be able to withstand their formidable power.

All around the bats were biting, scraping and interfering with the crows who in turn were cuffing them away with their wings, catching them in their talons and trying to kebab them on their beaks. The two sides were evenly matched but the higher they went the more the crows began to get the upper wing.

Strelle and Tragus, now flanked by eight others, kept their eyes firmly on Borb and Grod who continued to urge their kin upward.

"We're going to have one go at this," said Strelle.

"Tragus take your men and aim for Borb, we will tackle Grod. May Odhran be with us now."

The ten of them split into two groups about five feet apart. The cloud had almost revealed the moon again and the strange blue white light was surrounding them once more. They flew as high as they had ever flown and were briefly above the whole affair. They began their descent just in time. Borb was busy fending off a number of bats who carefully did not engage his talons but did enough to keep him busy.

Sadly for him it was too late to notice his visitors from above and they landed on him at full tilt. They bore their sharp teeth into him as quickly and as powerfully as they could. They heard his foul caws of pain and knew they had hit their mark. In another moment they began to fall. Borb, now unable to flap was covered by five of Strelle's finest. Strelle himself had Borb's left eye loosed from its socket and was working his way around to the other one. Still they fell and were only a few feet from the branches.

"Get off. Off now. All of you," yelled Strelle and the bats seemed to explode off his dark body, which now plummeted through the leaves, off branches and into the river where his caws were forever drowned.

Tragus's team had not been so lucky. Their descent was just the wrong side of the cloud cover and at the very last moment Grod caught sight of them. It was all the time he needed. Instinctively he flipped himself around and caught the unfortunate Tragus in his talons. However, he had exposed his weakest side and as he grabbed Tragus the other bats went about their work on his stomach. Still, he had the wherewithal to flip himself over again loosening a couple of his attackers. He began to squeeze the life out of Tragus.

"Enjoy your last breath, bat."

His strength was more than the bats could handle in spite of their best efforts. He was able to brush them off and had mortally wounded a few more with his beak. His talons had ripped through Tragus's wing and he now feared certain death. Indeed certain death would have been delivered upon him if not for an unexpected intervention.

Frustrated by the darkness, because they never flew at night, Rithacus and the other robins decided to risk all and use the moonlight for the first time.

"We will sit here no longer," called Rithacus suddenly.

"Smól of the Thrushes, Drood of the Starlings let us fly together. Let us fly together for the sake of our friends and Nut Hollow. Those black curs have flown above the mesh, let us meet them."

The thrush and starling leaders agreed and took off immediately. Now I'm sure you've seen a flock of birds fly off a wire? Well this was just like that and there was a great gush of wind as they flew upward into battle. Just as the crows began to think they had the beating of the bats up from the trees now came a new enemy.

Like the bats, the thrushes, starlings and robins all converged in groups onto the unsuspecting crows who were now hopelessly outnumbered. There would be little sympathy shown to them this night. It wasn't long before their black bodies began to fall through the night sky and into the river. The flames bestowed by the Banshee flashed yellow in the night. Many crows got a roasting they wouldn't forget and a smell of burnt feathers filled the air. Rithacus then noticed the terrible predicament Tragus was in and without a thought for himself swept downward at Borb. As he changed direction so the secret message that all flocks have was shared and as one they changed direction with him.

Tragus shut his eyes and prepared himself for death. In this way he heard the sudden rush of wind, feathers, chirps and caws. He felt the talons around him loosen and suddenly was falling. He opened his eyes and all at once could see moon, earth, trees, clouds and stars as he spiralled downward.

To have escaped the crows and die from a fall, he thought. This being the worst possible end for such a skilled flyer.

He waited to be dashed against a branch or stone for it was inevitable when he felt his body jerk and then defy gravity. He was no longer falling and then heard a familiar voice.

"You'll be ok."

It was Strelle.

"Can you see? Look."

More bats quickly joined Strelle and between them they held him. Tragus had now recovered sufficiently to realise what was going on. Of course he could see perfectly in the dark and here was a sight he could hardly have imagined. This massive flock of birds of different kinds united now with his fellow bats getting at the crows like nobody's business. He saw Borb, well to be honest all he could see of him were his talons which were now empty and weak. The rest of his body was a feathered mass of red breasted avengers. In another moment Borb was upside down as they carried him away from the fight. This was done to show the other crows what had become of their leader in the hope it would knock the stuffing out of them.

"Get out of here. Fly for your lives!" came the first desperate caw from none other than Borb himself.

The crows on seeing and hearing this had suddenly had enough and took flight away from the Hollow. There were now just ten or so left and they retreated as quickly as their injuries allowed. The bats, robins, thrushes and starlings began to land in the branches and the air became calm again.

"Wreck that cursed mesh," cried Rithacus.

Soon almost two hundred little beaks were pulling apart the crow's foul masterpiece. Beside him on the branches of the nut trees landed Strelle and Tragus.

"We had best watch out, do you see them down there?" asked Rithacus.

"I do indeed and they don't look pleased," answered Strelle.

He peered down through the leaves and saw a very angry father and son staring straight back.

62

Out Front and Behind

The father and son were surprised indeed at the sudden turn of events. No matter what the planning, when the unexpected happens it can take a bit of getting over no matter who you are.

"Look sharp you snipes!" yelled Nefairious.

Immediately the rats and weasels stiffened themselves in readiness.

"There are fairies about and no mistake," said Neroh gravely who had not counted on such unity between bat and bird.

"It would appear Strelle has made his choice," he said. "It will be up to us to show him he has made the wrong one."

Nefairious flew up to the top of the Learning Tree and witnessed for himself the crows shambolic exit back to their stronghold away across the fields. It would be a while again before they thought to venture near Nut Hollow.

"Useless cowards," he mumbled.

Even the keen eyes of Strelle and Rithacus lost him in the green gloom. He was careful to stay out of sight beneath a large leaf. He did not want to risk the wrath of the birds and bats nor be pecked at by some whippersnapper robin. It would be impossible for them to see him amongst the canopy. Had their numbers been less he would have killed a few for sure with a bolt or two of the Draykt but that would reveal him and trouble would surely follow.

No, not yet, Strelle, he thought and quickly flew back down.

"Father."

"What?" was Neroh's blunt reply.

"Father, the crows are fleeing and the trees will soon be lost to us. Even now they are tearing down the mesh. They are too many of them for one of us but together we could get rid of them?"

"Hmm, this is an unexpected twist and no mistake. I did not think the birds would be bothered who ran the Hollow but it is obvious they are. I have magic enough to wipe them all out but such a spell would weaken me further and we yet must face Greagle and the others. However, there's nothing to say we can't rid ourselves of a few from here."

They stood again at the front door and flapped their wings until their hands crackled blue. They then took aim and the Draykt shot out from their fingertips at the birds undoing the mesh. The blue beam flew straight into the birds and bats and several of them were blasted to pieces.

"What the . . . ?" exclaimed Rithacus.

"Everyone, fly. Fly now!"

More blue streaks whizzed through the trees and a fair number met a swift end. The bats and birds quickly flew from the Hollow and found refuge in a clump of trees across the river out of the line of fire.

"What in the name of Odhran was that?" asked a clearly shocked Smól.

"I don't know but whatever it is I'm not for testing it again," answered Strelle.

He had heard of such magic but never witnessed it until now.

"We need to get Tragus out of here, he needs medicine quickly," he said and quickly sent out a series of sonic bleeps.

Six of his bats flew off into the night with Tragus.

"Well, we have done what we can for now for the fairies," began Rithacus, "but I can't risk anymore lives against that blue magic."

"I know, we will have to bide our time for a while. How will they ever overcome those rats and weasels?" asked Drood.

They realised that even in spite of their victory over the crows their work was far from over.

"Well it would seem that we must trust to hope for the time being. Druhin would not have blown the whistle had he not been told to by Greagle. We will soon see if he can live up to his reputation," added Strelle.

"We will hold here and answer again if they call."

And so the birds and bats who had survived regained their wits in among the tall sycamore trees. They could see the weasels and rats now marching about down along the banks of Nut Hollow.

*   *   *

"Well did you ever see the like of that?" exclaimed Greagle, delighted to see the back of the crows.

"No," I answered, "but there were two bolts of the Draykt at once and that can only mean Neroh is back at full strength."

"Hmmm," began Tridge, "we have rats and weasels in front of us and should we somehow manage to overcome them we are left with Neroh and Nefairious and the Carving Knife."

"We must push on," said Greagle.

"Strelle has shown courage tonight that should be an example to us all. We all have the Draykt, we should go out and face them. They will not be expecting a ground attack."

I agree," said Síoda, "the time has come."

Laijir and Ionta did not appear so ready, nor did Blalim, who shook his head.

"We can't do anything unless we do it together," I said.

"What do you mean? Sure we're as together now as we'll ever be!" exclaimed Greagle impatiently.

"Greagle, I have always listened to you and benefited from your advice but now will you please listen to me?"

Greagle said nothing for a moment. He was hot in the desire to get at Nefairious and the rest. He looked at me and nodded slightly.

"I have no doubt that we could do serious damage to a lot of those animals out there but surely we would be overwhelmed, Draykt or not. I think that a diversion is our best hope. We must get to Nefairious and Neroh somehow and get the Carving Knife. After that it will be a more even fight. We have only another half hour or so of darkness before the dawn breaks. It will be too bright then for this to work."

"For what to work?" interrupted Laijir.

"For us to use the darkness against two dark hearts," I answered.

"But they can see in the dark as well as we can," said Greagle. "Surely it would be better to go for them now?"

"Go on Graneff," said Blalim, before Greagle could say more.

"Well I think if we can cause enough of a disturbance on the ground amongst the rats and weasels and whatever other crawling nasties there are it will give a couple of us the chance to get close to them. Greagle, I have no doubt that you are the one to lead the assault."

Greagle's demeanour brightened considerably. He would get his chance to fight after all.

"However, those not involved in the battle will have the even more dangerous task of confronting those two scoundrels and getting the Knife. Blalim this is where you come in."

He looked at me keenly.

"You know Neroh better than most and have seen his trickery first hand."

"Aye, true enough but do you suggest we just walk up to your house and knock the door?"

"No. It is my hope the threat from Greagle will draw them out to us. Now if I know Nefairious he will not want to get too close to the actual fighting bit and will stay at the back near the house and shout orders. If however, we can keep his eye away from the back of the Learning Tree I'm sure I could get us close enough to him to blast him with the Draykt or even capture him."

"You mean there is a secret way from here to the Learning Tree?" asked Síoda.

"There is. You remember the stories of the rabbit wars? How they would fight each other to gain control of the warrens? Well they dug many burrows and tracks at that time and most of them have fallen in or are impassable but there is one still that will give us safe passage."

"Where is it?" asked Tridge.

"About twenty wing beats from the back of this house," said Blalim.

"Of course! I remember that old track but its been many's a long year since anyone went through."

"Greagle, Tridge, Laijir, Síoda and Ionta there are no five better or braver fighting fairies in the whole of Ireland, the diversion I will leave up to you but we need time, can you do it?" I asked.

Before they could answer a younger voice spoke,

"What about me?"

It was Druhin.

Greagle answered both questions at once,

"Of course we can. Druhin get your knife ready, you're coming with us."

I felt a little uneasy at the young Druhin's role in all this but knew that Greagle would do his best for him.

"That's it then," I said.

"Remember Druhin you have the bat whistle. Use it only on my instruction," said Greagle. "Let's go."

"May Odhran be smiling on us," I said and watched the six fly up into the night.

Blalim and I went to the back of the house and looked down the Hollow. There were rats on duty but even they would hardly notice two swift fairies in this darkness. We walked quickly through the grass and rushes,

"There it is."

"Where?"

"Here, I'll show you."

To any rodent eye under order to block up all such burrows all that would've been seen was a large boulder. They would not have noticed the hairline crack in the rock itself which when pushed by a fairy with a little know how in these things slips away to reveal a dark hole in the ground.

"I had forgotten about that," said Blalim.

"Oh you have to be busy when you're the mayor you know," I smiled back, "lots of little things to be keeping an eye on."

Into the darkness we went as the first blast of Greagle's Draykt smashed into a platoon of rats. We heard their squeals and ran.

63

The Hand of Fate

"Greagle!" said Neroh coldly, eyeing his erstwhile neighbour. "Only he could be so bold."

"Yes and there are quite a few with him," said Nefairious. "Are you ready father? This is it."

Neroh did not answer with words this time instead he conjured up the Draykt and let go a blast that went straight at Greagle.

Greagle saw it coming of course and moved out of the way at the last second. The blue streak walloped into the leaves and branches behind him and they came crashing down into the river.

"You'll have to better than that old man," shouted Greagle who now amazingly flew straight at the pair of them. Wisely, Druhin did not follow.

"Greagle . . . No!" said Síoda.

"Cover me."

Síoda fired her own Draykt at Neroh and Nefairious as Ionta shot her arrows at the swarm of rats beneath them. The air was thick with sharp and shining edges. They were spread out in that very awkward place between the ground and the bottoms of the lowest branches. However, they were just high enough to be safe from the rats spears but not high enough to avoid their arrows which had started whizzing about them.

Laijir and Tridge were firing their own arrows as quickly as they could and were relieved each time they heard a squeal from below. They did not have long though as the rats began to find their range and as an arrow ripped through the bottom of Tridge's coat that was the signal.

"Up among the leaves and be careful," yelled Laijir.

Greagle flew as if riding the wind. His head clipped through the leaves and in a moment he was hovering on the opposite side of the river staring directly at Neroh and Nefairious. Nefairious did not wait for diplomacy and shot two bolts at him. This time Greagle barely managed to avoid them. They flew past his head and into the startled whin bushes behind.

"Is that the best you can do? After all this time Neroh I see you're as ugly as ever, both of heart and of looks."

By now the air was full of rat squeals and weasel cries and arrows and spears. The fairies fired back their own and as much Draykt as they could but the tide was swinging against them. They were too many and had now begun to climb the trees and were hunting down the fairies. Druhin, who had stayed at Laijir's wing was terribly afraid but had enough about him to speak.

"Laijir, look at them all, we are outnumbered. Greagle is on the other side of the Hollow. We must call for help."

"Good man, Druhin, you're right. I don't think old Greagle will mind you giving the bats a call without his permission . . . blow."

Druhin took the whistle out and gave it four long hard puffs. He smiled and looked at Laijir but Laijir did not smile back. Instead he had a look of complete shock on his face. The blue crackling Draykt in his hands was fading and he was falling . . . falling out of the sky.

"Laijir!" called Druhin but it was too late.

The mighty fairy looked blankly up at him as fell. Druhin saw the spear. It had hit him in the centre of his chest and went through him. His hands grasped it as if in an effort to pull it out which sadly he could not. The last thing that Laijir did was release his bow and throw it up high into the air. He looked up desperately at Druhin.

"Use it well."

Druhin was too shocked to move and watched in horror as both Laijir and his bow fell. Suddenly from the side with amazing speed flew Síoda and she grabbed the bow just as it seemed destined to smash on a wet boulder. There was nothing she could do for Laijir and his body hit the river and was taken.

"No!" yelled Druhin. "No!"

Druhin felt as if his heart would burst in his chest. This was not supposed to happen. He quickly went through the dizziness of emotions, from shock to sorrow to anger and it would be anger he would converse with. He did not have the Draykt yet but he did have a good knife and a found temper. The rats were not far from him now. They had been eating at their rations of nuts and had taken to the trees. Their arrows and spears were flying faster and higher and their ear piercing shrill shrieks were getting louder.

"In the name of Odhran, you will pay," yelled the young fairy and immediately headed down to do battle.

Well, he would have had he not felt a sharp tug at the back of his neck. *What the . . . ?* he thought.

It was Síoda.

"Get up here you young fool. Are you going to fight them all?"

"Get off me!" snapped Druhin, trying to wriggle free of her grasp.

She gave him another strong tug which knocked the red haze out of his eyes somewhat.

"You are no good to anyone dead. There is no glory or use in such a hopeless chase. Use your head, not your heart as sore as it may be."

Druhin now felt very confused. He wanted to go and crack rat skulls but here was Síoda, a fairy for whom he had the utmost respect, telling him to wise up.

"This is no place for lectures and lessons," she went on, "now c'mon."

She was just too late. A rat arrow flew up through the leaves and pierced young Druhin's wing sticking him to the tree.

"Owwww!"

Oh great, thought Síoda.

She quickly pulled out the arrow forcing another yelp from the youngster.

"You'll live," she said but really that was not her concern.

The injury would prevent him from flying, and here they were high in the branches with rats closing in and no obvious escape route. She quickly climbed, pushing the injured youngster in front of her to the higher thinner branches, letting forth a couple of blasts of the Draykt at the weasels who were almost within jumping distance of them.

"We should be safe for a moment here at least," she said sharply.

If there ever was a determined creature in the world surely it has to be a rat. Mankind has for an age tried to deny them access to their food stores and houses and consistently failed in spite of his so called wisdom. The rat it seems, will not take no for an answer. Here the case was soon proven yet again.

Even though Síoda and Druhin had settled on the thinner branches which would not support a well fed rodent, it only served to annoy them more. They started chewing on the branches until they began to snap off and fall. With each one the fairies were forced higher and higher. Soon enough they would have nowhere to run. The mesh was still up and the rats were climbing up it too. In no time there began a shower of branches and leaves from the very nut trees that gave the Hollow it's name.

Damn fool creatures, said Greagle to himself. *They'll have the place wrecked in no time.*

He could see the predicament that Síoda and Druhin were in. He could see Ionta and Tridge who also had their hands full and could not help either marooned pair. Speed was of the essence. He hoped that whatever Graneff and Blalim had planned would happen soon.

"Give up Greagle and they will be spared," shouted Nefairious at him suddenly.

"Give up? Are you mad? You know me better than that boy. Anyway how could we yield the Hollow to someone who looks like his head was made from the rumblings of a mole's behind?"

"Well, well, the great Greagle reduced to insults. I have every intention of cutting out your tongue. You're no longer the master here," shouted Nefairious who did not notice Neroh take a step back closer to the door.

"Oh I don't know about that, Nefairious."

He had heard a commotion in the trees behind him and guessed that Druhin must have blown on his whistle. The birds and bats were coming again. Soon the gush of flapping wings was heard in the air around them in harmony with the sound of the river. Nefairious saw them approach and immediately pulled out the Carving Knife.

"Father this is our moment, let us stand now and be rid of our enemies once and for all." Silence.

"Father," he said turning quickly. No sign of Neroh.

Where? he thought and then noticed Graneff's front door quickly closing.

He turned again, cursing his father as he did so.

One blast of the Draykt will do it, he thought and with good reason too.

The power of the Carving Knife was in his veins. If he struck the centre of the on coming flock now it would surely be it's ruination. He began to flap his wings at great speed until the Draykt was crackling at his finger tips. This time however, the magic was not blue but deep red. It was the power of the Carving Knife.

The flock was closing in on him now . . . closer and closer. Rithacus and Strelle, Smól and Drood at the front flying as fast as they had ever done.

Most amazingly of all they were flying to their doom but it did not cause them a thought. Closer and closer they came. Greagle began to fly over the river keeping his eyes on Nefairious whose hands now crackled red. He was ready to fire.

"The Hollow *will* be mine," he yelled.

He raised his hands, the left one holding the Knife.

"It will all be mine," he screamed with a new ferocity.

Blalim chose this very moment to fly from behind the Learning Tree straight at Nefairious. He approached him at speed from behind with a lump of blackthorn that he held in his fist and brought it down with all his might over the back of his head. Just at that moment the red Draykt flew from his hands but instead of crashing straight into the oncoming wings and feathers it flew above them cutting in half six sycamore tree tops in it's anger.

There was not a second to lose. Nefairious sank to his knees and his hands were wrist deep in the muddy ground.

"Get the Knife," shouted Blalim.

The force of the blow had knocked him over and he lay in a heap at the river's edge. I flew down to the bent figure not knowing what to expect. It had been years since any of us had seen him and now suddenly he we were, thrust together again. The Knife was still in his hand. The look of it captivated me and I could hardly breathe.

"Pick it up, you fool," roared Greagle, now fast approaching.

The flock whooshed over my head and on seeing the prone figure of their tormentor got stuck into the rats, weasels, wasps, slugs an whatever else they could. The battle was joined once more. Greagle's urgent voice shook me briefly from the lure of the Carving Knife. I stepped closer to Nefairious who still had made no sound but I could tell he was still conscious as he held his kneeling position in the mud.

Suddenly he spoke, his head still bowed,

"You cannot take the Knife from me Graneff. Don't you see I am the Knife and the Knife is me. You could not knock me over from the Learning Tree because my Cree is joined with it."

He slowly raised his head.

If he comes round we are all done for, I thought.

Greagle landed beside us. Blalim raised the blackthorn over his head.

"Nefairious," he began.

But he got no answer. Nefairious was moving slowly. His mind was again setting itself on our doom.

"Nefairious," said Greagle again. "You have but one choice, give me the Knife. You know it was not made for cruelty. You know it Nefairious, think for goodness sake. Think of your fellows. Think of the Hollow. The one you grew up in. It is for us all to enjoy, not to be ruled by greed or anger. Your heart is as ours. You share more in common with us than you do with the creatures at your command. Fight for your heart Nefairious, fight against your anger."

Something in my mind told me to say it, from where it came I do not know but out it came nonetheless.

"Thig leis an croí macánta an scian is ribeanta a mhaolú."

(Hig lesh un kree makkanta an skin is ribbinta a whale-oo)

"An honest heart can blunt the sharpest Knife."

"You have no need to translate Graneff," said Nefairious, his voice weak.

"I didn't spend my time idly on top of Knock Layde. I have some understanding of our old tongue, though I don't know why you would speak it now . . ." his voice trailed off suddenly.

He then began to repeat the sentence slowly,

"Thig leis . . . an croí macánta . . . an scian is ribeanta a mhaolú . . ." and then again . . . and again.

I glanced up at Greagle wondering what he was doing.

"It's the spell," he whispered.

There was something going on alright. Nefairious was now chanting the line over again as if his mind was trying to understand its message, perhaps trying to believe it himself. He began to shake his head as if against the line but still he chanted.

"Give me the Knife Nefairious," said Greagle again.

Nefairious gripped the Knife tightly and we could see he was battling with himself. Was there some honesty left in him? Could whatever goodness in him escape the darkness he had been shrouded in for so long?

I withdrew my sword and stood over him. As much as he seemed to be battling this was Nefairious after all and if he were to use the Knife against us now we would be killed.

"I can't do it," he whispered.

"Yes of course you can," urged Greagle

"If you can give up the Knife there is hope for you in spite of all."

"You must take it Graneff, I can not give it to you. You must take it."

I bent over to pick it up with my hand but Blalim put his hand on my shoulder.

"If you touch that Knife you will surely die. It is tied to him, Graneff. You must take it off."

"What? You mean take his hand off?"

"I do Graneff and if you can't I will."

"But, what about . . . ?"

"A small price for his salvation wouldn't you say?"

"We will need it to fight Neroh, I fear he may be headed for Fween Talav."

"But the children," I gasped.

"Exactly," said Blalim.

At that moment Tridge landed beside us, his sword drawn and raised above his head. He made straight for Nefairious.

"I'll take his head off, 'twould be a good deal safer than any of this messing about," he shouted and brought down his sword.

"No," I yelled and just managed to deflect the sword with my own so that they clashed violently but bounced off to the side without damage.

"Hold your temper, fairy. This is not the time for revenge. If you ever do that again I'll cut off your head myself!" barked Greagle.

Tridge was shocked to say the least. More shocked still when smoke began to come from his pocket.

"But its Nefairious, and on his knees. What in the name . . . ?"

He reached into his pocket and pulled out his shard of the Stone of Pity. It glowed red and burned his fingers.

"Aaaccch!"

He dropped it onto the sand at the riverside where it hissed in the mud.

"There is no victory in revenge my friend," answered Greagle. "I understand your need but you may find him more use to us all alive."

"I hope so, 'tis unlikely we'll get a better chance to finish him," answered Tridge dipping his fingers into the river.

"Do it Graneff," said Greagle.

I raised my sword and fought against my thoughts telling me not to harm him but there was no choice. The children were in danger. Neroh was on the loose and we needed the Knife. The blow was swift and went straight through his wrist. Nefairious's yell was but one more in a night of pain. The Knife sat in the hand that had grasped it. I peeled off the still warm fingers one by one until the hand fell. I held the Carving Knife once more.

"I'll sort him out," said Blalim, "now go the rest of you and get Neroh."

64

An End to Things

"Did you hear that?" asked Katie.

"Yes."

What they heard was no more than whisper but it was as clear as day. They heard the words in the old language.

"Someone has used the first part of the spell," exclaimed Clumsill. "I hope it works."

"But how could we have heard it?" asked Katie.

"After all that's gone on, nothing surprises me," answered Dara. "Must be a link between all of us who were at the Towers and the spell I'd say. Remember Sheana said we were all the spell? Are you both OK?"

She got a couple of very low 'Um hmms'.

"I hope there is still some toffee left," said Katie.

"Aye me too," agreed Dara.

Down they went as their flame flickered above them.

"There's light ahead," said Clumsill excitedly.

They quickened and were soon at the bottom of the stairway. They entered Fween Talav and delighted in seeing everyone.

"Well, well," said Gráinne, "our visitors have returned."

All heads turned toward them and when Silleyn saw her son she nearly went blue with excitement.

"Clumsill, my boy," she squealed and ran to him quickly smothering him with cuddles and kisses. Pog and Fer ran over to Katie and Dara and there were hugs all over the place.

"Wow, have we got stories for you," said Katie

"Ha, wait 'til you hear ours," replied Fer.

"Come on children, I'm sure you are hungry," said Gráinne and they headed over to the table, eventually being joined by a kiss soggy Clumsill.

Gráinne decided to let them have a quick bite before she asked them any questions.

Dara would have been more than happy to recount their tale but just as she was about to sink her teeth into a healthy slice of Rowanberry pie a most dreadful sight filled her eyes. Walking slowly into Fween Talav via the Graneff's own stairway came Neroh.

There was dead silence. He looked at them all coldly and confidently. He would be safe in here for the moment. He had left a locking spell on the trap door above and it would take the fairies a while to break it. He would have his revenge at last.

"All of you, get over there," he said pointing to the small room that had previously been host to a recovering Greagle.

"Of all the curses, what has brought you back on us?" asked Sherene, who was old enough to recall Neroh's exploits.

"Let us call it destiny. Now move, all of you."

Though there were plenty of fairies in Fween Talav they knew it was pointless to resist. This was the man of nightmares, the fairy that had been locked in a Thorn tree never to return. He was cruelty itself, the very essence of fear and now here he stood in front of them.

"The years have not been kind Neroh," said Frenel, "and neither will be your justice."

Neroh gave her the most withering of looks.

"Justice? Justice you say, Frenel. Just who do you think is going to deliver justice on me? Graneff? Blalim? Grochin? No my dear your brave brigade are probably now just stuck in some rat's teeth with any luck."

"You lie," said Fer.

Neroh's eyes fell on the young fairy.

"You have the look of Graneff about you," he began, "a daughter I'd say and a granddaughter of Graunad. You will enjoy a particularly delicious end."

"What sort of creature are you that would harm a child?" asked Gráinne suddenly.

"A surviving one. Yes and one about to sup the cool waters of revenge. Now you too have the look of Graunad. A daughter I'd say, this gets better. And what do we have here?" he asked as his gaze now rested on Katie and Dara.

"Humans. Well of all the creatures. I did not expect two humans to be here of all places. I hope you have enjoyed your lives . . . they are now at an end."

*   *   *

"Quickly," said Greagle, "we must get to Fween Talav. The pup is tamed but the old hound is still on the loose."

"He has some spell on the trap door!" said Ionta.

"No doubt," replied Greagle. "Graneff, hurry."

I ran over to the trap door. Behind me Blalim locked the front door and the now bound Nefairious walked silently in front of him. Blalim had fastened a healing docken leaf bandage on his wound. The severed hand was in his pocket.

"Sit," he ordered.

Nefairious sat as he was told and stared emptily ahead.

"Can you keep an eye on him?" asked Greagle.

"Yes brother, can you do your own work instead of asking me silly questions?" replied Blalim, drawing his sword. "Graneff, you are keeper of the Knife from now until we can return it. Use it son, use it now."

I had never felt power like it. My right arm felt twenty times bigger than normal. I stuck the Knife into the sparkling clear bubble that sat atop the lock of the trap door. It popped immediately and for good measure the Knife cut through the actual bolt.

"C'mon, let's end this," urged Tridge who jumped down the first few steps determined to lead the way. Greagle, Ionta and I followed into the darkness.

*   *   *

"Druhin, this is not the best place we're in you know," said Síoda rather ironically.

"I'm sorry," replied Druhin, his eyes just on the verge of tears. "You must go on Síoda, the others can't afford to lose you too."

"My young friend, whatever happens you will not be alone," she answered and withdrew her sword. "Fire as many arrows as you can and aim between their eyes."

The rats had now snapped and eaten their way through the smaller branches forcing the two onto the very edge of the last branch that would hold them. It would not hold them for much longer for none other than Rant himself was at its base gnawing furiously. Síoda went straight at him.

In the fury of the battle the gleam of her sword so high in the branches caught Strelle's eye. He feared an attack from above an immediately shot up to investigate. It was not a moment too soon either. He saw Síoda at the end of the last branch fighting against the mighty Rant and the young Druhin whizzing arrows from his quiver as quickly as he could without much direction.

This won't do, he thought and flew up beside Druhin.

"Are you going to stay there all night?" he shouted.

A shocked Druhin looked back in shock and an answer would not come.

"Jump!"

Druhin stood up and looked worryingly at Síoda. She could not hold off something as grotesque and as strong as Rant much longer. However, she did notice Strelle and without need of further encouragement took flight. Druhin stood and jumped for all he was worth landing fairly and squarely on Strelle's soft furry back. Away they flew to the Learning Tree and as they landed they heard that unmistakeable high pitched shriek from above. The buzzards had arrived with Rant the first to feel their fury.

*   *   *

It is a curious thing the power of a young mind. In almost every circumstance the sight of Neroh alone should have been enough to scare the life out of them but Katie and Dara were not scared. They did not see a monster but instead a decrepit, bent old fairy. They had flown with the swans of Lir, they had swam with the great Saroist, conversed with Rachary no less and seen the beauty and wonder of the 'daoine maithe' (deenee myhuh), the good people . . . the fairies. They were not now going to give this horrible old bully his way without a damn good fight.

"It seems you have befriended this rabble," began Neroh, "well more's the pity for you. Any friend of the fairies is no friend of mine."

He reached his wiry hands into his pockets on either side of his long coat and brought out the Ogham stones. They had heard his voice and were now glowing a dark red as they sat in his open hands.

"He has found the Ogham stones," gasped Gráinne.

There were now many concerned whispers amongst the fairies. They had not seen an Ogham for many years but knew of their power and links to the ancients that lived here before them.

"It will not be long now before Nefairious brings me down Greagle's head," he said aloud.

He had neglected to tell them that he had abandoned his son on seeing the flock of birds and bats come tearing up the glen at him.

"No doubt he will use the Carving Knife for the job, as I will use these stones and be rid of the rest of you."

"What do we do?" asked Clumsill, who was in no mood to give in now after all his adventures.

"I know," said Katie, "we should say the line, the second one . . . together."

Dara and Clumsill nodded and the three of them held hands and took a couple of steps out in front from the others.

"Children please," said Gráinne, "come back here now."

The glowing Ogham stones had transferred their glow all round Neroh now and he stood before them with his hands outstretched as if drawing in all dark power to him.

"Ok after three," said Dara.

"One, two, three . . . 'Cinnte, níl an obair crua chomh furasta sin' they shouted together as loud as they could and waited to see what would happen.

* * *

"Did you hear that?" said Ionta.

"Hear what?" asked Greagle who of course was not part of the group at the Towers.

"It's the second line," said Tridge, "the children must have used it against Neroh."

"C'mon quickly," I said, "our friends need our help, it will take us all to stop him."

We rushed down the steps and could see in the distance the jigging lights of Fween Talav.

"There is no point in rushing Neroh," began Greagle, "no doubt he will have some protection about him, some old spell he'll have conjured up. Tridge as soon as you see him, fire your arrows and spear. Whatever you do keep him busy. If the rest of you have a spell in mind use it together. More voices, more power."

We were at the doorway into Fween Talav and saw them there in front of Neroh and him surrounded by a reddish glow.

"Oh great!" sighed Greagle.

"Ogham stones. They will protect from almost anything."

"Yes, almost. I don't think he'll have bargained for this," I said, holding up the Knife.

Tridge did as Greagle had ordered and began to fire. The arrows bounced off him and stuck in the wall and ceiling but they did get his attention. I could hear the three children repeat the line again and again.

"Quickly, everyone say it and keep firing Tridge," I said quickly.

Síoda and Ionta flew above the glowing Neroh and hovered on either side of the three youngsters. They began to chant with them and encouraged the fairies to do the same. The hall echoed to their voices.

"Cinnte, níl an obair crua chomh furasta sin."

(To be sure, hard work isn't easy)

Once again the voices of Nut Hollow united and sounded as loud as the north wind itself.

Neroh's eyes remained closed and he glowed as red as before.

"Perhaps he can't hear us," I said to Greagle.

"Oh he can hear us alright, look."

Neroh's eyes opened wide and white. His face was a picture of anger and he began to move his wings behind him.

"Oh no, he's calling up the Draykt," exclaimed Tridge who continued to fire arrows at him.

"If he releases it in here we'll all be done for," said Greagle, "time to sort this bloody thing once and for all."

Up he flew straight at Neroh who could see him coming.

"I've been waiting a long time for this," said Neroh suddenly.

"No Greagle he's too strong," came a cry, it was Gráinne.

Greagle flew head first into the Neroh's chest and rather like a large arrow he too bounced off him and clattered across the top of the great table scattering cups, bowls and all manner of food.

"Is that all you have?" roared Neroh.

The voices continued the chant. Greagle's action was the ultimate distraction for although he had not harmed Neroh he did knock him off balance and even as he shouted his defiance he began to totter backwards. One leg went back to support the other but his momentum carried him back and he landed on his backside with a thud. The two Ogham stones shot up into the air.

Immediately Pog and Fer darted out from the crowd and just before they both landed and smashed on the stone floor they each caught one. Any great hurling goal keeper would have been proud of two such saves. The red glow disappeared immediately from Neroh.

"Give me back those stones," he yelled but Pog and Fer were safely back in amongst the crowd.

Neroh was not to be denied and soon had the Draykt crackling in his hands but he did not fire. He stood motionless and listened. The spell had got to his ears at last.

"Cinnte, níl an obair crua chomh furasta sin," they all shouted.

The old language. Old magic. New power. His mind was now telling him indeed that hard work was not easy. Suddenly it would be too hard to fight them all. He wanted to give up. He wanted to fight on. He didn't know what he wanted. He shook his head as if blocking out the message but his shoulders soon drooped and his hands covered his face.

"No, no, no," he yelled. "Nooo!"

With a burst of speed none of us expected he flew for the entrance we had come through earlier that led to my house where Blalim was alone with Nefairious.

"Stop him," came the call but he was gone with Greagle hot on his tail.

*   *   *

We all flew up the steps again and I heard in the distance the trap door being broken through. Blalim turned quickly but did not expect to see the cruel fairy. Neroh flew at him and knocked him over with a blow to the head. He grabbed Nefairious and flew out through the front door. If they escaped now goodness only knew what they would do. They sped out the door and saw the ranks of birds and bats settled in the branches above. The bodies of their rat and weasel army were strewn at their feet. Nefairious was awake again, the shock of the release had broken the spell of the line and his wings began to flutter.

"We will return, we will return," shouted Neroh for us all to hear.

"Just you wai . . . !"

I think he would have said 'wait' had he had the chance for at the very moment they were about to fly under the bridge up from the water as if he was a golden spear came Saroist. He got a hold of Nefairious's leg and pulled him down. Neroh was forced to let him go and soon regained height but he too was stopped all of a sudden and in a second found that he was back on solid ground underneath the talons of Brandon himself.

Saroist shook his head and a very soggy Nefairious landed at our feet as we came out my front door. No sooner had he hit the ground when bounding from the bushes came a giant weasel. It was Welset and he made to pull off Nefairious's head.

"Curses on you, you fairy devil, my men are done for. I have lost all because of you."

He revealed his two longest gleaming white teeth and went for his neck. Luckily for Nefairious, Blalim had recovered enough to grab Welset by the tail. Amazingly, he swung him round his head and bounced him off the Learning Tree knocking him clean out. We drew our breaths, there would be much to sort out.

65

Back through the Garden

Brandon moved his great beak to within a hair's breath of Neroh's nose. The great bird towered over the old fairy who suddenly looked all his years and more. His talon was over Neroh in such a way as to make any movement impossible. He was not about to take any chances. The rest of the Nut Hollow fairies now slowly came out my front door until we all stood together. In the furore of it all we had failed to notice that dawn had broken and the darkness was being ushered away for another while.

Nefairious moaned something about the Knife and his father got a curse that I shall not repeat here. He was broken. His dreams of ruling Nut Hollow were as damp as his great cloak that now was almost as soggy a mess as he. Neroh did not say a word. Anyone who could stand to look at him saw an unrepentant face, his eyes still burned cruelly at us all. But he was powerless too. Brandon picked him up and hopped over to Nefarious and with his other talon picked him up. We knew that justice would be swift.

Brandon's fellow buzzards, Clav and Gearr were waiting atop the Learning Tree and as Brandon flew up to them he beckoned us to join him. Greagle, Blalim, Síoda, Tridge and Ionta flew up alongside and sat on the highest branches. On the ground below the dazed faces slowly gave way to smiles and hugs. I saw Katie, Dara and Clumsill and Druhin and Pog and Fer. Druhin's friends and parents were now all chatting and holding each other. I was a little concerned at the kiss the Fer gave him but decided I would deal with that later.

I noticed too Lirna walk along smiling sadly with Gráinne. Many had fallen in this battle and our joy was tempered at their loss. A gentle breeze blew through the leaves and we moved together on the branches.

"There have been great deeds done here this night," began Brandon. "The bravery of the Nut Hollow fairies will go down in legend for ever more. It is fair to say however that given the choice none of you would have been involved in such a battle and the reasons we find ourselves here both now lie in my grip."

To emphasise the point he tightened his talons around the two until they wheezed and groaned.

Good enough for them, thought Grochin who, unable to resist, had flown up to the lower branches to get a closer eye on proceedings.

"The law of the fairies and of those who would live by it has been broken and the consequences are clear. Death. There is little doubt that anyone as cruel as Neroh would bring anything else but sorrow should he get the chance. What say you my fellows?" he asked and looked at the other judges.

"In the case of Neroh death is the only option," said Gearr, who opened his wings out as he delivered the sentence.

"I agree," said Clav who did the same.

"What say you fairies? The last word will be yours for it is upon you that he has delivered such pain."

As mayor of the Hollow it was my place to speak but before I did I received a few whispers from each of my friends there in the high tree top. I felt the stone of pity cool in my pocket.

"On advice from my friends and with memories of the fallen in my heart I can say only one thing, Neroh will not be killed."

The buzzards were not overly impressed but in spite of a 'humph' or two they nodded.

"And what would you do with him?" asked Brandon.

"He will return to the Fairy Thorn and remain there as long as the sun rises in the mornings."

"So be it."

Neroh let go a yell of anger from the talon but it was a defeated cry at best and soon he was silent again.

"And what of Nefairious?"

"If I might answer," said Greagle.

"Of course," I said.

"Your honour, I have lived a long time in this Hollow and never before came so close to losing it. We have lost friends and family and their spaces at our tables can never be replaced. I have learned that no matter what judgement we deliver upon Nefairious that it will do little to ease our pain. Do you agree?" he asked turning to us.

We nodded and below on the ground there were nods from the other fairies.

"Take him from here back to the top of Knock Layde and let him stay in exile there until perhaps he finds it in himself to come back as a friend."

"You're sure of this?" asked Brandon.

"We are."

"Have you anything to say Nefairious?" asked Brandon raising him up in his claw in front of us.

He was a pitiful sight as far removed from a fairy as you could ever imagine and yet I wondered was there anything good left in him at all.

He stared at the ground.

"Thank you," he said quietly.

"Go ndéanfaidh seo maith duit (Guh nyanni shuh my ditch)

(Might it do you some good)" said Síoda. The lady of few words had chosen well. The third line!

"Send this with Neroh," said Tridge removing the jar of embers from his pocket, "may it brighten his heart. He will have little else to look on."

We hoped their power and that of the old spell would indeed do him some good. The buzzards were truly impressed. Such dignity in the face of an enemy was rare.

"Just a minute," I said. "I have one more thing for Nefairious. I found this up in his house on Knock Layde."

I walked up to him and hung the little silver chain around his neck. He touched the locket gently with his fingers.

With that up flew the buzzards firstly to the Thorn where we watched the runners come for Neroh. In a moment, after getting a good sting from the nettles the nasty old fairy was gone. Then off they went with Nefairious in the direction of Knock Layde disappearing into the distance.

*   *   *

We flew down and the job of tidying up was soon on everyone's lips.

"Why did you let him go?" asked Fer.

"I mean he'll just get his magic back and we'll all be fighting again."

"No Fer, he left his magic here," I answered taking the Carving Knife out from my belt. He invested his Cree in it. His very essence is here, all his magic, all his hopes and dreams as cruel as they were. He'll not be much of a threat to anyone or anything now."

"But what about the Knife daddy, what will happen to it?"

"I'll take it thank you," came a deep voice.

From above we saw the wide face and kind eyes of Odhran himself. Even in the early morning light his colours were almost too bright for our eyes. His wings were half sun yellow down to the tips while the other half of the wings were rust red with a grey stripe down the middle. His face was as white as the wood of the inner Learning Tree and his eyes as deep and dark as the sea of Moyle itself.

Immediately we bent our heads as he landed.

"I shall replace the Knife, Graneff. You can all be very proud of your efforts here. Please try not to worry about those you have lost, I will take good care of them," he said looking at Lirna and all the others from whom someone special had been taken.

He flew over to the Learning Tree and tapped his wing against it whispering an ancient spell we couldn't hear. In a moment the old tree opened up and we saw the swirling white wood again. He placed the Knife in blade first and it slowly withdrew to safety.

"My friends, I am happy to say Nut Hollow is back in safe hands, fare well."

And as quickly as he had come he was gone again, flying straight for the early morning sun.

*　　*　　*

Katie and Dara now walked toward me. I think we were all in a state of shock at Odhran's visit but youth soon wakes you up.

"Graneff," said Dara, "we were wondering if it might be possible for us to . . . to ehm . . . go home?"

Katie held Dara's hand and nodded in agreement.

"I think Granny will be getting worried now you know."

"Ha! Indeed she will girls. Now let me see," I said and give a shout up to Rithacus.

He flew down beside us.

"Rithacus, if I might ask one last favour of you."

"Oh and what would that be?" he answered, obviously tired from his exploits.

"Would you mind giving the girls a lift back to the top of the glen?"

"You mean back up to the humans?"

"I do."

"Of course I will and I don't mind saying it girls I will be sorry to see you go. You have done your kind proud indeed. Will you not stay?"

The girls smiled but shook their heads.

"Oh well, on you get then."

"Just a minute," they said together and ran off in to the arms of their now many new friends.

Well, didn't they hug and get hugs and kiss and get kisses (especially from Clumsill). They got little souvenirs and trinkets so much so that in no time had pockets full of toffee and hearts full of good wishes. There were plenty of tears too but isn't there always sad fondness at parting? They stood in front of me again.

"We can't thank you enough for your help and I am not sure of a reward you could use but I promise that you will always have friends in Nut Hollow and I'm sure we will meet again very soon. We will keep an eye on you on your visits and you might want to keep an eye out for us," I said smiling, and from behind me the fairies clapped and cheered.

I gave them each a kiss on the forehead and we watched and waved them take off into the morning.

"Wow," said Katie.

"Bye everyone," shouted Dara.

"But . . ." gasped Katie, "we are too little. Mum and dad and granny and granda will never see us."

"Leave that to me," shouted Rithacus over the wind.

They flew quickly up Glenmak Mountain and past the great sycamore tree of Sronamona.

"I can see the house," said Katie excitedly.

Rithacus then detoured into the garden at the side wheeling round the branches, over the goldfish pond and eventually through the little arch under the pine trees, whispering to himself all the while. The girls were not at all sure why he did this but guessed deep down that there was magic in it.

He landed very quickly and Katie and Dara got off. They had hardly dismounted when they began to feel very odd. The many huge flower heads above them were shrinking. The branches of the trees were getting closer and closer and in another moment they realised they were standing up as tall as they had ever been beside the steps at the front of Katie's house. A second later they were trying to dry their faces from the delightedly excited licks of Finn, their wonderful and gentle black dog.

"Oh Finn," they laughed, "and we are glad to see you too!"

"Fare well my friends . . . but before I go . . ." the robin gave a series of chirps.

In another instant the birds of Nut Hollow began to land on the branches around them.

"Time for another song," said Rithacus, "fairies aren't the only ones who can use music you know."

With that the thrushes, starlings and robins all began to sing just as several extremely worried, relieved, angry, tearful, happy and astonished parents and grandparents saw the children and made toward them. Before they could interrogate Dara and Katie with a thousand questions regarding their whereabouts these last days their faces relaxed and smiles replaced frowns. The bird song was working,

"Worry not, do not fret,

You are together again

It doesn't matter how or why

Let joy replace your pain

Remember not anxiety,

Let no words complain

Hold you dear ones tightly now

In time they will explain."

It may be said that humans rarely hear such magic, those few that do can count their ears very lucky indeed.

"It's a bird spell!" gasped Katie.

"Yes, so the oldies won't remember where we've been," agreed Dara. "Clever."

They did not say another word and gave each other a hug. They smiled widely and enjoyed the music of their many new friends. They were home, safe and sound.

CPSIA information can be obtained at www.ICGtesting.com
Printed in the USA
BVOW071205031111

275216BV00002B/225/P